JUSTIFIED

Wendy Turner-Hargreaves

DEDICATION

For my Dad, Jack, whose creativity endlessly inspires me.
and my Mum, Joyce, who taught me that rejection is just
another hurdle.
For my partner Chris, whose input, support and belief I
appreciate beyond measure.
For our daughters, Matilda and Pippa who fill my life with
love, fun and magic.

Thank you.

Justified by Wendy Turner-Hargreaves

Published by Retro River

www.wendyturnerhargreaves.com
Copyright © 2023 Wendy Turner-Hargreaves

Cover by Khalid
Copyright © 2023 Wendy Turner-Hargreaves
All rights reserved.

Contents

Chapter One

Storm Clouds

Suspicious death in Broadstone. As rare as waking up in your own coffin.

DI Robin Scott accepted the call out and diverted from his regular route to the station, cutting across two lanes of snarled commuters already inching miserably towards the town centre. A rapid U-turn and he was free again, hurtling down the empty carriageway as invigorated as a skydiver stepping out into miles of fresh air. He cranked up the volume on his radio to drown out the thrash symphony of raindrops drumming on his car roof, and his sound system accepted the challenge with a brief crackle of protest. Screechy guitars battered his ears instead, so loud the vibration rattled his travel cup in its holder. If thunder clattered around overhead, he didn't want to hear it.

Broadstone rushed by. Charming, vibrant but criminally unexciting. Tearooms full of tourists and trendy bars where the commercial quarter did lunch and Zoomed in quieter corners. His satnav sent him towards the older, affluent suburbs, ten minutes out of town. He turned into a sloped avenue lined with high trees and checked the address with the control room. It didn't feel right. Suspicious death? The occasional break-in or a nicked Range Rover maybe, but this was a peaceful collective of empty nests and executive hideouts. While control checked, he took a quick glug of the caffeine oil-slick his partner Catherine had made him just before he left her house. A pleasant mental image. Mad hair everywhere, deliciously dressed in just the shirt he now wore, singing to Bowie while the kettle boiled. A morning person. He inhaled her scent on the fabric and enjoyed the memory.

The address checked out so he continued, wipers swiping on double speed.

Fifteen seconds later, he floored the brake and skidded to a slippery stop alongside two drenched women grappling on the pavement. Another charge of adrenalin thrummed in his ears. He yanked the handbrake and shoved open his door against a weighty wind. An icy smack of rain punished him for his arrival, mugged him of breath, and made his face hurt. The elements were raging.

The fight spilled into the road. A stocky Merc going the opposite way swerved, alloys scraping on the high kerb. The women looked wretched, like they'd been out there a while, gusting around in the deluge. Robin waded in and pulled apart the uniformed female officer and her fugitive, an apple-shaped woman with the face of a wrestler. His fingers barely circled the woman's chunky wrist as she yanked and writhed in his grasp, half crying, half snarling. Maintaining hold, he twisted towards the police officer, who bent over to get her breath back.

"What's going on?" he shouted. A roar of wind swallowed his words and forced the nearby trees to sway and bow in submission. "Are you OK?"

"Yeah, I'm fine, Guv." PC Judy Smith grabbed air back into her lungs. "She's a care worker. Found her client dead. Back there, number seven. I've not been in yet."

Robin glanced up the street to the marked car with its lights still on. The woman jerked his arm again. He might be half her width, but he was twice her height and ten times stronger. A pointless struggle.

The label on her saturated jacket bore the name 'Karen Taylor' under a Bluebird Homecare logo.

"Karen, I need you to calm down. What's happened to your client?"

"She's dead; she's been … oh God."

Judy straightened up and shoved back her hair. "Killed she said. That's why I called it in."

"Let's go inside …"

"I'm not going back in there." Karen tried again to snatch herself out of his grasp. Tough but tiring, she let out a shriek of frustration when her efforts failed.

"Did you see what happened?"

"No! I didn't do anything. I just found her."

"Great, then let's go and sort this out." Preferably somewhere dry. The rain battered his cheeks like a nasty cloud demon was peppering him with ball-bearings.

With an arm each, they led her back to the house, a decorative detached with an overly grand entrance to the side. Karen shoved herself into the corner of the porch next to a statue of a pissed off angel holding a plant in its stone basket.

"I'll check on the deceased." Robin slicked back his hair and swiped water from his face. "Sort her out please, and get some details. Don't let her leave."

"Guv."

As Robin turned to go inside, DS Jack Tanner's red Ford Capri chugged up the street, encouraged by a crunchy gear change. He stopped to wait for him and tapped his weather app. No end to the rain, a 20% chance of thunder. He'd take that.

Jack parked the Capri behind Judy's patrol car. Face screwed up, he jogged towards Robin, doing the weird, hunched thing people do when they're trying not to get wet. He'd withdrawn into his overcoat, several chins tucked behind a high collar, hands shoved deep in his pockets.

"Have you lost the seventies, Starsky?"

"Very funny. Have you been in?" Jack nudged his head towards the door and wiped his craggy face.

"Not yet. I've just arrived too."

Inside, the house was pristine, nothing out of place. Pale grey walls, clotted cream carpet, watercolour paintings of landscapes and gardens. Robin stuck his head into the two rooms on the right of the hallway and found the same. Chintzy rich. Whoever owned this house had old-fashioned but expensive taste.

"Nothing here," Jack shouted, "Kitchen, conservatory and utility room, no sign of disturbance. Back door and patio doors are locked."

Robin bounded up the stairs, and as soon as he reached the upper landing outside the front bedroom the smell beckoned him. Death presented itself differently every time their paths crossed, and today it crawled into his airways from a smothering rag of crushed lavender and fear. He stopped at the doorway. Claggy old lady perfume with top notes of dirty meat.

Death breath.

A dainty cup lay in a puddle of brown liquid on the floor, just inside the room. He stepped over it and sensed Jack come in behind him.

They edged through a two-second time warp. In the bedroom, all sense of modernity vanished, replaced by Gatsby-era furnishings and art done so meticulously it resembled a film set. A mahogany bed with a fanned art deco headboard and pompous gold feet dominated centre stage. Nailed to this spectacular statement piece was an elderly woman dressed in a cream satin and lace nightdress.

Robin froze. Jack took a few steps backwards and banged into a set of drawers.

"I thought I'd seen everything."

Robin stared at the woman, transfixed. "Me too."

Her body weight had dragged against the thick nails, forging a path through her palms, and the sleeves of her glamorous nightgown draped from her arms like blood-soaked wings. The sight of her pinned into place repulsed him, but he couldn't help but be fascinated by the bizarreness. She reminded him of a broken butterfly, vulnerable and frail but beguiling still. Hair, the colour of brushed steel, hung to her shoulders, styled on one side but hacked off to her scalp on the other. A miniature bible with pages bordered in gold balanced between the clawed fingers of her left hand.

"Who is she?" Robin's attention shifted downwards. The bed covers had been pulled back, her nightdress hitched up to her thighs, and both knees had been battered.

"Ursula Harrison. Used to be CEO of Harrison Engineering." Jack parted the curtains and peered outside. "Spectators are out already."

"What did you do to deserve this?" Robin asked the dead woman, and his mind raced over possibilities, none of which merited this death, not even close. She had to be eighty at least. Frozen terror shrieked in her eyes, yet her lips scrunched together, her scream denied.

"Her lips have been glued, look." Hair stuck to her lips, like she'd eaten some by accident and tried to spit it out.

"This was planned. Unless she kept 5-inch nails and a hammer in her bedroom."

Unlikely. The room was this woman's world, abundant with vintage indulgence, where she spent much of her time. An ornate walking stick lay on the floor by the bedroom chair, snapped into two pieces and bloody. It had probably been used to smash her knees. Was it possible for a solid piece of wood to snap against human bone? Robin stepped over it and moved around the bed.

"How do you nail someone to their bed? asked Jack, "They'd either struggle if they were conscious or be a dead weight if they were out cold."

The woman's arms were creamy smooth, and she'd been in good shape for her age, her body still slender. Ursula Harrison had taken care of herself and refused to age or give up her passions. She'd had enough money to indulge herself, just not enough to guarantee her immunity from evil.

"She was alive when this happened. She bled out for a while."

Blood puddled on the bedsheet beneath the deep holes in her hands and slopped down her arms. More congealed in the sleeves of her slinky nightdress. Not your usual old lady nightwear. Hers, or had her killer made her wear it? No immediate sign of sexual abuse, and no other clothes tossed aside. Robin snapped on gloves and opened the bedside table drawer. A packet of tissues, a pot of Vaseline and a vibrator. Not your usual old lady possessions either. He pressed the 'on' button, and the vibrator hummed in his palm.

"Check this out."

Robin returned the vibrator, closed the drawer, and turned around. Jack held the laundry basket lid in one hand and a wine-red basque dangling from his pen in the other. "Sex game gone wrong?"

"Call me naive, but I don't know of any sex game which involves nailing a woman to her bed. Can you call Joseph Carling please, Jack? We need forensics in here and this house sealed off right away."

"Guv."

Jack left the room, his phone already to his ear.

Alone with his dead companion, Robin tried to see the scene through her eyes, to imagine what she'd been through as she'd taken her final breaths, who'd watched her die. Someone she trusted enough to let into her home or a stranger who knew she'd been alone.

Whatever had happened in this room hung in the air, like the pungent lavender scraping at his throat. Where was it coming from? He panned around, taking in the luxury. Billowy curtains in a metallic print, gold wall sconces, a chaise longue under the window. Then he spotted it. A large bottle on the mirrored dressing table lay on its side, and the perfume pooled out around a collection of jade bottles. Lavender. He would never smell lavender again without thinking of Ursula Harrison, crucified and pulverised in her beautiful room, surrounded by her beautiful things.

Tinny fingers of rain chimed against the bedroom window, calmer now after the earlier deluge.

Ursula. An unusual and feminine name. It suited a woman who still wore glamourous nightwear and cherished her luxuries. Being alone in her room, sharing her death and vulnerability, brought him closer to her. An unusual intimacy. He stared at the one breast sagging outside the neck of her gown. Her chest had been exposed as she'd fallen forward and made her position brazen and lewd. He resisted the urge to cover her up. She would be photographed and catalogued from every angle, and he couldn't give her back her dignity. Sadness dragged in his guts as he moved away, out of her personal space.

From the foot of the bed, Robin burned Ursula's image into his memory.

"Forensics on their way." Jack peered around the doorway, phone still against his ear. "And Joseph Carling."

*

"This is the strangest death I've ever seen."

Joseph Carling, Broadstone's coroner, straightened and flexed his back. He looked more like a surfer than a medical examiner with sunny blonde hair, several leather necklaces, and a paisley patterned headband. Scene Of Crime officers were now all over the house and three of them in the bedroom mutely dabbed and swabbed.

"She's been dead about seven hours. Currently in rigor mortis, although it's warm in here, so I may be out by an hour or two. There's also evidence of cadaveric spasm," he pointed at the victim's fingers around the bible, "You see it with drowning victims. They're often found still gripping whatever they hoped might save them, like a piece of wood, or in suicide cases where they're still clutching a knife."

"But her hand was nailed down," said Jack.

"Yes. I'd say nailed first, then the bible was put into her hand. The nail's gone in clean on this hand, not so clean on the other. There would still be movement in the fingers."

Joseph's eyes shone, as if he'd discovered a chest of ancient treasures and a cure for cancer on the same day.

"No defence wounds," said Robin, "No sign of a struggle."

"Maybe she wasn't conscious. The injuries to her legs are all on the front. If she'd been moving, trying to get away, there would be bruises all the way around. I think she was alive for some time after she was nailed, then battered once in place. No struggle here."

"She had to be out cold."

"Tough job, but not impossible," said Joseph. The three of them were silent in shared perplexity.

"It's a strange one for sure. Fascinating."

"You're enjoying this?" Jack didn't hide his disgust. "Fucks sake, Joe."

"Enjoying? Hell, no. It's dark and nasty. But something exceptional happened in this room; physically, mentally and medically. This is not normal, and to me that's fascinating."

Robin admired Joseph's honesty and was about to probe further when a commotion erupted downstairs. He broke away and followed the noise back to the hallway where a uniformed officer was arguing with a newcomer. The woman, in her fifties, so distinctly resembled the woman upstairs Robin catapulted back in time again. Now he saw Ursula when she'd still been able to enjoy her passion for art deco, maybe had a lover to seduce in her glamorous lingerie.

"I'm sorry, you can't come in. You shouldn't have crossed the cordon."

"This is my mother's house; you can't stop me. Where is she? Who are all these people?" She edged in further and craned her neck to peer up the stairs.

"I'm DI Scott from Broadstone CID. Maybe you should come in ..."

"Oh, now I'm allowed in, am I?" Clenched jowls nestled in the high neck of her cream blouse. "Well?" Hands on hips, thin eyebrows raised in question.

Not an ideal scenario for a family death notice, but he had to tell her. A quick mental search around his usual phrases didn't throw up anything suitable. He'd never told a relative their loved one had been crucified before, especially one who glowered with eyes like storm clouds.

"I have some bad news. Your mother's carer found her dead this morning."

A blink, nothing more. Had she heard him?

"Why did no one call me? A neighbour told me, which is deeply embarrassing."

Yet she still had the time to dress, do her hair, squirt some perfume and stomp over in her polished boots. The eyebrows were still raised.

"I'm sorry for your loss. Now..."

"That bloody care company. I'll sue them for incompetence..."

Robin held up a hand to stop her, baffled by her reaction. "There's no evidence to suggest the care company were to blame. Now, Mrs ..."

"Barbara Rickman."

"Mrs Rickman ..."

"It's her fault, isn't it? The fat one with the bleached hair. She never liked my mother. Where is she?"

Barbara Rickman spun on her heel and strode down the hall. She barged past Jack, who spun around and reached for her arm. She shook him off without a glance and shoved open the living room door. Judy narrowly avoided getting smashed in the face, and collided instead with Barbara, who disentangled herself with a huff.

"You!" Barbara spat, pointing a burgundy talon at the carer, "This is your fault."

Karen Taylor swallowed, perhaps grateful now for the presence of Judy, who became a helpful barrier between her and the enraged daughter.

"This had nothing to do with me. I just found her."

Barbara Rickman spun around towards Robin. "I want to see my mother."

"That's not possible, I'm afraid."

"You have no right to stop me!"

She took a step, considered shoving past Robin's considerable six-foot-two frame. But he didn't budge, and for the first time, she hesitated.

"I understand this is a shock, but I can't allow it."

People dealt with unwelcome news differently. Perhaps anger was her way of controlling the situation because facing other feelings such as grief and loss meant accepting vulnerability, and this woman didn't have a vulnerable bone in her body. He stared at her in a silent challenge, wanting her to reveal more of what lay beneath the veneer. But, maybe sensing she'd met her match and with nowhere else to go, Barbara Rickman threw herself into an armchair. An invisible tripwire of hostility separated Karen and Barbara.

"When did you last see your mum?" Jack sliced through the tension.

"Yesterday. And she was fine."

"Were you close to her?"

"She was my mother. What do you think?" Mrs Rickman checked him over and sighed. "She depended on me. I moved close by to help her as much as possible."

"Does she have a partner?"

"No."

"Who knows the code to the key safe?"

"The carers do," another venomous glare, "The cleaner, and me of course."

"Could she have given the code to anyone without your knowledge?"

"How the hell would I know, if it was against my knowledge?"

A smile twitched on Jack's lips, and he turned away to write in his notebook.

Another CID car arrived, and the FLO got out, holding her hood up in a battle with the wind. Robin spotted a chance to escape. "Our family liaison officer's here, Mrs Rickman. I understand this is difficult, but ...."

"I demand to know ..."

Robin held up a hand to stop her as his phone rang and indignant jaws snapped shut. Clearly Barbara wasn't used to being silenced. He took the call in the driveway, finger in one ear to block out the wind. DC Vic Mason babbled out information in a verbal stream which only subsided when he took a breath.

Jack appeared beside him and puffed out a breath. He looked relieved to be out of the toxic environment indoors. He scanned the road as Robin managed to end his call with Vic.

"This wasn't random. She's minted."

"Do you reckon this was just about her cash?" asked Jack.

"If she'd been clunked on the head or stabbed, maybe. One of these curtain twitchers must've seen something."

Diagonally opposite, a woman in a massive bathrobe watched the unfolding events from the shelter of her porch, cradling a mug. When Jack made eye contact, she released one hand and beckoned him over.

"You've pulled."

"It's the bald thing. Women love it."

"Vic's so excited he can't breathe."

"He gets like that. He nearly passed out once over a stolen mink. He thought he'd busted an international fur smuggling ring." He took a deep breath. "Right, if I'm not out in fifteen minutes, come and save me." He crossed the road, doing the hunched up half-run again.

A message buzzed on Robin's phone. Catherine reminding him they were going to her cousin's wedding reception and offering to collect his suit from the dry cleaners. Life is taken, yet life goes on with its mundanities. People still go to work, walk the dog, laugh on their phones. He'd experienced a similar sense of disengagement with life when his wife had died, and he'd been so angry at everyone for carrying on as usual when his world had been shattered.

He closed the message. No chance he'd make the reception. Two seconds later his phone rang again, just as the heavens opened and unleashed a fresh barrage of cold venom. He did a quick jog down the road to his car and ducked inside to wait for a gap in the noise before he spoke. Their office manager Janet had taken two calls already about police cars and SOC vans blocking the street, and could they speak to number twelve about the height of their gazebo while they were there? Ten minutes later, Jack opened the door and filled his car with the whiff of wet dog from his overcoat.

"Anything useful?" Robin asked when he'd finished with Janet.

"Not much. She woke in the night and went to the bathroom. Reckons she saw a light in the bedroom at Ursula's around 3 am, but she didn't see anyone. Jack opened the glove box, didn't find what he wanted and closed it again. "I'll go back in and get a full statement from the carer."

"I'll deal with the daughter." The glove box rummage puzzled him but not enough to say anything. "Then we can get back and brief the team."

Jack dashed back to the house, backlit by a flash of lightning. Robin closed his eyes and focused on the rhythm of his breaths, doing the old trick he'd done as a child; count the seconds between the lightning and thunder. Five seconds for each mile. It was moving away. Satisfied, he shoved open the door and followed Jack through the rain.

*

The incident room at Broadstone station was rammed. Almost the entire payroll gathered in the seats and stuffed into standing room at the back. No wisecracks, no banter. Everyone focused on the crime scene and the grim images of the crucified woman. Tasks allocated, roles established, they dispersed to work on their own piece of the case.

CID lurked in the oldest part of the building with a lovely view of the bins and fleet garage. Jack had beaten him there, grumbling about someone nicking the biscuits he'd hidden in a filing cabinet.

"Christ, you move fast for an old boy."

Jack smirked. "Your exit strategy is all wrong. Last in, first out. Schoolboy."

Robin sat at the table in what his immediate team called 'the cave' while Jack redirected his scowl at the rickety coffee maker. The tiny room off the central office had previously been a graveyard for dead fax machines, dodgy swivel chairs and boxes of PC cables. Robin had moved out the junk and turned it into a tiny meeting room/break room under the radar of the buildings manager, who'd been preoccupied with the admin refurb.

DS James Witney, their tech brain, fired up a laptop labelled 'Do not remove from Traffic', while Vic scrolled through his phone at the table. DS Ella Montgomery plonked down a bag of sandwiches, narrowly missing his fingers.

"Breakfast." She dug a greasy packet out of the bag. "Not that I feel like eating much after seeing that."

Robin waited until they were all happily munching. "So, we've heard all the facts, and we have the practicalities covered, but I want to start with why. Why did someone crucify an eighty-year-old woman? Vic, talk us through what you have on her so far."

Vic licked ketchup off his fingers, rearranged his fringe and opened his notebook with a fancy flourish. He loved the spotlight. Robin prepped himself for a potentially arse-numbing monologue.

"Well first, she was known to us. She's made a raft of calls to the station about minor things over the years. I remember them from when I was in uniform. She pissed everyone off with her constant complaints. Anyway, her late husband Maurice started Harrison Engineering back in 1966 when he was just twenty-eight. She's still a major shareholder, along with her daughter Barbara Rickman. She owned the house in Billingsworth outright –valued at over half a mil by the way - a property in France, one in Malta and a holiday home in Cornwall. Well, a log cabin, in a fancy forest park. Anyway, I'm waiting for a financial report, but her estimated net worth must be close to five million, excluding her share in Harrison Engineering."

"And her daughter's sole beneficiary," said Ella, trying to clean a blob of egg off her top.

"Wrong," Jack managed through a mouthful of bagel, "A neighbour reckoned she included a 'significant' donation to the church in her will. She bragged about it."

"She had grandchildren too," said Robin, "But they're not listed on Companies House as having any significant control. Any scandal?"

"Nothing yet, but there's a ton of stuff to go through. Loads of news stories about the company's success, about how it regularly made charitable donations and contributed to the community. Massively active with the church. Harrisons paid for the repair of the tower and extensive renovation works at All Saints church in Broadstone. It was built in 1847…"

"Do we have any video footage of Ursula?" Robin couldn't take a history lesson. "I'd like to see her alive."

James' fingers skittered across his keyboard, and after half a minute or so he spun his screen around. "This was on the news when the church tower reopened two years ago."

They all hunched up. The video started with a before and after sequence, showing the extent of weather damage the church had suffered, followed by an overview of the renovations. Then the footage cut to the priest, a local MP and Ursula Harrison standing next to a tiny, curtained plaque. Robin leaned in further. She was immaculate and attractive for a woman pushing eighty, wearing a slash-necked blue dress with low-heeled shoes, platinum hair perfect. She used a walking stick for support, but it didn't diminish her. It gave her gravitas and elevated her more.

Ursula began to speak, and James turned up the volume.

"I'm delighted and honoured to be able to fund this project for the church through Harrison Engineering. I've worshipped here all my life and this donation exemplifies my dedication to the church and our Lord."

Clipped and clear voice, her words delivered with the intonation of an experienced public speaker. She opened the curtains, prompting a ripple of applause. The camera panned out to Barbara Rickman standing behind her mother with a tall, good-looking lad struggling to hide his boredom. Barbara's smile appeared practised and phoney.

"Reminds me of Margaret Thatcher," said Jack, "Like it's a performance, each word and move scripted."

"Cracking figure for an old woman," said Vic, and Jack shook his head at him, "What? I'm just saying she looks awesome for her age. I wouldn't do her. Well, I can't obviously …"

"Thanks for that insight, Vic." Robin pulled Vic out of the hole he'd dug. "You're right though. I noticed it this morning," he turned to Jack, "I get you about the staged thing, and think about her bedroom. Another place, another stage. Let's watch the end, James."

James resumed the footage which finished with a cutaway of Ursula Harrison, accompanied by Barbara this time, pointing towards the top of the tower. More staging. Robin ignored what they were doing and studied what they were hiding. Barbara hovering behind the matriarch, allowing her to dominate the scene while she carried two handbags, one matching her mother's dress. The way her jaw clenched, how she painted on a happy expression, suggested she didn't enjoy the submissive role.

"It's all very corporate," said James as the video clip ended, "I wonder what she was like in private?"

"A tyrant apparently," said Jack, "No one could stand her."

" 'exemplifies my dedication'," Ella quoted, checking her notes, "Who says that?"

"Convincing herself as well as others." Robin leant back and studied the paused image of Ursula, splendid in electric blue. "Like when people rattle off their achievements or earnings. I think she was confirming her list of good deeds, reminding herself of why she helped. Buying her way to heaven."

"And then she was crucified," said James.

Who did she piss off so much they had to make her death a statement? Robin struggled to assimilate the woman on the screen with the one he'd seen earlier. Dead Ursula had been soft and vulnerable. This woman oozed authority.

"It's personal," said Ella.

Robin agreed. He'd felt like an intruder just by being in her bedroom.

"Any signs of sexual activity?" asked James.

"Joseph doesn't think so. Just some kinky lingerie in her laundry basket," said Jack, "Vibrator in the drawer."

"You were right." James winked at Vic. "The old girl was foxy."

Vic looked sick at the thought.

"If the daughter's involved, she paid someone else to do it," said Jack.

"Any related crimes on the system?" Robin asked James, "Crucifixions?"

"Nothing in the UK except a paedophile who had a crucifix rammed down his throat. There was a case in Italy involving a prostitute who was crucified back in 1987. Check this out though." James tapped and clicked until he found the right site. "It's from John 19.31. Might explain why he smashed her knees."

They all huddled over the screen to read the quotation.

"The Jews therefore, because it was the preparation, that the bodies should not remain upon the cross on the sabbath day, (for that sabbath day was an high day,) besought Pilate that their legs might be broken, and that they might be taken away."

"He did it to make sure she was dead," Vic said.

"I'm not sure it's literal," said Robin, "But there's a link. Either this guy, or the person he acted for, knew Ursula's religious beliefs. Vic, stay with Harrison Engineering, James on the tech please and Ella, see how you get on with the church connection. All the adoration is fake. No organisation is that squeaky. Let's find the truth."

Chapter Two

Sucked in

Once they'd gone through their tasks, Robin made another coffee and was on the way back to his office when his phone beeped.

"I'm downstairs. Do you have 2 mins? x"

Catherine again. The station in Broadstone was in the centre of town and around the corner from the dry cleaners he used. Shit, he'd forgotten to message her back about the wedding reception. He dumped his coffee on a battered filing cabinet and headed downstairs, trying not to be pissed off by the interruption, but he wanted to push on while he was pumped and focused.

She waited on the steps outside, windswept and lovely in skinny jeans and a tan jacket. Chestnut curls whipped around her flushed cheeks, and they laughed as he leant in to kiss her and got a mouth full of hair. His irritation blew away on the wind, and he fought his way through. He enjoyed how she tasted of fresh air and her favourite lemon lip balm.

"You look hot. If I wasn't so busy, I'd take you round the back of admin for a quickie." He was only half joking.

"How romantic." Her laugh swept over his lips. "But I'm not staying. I just brought you some lunch." She passed him the brown bag dangling from her wrist. "I rang your landline and Janet answered. She said a major incident had come in."

A tinge of curiosity in her inflection. The ex-reporter in her still perked up at the sniff of intrigue.

"A strange one, yeah. I'll tell you more later."

She smiled, he smiled, and they both knew he wouldn't. Robin rarely talked in detail about work. His usual excuse was he didn't want work to interfere with his home life, but it was more the belief that if he kept the two worlds apart, everyone would be safer.

"Were you caught in the storm earlier?" She inspected him as she waited for his answer, green eyes merciless in their scrutiny.

"Yeah, I put the radio on full blast and drowned it out. There was so much going on I hardly noticed it."

She nodded, not giving away whether she believed him or not, and retreated into her jacket as a gust of wind whipped curls around her face again. He suspected the weather was another reason for the impromptu visit. Catherine was one of few people who knew how much he hated thunder.

"I'm meeting Clive for coffee in five, so I'm off. Drop me a text when you're leaving work."

He wouldn't make the reception, and the way she lingered as she kissed him suggested she knew it too.

*

Catherine Nicholls watched Robin go back inside and almost called him back. She hated to see him go. She hated goodbyes, full stop. Ever since she'd been a child, she always had the same anxiety when she left someone, a fear she would never see them again. Totally irrational. Like Robin and thunderstorms. When he'd first told her about it, they'd been away for the weekend, glamping at a music festival. The storm had hit during the night, and she'd found it impossible to believe such a strong and steady man - a policeman – had such an illogical fear. He'd been embarrassed and tried to hide it, but she'd loved him more for showing some vulnerability.

Her ex-boss and old friend from the Broadstone Daily Post skulked in a corner of Bakers Bistro, vaping covertly inside his jacket. He shoved his ecig back in his pocket and bear hugged her, dwarfing her with his six-foot-three mass. Clive Darwin was an old school editor, and as tough as he looked. He used every inch of height and bulk to bulldoze his way through whatever shitstorm blew his way, didn't suffer fools and was relentlessly loyal to the paper and its publishers.

"When will you come and work for my paper again?"

"In your dreams, Clive." Catherine grinned. Their conversations often began in the same way. "I'm starting work on the castle contract next week. Sorry, but that's much better for my soul than school fundraisers and interviewing councillors about parking restrictions."

Clive clutched his chest like he'd been stabbed. "That's a dagger to my heart, it really is."

"Behave. There's a wall of steel around your heart."

Clive's eyes twinkled from deep within a face so rugged they almost disappeared in the furrows when he smiled. On the table between them, an ancient Blackberry vibrated. Catherine ordered coffee while Clive took a pair of battered glasses from his pocket and read his message. His appearance was deceptive. While he didn't spend money on basic possessions (barring his weird shirt obsession) he made up for it with his love of expensive food and wine.

"Interesting," he said, removing his glasses again, "Have you spoken to Robin today?"

"I couldn't possibly say."

"Two words: major incident."

"I've just seen Robin actually, but he didn't mention it. I've told you before, he never does."

"You're the worst spy ever. I trained you better."

"No, you trained me to recognise the difference between a Merlot and a Malbec. Anyway, I thought I was a friend, not a mole."

"It's a good job you are, because you're a shit mole. There's a press briefing at five, so I'll have to bail a bit earlier," he sipped his coffee then added, voice raised a pitch, "Come with me; you still have your card."

Catherine's drink arrived, giving her a moment to think. She didn't want to admit how much she was tempted. Although she loved freelancing and her new contract with Broadstone Castle excited her, she missed the thrill of the chase. Clive took another sneaky pull on his vaper while she sprinkled nutmeg on her coffee.

"How long have you been off the fags for now?"

"Question avoided. Don't think I didn't notice."

Catherine sipped coffee through a frothy cloud of nutmeg flavoured milk.

"I've moved on," she said, filling the silence which confirmed Clive wasn't about to let it go, "And it was the right decision."

"For whom?"

"Clive …"

"No, let's go there. For whom? For your family? For you? Or for your boyfriend who didn't like you being a journalist and persuaded you to quit?"

"For me," Catherine bit back, "After … well, you know. I didn't feel the same."

"And your family and boyfriend pressured you into sacrificing a successful career because once, just once, you ended up in a scrape."

Catherine stared at him, stunned and hurt by the understatement. After a few seconds he dropped his gaze and held up his hands.

"OK, I'm sorry. It was more than a scrape, and I know the distress it caused, but you came through it. Back at your desk a week later, right as rain."

Obviously not as 'right as rain' as Clive inferred, because a month and much soul-searching later, she resigned from the job she loved.

Clive squeezed her hand in his huge paw and smiled with genuine affection.

"I miss working with you. We were a great team; you make a cracking brew, and I miss that green top I could see your bra through."

"Perv," Catherine said, smiling.

"When you get to my age, you take what you can get. Seriously, think about it."

"What? The green top?"

"You know what I mean."

"I like the freedom, Clive. I like working all day in my scruffs with no makeup on. I like being in control. I don't want to go back to someone else's rules …"

"You can't control everything," Clive enunciated each word with feeling.

Catherine sighed. "Can we change the subject?"

Clive refilled his coffee and spooned in two sugars. "How's things with Robin?"

Thorny question. Most of the time they were happy, except for when the ever-present shadow of Robin's dead wife appeared. Young, popular, taken in tragic circumstance. Tough to compete against PC Erin Scott. She didn't like herself for it, with Erin long dead, but jealousy gnawed at her. Catherine had Googled her often, fascinated by the woman who'd caused Robin so much pain. She wanted to understand why, because although she would never replace Erin, she needed to at least become her equal in Robin's affection. Google didn't have the answer.

"He works too much, and his apartment is too tidy, but no one's perfect. How's it going with your neighbour? Alice?"

"Alison. She chinned me off for the guy who delivers her prescription."

"Back to swiping then?"

"It's not easy at my age." Clive took off his coat. Underneath, he wore his standard uniform of weird shirt and plain V neck jumper. Greyhounds raced across today's shirt. "I'm glad you're happy, and I respect Robin. He's smart. Still not sure he likes me though."

"Because you ripped the piss out of me at the Christmas party, and he thought you went too far."

"You didn't think so."

"Of course I didn't, which didn't help."

"Come with me later," Clive leant towards her with sudden eagerness, "We can sit at the back so you won't be seen, and you can watch him in secret. For old times' sake?"

"Clive. Enough."

Clive held up his hands again. "OK, but I'll never stop trying to tempt a talented writer back to her craft." Cheesy grin, on the cusp of creepy.

"Prepare for the rejection. And I'm still writing anyway. There's a raft of copy needed for the castle re-opening."

"Fascinating. Some crumbly old building full of crumbly old shit. Dull dead people no one gives a shit about and one vaguely salacious tale about witches. I know you love your history but Jesus Catherine, really? Where's the thrill? It's not sitting in your jammies trying to make a family tree sound interesting."

"I don't wear 'jammies,' whatever they are."

Clive fixed her again with his wise gaze. "You're better than that."

"We're going to fall out soon, and I don't want to argue."

"Fine."

Clive picked up his phone again, and Catherine twisted around as a bunch of men in a booth erupted with laughter. Plenty of truth in what Clive said, and it came from a good place, but it pissed her off. She'd made her decision. No point doing all the soul searching to go back on her decision six months later. A tough temptation though.

"I don't want to fall out." Clive's tone softened. "You know me, I'm a persistent old bugger," he held up a finger to stop her next protest, "And it's a murder. A juicy one."

"Who told you?"

Clive tapped his nose with a mischievous grin. "It's better if you don't know. So, are you coming? Total anonymity. You could chuck in a few dodgy adverbs, so no one knows it's you."

"I thought I was just going for a nosey."

"So you're in?" Clive sounded like an eight-year-old who'd been told he could have a dog.

"This is a serious decision Clive."

"I know, and I'm so fucking proud of you for even considering it."

"I'm not writing for you …"

"Fine."

Catherine sighed as the rest of her afternoon crumbled away, like a cliff-edge beach house disintegrating into a greedy, corrosive sea.

"If you tell anyone, I'll never speak to you again."

"I'd expect no less."

*

Barbara Rickman filled the interview room with her attitude and perfume. She placed a leather-bound notebook on the table as if attending a meeting and not a formal interview about her mother's murder. She'd dismissed the FLO and arrived at the station demanding answers, changing first into a black power suit with another high-necked blouse, makeup perfect. If Barbara Rickman had spent the day mourning the loss of her mother, she showed no visible sign of it.

She leant forward towards Robin and Jack.

"Let's cut to the chase. You want to know where I was last night, don't you?"

The direct approach didn't surprise him. He'd expected her to be a challenge. Robin opened his case file and allowed the force of her question to dissolve in a few moments of silence.

"We always ask everyone associated with or related to the deceased the same question," he answered, and he eyeballed her, undaunted by her fierce expression.

"I was at home, in bed. Alone. Am I a suspect?"

"Why don't you relax a little Mrs Rickman? We're investigating your mother's death, not trying to frame you for it."

"Relax? My mother's been murdered, and you want me to relax?"

"I think you know what I mean."

Barbara sat upright in her plastic chair. She glanced at Jack, assessed and disregarded him, turned back to Robin. She was wrong to dismiss him. Jack seemed like the harmless one, the retro-clad old-timer who trundled around town bollocking pissheads and gave directions to tourists while he waited for his pension. He enjoyed the empowerment in being underestimated.

"You still haven't told me how she died, and your family liaison officer keeps reeling off lines from her platitudes and clichés manual."

"We're still gathering evidence ..."

"Yes, I've already heard that one."

Robin met Barbara's eyes again. Just when the friction began to feel uncomfortable, she rubbed the back of her neck and adjusted her scarf, pacifying herself.

"Your mother was murdered, Mrs Rickman. She was restrained and beaten in her bed." Barbara recoiled from the information and sank back in her chair. Interesting how far she had to be pushed before she presented an external emotional reaction. "We need your help to understand why. You were the closest person to her."

Barbara shook her head and frowned. "She wasn't close to anyone."

Robin waited while she processed her thoughts. He'd glimpsed beneath the veneer, and he wanted to crack open the breach.

"Could you give us an overview of your mother's last year or so. Where did she go, who did she meet? How involved was she in the business?"

"For years she was an exemplary and inspirational leader, and I can assure you no one at Harrison Engineering, or its suppliers, had anything but the utmost respect for her.

And there, in an instant, the breach snapped closed again. Had she rehearsed that little speech? It sounded like she'd been reading a statement rather than remembering her mum.

"We have to consider all avenues, and with respect, you might not know if an employee at Harrisons harboured a grudge against your mother."

"I'd know."

"Like you knew someone who wanted your mum dead had the code to the key safe?" said Jack.

Barbara bristled and assessed him again with a chilly stare. Jack returned the glower with a warm and amiable smile. "What's your point?"

"My point is you can't know what everyone at Harrison Engineering does, thinks or feels."

Barbara sighed like she had to indulge a persistent child. "My mother was the CEO and company accountant for years, a pioneer for women in business. As a woman at the helm of a company, you must be a strong visionary leader. When she started to have health problems, she retired, reluctantly, but she always maintained an interest. We often talked about the business. It made her feel involved."

Or in control. Two tough women at the top table in an otherwise male-dominated business. Bet the sparks had flown when those two disagreed.

"She's made lots of calls to the police over the years about various trivial matters. Why do you think she did that?"

"They weren't trivial to her. And she paid a fortune in taxes in her lifetime, so she saw it as her entitlement to receive a service she'd helped significantly to pay for."

Explaining that wasn't how it worked wouldn't get him anywhere. Robin had met plenty of people who thought the police were just public servants who should be available at the snap of entitled fingers.

"Was there anyone she argued with, or who might have an issue with her?" he asked.

"As I said, she hadn't physically worked there for years. It would've been impossible for her to argue with anyone. Naturally, there's conflict over operational issues, staff, or finance in any business, but nothing which would result in … this."

"Any personal disputes?"

"Only with the care staff. She didn't see anyone else. Have you read the visit log?"

Robin had read the file. The catalogue of complaints, like the calls to the police, seemed to be Ursula's way of asserting power because she felt powerless.

"Your mother was religious, wasn't she?"

Barbara blinked, knocked off guard by the switch in questions. "What does her faith have to do with this?"

"Deeply?"

"I'm not sure how you define the depth of faith. She always attended church and read her bible. She was a good Catholic. When she couldn't go to church, her priest used to visit her at home."

"Did she read her bible in bed?"

"What a strange question." She waited for an explanation but gave it some thought when she received none. Robin had asked a vaguely personal question, and Barbara didn't know the answer.

"I don't think so. She had a large print bible for day-to-day reading and a vintage one with gold-tipped pages in her room. The text is too small for her to read comfortably, but it's pretty. She mostly read gardening books."

"Her gardens are stunning."

"They should be with the amount of money she spent on them. I do hope your people are careful in their work. I have to sell the house now, and the fact there's been a death there, a murder even, will affect its saleability."

It took some effort not to react. This woman didn't have a veneer. Veneers were surface level and chipped easily. Barbara was as guarded and impenetrable as a steel-clad vault, and he was determined to break his way through. Perhaps not today. He might have to play the long game with her, but he would get through.

"Karen Taylor mentioned your mother could be attention-seeking. Said she shaved her eyebrows off once as a protest. Did she cut her hair recently?"

"The woman's an idiot. My mother did it because she adored 1920's style. Clara Bow, from the silent movie era, used to do it. And no. I saw her yesterday, and her hair was like it normally is. Styled. Perfect."

"It wasn't this morning."

Barbara shrugged. "She took great care with her appearance; I can't imagine her doing that."

"You're remarkably calm about your mother's murder," said Jack.

"I've survived in this world by learning to keep emotions private. I'd prefer not to share my feelings about my mother and her death with you."

Robin found her as cold as Jack did, but she did have a point. He'd met plenty of people who dealt with their emotions by presenting an alternative exterior.

"You have two sons," he said.

"A son and a stepson. My husband, his father, died when John was eleven."

"That's admirable, Barbara. It takes real love and dedication to raise someone else's child."

"It's what my husband would have wanted. It was my duty."

Duty. A distressed child, orphaned at eleven, and taken in by a woman who considered him a duty. Perhaps Barbara resented the child she'd been duty-bound to raise. Would he have taken on Erin's child if she'd had one? Hell yes. He wouldn't have hesitated if it would've meant having a part of her still close to him. It would even have helped with the grieving process. Might turn into resentment though

"Is he involved in the business?" Jack's question jolted Robin out of his thoughts.

"Not at all. He has no aptitude for business." She sneered with distaste. "His father had a brilliant mind. He established the Harrison Technical part of the company and John receives bi-annual dividends as part of his inheritance. I don't see him much now."

"What about your other son?"

"He's fifteen, and my mother adored him. His father also left him an inheritance and part of his shares in the business. The same as John."

She shifted as she spoke, as if the outrage at her late husband's sense of equality made her squirm. Odd how the descriptions of both sons were financial statements. Nothing about them as people.

"Any other relatives involved in the business?" asked Jack.

"No." Barbara drummed an irritated beat with her pen against her notebook. "Why did you ask about my mother's faith? What are you not telling me?"

Robin leant forward. The religious question resonated with her. "Your mother was holding a bible when she died, the gold-tipped one you mentioned earlier, and her body was positioned in a manner similar to a crucifixion."

Barbara swallowed, and this time her attempt to conceal her feelings was more difficult. She stared straight through Robin, visualising what he'd said. Her eyes flickered left as if she was recalling a memory, but she forced herself back.

"Did she suffer?"

"I'm sorry, we don't have the details at this stage."

Barbara swallowed and rubbed her throat.

"Would you like some water?" Robin filled a cup for her from the water machine in the corner of the room. She drank it in one go.

"You're critical to this investigation. We need all the information we can get, no matter how insignificant you feel it might be."

She nodded but she looked elsewhere. "Her priest might be able to shed light on it," she said finally, "Father Michael Heath. He's at the All Saints church in Broadstone now, but he used to be at Our Lady's in Billingsworth."

"Who inherits your mother's estate?"

Barbara had been midway to her feet. She froze and stared at Jack in disbelief, then straightened to her full height. Robin and Jack remained silent. Barbara didn't move.

"I do. There. But for your information, I'm also wealthy in my own right."

"Just you?"

"Yes. The houses, her properties overseas, her shares in the business and her collection of ugly Lalique glassware." She snatched her notebook and shoved it into her handbag. "If you don't mind, I've things to do."

"Of course." Robin wasted a smile. She looked like she wanted to punch him.

*

"What do you think?" asked Robin as he and Jack squeezed through a group of earnest newbies on their way to the briefing room.

"Not involved, not physically anyway. Her nails were perfect."

The grandly titled briefing room served as refectory, classroom and dumping ground for shit without a home, stuffed with rows of chairs for the lucky few who grabbed them first. Robin loved the challenge of media briefings. Time to conduct the orchestra of hungry stringers. Mostly freelancers these days and the odd regional hack still doing things the old way, still talking about the dark ages when editors smoked in their office, lunched on vodka, and used shorthand. Like Clive Darwin. He might've progressed to vaping but there he was, right at the back, towering over everyone like an old school headmaster …

Robin did a double take. Catherine? What the …? She stood next to Darwin, talking to a woman whose hair didn't move and had airbrushed skin the colour of Barbie plastic. Cindy Shelby, Post colleague and Catherine's friend. The pack had circled and drawn her in, which didn't surprise him. They'd been trying for months. Just when Catherine had found a new project to be excited about. It had been securing the Broadstone Castle work that had pulled her out of a pit of darkness, and Robin couldn't have been happier for her, yet the paper's allure hadn't gone away. Whenever she met with Darwin, it made him uneasy, but he always held back, determined not to be a controlling, overprotective dick. Well, that had worked.

"… so what I intend to do today is read out a short statement of the facts as we know them so far…"

Superintendent Anna Collins took over, but Robin was no longer in the moment. He answered questions which followed with his usual ease, but internally his focus had wondered.

"You never said Catherine was coming," Jack whispered as Collins wrapped up and people began to leave.

"I didn't know."

"Is she back at The Post?"

She filed out, flanked by Cindy and Darwin.

"I'm about to find out." Robin broke away from the team, earning him a scowl from Collins, and left the room through a separate entrance. Outside in the corridor, the chatter increased as people discussed what they'd heard, several already on their phones. Robin pushed his way through, looking for Darwin as a marker. Eventually, he spotted him with Catherine at his side.

"Cat." She spun around and Robin nudged his head in the direction of a quiet corner, just off the stairs. "What are you doing here?" Robin took her arm and eased her away from the pack.

"Clive asked me and ... I don't know. I was already in town. And I miss it."

"What, hanging around at media briefings?"

"You know what I mean."

Robin scanned the foyer, fighting off a bitchy come-back. What was so fascinating about that paper? Darwin pretended not to be listening, chunky fingers stabbing the keys on a knackered Blackberry.

"Don't miss the opportunity you've been waiting for. Give yourself the chance to find the excitement elsewhere."

"I came out of curiosity, that all."

Vic was trying to get his attention, arm-waving with the subtlety of someone sent to collect a partially sighted relative from airport arrivals.

"I have to go. Look, I don't think I'll be able to make it to the reception."

"I know." An unconvincing smile.

"I'll call you later."

Chapter Three

Fatal Collision

"Please Marcia, you have to stop this."

John Rickman edged closer to begging. Extremely close. He'd tried reasoning with Marcia Clarke, and it hadn't worked. He'd ordered her to go, but she'd laughed in his face. What did he have to do to make her leave? His inner pragmatist screamed at him to grab hold of her and launch her out of the front door, but he couldn't touch her. So, all he had left was to beg like a pathetic sap. His self-esteem crawled out of the room in disgust.

His day had darkened with a phone call from Barbara. When her name had appeared on his phone's screen he hadn't answered. He'd waited a full hour before he listened to the voicemail.

"John, it's Barbara. Your grandmother has died. It's complicated, and I need to brief you. Call me."

Brief you. Who speaks to their family in that way? The call had left him as cold as her clipped tone and the emotionless message. He hadn't called her back and had no intention to; at least not until he'd dealt with the monumental fuck up unfolding in his living room.

Marcia Clarke stared at the street through rivers of rain streaming down the window. She toyed with a loose thread hanging from the hem of her cropped jumper. This tiny gesture irritated him so much he had to look away.

"Are you saying I mean nothing to you?"

A tricky question with unfavourable consequences in all directions. Yes, she meant nothing to him, except in this moment she meant everything. She had the power to destroy him and his career and all he'd ever worked for. She had his balls in her hand, metaphorically of course because thank Christ he had morals and self-control. Marcia was an attractive girl, curvy and sumptuous like a mini Marilyn Munroe. She might be brassy and bold, but she could turn heads, and if she'd had her way, she would be caressing his balls right now.

If you stick to the truth, you can't go wrong, right? His inner sceptic bristled, but for now the truth was all he had to go on.

"Marcia, I care about all my students, but not in the way you're suggesting."

"You're a leching, pervy bastard!"

She liked to shock, and her vitriol disturbed him, like when she'd undressed, and her little denim mini skirt had hit the floor. She'd demanded his attention. Her fierce confidence reminded him of the boldness of the women who beckoned in passers-by from behind glass doors in Amsterdam's red-light district. Cheap red thong partially buried in puppy fat, and still visible, even though she'd dressed again. It screamed at him from above the low-slung skirt skimming her hips.

How had she found his house? It had to be a good ten or fifteen miles from where Marcia lived, and he'd never given out his address at work. Not to students.

Marcia turned, blue mascara tears streaking her cheeks, massive hoop earrings smacking into her jaw. Her scorn made him feel like a scumbag. She grabbed her bag from the floor and stormed out of the room.

"Marcia …"

"You've led me on."

"Are you serious? How have I led you on?"

She stopped at the front door and shoved back her platinum blonde curls. She looked at him like he'd morphed into a stupid spaniel.

"I've seen you leering at my tits." She pouted and jiggled her ample chest. "The way you lean over me in class, the way you smile at me when we see each other. You've been crushing on me for weeks."

John stared at her, suddenly cold to his core. Mentally he flicked through all their encounters, fast-forwarded through hours of teaching time. He searched for one moment when he might have overstepped the mark, but he couldn't find one, despite her attempts to get his attention. He'd seen her flaunting herself, all the male teachers had. Hard not to see the ample breasts spilling from her shirt like mesmeric beacons. But he found her in-your-face approach borderline aggressive and about as attractive to him as a guy in a tutu.

"That's a pack of lies and you know it. If I've glanced at your chest I sincerely apologise, but it's hard to avoid when your blouse is undone. You're inviting men to stare at you, but you have much more to give. Respect yourself."

Marcia cried harder. More blobs of make-up slid towards her chin, and she swiped at the tears. He wanted to give her a hug and help her but couldn't. Physical contact could be misconstrued, and he couldn't take the risk.

"I think you should leave."

She scrunched her face like she'd swallowed a sweet made of vinegar.

"It's pouring down out there. Can't you give me a lift?"

"It would be better if you caught the bus."

Marcia flung the front door open, and the chill autumn night rushed in. "You don't care about me, just your shitty job at that shitty school. Let's see what Maloney thinks of you and your precious job after this." With one last sneer of contempt, she ran down the steps and onto the street.

John rested his head against the door frame as a strange blend of relief and fear flushed through his system. She'd gone, but what had his rejection done to her warped little mind? He had to follow her.

I need to brief you. Barbara's words bounced around in his head again. He thumped the heel of his hands against his temples, but it wasn't easy to get rid of her either, it had never been. He wanted to sort his head out but instead, he had to go chasing after someone else he wished would disappear.

Brutal rain swept across the street and the road blurred through his windscreen, like an impressionist watercolour. A handful of glum cars inched along the wet streets. He passed a teenage couple giggling under dripping fringes, huddled in a bus shelter, and he envied the simplicity of their lives. Why wasn't Marcia just being a teenager, necking some spotty lad or binge-watching rubbish on YouTube? No sign of her. She'd fused into the deluge and become aptly part of its nature.

Maybe she'd thumbed a lift, enticed a lonely motorist with her provocative outfit? If anything happened to her, it would be his fault. He should've called her dad and taken her home. He crept on, wipers on double speed.

He'd almost reached the top of Broadstone Bridge when a figure in white appeared on the kerbside, a distorted and faceless apparition, arms flailing. The figure paused for one breath then stepped calmly into the road. John jammed his foot towards the brake, but it slipped, the sole of his shoe slimy from the rain, and instead he pushed the useless space between the brake and the clutch. It took a second to disentangle himself, he recovered too late.

Blackness engulfed him.

*

Halfway home, the rain battered the town again, sweeping across the country lane leading out towards Catherine's village, Camber. She slowed right down and flicked her wipers to full speed, but she could've been driving through a car wash. Angry nails of rain hammered on the roof and drowned out her music. She considered pulling over for a second, then a phone call came through the sound system. She checked the screen, expecting it to be Robin. It was Clive.

"Christ almighty, what's that noise?" Clive shouted, loud enough to make the sound distort.

"Rain. Two secs, I'll pull in."

A loud car horn made her jump, and she slammed on the brakes, a reflex action which jarred her spine. The sudden adrenalin surge made her stomach lurch and her pulse throb in her ears. Some dick who'd been up her arse for a mile or two, overtook her and disappeared into the distant vortex. The pretty lane, lined with trees and tumbledown cottages was normally a tranquil landscape. Today it had become a scene of elemental carnage.

"Who's a fucking nob?"

"Sorry." She parked under a cluster of low-hanging trees. "Some idiot trying to kill himself. Can you hear me better now?"

"Just about. I just had an interesting call with a guy who used to work at Harrisons and I wondered if you could do me a favour? He lives near to you and he's in right now. Any chance you could pop round and tie up loose ends with him? He doesn't want his name mentioned, but he ripped into the management there. Sounds like Ursula Harrison was a bitch."

"I don't work for you anymore …"

"You're a freelancer. You can freelance."

"I'm almost home, and I'm going out tonight. No chance."

"Don't you see I'm trying to help you?"

"No, not really."

"I know you better than think. I know deep in your lovely soul, in a place hidden even from yourself, you're bitter about quitting because you did it for everyone else except for yourself."

"Profound, Clive."

"Am I right?"

Catherine sighed and stared out of the window. Rain enclosed her in a claustrophobic bubble like her car had become submerged in water. "You won't let it go, will you?"

"No. Like I said earlier, I'm not willing to give up on you, even if you've given up on yourself."

"You've gone very fluffy these days."

"I've always been fluffy."

"Fuck off," Catherine glanced at the clock. Pushing it, but she could spare about half an hour which gave her an hour to get home, get gorgeous and get back to Broadstone for eight. And she couldn't deny it, her head spun with angles on the Harrison story. Rare for an eighty-year-old woman to be murdered.

"Where does this guy live?"

"Off the park road."

"OK, I need to turn around. Fill me in on the way."

"So, he was a commercial manager, working under Ursula Harrison …" Clive rattled off the details, excitement in his voice. She turned around and headed back towards Broadstone. The road would take her past the castle and over a narrow bridge in one of the main tourist areas outside the town itself. Steeped in history, it lurked eerily in the relentless downpour. People darted around, defiantly battling through the rain, encased in gaudy waterproofs.

The electronic sign before the bridge reminded her to slow. As she passed it, a figure appeared on the narrow pavement and his face flashed in her headlights, oddly recognisable, like an old nameless enemy popping up in a bad dream. His bare foot, slab-white against the tarmac, left the kerb and he stepped into the road. She floored the brake and time froze in a blurry split-second tableau. Oncoming headlights bleached his profile in dazzling brightness. Then he was gone.

The crunch of battered metal added to the roar of the rain.

*

Robin pushed open the doors to the morgue as darkness fell. Most of the lights were off and the little reception room was empty. He dug out his phone and checked his messages. No missed calls from Catherine. He opened the weather app. 90% probability of rain, no thunder. Miniscule chance of another storm occurring on the same day.

Joseph Carling, looking as sunny as he had that morning, stuck his head around the door just as he'd started drafting a text to Catherine. "Check this out."

Robin followed him to his desk and peered at the report on his screen.

"Both tibiae are broken, the right fibula is also broken, and both scapulae are shattered. This was a vicious and sustained attack, but look at this. We have an unknown substance. At first, I thought it was nicotine because of these." He tapped his screen and pointed to some unrecognisable hieroglyphics, "Piperidine alkaloid toxins are similar in structure to nicotine, but she was a non-smoker. No match against any common drugs or any of the prescription drugs found in her house. Shortly before death, her entire respiratory system began to shut down. Cause of death – heart failure." Joseph's fingers skimmed over the keyboard and a photograph appeared on the screen. "This shot is of the victim's left earlobe. See this?" He pointed with his pen at a tiny dot. "It's an injection site, and a recent incision."

Robin leant forward and squinted. "We need to identify that unknown substance as a priority."

"It's on its way to the path lab as we speak, but don't hold your breath. It's skeleton staff over the weekend."

"OK, but I'd appreciate it if this can get priority on Monday," Robin stared again at the screen. It could've been given by one of her carers earlier in the evening, to calm her down maybe. Maybe she'd been prepped and already sedated when he arrived. Made the job easier.

Joseph tapped his pen against his lips, thinking. "People smoke to relax, because nicotine activates the reward pathways in the brain and makes us feel pleasure or wellbeing. Whatever this is, it was administered to calm her. I'll make sure we prioritise the identification. It'll help you understand when it was given too."

Questions and possibilities pinged around in Robin's head but no answers. "Anything else useful?"

"There was a clump of hair in her mouth – her own hair - and in her stomach. And she was clean. No contamination from the killer. I've found no trace on the body. Bearing in mind how physical this was, it's extraordinary there was no exchange."

"He suited up?"

"From the moment he entered yes."

So this had been more business than pleasure, about killing her rather than enjoying the moment. Someone doing this for fun would want to be more physically involved.

They were still staring at the screen when a door clanged, and rubber shoes squeaked as someone approached. Joseph's assistant Kane opened the door, a phone tucked under his chin.

"Fatal collision out at Broadstone Bridge." He covered the speaker as his caller continued the update. "Two cars and a pedestrian."

"I'll leave you to it," said Robin, "Thanks Joe."

Robin dug his phone out again as he headed out of the door. Ten missed calls from Jack. Ten? What could've happened in 30 minutes to merit ten missed calls. He redialled, and Jack answered after one ring.

"Have you heard about the crash on Broadstone Bridge?" asked Jack, without any preamble.

"It was called in just as I left the morgue. What's up?"

Too long a pause. Robin's pulse quickened.

"One of the drivers was John Rickman, Barbara Rickman's stepson." Jesus, talk about coincidences. Ten missed calls though? "The other ... the other was Catherine."

Robin stopped. The world became noiseless as two words looped in his head.

Fatal collision.

*

Robin burst into the side ward and had to swerve to avoid colliding with the massive bulk of Clive Darwin.

"What are you doing here?" Robin snapped, and strode straight past him. He dragged a chair closer to the bed and took Catherine's hand. Her eyes flickered open, then closed again. Cuts blazed across her pale cheeks and a large dressing covered her forehead.

"I was on the phone with her when it happened," Darwin said, "I heard it all."

"Great story for you."

"She's fine by the way, no serious injuries. She's had a sedative."

Darwin leant on the wall by the door not bothering to hide his disdain. He wore the same clothes he'd worn earlier, arty greying hair dishevelled. You wouldn't think he was a well-connected, shrewd journo with both high-standing politicians and murderers in his phone contacts. Robin ignored the loaded comment. He could take Darwin on, but it had been a long day, which was now the next day, and he couldn't be arsed with a pissing contest.

"Why was she heading back towards Broadstone?"

Darwin sighed and stared at the wall opposite him. "She was going to speak to an ex-employee from Harrison's, a guy who reckoned he'd seen Ursula twat an employee with her walking stick."

Robin didn't know which of those bombshells to deal with first. He placed Catherine's hand gently back on the bed and rose to his feet.

"You can't wrap her in cotton wool."

"You haven't been with her most days and seen how deeply all that shit last year affected her."

"Maybe. But I've seen how conflicted she's been over her decision to quit. When you saw her today did you not see the cloud lifting, the shine in her eyes?"

"Jesus. Do you want to fuck her Clive, is that it?"

Darwin straightened, returning to his full height. "Is that what you think's going on? Seriously Robin, that's so beneath you."

Patronising bastard. Robin turned away and stared out of the window. Darwin's words stung, mostly because of their truth. It *was* beneath him, and he already regretted the uncharacteristic comment. His irrational dislike for Darwin hinged solely on him being a journalist. When Erin had died the newspapers had covered her death for days, burrowing into all corners of her life. Robin had despised the intrusion and years later his hatred for the media had barely faded.

"Sorry. I shouldn't have said that."

"It's OK, I get you're stressed," Darwin said reasonably. Skin thicker than a rhino. He pulled out a chair on the other side of the bed and folded himself into it. "Do you know what happened?"

Robin admired Darwin's magnanimity. Begrudgingly. "Just the basics."

"I heard her scream, the impact, and him trying to get her out too, before the car fell over the side. Do you know who the guy was?"

Robin nodded, lost for words. Eyes bloodshot, Darwin waited for an answer.

"The guy's a hero."

"I know, and it's a good story, I get it."

"Better I tell it than have the nationals dredging up old news. And they will once they make the connection."

Of course they would. More intrusion. The last thing he wanted for Catherine. And when they found out who else was involved, they'd invent even more toxic word cocktails to share online with thirsty followers.

"It was John Rickman."

"Rickman?" Clive frowned, his mind spinning. "This is connected to Ursula Harrison's murder?"

"I don't know." Robin looked up at him, "But whatever you can do to divert attention off her Clive, do it. Please."

By the time Robin left the hospital, Catherine had woken, lethargic and teary. Her parents arrived and took over at the bedside, and he welcomed the opportunity to snatch a few hours' sleep. He desperately wanted to talk to her, but she needed time to recover.

He sank into his huge leather sofa when he reached his apartment, and considered sleeping there, fully clothed. Tomorrow had become today. Barely worth the effort of going to bed.

His building slept. The old thick walls of the converted factory, together with the industrial steel pillars provided the framework for the airy, minimalist space Robin had instantly loved. He recalled the moment he discovered the incredible the acoustics, two days after he'd completed the purchase. Queen, Bohemian Rhapsody. He'd stopped unpacking boxes, laid on the wooden floor and let the song blissfully reverberate through his entire body.

Catherine hated the place. OK, maybe not hated, but it couldn't have been more different to the quaint cottage she'd inherited from her grandmother. Catherine loved period features and quirky décor while he preferred the calming expanse of clutterless space and the honest simplicity of brick and steel. Plus, the floor was perfect for tai chi and karate training, the wood a joy beneath his feet.

Catherine was fine. Mildly concussed, a few cuts and bruises, but otherwise unscathed. So why did he feel so uneasy? She'd excluded Robin from her decision to work with Darwin, which he didn't like but could handle. The potential press intrusion was a concern too, but the uneasiness came more from John Rickman and how she'd now become connected to his case. But according to Darwin the decision to turn around had happened less than a minute before the collision. It had to be a coincidence but how rare were genuine flukes?

The image he'd burned of his crucified victim reloaded with crystal clarity. The pressure was on for a speedy result.

Robin forced himself to undress and collapsed into smooth black sheets.

Chapter Four

No hero

Robin could power sleep for three or four hours and feel like he'd had a solid eight. He showered, called Catherine's ward at the hospital and was back at the station for the handover from night shift. Jack was at his desk when Robin strode back into CID. He ended his phone call and spun around.

"I thought you'd be at the hospital. How is she?"

"She's good."

Jack frowned.

"I called but her dad was there."

"Oh."

"Don't."

Jack got it. He switched modes. "Couple of witnesses last night, both claim Jason Eaves stepped out into the road deliberately, and it does make sense. Jason used to be a local celebrity. He was injured four years ago in a boat accident and left with brain damage. He didn't know what he was doing."

"Or he knew exactly," said Robin.

"Also possible. His mum said they'd had an argument, and he'd stormed out, distressed. She also said, when he was thinking clearly, that he wanted to end his life."

"I'd like to talk to her myself later. What about Rickman? What did he have to say? Any link to what happened to his grandmother?"

"He'll be here shortly. Both cars will be checked obviously, but there's nothing suspicious about the accident. I don't see how Catherine or Jason Eaves could be linked to the murder inquiry."

"What about me being SIO on his grandmother's case, and Catherine's my partner?"

"You're the link?" Jack's face bulldog wrinkled. "I don't buy it. Oh, three years ago, Karen Taylor broke a woman's nose in a pub fight, and last year a neighbour reported her. She had a go at their teenage son for kicking his ball against her fence and had a pop at him too."

"Let's get Vic on it. Check her employment history and see if she's ever lost her temper with a client."

What should he say to John Rickman about Catherine? He was about to ask Jack's opinion on telling him he was Catherine's partner, maybe thank him for saving her life, when Jack's phone rang.

"That'll be Rickman now."

Even though John Rickman wasn't Barbara Rickman's biological son, Robin had expected him to be like her. Middle-class upbringing, surrounded by strong women like Barbara, influenced by other wealthy people and their privileged lifestyles. He'd expected the stepson to be a right tosser. So, when he shook hands with John Rickman and offered him a seat, his laid back, charming ease surprised him. While Barbara bubbled with attitude, John carried himself and spoke with calm confidence. He reminded Robin of an old-style film star he couldn't name, classically good-looking and sophisticated for a young bloke.

Robin spent a couple of minutes on preamble, keen to relax him and benefit from his insight. John responded amiably, engaged with eye contact. He took a moment to weigh up his first impressions. John was pale and seemed tired, but he warmed to him instantly.

"Talk us through what happened last night."

John let out a long breath, crossed his legs and twirled an ornate silver ring round and around his middle finger.

"The rain last night was something else, like driving in a car wash. When I reached Broadstone Bridge my wipers were on full, but I could hardly see the road. Just as I drove onto the bridge itself, a blurry, distorted shape appeared. I didn't realise it was a person at first until his face flashed in my headlights. I braked, but my car slid from under me. The other car swerved left and crashed through the bridge wall. I hit its back end."

He would make a great narrator. John's softly spoken words drew him in, like an enraptured child at story time. He exuded a soothing but authoritative gentility.

"You live in Castleton, don't you?" asked Jack, "But you were heading towards Camber. Where were you going?"

"I don't know. I had words with a friend of mine, a misunderstanding really, but she stormed out. I couldn't let her go like that, especially in such horrendous weather, so I went to find her. I drove the other way first, towards Broadstone, but I couldn't see her, so I turned around and drove in the opposite direction."

"What speed do you think you were doing?"

John stared at the wall over Robin's shoulder, visually reconstructing. "I don't think I was in fourth. Twenty, twenty-five at most."

"So, your car stopped on impact. What did you do next?"

"My door was blocked, so I climbed over the passenger seat to get out. The other car looked like it could fall through the wall at any moment. I managed to shove some of the stones aside, yank open the door and pull her out."

"You were incredibly brave," said Robin, "A hero even."

John stared at him as if only just realising his own actions. He dipped his head, hair partially shielding his face, and he swallowed back a swell of emotion. Robin glanced at Jack who disguised a slightly perplexed head shake by cricking his neck.

"I just did it. Instinct kicked in, I think, something primal. I didn't act consciously, and I didn't feel heroic. It was profound."

Robin didn't entertain the ethereal, but the sincerity in John's tone gave him goosebumps. He was twenty-six but his demeanour made him appear much older. A striking blend of fresh-faced youth with an old-fashioned soul, and an interesting case of nature conquering nurture.

"We're sorry for the loss of your grandmother," said Jack, "Tough couple of days for you. Were you close?"

"Ursula was close to no one. Incapable of normal relationships." All the warmth and mellow civility drained from John in those few seconds. His tone hardened, his face darkened, and the shift in his composure changed the atmosphere in the room.

"What do you mean?"

"She didn't like people. All pawns on a chessboard to her, to be moved around and played with."

"Would any of those people want to hurt her, in your opinion?"

"Most of them I imagine."

Robin blinked, surprised more by John's indifference than the information. "Enough to want to kill her?"

John raked his hair back with his fingertips and gave the possibility more thought.

"She wasn't a good person. She had a pleasant public persona, and she donated regularly, generously, to the church. But it was for show. Her heart was empty."

The developing picture of Ursula recoloured in Robin's mind, darkened by the stark description. Still hard to think the tiny old woman had been as unpleasant as everyone made out.

"What about her business relationships?" John's comment added credence to what Clive had said. "Have you spent much time at Harrison Engineering?"

"As a child yes. Her relationships were fake and built on fear. Everyone pretended to like her, afraid of losing their expense accounts and benefits, I imagine. She intimidated most people, snubbed the rest."

"During our inquiries, someone mentioned she may have assaulted an employee with her walking stick. What do you make of that?"

John shrugged like he'd asked what he thought of the colour of Ursula's curtains.

"I wouldn't put it past her." He dismissed the question with the same indifference as before.

The admission surprised Robin. "Was she aggressive or violent at work?"

"She knew how to get what she wanted, and the business thrived under her leadership. But she didn't tolerate mediocrity or underperformers. She chewed up anyone who didn't meet her standards."

"Surely people challenged her?"

"Of course, but they were squeezed out. Face doesn't fit syndrome. Ursula chose people who wouldn't oppose her and binned any who did. Constructively of course."

"Did anyone you know of hold a grudge?"

"I remember a few arguments."

"Any names?" asked Jack

"Sorry, no, but past employees might be able to help."

"When did you last see Ursula?"

"About three years ago. I was summoned to Barbara's to sort some paperwork out regarding my dad's estate. She was there."

"Do you think your accident and Ursula's death could be connected?"

"You think I was targeted?" John spun the idea around but shook his head. "The only connection is our shares in Harrisons, and my allocation is insignificant compared to hers or Barbara's."

But Barbara, or the younger brother could benefit considerably. He flicked back through his file. William Rickman was 15, feasible that a young man could top off an elderly woman. He might've collaborated with his mother. Interesting to find out which direction the nature versus nurture balance tipped with him. Doing away with his gran and brother would give the two of them full control, full shares.

Robin needed to move on and go digging. "Thanks for your time and your honesty John. We'll be in touch if we have further questions."

*

John threw his keys on his kitchen table and leant over, staring at the swirls and lines in the smooth oak, cool beneath his palms. Had he been stupid to tell the police about Ursula and what a tyrant she'd been? And he'd given a snippet, the sanitised version of the truth.

And why had the older guy asked where he'd been going when he crashed? What did it matter? He'd made an instant decision not to tell them about Marcia and now his guts were in knots because he'd lied. If they found out, it would seem like he was guilty. Thinking about Marcia's accusations made him feel dirty again and he wanted her to back off so much it made him physically ache. But she wouldn't quit easily. She was too obsessed to back off at the first sign of rejection. He longed for the basic simplicity of last week.

He took a long, hot shower and embraced the stinging pain of heat on his skin. A fitting punishment for getting himself into such a colossal fuck up.

Someone knocked at the door as he grilled bacon and made coffee. The anxiety slammed back in. They already knew he'd lied. Another knock, louder this time, twice as persistent. He pulled the tray out from under the grill and with a gutful of dread, he opened the door.

"You have to see this." His friend Rich blustered past him clutching his iPad, heading straight for the kitchen. "Oh Bobby's here too. He's brought some plants for you."

Relief drained from him like a glorious purging.

Bobby climbed the steps carrying two large pots, one in each arm. He put them by the door and pulled John into his arms for a hug. They held each other in silence and John did what he always did when Bobby hugged him. He imagined his dad was back.

"Are you OK?" Bobby asked.

"I think so."

Bobby released him and checked him over in a fatherly way which warmed John's soul. Bobby had been Ursula's gardener for years, and he'd had been there for him more than anyone else. Bobby wasn't his dad, but he filled that void in his life, and in turn John became a substitute for the child Bobby had always ached for. For years John believed Bobby had been sent by his dad to care for him. On days like today, he still did.

"Are you coming in for a coffee? Thanks for the plants by the way."

Bobby studied him from behind his small black glasses. His impromptu visit wasn't about plants. "I thought they'd look good by the door." He squeezed John's shoulder. "I'll have a quick one."

Rich was at the kitchen table unzipping his iPad case, dressed as usual in a band t-shirt, skinny jeans and a beanie hat over a long ponytail snaking down his back. He rubbed his ginger goatee and sniffed.

"Food smells good."

John pushed the bacon back under the grill. When he'd met Rich at Uni, he'd gravitated towards the quirky outsider occupying the same space as him at the edge of the pack. He'd been grateful for their friendship ever since and knew Rich felt the same.

"So, what's this amazing discovery?" He dumped a milky tea in front of Rich, a black coffee for Bobby. "Let me guess; it's a suit of armour on eBay for fifty quid."

"Do you think I'd be round here if there was? No, but you're on the right track." Rich swiped and tapped then spun the iPad around to show John.

"A re-enactment? This is what you're creaming yourself over? Last time we joined one you got us evicted. Who the hell gets evicted from a historical re-enactment?"

"It got a bit out of hand."

"Yeah, because you got arsey about the historical accuracy and pissed off the Roundheads."

"Bunch of nobs, anyway this is different. It's more professional, and you're missing the point." Rich swiped and prodded some more. "Look."

John sat and checked out the screen again.

"Broadstone Castle. When it re-opens, this re-enactment group are part of a weekend of activities. They're building a jousting arena with proper lists. You never know, they might have a Henry Stanton."

"Like I've told you a thousand times Rich, he wasn't well-known. They're more likely to have one of the St. Stephens, the Duke probably."

"Whatever. Don't tell me you're not excited. Now who's creaming?"

OK, his day had brightened. He had a long-standing fascination with jousting and with Henry Stanton, a little-known knight from the thirteenth century who he'd come across during his studies. Stanton had spent a brief time at Broadstone Castle not long before his death.

"I've put a quote in for the landscaping work at the castle." Bobby peered over Rich's shoulder, "They want a garden and picnic area for after the refurb. Where did you hear about this Rich?"

"I came across these guys in a chat room talking about it." Rich grinned at John. "Bacon." John snatched the spitting bacon from under the grill and tiny bombs of hot fat pricked his skin. "Don't worry, I like it crispy." Rich took bread from the cupboard and began buttering. "I thought you'd be more excited."

"I've had a shit few days."

"How shit?"

Where should he start? The two people closest to him waited, concerned.

"I was in a crash. Knocked another car through Broadstone bridge, and a bloke who ran into the road died. Wrote my car off too. Next: Ursula was found dead yesterday, not from natural causes either. Suspicious death. Then, on top of all that … one of my pupils followed me home. She's got it in her head something's going on between us. She came here and … it was messy."

He was relieved to get it all out, and lighter for sharing the load. Rich sat with a bump. Bobby pulled out a chair and sat too.

"Shit, man. Why didn't you ring me?"

"I kept meaning to, but everything exploded all at once."

"What happened to Ursula?"

John glanced at Bobby. He'd spoken with Bobby briefly the previous night, so he knew about her death.

"I think they're investigating her carers."

Rich blew out a long breath and picked up his sandwich again. He took a bite then pushed back his chair and hunted for sauce. "And how did the accident happen?"

"I went chasing after the girl from school. The only upside to all this is the woman would've died if I hadn't dragged her out of her car before it fell through the wall."

As he spoke, memories returned. The rain stinging his cheeks, wrenching open the door, dragging her out onto the road.

Rich stopped, sauce bottle aloft, eyes widening. "Who was she?"

"Well, that's an interesting question. When I found out her name, I Googled her."

"Is she famous?"

John took Rich's iPad and did a quick search. "That's her." He pointed at a photo of Catherine Nicholls.

"She's fit."

"She is. But check out the news stories. She's a journalist, and last year ended up in a universe of shit for retweeting a pro-gay tweet. Turns out her brother's gay, but that's not the crux of it. She fell on the radar of some anti-gay activists who launched a terror campaign against her and her family. I'm talking nasty shit; emails, texts, voicemails threatening to sodomise her, threats against her brother too. They weren't just threats though. They jumped her brother, battered and raped him and left him for dead."

Bobby stared at him in shock. "I remember. That was her? Jesus."

"Do you think I should ... oh, I don't know. I feel like I should do something."

People come into your life for a reason, like the two oddballs sitting at his table. They'd been brief, but those seconds in the car as he'd struggled to drag her out, those few minutes waiting with her for the ambulance, they meant something.

"What more can you do than save her life?" said Rich.

"It was an amazing thing to do." Pride cracked Bobby's voice. John swallowed hard, touched as always by Bobby's affection. "Look, speak to the Head, first thing on Monday and get it all out in the open. He's not daft, he'll deal with her, and he'll appreciate you being honest about it."

Yeah, like being honest about why he'd been on Broadstone bridge last night. He couldn't tell Bob and Rich he'd lied to the police about it. He didn't want them to be ashamed of him.

Rich zipped his iPad back into its case and drained the last of his coffee. "You're strong, credible and above all else, you're a good bloke. You'll sort this. Have a think about the re-enactment. It'll keep you sane while all this is going on. And you can ring me. Any time."

"I know. Cheers Rich."

A stab of envy at the blissful simplicity of Rich's life prodded him in the ribs. He had a job he loved, a family he loved and a carefree, childlike approach to life. Rich always seemed light and unburdened.

"I'm off too." Bobby turned to John, "As long as you're OK. I'll call you later."

*

"Rickman's car wasn't tampered with," said Ella, as Robin and Jack returned to the incident room, "Old but roadworthy. Nothing suspicious."

Robin surveyed the board where a visual map was building in the form of lists, photographs, and an actual geographic map of her neighbourhood. He took off his jacket and gave the others a quick update on the accident and the interviews with John and Barbara.

"We need a more thorough dig around Harrisons. HR would know if there were complaints against Ursula. Check for financial or employee disputes Vic. Court cases, disgruntled clients."

"Guv."

"Any joy with the church group?"

"Not really," said Ella, "The church secretary was complimentary at first, but when I asked about Ursula personally, she said she didn't really know her, but she seemed 'nice'."

"Rubbish," said Jack, "Funny how everyone who benefits financially from the Harrisons won't criticise them."

"Scared the money well will dry up," said Robin, "See if you can meet Michael Heath on his own Ella. Run the religious theories past him. James, anything to report?"

"We've had a brief look at Ursula Harrison's computer. She was active online until 5.15 pm on Thursday. She didn't use any social media, but she browsed the news sites, googled 'tingling fingers' and visited a couple of symptom checker sites. She ordered three books off Amazon. All Kindle biographies."

"Tingling fingers?"

"Circulation problems apparently. Tons of spam emails, mostly from shopping sites. A couple of emails from the church group. Just one personal email, from Barbara, forwarding her a link to a site selling medical support tights."

"For circulation problems," said Ella.

"She'd replied with three words - 'what vile colours'."

Robin recalled the mental image of Ursula Harrison, the one he'd burned into his memory. The broken doll dressed in vintage finery, with a fully charged vibrator in her drawer and a basque in her laundry. If there a shred of truth existed in what Darwin had said, she had an aggressive, dominant side.

"I'm seeing the carers tomorrow," said Robin, "Has anyone spoken to the other people who worked for Ursula? The gardener and an ironing woman. Have we traced them?"

"The ironing woman is Jeanna Moss, but she's on holiday in Portugal and has been for four days," said Ella, "The gardener Bobby Trent is a one-man band called Green Tips. Last there five days ago, according to their timesheets. They gave me his home number and a mobile, but he's not answering."

"Let's send someone round. I'm waiting for another update from SOC but so far, we've sod all to go on, no real suspects.

Let's keep digging into the religious references, her personal relationships, find any enemies. Old lovers, or even current ones. Ursula had needs. Who was fulfilling them?"

Tasks allocated, they all gathered their stuff. Jack nudged his head towards Robin's office.

"Do you have a sec?"

Puzzled, Robin headed for his office and Jack followed, closing the door behind him. Robin perched on his desk waiting. Jack studied his shoes. He was a good fifteen years older than Robin and wasn't in bad shape, but he had the dress sense of a circa 1990 used car dealer. Today's tan leather jacket and suede loafer combo was a favourite.

"You can tell me to keep my nose out if you want, but if I was you, I'd get over to the hospital pronto. Don't let the job get in the way. She's going to need you."

Jack's heartfelt advice came as a surprise, and he had to stop himself from being defensive. From anyone else, Robin might have fought the suggestion, but coming from Jack the words had a different impact. He'd woken on autopilot and had remained that way throughout the morning. He hadn't questioned his own behaviour.

"I was there till three this morning."

"Which was when her parents arrived."

"Pretty much."

Jack just nodded.

"What?"

"I think you know."

"I've had three hours sleep and I'm not in a self-counselling place right now."

"Stop punishing yourself. Just stop."

Whether he wanted to or not, Robin didn't have the chance to reply to that cutting insight. Jack launched his grenade and departed, leaving him to deal with the impact alone.

*

The temperature in Catherine's snug rivalled the bowels of hell. As Robin put down the bag of stuff he'd brought for her, her mum Liz shoved another chunk of wood in the log burner and pulled her pashmina around her shoulders. Christ, it had to be forty degrees in there. Catherine didn't seem to notice. She lay on the sofa, with a blanket over her legs and a lost vacancy in her eyes. When he hugged her, she seemed smaller in his arms.

He eased away and checked her over. She squeezed out a smile. "Mum said you were at the hospital all night."

"Most of it yeah. I didn't even know they'd discharged you. Why didn't you ring me?"

"My phone's in my car." Catherine bent over and poked into the bag he'd brought, but he could tell she wasn't really looking.

"I popped into Rituals. I know you love their stuff."

"Thanks. God, I need a bath."

Their eyes met again, and the emotion gushed out of her. He shoved the bag aside and pulled her back into his arms, holding her while she sobbed into his chest. Liz sat on the other side and stroked her daughter's back, lost for words. She was nice enough, and she loved Catherine deeply, but she had her fragilities and anxieties. She would make the right soothing noises, and be there to help, but offer little in terms of strength and support. Thanks Jack, for the not-so-subtle nudge.

"I keep seeing him in my headlights." Catherine's breathing chugged, sobs still catching. "I killed him."

Liz whimpered. She'd been through dark times, but Catherine needed to work through this without having to worry about her flaky Mum too. Her Dad had more balance, but he could be a snapper when his nerves were tested. They needed Simon, Catherine's brother. He would have told Liz to get a grip by now and marched them all off to the pub. Robin had a lot of time for Simon.

"He deliberately stepped into the road; witnesses across the road saw him. He had serious mental issues and he's tried it before. You didn't kill him."

"There you go see." Liz's forced cheeriness grated on his nerves. "I told you."

Catherine's fingers, clutched onto his jacket, tightened. "Would you make Robin a coffee please mum?"

"No problem," said Liz, and she picked up her handbag from the floor before heading for the kitchen.

Catherine released her grip on his jacket and sat up, shoving her hair back. Robin stroked her cheeks and reached for a tissue nestled among a pile of tablets, antiseptic creams and bottles of Lucozade on the table. Liz's home nursing kit.

"Do I look like shit?"

"Yep."

The tiniest laugh. Dark shadows swept beneath her eyes, matching the darker shadows within them. She dabbed tears on her cheeks.

"I'm so glad you're here. She's doing my head in. I know she's had a shock, but all she's done is cry. Bet she's necking diazepam in the kitchen." She took a couple of deep breaths, calming herself. "I knew Jason Eaves. I interviewed him when he won his first boat race. He was so lovely. Feels like he's had two deaths. Part of him died that day, the rest of him died last night." She shook herself off, took another ragged deep breath. "I know you're busy with work, so Simon's going to come over, otherwise Mum will either cook me alive or overdose me on …" She stopped, paling suddenly like Robin's niece on a car journey, about ten seconds before she threw up.

"Cat?"

"The guy who pulled me out of my car, I need to contact him. He pulled me out of my car and I haven't thanked him."

"There'll be plenty of time for that. Focus on you. Not your mum, or Jason …"

"She's terrified of losing us, it's why she's so stressed all the time."

"I know, but you're not responsible for your Mum." He glanced towards the door and lowered his voice. "She would've had a meltdown if you'd clipped someone's wing mirror." Robin's phone rang and he fished it out of his pocket. "Sorry, I need to take this." He headed for the back door, desperate for air. "Jack?"

"Sorry, I know this is a bad time, but … Karen Taylor's posted a photo of Ursula Harrison. It's all over social and Collins is flipping."

"Shit. She wanted a photo for Instagram, not to check if she was dead,."

"Can you come back?"

"On my way."

Back in the furnace, Catherine was struggling with one of the top windows, the old leaded light refusing to budge.

"Let me do that." He wrestled with the handle and shoved it free. Beautiful fresh air diffused the heat and the smell of her Gran's old cigarettes in the brickwork.

"You need to go." No criticism, just a hint of disappointment. "What's happened?"

"Tell you later." He kissed her burning cheek. "And buy a new phone."

Chapter Five

Water or blood

"Barbara."

Why had he answered the door without checking first? He stared at his stepmother and wished he had the balls to shut the door again. She glared back at him as the wind attacked her hair.

"You're not answering my calls." She waited for a response. He gave none. "Shall we go in?"

John pushed the door open, and she moved past him, heels clopping on the wooden hall floor. She strode straight into the living room and scowled around. "I see you're making the most of your dividends." She stared with distaste at an ornate long sword mounted on the wall.

"It's my money. I'll spend it however I choose."

She spun around. "You're frittering away your father's legacy."

"Is this why you're here? To talk about the business again, to try to persuade me, again, to sell my shares?"

"Your grandmother is dead."

"I spoke to her less than an hour ago. Aunt Lucy has gone to Cornwall to stay with her. They were shopping for duvet covers."

She swallowed her irritation. Good. He wanted to piss her off.

"My mother. Ursula."

John stared back at her. "I'm sorry for your loss."

Barbara moved a pile of books he'd been marking off the table and sat on the sofa. "Have the police been in touch?"

"Why?"

"Have they or haven't they, John?"

"I had a crash last night, and someone died, so yes, they have. I'm OK though, thanks for asking."

Barbara stared at her nails. John sat opposite her and waited. No way would he make this easy for her.

"They're questioning her carers." The effort of restraining her annoyance weakened her voice. "And they're also probing into the business. I thought they might talk to you."

"She pissed on a lot of people. Literally, knowing her."

"How dare you…"

"Oh, don't bother defending her. I saw what she got up to."

"If you say anything defamatory about her, I'll make sure you don't see William ever again."

She fixed John with her pale grey glare and John stared back, determined not to look away. The glare of his childhood. It had accompanied endless bollockings, over muddy football boots, sick on the bathroom floor, crap grades in French.

"Good luck with that. He's eighteen in two years and you'll be the one never seeing him again."

Barbara blinked but managed not to recoil from the truth. "You don't seem surprised or concerned about my mother's death."

"I've seen her twice in five years and let's be honest; we weren't exactly close, were we?"

"She helped me raise you!"

John jumped to his feet. "I think it's time for you to go."

Barbara rose too. In her heels, they were the same height. As a child, she'd loomed over him.

"William is devastated."

He didn't sound 'devastated' on the phone, but John let it go. He didn't want her to know they'd spoken, and Barbara had never approved of their relationship, like Will betrayed her by befriending the black sheep.

"And I suppose you know about the photo that useless bitch has posted on social media. William saw it, his own Grandmother exposed for everyone to stare at and share with their contacts. Think of the humiliation John."

"I'm thinking more of the irony."

Barbara turned away. "I expect you to attend her funeral."

"Over my dead body."

"Have some respect! It's her money funding your freaky fascination for old relics and dusty antiques."

"My father's money, not hers, and let's not begin on respect. This is a woman who made me wear my boxers on my head for a full twenty-four hours after I pissed the bed. I was grieving for my dad, having nightmares about him burning to death, and that's how she dealt with my trauma."

"She was tough, but it's how her parents raised her. She still supported you until you went to university. As I did. Not many women would take on their dead husband's child. And you weren't easy John, not by a long stretch."

"Well, I apologise for being distraught by becoming orphaned at eleven years old." John headed for the door. He had to move away from her before he regressed to a childhood he didn't want to remember.

"Don't speak ill of her to the police." Barbara stopped at the door. "Whatever you think of her, she deserves respect. She didn't die peacefully."

No way would he protect the memory of her toxic mother or her either.

"You're a rich woman now Barbara."

With one last glare, Barbara wrenched open the door and slammed it behind her.

*

"Do you know what this is?"

Jamie Clarke dug the tips of his fingers deeper into the flabby neck of a cocky bastard who smelled of Lynx deodorant and KFC. Oh yeah, Brad. Brad 'The Bradster' Flemming to give him his full title. The Bradster was close to pissing himself. Not so cocky now.

"What do you mean?" Brad managed, and he swallowed beneath Jamie's fingers. He shoved him harder into the wall, crunching his head against the bricks.

"It's called a death hand. And you have to put your fingers in exactly the right place. If I move them over your jugular … well, it's called a death hand Bradders. You work it out."

"You're full of shit."

Jamie shifted his index finger and Brad gasped. He had a trace of fight in him, but Jamie could feel him trembling like a dying fly, which was what he deserved. Jamie hated bullies. The best way to deal with a bully is to show them some fear. He slid his palm over Brad's crotch and squeezed hard enough to force the zip of his jeans into his sweaty little balls. Brad squirmed.

"Did you leave your cock at home Bradders? I can't feel it in here."

He leant in with his full body weight into and rubbed his face against Brad's, loving how much he hated it. Oh yeah Brad the alpha male, with his hipster skinnies and tatts up his arms, just edging over to the wrong side of 'chunky'. So tough, he found his kicks sleazing on younger girls and getting photos to brag over with his mates.

"If you go near my sister again, if you speak to her or look at her, I'll rip your fucking throat out," Jamie whispered in Brad's ear. He took a quick bite of his ear lobe and Brad spasmed like he'd been tasered. Jamie wiped his smile across Brad's cheek. "Take your pathetic little beers and fuck off."

He pulled away and Brad gasped for air like he'd been underwater for three minutes. He picked up the carrier bag by his feet and ran off down the alleyway, cans clanging against his legs. Jamie blew him a kiss and shooed him along with a flick of his hands.

Jamie had his Mini across the road, out of sight. His sister Marcia sat in the passenger seat waiting for him, radio on full blast listening to Beyonce.

"Get that shit off." He jabbed his finger at the radio, which was worth more than the car, "Have you re-tuned my stations?"

Jamie started the engine and the ancient banger coughed into action.

"Chill the fuck out will you? Did you speak to him?"

"Yeah. He apologised for being a dick, don't worry. You're well rid."

Job done, Marcia dug into her pocket and pulled out a packet of tobacco, papers, a lighter and a tiny bag of weed. She flipped down the glove compartment and started skinning up. He loved his sister, and he'd always protected her, but lately she'd gone off the rails. She was shoplifting more, and this teacher fixation was different from Marcia's usual crushes. She always fell for older guys, especially if they had a car, money, and a regular dealer. He didn't get why she obsessed on Mr Rickman though. She yapped on about him, in a weird way like they were actually shagging. Complete fantasy, but Marcia's imagination scared him.

They headed out of town. Marcia slouched in her seat and smoked through a gap in the open window. What the hell was he doing with his life? Stuck with his dad and sister in a shithole of a council house, wedged between desperation and resignation. His band had folded, his love life sucked shit and the most expensive item he owned was the knackered rot box they were sitting in. Twenty-three and already a failure. His old mates were dads now, or had proper jobs and travelled abroad. He saw them on Facebook, sharing their dull shit. Jamie took a quick drag on Marcia's joint. What would his Facebook status be? 'Jamie is too big a loser to have status'…

"Where are we going?" he asked. He'd been driving on autopilot and had no idea where they were.

"I'll show you."

"I'm not your chauffeur Marcia."

"What the fuck's a chauffeur?"

"Someone who drives people around for a living."

"You don't do anything for a living. You haven't got a job."

"No and I don't want to waste my petrol sightseeing with you."

"Next left."

Jamie chewed back his rising irritation and turned into a quiet street of tall, semi-detached houses. Expensive cars on the driveways, Beamers, Mercs and a gorgeous Tesla with a brand new reg plate.

"Pull over here," said Marcia.

"How do you know this place?" Then his heart sank. "Oh no." Jamie leant across and peered out of Marcia's window at the house where they'd parked. Darkness was falling already, and a lamp glowed inside. "The teacher, right?"

"I saw a house like this on Location Location. Kirsty Doodah was wet over period features. I didn't know what she was on about until I Googled it. Period means something totally different to me."

"This is your teacher for God's sake. Everyone has a teacher they fancy but why take it to extremes?"

"What if I was sleeping with him?"

"Are you?"

Marcia craned her neck so she could see the upstairs windows. "Not yet."

"Right, we're out of here." Jamie moved to take off the handbrake, but Marcia pulled his arm.

"Someone's coming out."

A tall woman in a business suit stormed out of the house and slammed the door behind her. She marched down the path and opened a silver Mercedes parked in front of Jamie. She drove off seconds later.

"Looks like your teacher's bagged an older woman."

"If he does, they've had a right barney. Did you see her face?" Marcia hadn't taken her eyes off the house. "He's following her."

Mr Rickman came around the back of his car and tapped on the window. Not following the woman then. Marcia's teacher was straight off one of those historical Netflix series their Nan watched, all swooshy hair and moody, a bit mysterious. He understood why Marcia was crushing over him.

Jamie wound the window down. Her teacher bent over and scanned the car interior. Heat radiated off Marcia's billion-kilowatt smile.

"What are you doing here?" He glared at Marcia. "Didn't I make myself clear?"

"Just showing my brother where you live. No crime against it is there?"

Rickman checked Jamie out. "Talk some sense into your sister, will you?"

"Been trying for years, mate."

Rickman sniffed. "This car stinks of weed."

Jamie opened his mouth to deny it but stopped himself. If he denied it, he'd stitch Marcia up and he didn't want her getting into trouble.

"I'm speaking to Mr Maloney on Monday."

"About the weed?" Marcia gave him some puppy eyes.

"About you, and this obsession of yours. Stay away from me, stay away from my house."

Rickman stepped back from the car as Jamie rammed it into first gear and pulled away from the kerb. In the rear-view mirror, Rickman watched them, hands on hips, hair blowing wildly in the wind.

"He's so fit when he's angry."

"You heard what he said, Marsh. Back off."

*

"Robin, what's this about a death photo all over social media? Your murder case I believe."

Superintendent Anna Collins matched Robin's strides as he headed for CID. He'd been hoping for an update before facing her. Mid-fifties, country Auntie vibe, soft Northern accent with a gentle tone, good for soothing animals and fretting toddlers. He'd seen her lose her rag a couple of times and her bollocking voice had the upper pitch of a pissed off violin.

"Just about to get an update Ma'am."

"How's Catherine? I heard about the incident."

"She's fine thanks."

"Good. I want your full attention on this case. If you need some personal time, we can assign a different SIO."

Robin stopped. Collins stopped. Tweedy auntie bore into him with eyes as sharp as knitting needles. He'd never been pulled off a case, and no way was she denying him this one.

"I can assure you, Ma'am, this case has my full attention."

Collins nodded and managed a Mona Lisa smile. "I know you were at the Met a while, but Broadstone's different. We're not just a tourist town. The commercial district is a huge employer, the historical attractions pull from all over the world. We don't want our reputation tarnished by this, and the media's all over it already. Let's get a quick result."

"I understand..."

"So, if you need help, let me know. My door's always open."

It sounded like a seductive invitation, poured from her lips like liquid velvet, but her passive aggressiveness irritated the hell out of him. Doubly insulting that she patronised him with the fluffy bunny routine. It pissed him off more than her insinuated criticism.

"Thanks, but I have this under control. Excuse me." Robin continued walking. Her eyes burned into his back all the way along the corridor.

Ella, James and Jack were already in the cave, all on their phones scrolling through websites.

"How bad is it?" Robin took one of the chairs and Ella slid a coffee over towards him.

"Well, the good news is it's just her face Guv."

"And the bad?"

"I'll show you," said James. He pushed his phone aside and turned to the laptop instead. It took a few seconds to come to life and load the image of Ursula Harrison. The cropped picture had the words 'ding dong the witch is dead' in red lettering across the bottom. It didn't show the full horror of her death, but it was bad enough. Why hadn't Facebook taken this down?

"The original post was deleted. But it's been shared more than forty times already. Classic viral. It'll take a while to track every posting of it. Facebook has allowed photos of corpses in the past. Remember the dead refugee child on the beach?"

"I do," said Ella, "I wish I'd never seen it."

"There's a market for it," said Jack, "People are sick, but none of us like to admit it."

"This is related to a live investigation though."

"Karen Taylor reckons she was fraped." Vic joined them, panting. He sounded like he'd sprinted over from the other side of town. "Totally denies it was her."

"Fraped?" said Jack, "And sit down for God's sake. You're so unfit."

"It means Facebook raped. Someone logged or hacked into her account and posted." Vic flopped into a chair with a dramatic sigh.

"I know what it means …"

"Sorry to interrupt sir." They all looked up from their huddle. Judy Smith hesitated in the doorway. "I have information which might be relevant."

"Grab a seat." Robin pulled out a chair and they all squeezed round to let her in. Red blotches crept up her neck and cheeks, so keen to impress she bordered on tongue-tied. He smiled, hoping to reassure her.

"I've just been to see Bobby Trent, Ursula Harrison's gardener. Lovely guy, been working at her house for years, although Ursula's made several complaints about him. Unfounded ones. He witnessed the end of a heated argument between Ursula and Karen Taylor. Ursula threw a glass at Karen, who retaliated by slapping her."

"No mention of that when we checked her out," said Jack.

"No Sarge, no one reported it. Strange, given how much Ursula complained."

"I wonder if Barbara knows about it," said Robin.

"She would have mentioned it," said Jack, "She's desperate to stitch up the carers."

"Motive," Ella said through a mouthful of crisps, "Karen admitted she didn't like Ursula, and she photographed her corpse."

Karen's behaviour at the house had seemed genuine. Hot headed maybe, and reactive, but not calculated. Maybe she had something on Ursula Harrison.

"Let's see what Karen has to say."

Chapter Six

Suspects

"Is it that time already?"

Robin had woken Catherine as he tried to slide himself from underneath her when his alarm beeped.

"Go back to sleep." He kissed her and tucked the duvet back in around her. He'd arrived at her house late the previous evening, but he'd been able to have an hour with Catherine and Simon before she'd fallen asleep.

He showered in her en suite and dressed, thankful for the clean clothes in the sliver of wardrobe space he had there. She'd nodded off again when he ducked under the low door frame and headed downstairs.

The house was full of exposed beams and he still had to concentrate to make sure he didn't forget where the low ones were. The one in the kitchen had a hanging rack full of pans extending from it. Doubly treacherous. Catherine's arty taste suited the unusual cottage, but he always wanted to push the walls back a little. Although a decent size, the rooms were small with steps between them or little hallways connecting one part of the house to another. It made him feel like he'd stumbled into a doll's house.

He put the kettle on to make a coffee to take to work with him and was skirting around the central island when a flashing blue light on her landline base stopped him. The phone had rung several times last night, even late on, with relatives checking on Catherine. Next to the phone was a chunk of multi-coloured post-it notes. John Rickman, 2pm Long Café. A phone number underneath. So they'd made contact already. It made sense she would want to thank him for what he did, but why not mention it last night? She hadn't hidden the note and the number, so maybe she'd just been exhausted and forgotten to tell him.

Robin took the note from the stack back upstairs. When he sat on the bed next to her, she was still half awake, and her hand snaked over his leg.

"Are you coming back to bed?"

"How do you know John Rickman?" She pushed her hair from her face, opened her eyes and frowned. "I'll rephrase. Why do you have his phone number?" He waggled the post-it in his fingers.

"He sent me a private message on Facebook last night."

"Why didn't you tell me?"

"What's the problem? He saved my life. I'm glad he contacted me."

"How did he know your name? You weren't mentioned in his interview at the station."

Catherine sat up, now fully awake. "You personally questioned him, but you didn't tell him who I was, or tell me who he was for that matter?"

"I didn't know whether to say anything or not. It was an awkward situation."

"What you mean is you didn't know whether to put work first or your personal life."

"Cat …" He put his hand on her arm, but she pulled away.

"If someone saved your life, I wouldn't hesitate to thank them. It's a human reaction surely? Where's the conflict?"

Robin frowned. Had the knock on the head affected her memory? Why did she not get it?

"The conflict? He's Ursula Harrison's grandson. Step-grandson." Her expression froze as she processed that bombshell. "Ah, I take it he didn't tell you?"

"Why would he?" Good recovery. She really was pissed off. "Hey, I saved your life, and my grandmother was murdered last night. Fancy meeting up?"

Catherine rubbed at her temples and Robin didn't push it any further. Plus, Simon slept in the next room, and he didn't want him to hear them arguing.

"I need to go. I'll call you later."

"I'm meeting him for a coffee this afternoon."

"What? You've been out of hospital for less than twenty-four hours. You should rest. Can't it wait?"

Huge mistake. She yanked the duvet back and stomped past him, heading for the bathroom. She changed her mind and came stomping back.

"Almost dying teaches you nothing can wait; you don't know when your time's up. You know that."

Robin stiffened at the dig, but he didn't want to fight. Maybe thanking Rickman couldn't wait, but this argument could.

"You'll like him, he's a nice guy." Inward cringe. That sounded so insincere. "Look, it's probably a good idea and it'll help you with your recovery. I'm worried it's too soon, that's all."

Her well-being bothered him, but was more concerned Darwin had put her up to it and she'd planned another scouting mission for the Post.

"I'm fine. I want to talk about it. Simon's taking me into town and bringing me back, so I won't be on my own."

Robin held up his hands. "Only you know how you feel." He gave her a quick squeeze and kissed her. "Go back to bed. Call me if you need me."

*

Robin slammed the interview room door and checked his watch, as Vic ambled off to the station desk. He hoped Karen Taylor had more to offer than her boss and Munroe, her pompous solicitor, who'd scribbled notes all the way through the meeting with a scratchy pen and avoided eye contact throughout. He knew his stuff though. Martina Banks, the owner of Bluebird, absolved herself and her company of any responsibility in Ursula's care, claiming all procedures had been followed and any deviations were down to individual staff. Her record keeping supported her position. Ursula had been cared for exactly as her care plan indicated. So, together they'd constructed a protective wall, made from bits of paperwork glued together with ingenious guile. They'd stitched Karen Taylor up royally.

Robin checked his phone. No messages. Catherine was either still in a pissy, total in love with Rickman or Simon had persuaded her to go to Wags and she was dancing on the pink piano necking jaeger bombs.

Interview room two smelled of stale cigarettes and BO, masked with a cheap air freshener that reminded Robin of Christmas candles. Jack had already gone through the preliminaries with Karen Taylor, who slouched in her chair trying to remain casual. But her body language betrayed her. One arm defending her chest, the other hand tucked under her chin, fingers partially blocking her mouth. He'd seen it countless times. Classic defence position. She half-smiled at Robin, but it didn't reach the mud-brown eyes propped up with more bags than an airport carousel.

"So, you took Ursula's tea upstairs, found her dead and ran to the bathroom. You hid in there for a few minutes then went back downstairs to get your phone. You rang 999 then went back up and took a photo of her. Then you started to panic thinking people would assume you were involved, and by the time PC Smith arrived you'd worked yourself up into a state. You thought she was going to arrest you. Is that right so far?"

"Pretty much."

It had taken an hour to drag out of her what he pretty much knew already. His stomach had started grumbling, the BO was beginning to smell like meat pie, and Jack stifled multiple yawns. Nowhere to go mooching. Jack hated the interview suite.

"How did a photograph of Ursula Harrison, deceased, ended up splattered all over Facebook."

"We do it all the time, don't we? Kids, pets, your dinner."

"I get all that, well maybe not the dinner photos, never have. But you posted a photo of a murder victim."

Karen blinked at the blunt description. "I just didn't like her."

"Is that since the incident where you slapped her?"

She begun staring at a fascinating coffee stain circle on the table, but her head shot up. "I've never slapped her. I'd get sacked!"

Robin sat up, piqued by her sudden animation. "There was a witness."

"What witness? The pervy gardener? He creeps around the place watching people."

"Ursula loved complaining. She reported a delivery guy who knocked a flower off her rose bush. Why do you think she didn't report this?" He was rewarded with a shrug. "It sounds like a serious incident."

"Is that what Bobby said?"

"We're interested in what you have to say." Robin waited, but Karen stared at the wall behind him, one leg swinging with nervous energy. "This is important. You have a history of aggressive behaviour, which you've hidden from your employers, and your version of this argument doesn't match Mr Trent's. Can you describe what happened?"

Karen filled the expectant silence with a huge sigh.

"She smacked her walking stick over my knuckles like an angry old schoolmistress, tried to pass it off a joke. I didn't report it because I need the job, OK? Most of my hours are with Ursula. I knew no one would believe me if I reported it. Which is true, isn't it?"

"She assaulted you?"

"It didn't hurt. It was just embarrassing."

"Was there another argument?" asked Robin, "Because the 'pervy gardener' – and we'll come back to that – said she threw a glass at you. So, there were two incidents, or more?"

"No, just those two." She swallowed and pulled her lips inwards until they disappeared, biting her words back.

"Did she hit any of the other carers?" asked Jack.

Karen shrugged again. "She used to leave big tips, so if she did clobber a colleague, they might've kept it quiet. For the money."

"How big?"

"Twenty, thirty quid. Often more like a hundred. We had a bloke working with us. Ryan. Young, late twenties. She paid him two hundred to take her out for the afternoon. He wasn't supposed to, but he did it a couple of times. Another time she asked him if she could see his cock."

Robin blinked, momentarily blindsided. He couldn't resist a quick glance at Jack. He'd definitely woken up.

"And what did he say?" Jack managed to keep his cool.

"For fifty quid, are you kidding? He got his cock out."

"Where is he now?"

"Dead. He went mountain climbing with his mates, had a massive heart attack and died. Ursula was gutted. She asked if more male carers were available."

Robin leant forward. Karen had become much more expansive on this line of questioning. She'd relaxed now she'd introduced the subject, was enjoying it even.

"Did she pay you to keep quiet about the smack?" A nod. "So, to be clear, you're saying Ursula manipulated and assaulted her carers?"

"More of power trip. Like showing she was the boss. I never heard anyone complain about it either, the tips for extras I mean."

"And were they always of a sexual or aggressive nature?"

"Sexual with Ryan obviously. What she did to me ... it wasn't aggressive really. More like she had to be dominant. Controlling. Maybe she got off on it." Her face screwed up. "Ugh, I've never thought about that until now."

"Did Martina Banks know about the extras?"

Karen laughed but stopped abruptly when the laugh turned into a cough. She unzipped her shiny bubble jacket and whacked her chest with a beefy fist.

"Miss prim and proper, butter wouldn't melt? Dead right she did. She kept Ursula sweet because she was a good earner. Bet she's devastated she's lost her best client."

"And what about the 'pervy gardener'?" he asked, "In what way is he pervy?"

"It's the way he talks to your chest."

"To be fair," said Jack, "Most blokes will sneak a look if they think they can get away with it."

And Karen's chest was massive. Hard not to.

"He's always there, like a couple of days a week at times. Her garden looks like it's off a TV programme."

"Sounds like he's good at his job. Doesn't make him pervy."

Karen scratched at her neck with stubby nails bitten to bits. He gave her time to elaborate but the scratching led to fiddling with her bra strap. Either she'd made up her story about Trent or didn't want to go into it further.

"Were you involved with him?" Robin took a punt.

She sneered in disgust. "No chance."

"Was Bobby Trent doing favours for Ursula?" Karen pulled another contemptuous face, this one more like she'd licked shit off her finger thinking it was chocolate, "What? She obviously had desires. You saw her lingerie. You knew what she asked Ryan to do."

"She spent a load on underwear, all of it sexy stuff. Barbara would buy her more practical, old lady things and she binned them. Not cheap stuff either."

"But from your reaction, you don't think Bobby Trent was involved with Ursula or the sexual favours?"

"Nah, he's too nerdy and dull. Always reading when he's on a break or listening to stuff on his phone."

The door opened and James stuck his head in. "Sorry to interrupt Guv, but I really need to speak to Jack."

"No problem, we're almost done."

Jack left, giving Robin a moment to think. Karen's comments about Ursula had thrown the case open wider. There could be countless people out there who she'd manipulated and upset.

"You've been really helpful." Robin sat back, and Karen relaxed now the end was in sight. She smoothed down her stretched-to-the-max black leggings and zipped up her coat. "You saw what happened to her and I understand it's been traumatic for you. But can you think of anyone who might have wanted to hurt Ursula?"

"Hurt maybe." Big hoop earrings clunked against her cheeks as she shook her head. "But not like that. I'd ask PC Mason, if he's still around. He went round a few times when she complained about stuff, and there was a guy from the council, Andrew Goddard. She had a right go at him over the park at the back. Kids on there at night with music playing, doing laughing gas canisters. His wife worked at Harrison's, and she threatened to sack her if it didn't get sorted."

Robin made a note of the name. "Do you know what happened?"

"She got sacked."

*

John had never been in The Long Café before. He pulled the door open, and a delicious waft of coffee and warm bread blew across his face.

Catherine sat at the back of the café, reading her phone on the table. He stopped as the enormity of his actions hit him. The woman he'd dragged from the smashed-up car had been barely conscious. She'd slumped to the tarmac like a slain carcass, and although he'd known she was still alive, there'd been a detachment. A survival instinct had kicked in, and as he'd tried to explain to the police, it had been profound. Seeing her vibrantly alive, because of him sent a rush of happiness flooding through him. He couldn't imagine being more at ease with the world.

When she saw him, she hesitated, and he understood. He took the uncertainty away and hugged her, holding her in silence as the café buzzed and hummed around them. She returned the hug with strength and felt good in his arms. When they moved apart, she pushed back her hair, and her eyes were glossy.

"Thank you for saving my life."

Her simple words were laden with sincerity.

"It was a pleasure. Well, not a pleasure, not an enjoyable pleasure … oh, you know what I mean."

He laughed at himself, and she smiled too, the ice broken. She must've felt as overwhelmed by their strange meeting as he did. Dark shadows beneath her eyes and the puffy eyelids belied the smile. Her gratitude was implicit, but the effects of the trauma were obviously still raw. Survivor's guilt or just lack of sleep? Whatever caused the sadness, it didn't detract from her earthy appeal, nor diminish her curious energy. She oozed an unusual vibe.

Coffee ordered, he slid into the booth opposite her. "I like the atmosphere in here. I've seen this place loads of times and I don't know why I've never been in before."

"Yeah, I love its quirkiness and the owners are lovely."

Framed articles covered the walls along with photos and paintings of Broadstone and the castle. An unusual mixture of café and museum. People were reading the pieces as they drank their coffee.

"They have live music on most weekends. Indie folk stuff usually. It's a great night."

"I'll have to try it sometime."

She drank her odd-smelling tea and topped up her cup from the pot. Her arm shook as she poured.

"Are you OK?"

She nodded, visibly battling with her emotions. "I keep thinking about Jason, who … died. I keep seeing him too and hearing the sound when …" She swallowed hard, took a deep breath, and let it out in a shaky sigh. "I'm sorry, it must be tough for you too."

Straight to the heart of the matter. He liked that she'd opened up with him already. He reached over the table and rested his hand over hers. She swiped at her eyes with her other hand, but she didn't pull away.

"It's raw right now, but don't let it destroy you. Part of me will always feel guilty, but I believe he made the choice, and we were the means to his end. We were just there when he died Catherine."

She silently challenged him, experienced bullshit radar scanning for lies. She would find none. He genuinely believed what he'd heard about Jason Eaves and wanted her to find peace with it too.

"Has it affected you?" she asked.

This wasn't the time to spin her a story, but honesty would sound so cold. He wavered for a second. She sat back and withdrew her hand, maybe misreading his hesitation or concerned she'd upset him.

"I've so much going on now, stuff I don't want to bore or burden you with, it's become swept up in a tsunami of other troubles." She must've had a dozen questions, but she asked none. "Work problems, family problems."

She accepted his vague explanation, too polite to push him any further. Had she looked him up too? He wasn't on any social media and none of the news stories about Ursula connected him to her. Not yet. Interestingly, when he'd Googled her, he'd come across several images of her with DI Scott who he'd met the day before.

A waitress brought his coffee over along with a plate of green star-shaped … biscuits? When she'd gone, he picked one up and sniffed it. Funky.

"What the hell are these?"

She smiled. "Another Alice creation. Last week I had cheese and aubergine crisps." She sniffed one too. "Herbs. Legal ones probably, but you never know. Alice and Jim are a bit unconventional."

"They sound like a laugh. I'm definitely coming back. Do you live in Broadstone?"

"No, Camber. I took on my Gran's old cottage when she died. It's wonky and odd but I've loved it since I was a child. Living there makes me still feel close to Gran. I live on my own, but I don't feel alone. Does that sound weird?"

"Not at all. I know what you mean. Well, I think I do. No, I wish I did," he shook his head. What had happened to him? He was bumbling like Hugh Grant on overdrive. "I'm envious actually. My family are either dead or distant, and I'd love to feel that way about someone, although it's sad you miss her. My younger brother is the only close family I have. Apart from Bobby, he's my surrogate dad."

"A surrogate dad? How does that work?"

She asked the question with refreshing, genuine interest. He was enjoying her company more than he'd expected.

"My mum died when I was a baby and my dad when I was eleven. I lived with my step mum and my little brother until I left for uni. Bobby was our gardener and we just clicked. I didn't realise I needed a substitute dad, and I don't think he was looking for a substitute son either. But he's amazing."

"How lovely that you found each other."

The first person who'd responded without a hint of implied judgement or sleaze.

"I feel blessed to have him. I just wish he could find someone to share his life with. Well, he has but she's married. Long story." Time to change the subject. He suddenly had a lump in his throat that he struggled to swallow. "So, are you a writer? I've just spotted your name on an article over there."

She turned around to see what he was looking at. "I used to work for The Post, but I freelance now. Local history is my specialism."

"Really? I teach history."

"At Broadstone Grammar?"

He laughed. "No, Toncaster High. Rough comprehensive in a grim area, but it's been such a valuable training ground for me. They're a difficult bunch, mostly from tough backgrounds, parents struggling, disruptive peer groups. But I love when a subject clicks with them. They think history is stuffy and boring, then a story resonates, or a spark ignites. It's a reminder they're still just kids, still capable of wonderment. It's a beautiful thing."

"You feel you can make a difference."

"This sounds wanky, but I feel more like I'm championing history. I try to make it exciting and current, to get the kids to feel a connection. I'm doing what I love and hopefully along the way I pass fragments of my passion on to others. My soul likes that. Anyway, enough about me. Tell me more about what you do."

"I've been lucky, I guess. I came out of papers and landed work right away. I'm about to start working with Broadstone Castle Trust, doing the PR and marketing for the re-opening of the castle."

"That's a coincidence. My friend and I were talking about Broadstone Castle yesterday. He'd heard about a historical re-enactment taking place there."

"Ooh impressive snooping skills," she laughed, "Yes, there are plans, but they're under wraps still."

"Rich has a knack for unwrapping the unwrappable."

"It will be spectacular if it comes off. Are you into re-enactments?"

John raked his hair and sat back.

"I've been to five or six, but they never quite hit the mark for me. It kills it when everyone breaks for coffee and gets their phones out. I have the same feeling when I visit a castle. In a historical building, I want total immersion. I want to be back in time, living it for real. Fake styling winds me up, which is irrational I know. What I want is beyond impossible."

"I know what you mean, but at least people can still go and visit these places and get a feel for how it used to be."

"You're right. It's my failing. I'm a purist … God, that does make me sound like such a wanker! I'm not, honestly ..."

"I feel the same when I see a Shakespeare done in modern dress."

"Exactly! It's infuriating."

He needed to shut up and stop talking about himself. Easy to see how she'd been a reporter. Talking to her was effortless, like he'd known her for ages.

"So, which period would you like to be transported back to?"

"Early to mid-1300s," he replied without thinking, "My thesis focused on this county in 1235-1248ad."

"Interesting period locally. Dark times for the inhabitants at Broadstone Castle."

"Extremely dark. I love how this small place, unimportant in its time, had such a rich cast of characters. I'm sure you have it covered but I'd be happy to help if you want a brain to pick."

"I may take you up on that, thanks."

They ordered more drinks, and she left the table for a moment. She headed towards the ladies, saying a quick hello on the way to a woman she knew. Why had he'd been so strongly compelled to meet her again? Maybe because she represented an instance of goodness in his life, and he didn't want to let it go. Like an amazing day you wish would never end.

She came back as their drinks arrived and chatted with the waitress, whose armful of bangles tinkled as she spoke. She introduced herself as the owner, Alice, then discreetly withdrew.

"Do you believe in fate?" he asked her when she'd settled again.

She blinked, blindsided momentarily by the left-field question, but didn't take long to answer. "Yes, I think so."

He nodded, swirling froth around his cup. "When extraordinary events happen, life-changing moments – I always wonder why. It's the small moments. A simple choice made without more than a second of thought and – bam – your life has changed. How much of what happens as we make our journey is predetermined?"

"Life's just a series of choices."

"But do we make them completely or were we always meant to make them?"

"Make a wrong decision but blame it on the universe? I feel that's a cop-out."

"Depends on your filters, doesn't it?"

"OK, so why were you on the bridge on Friday night? What choice led you there?"

He took a deep breath, let it out slowly, buying some time. "It's complicated."

"If you don't want to talk about it …"

He did. Like a willing patient settling into his shrink's comfiest chair.

"This sounds wrong no matter how I say it, so I'll just say it. One of my pupils has a crush on me." He anticipated a reaction, but her expression didn't change. "She turned up at my house and … came on to me. I told her to go home, and she ran out, threatened to go to the police. I chased after her and that's how I ended up on the bridge."

"Shit. Sounds heavy."

He smiled. "Yeah. This girl has more sass than a woman of thirty. I've told the Head, and he'll speak to her, but you know how it goes; no smoke without fire."

"Is it all lies?"

He stared at her, impressed with her for asking. "Completely."

"Then you have truth on your side, and it always comes out eventually. Don't let her beat you, John."

He drank his coffee. "Thanks, and I won't. No way will I let her ruin me or my career. So, that's me. What about you?"

"It's boring. I was on my way to the dry cleaners."

"God, that is boring. You could've made something up."

Catherine laughed. "I'd been for lunch with a friend and forgotten to pick up my dress for my cousin's wedding reception. So, I turned around to head back to Broadstone," she paused for a moment, "Why did Jason choose that moment?"

"Catherine …"

"But was he always meant to be there or did a last-minute change of decision alter his path too?"

"We'll never know. The dry cleaning you forgot, my crazy stalker; all sliding doors."

"This is deep for a Sunday afternoon."

Nice one. He'd made the classic mistake he always did. Heart on sleeve, open book. He couldn't help himself. The first woman in a while who he found both attractive and intriguing, then within minutes, he'd scared her off by going too deep too soon.

"You're right, forgive me. You're easy to talk to and I suppose I don't find that often," he checked the time on his phone, "I'd love to stay longer but I'm collecting a new car and the dealer closes in half an hour." He reached for his jacket. "Well, you have my number. Message me if you need a brain to pick, or if you want to talk about … , you know. Stuff."

"John …"

Halfway to his feet, he stopped. Sea green eyes laden with intensity communicated more than words could.

"It's been lovely meeting you, and I've enjoyed talking to you. A lot."

He sat again, bathed in relief. "I thought I might've scared you off." She shook her head, and he trusted her honesty as much as his own instincts. "I don't want to complicate your life, but if you need a friend … well, as I said, you have my number."

Outside, the pale sun had broken through the rain clouds, and it pooled on the riverside. Its gentle rays warmed her face as he leant over to kiss her cheek. When he turned to leave, a sadness darkened her eyes, or maybe he was projecting his feelings onto her.

He missed her the moment she'd gone.

*

"Wow, this car is cool!"

Will Rickman slid into the passenger seat of John's new Audi coupe and threw his sports bag onto the back seat. He opened and closed the glove box, flipped some switches and checked himself out in the vanity mirror. "When did you get this?"

"Half an hour ago."

"Your old wreck was embarrassing."

John grinned and headed out of the car park into the traffic.

"Will you put me on your insurance when I'm seventeen?"

"No." Will pouted. "Anyway, Barbara will buy you a sensible old lady car."

Will pulled another face. Hard to believe in just over a year he'd be old enough to drive a car. He swept his mop of dark blonde hair ingeniously across his head. Straight out of a boy band. Battling teenage spots, but still a good-looking kid, with inky blue eyes and the Rickman cheekbones. Will had their dad's baby face too. When he'd died at thirty-seven, he could've easily passed for under thirty.

"How are you feeling about your Gran? Barbara stopped by yesterday and said you were upset."

Will stared out at the road and John let him think for a moment. "Can I say something bad? Like, really bad?"

"Nothing's taboo with me, you know that."

"I don't have any feelings about it. I'm not sad, I'm not upset. I feel, like, empty." Will turned to John. "That's shit, right? She was my Gran."

"It's how you feel. That's not shit."

"When Jake in my class lost his grandma, he had a week off school. He was gutted."

"Don't feel bad. She was a tough lady, and Jake was close to his grandma."

"Mum won't tell me what happened. She said Karen found her dead, but the police think she was murdered."

"She pissed off a lot of people in her time."

"Tell me about it."

Will stared back at the road. His silenced stretched on, and John could tell he didn't want to talk about it any further. Will talked in his own time. Pointless pushing him until he'd had time to think.

"Where've you been anyway? You look cool. Have you been to meet someone? What's she like? You so need a girlfriend."

John laughed at the barrage of questions. "Yes, I met someone, but before you start texting anyone the good news, I have bad news too. She's not single."

He didn't tell Will he'd already met her other half and found it curious neither of them hadn't mentioned the other.

"Ah, shit man. Married?"

"No."

"Living with?"

"No."

"Fair game then."

"Will!"

"Do your whole schmoodling thing, get rid of the boyfriend and you're in. What's she like?"

"I don't have a schmoodling thing …"

"Do you have a picture of her?"

"No, because I'm not thirteen." He took a deep breath. "Actually … I crashed into her car, and a guy was killed."

"No shit?!"

"Will, your language is appalling …"

"You didn't tell me any of this on the phone."

"I thought you had enough to deal with."

"I'm not a kid John."

To John, he would always be the little boy he'd watched grow up and loved from the second he first saw him. Will slouched in his seat as they turned into John's street.

"You might be older, but I'm protective of you too."

"I know." John parked outside his house. "I'm sorry. You're right, I should have told you, but I didn't want to worry you. I'm good."

Will gave a sniff and didn't seem convinced.

"I lied before." He fixed his gaze on the trees in the distance. "About Gran. I don't feel empty. I feel free."

*

A quick half-hour run gave Robin an invigorating burst of energy. Bit of a luxury to sneak out but worth it for the adrenalin boost. The team were in the central office when he returned. Jack was on the phone, but he held up his hand to stop Robin as he walked in. He rolled his finger in the air as if he couldn't get the person on the other end to finish whatever they were saying. Vic leapt up from behind his desk like someone at a surprise party when the lights go on.

"Guess what? The gardener's alibi doesn't check out."

"What?"

"When he's in York, Trent always stays at the Spinnings B&B. Always. He knows the owner and gets a discount because he 'gives their front garden a tickle' while he's there. He hasn't stayed there for weeks."

"Maybe he stayed somewhere else."

" 'Always' the guy said. He's known Trent a while," Vic countered, jigging enough to make his fringe bob against his forehead, "He drew the designs for his house back in his architect years."

"Alright Vic, calm down." said Robin as Jack escaped from his caller, "Checking an alibi isn't ground-breaking stuff."

"Puts him as a suspect though, yeah?"

"It puts him as a liar." Robin thought for a second. "By the way, how come you never mentioned that you'd met Ursula Harrison when you were in uniform?"

Vic frowned, stopped jigging. "I did. I said the other day she was always ringing back then."

Did he? He'd missed that one...

"Reports of a guy throwing up in a layby on the A56 at 3.04am on the night of the murder." said Jack, joining them. "Clipped a truck on the way out. We're trying to get hold of the dashcam footage from the truck. Also, the CSOs have found a footprint. Rain's washed most of the ground to mush but the porch is largely dry. Size ten, some type of boot. Guess whose wellies in the shed are a size ten?"

"Bobby Trent's?" Jack nodded. "Let's hope they match. Any prints?"

"No, but we do have several hair samples which aren't Ursula's, Barbara's or Karen Taylors. One unidentified is a close match to Barbara so we're assuming it's William Rickman's. We need a sample to eliminate. The other is short and mousy brown, found on the windowsill. I checked with the gardening agency, who I was just on to, and Bobby Trent has short brown hair."

Could all be circumstantial, but it did suggest another angle.

"Trent doesn't have a record," said James, "He was an architect for most of his career then started Green Tips. Divorced three years ago, no kids. He has a website for his gardening services. Fancy stuff. Creative."

"Giving up a career in architecture for messing around with plants is a real leap, in both salary and career."

"His work is more in landscaping and garden design. You can see the architectural influence on his website."

"It's not like he was under pressure to pay the mortgage," said Jack, "He lives on Bankhouse, bought an ex-council house dirt cheap."

"Maybe he just enjoys working outdoors." Ella ripped open a pack of sandwiches with her teeth. "Bail out of the rat race and do what you love."

Robin hadn't picked up Ella's sneery tone before. Was there more to her comment or was she just having an off day? Tough working long hours with a baby.

"You don't get many architects living on Bankhouse though."

Maybe Ursula tried her bossy routine on him and pushed him too far, but did they have enough to arrest him?

"Ursula complained about him to the agency who contracted Green Tips," said Jack, "accused him of spying on her. And she kicked off about him treading dirt through her house."

"Why did all these people take her shit?" asked James.

"Because she was flash with her cash. She slipped them a few quid and bought their silence. Or a cheeky add-on."

"She binned him off then, and he took it badly."

"Possible." Jack stretched and cracked his back. "But no one's mentioned it so far. Not her daughter, the carers, any of the neighbours …"

"People do keep affairs secret," said Vic, but Jack was still shaking his head, "And if she was paying him … well, he won't want to admit it. Even if it was consensual."

It was all speculation, and they had no idea whether it was consensual or coercion. "What about Andrew Goddard, the councillor Karen Taylor just mentioned? He sounded interesting." Robin clutched another handful of straws.

"Diagnosed with MS three years ago," said James, reading from his laptop, "He's retired now, so's his wife. Big in am-dram. Serial panto Dame. Sounds like a colourful character."

But would a former civil servant turn to murder because his wife lost her job? It seemed a stretch, no matter how colourful he was.

"Let's go and have a chat with Bobby Trent."

Chapter Seven

Dishing dirt

"Marcia, let's go home."

"This is the last one, I promise."

Jamie sighed. They'd been in six bars already, all clustered around the Broadstone Post's offices in the centre of town, drinking the cheapest drinks available. Marcia's mission: to find Catherine Nicholls. So far only one of the bar staff Marcia had shown her picture to knew her, in The Elephant and Castle, a dingy dive down a back street behind the Post's offices, and popular drinking hole for Post staff. But she'd not been in there in a while the barman said.

"Why would she be out on the piss on a Sunday night anyway? If she had a crash three days ago, she'll be on the couch in her poorly clothes."

"At least if I know where she goes, I can come back."

"She won't go in here." Jamie scanned the fancy bar. "It's a gay joint."

"She's pro-gay, I've looked her up. So, I bet someone knows her at least."

"Last one Marcia."

He instantly liked Wags. It had a cool retro style, with walls covered in album sleeves, mixed in with black and white photos of musicians. Dark wood and warm lighting made the place feel cosy. There was even a dusky pink baby grand in the corner ready for anyone to wander up and have a play.

The guy behind the bar was chatting to another customer but he came over to serve them, smartly dressed in head to toe black with amazing grey hair crowning his head in perfect spikes. He welcomed them with a smile, although they were totally out of place. Jamie didn't have chance to speak.

"We're looking for Catherine Nicholls. Does she come in here?" Marcia showed the barman the picture she'd saved on her phone.

The smile died down a few notches. The guy didn't look at the photo. "Why do you want to know?"

The customer at the end of the bar spun around on his stool to listen in, frowning. Jamie gave him daggers. Nosy bastard.

"I just need to speak to her."

"About what?" asked the customer, getting up from his stool. He came towards them, and as the light fell on his face Jamie couldn't stop himself from staring at the scar running from his eyebrow, along his nose and through his upper lip, like someone had sliced his face in two.

He was still staring when a hot woman with big hair came through the door behind the bar carrying a vase of flowers. She put the vase on the bar and frowned.

"What's going on?" she asked.

"These two are asking for you." Scarface nudged his head their way.

Marcia glared at her, hands on hips in a 'Pauls Boutique' bomber jacket (fake or nicked, probably nicked) and cheap purple leggings with a hole on the butt. Catherine, in skinny jeans, boots and a funky jacket outshone her, despite being at least twice Marcia's age if not more. Nice rack, good legs. Obvious why Rickman liked her.

"If I had a story about a teacher who was a kiddy fiddler, who should I go to? A local paper, like the Post, or The Sun?"

Catherine stared at Marcia, then shifted the scrutiny to Jamie.

"I'm her brother," he said, feeling the need to make that clear. He immediately regretted it. She must've thought he was a right dick.

"I'd recommend you go to the police, your parents and your school."

"Yeah, but the police wouldn't believe me. My parents – well, fuck knows where my mum is, and my dad wouldn't give a shit – and I've already told my headteacher."

"Well, we're not social services love." Scarface moved closer. "This is a bar and you're underage. I think you should leave."

"It's OK Simon, let her say what she came to say." Catherine came to the end of the bar, nearer to Marcia. "What school are you from?"

"Broadstone Grammar," Marcia lied, and Catherine smiled. As soon as she smiled, Jamie knew none of this surprised her. Rickman must have given her the heads up on his crazy sister already.

He pulled Marcia's arm. "Come on, let's go."

"I thought you might want to print my story so people will know what a dirty perv he is. His name is John Rickman." Marcia smirked with victory, and he cringed.

Catherine's expression didn't change. She studied Marcia, sussing her out. "He doesn't teach at Broadstone Grammar."

"He won't be teaching anywhere soon."

"And he's behaving inappropriately with his students you say?"

"Yep."

"Including you?"

"Just me."

Catherine nodded. "You should think carefully about destroying his career and reputation before you take it any further. Especially if it's all fantasy and lies."

Everyone was staring now, earwigging the free show. Two other guys who'd been in a booth were on their feet, ready to wade in if it kicked off.

"He fucking raped me!"

Ouch, too far. Jamie pulled harder on Marcia's arm and dragged her away from Catherine just in time to stop Marcia from launching herself across the bar. Shit, she was strong. He had to use all his weight to shove her towards the door, but she came back again like a spitting cat.

"So, you want to get involved with a rapist, do you?"

"Grow up sweetheart. You're making an idiot of yourself." Catherine didn't move, calm and unfazed by his furious sister.

"Tell the kiddy fiddler I am going to destroy his fucking career. No one will believe him when he denies it. No one!"

"A credible, respected teacher or a cheap little girl with a big mouth? We'll see, shall we?"

"What? You bitch ..."

Jamie wrapped both arms around his sister and spun her around, ducking her swinging arms. The brother and barman followed behind them. Simon held the door open while Jamie wrestled her outside.

"Don't ever go near my sister again or you'll regret it," he sneered, and with the scar he looked like he fucking meant it. He slammed the door shut behind them.

"Did you hear what she called me?"

"Sort yourself out! You got what you deserved there Marcia." He wanted to die of embarrassment. He'd never felt like such a scutter.

*

John and Will were engrossed in a tennis match when his phone rang, in the middle of debating a decision from Hawk Eye. He grabbed it off the table. Catherine? Already? Will peered over at the screen too and wiggled his eyebrows at John in encouragement.

"Hey."

"John, I just had a run-in with your pupil and her brother. They came to my brother's bar in town."

John jumped up from the sofa and Will looked at him in alarm. She told him about the confrontation, and he had a strange feeling like the blood draining from his body. His guts clenched so tightly around his lunch he felt instantly nauseous.

"I'm so sorry you've been involved. Are you OK?"

He left the living room and continued the call in the kitchen, wrestling with a barrage of emotions, jaw clenched so tight he had to force his words out. Shame burned from within, despite his innocence.

"I'm fine. I see what you mean now about her obsessiveness."

"I don't know how to deal with this. Catherine, please can we keep this between us for now? I know it's a huge ask but …"

"I won't tell anyone, don't worry. It's not my business, or anyone else's either."

"Thank you, and again, I'm so sorry. I swear she's making this all up."

"I believe you. From the way she behaved, I'd say she was stoned or unhinged. Or both. I was a bit cutting with her. Hope it doesn't backfire on you."

Backfire? The situation couldn't be any worse, and he didn't blame her for retaliating. He liked it. She'd shown she had bite, which made her even more attractive.

"I'm sure you don't want anything more to do with me, but if you do ... well, you know where I am."

"Thanks. Take care. Hope it works out tomorrow."

John ended the call and slammed his phone on the worktop. He stayed there for a moment and stared at his clenched fists. No way would she call him again, and he didn't blame her.

"Why wouldn't she want anything more to do with you?" Will asked from the doorway, "I caught the end bit. And who's out of control?" John covered his face, still mortified. "OK, I get it. You don't want to tell me. Again."

Will stomped back towards the living room in a huff and John returned his head to his hands. What must Catherine think of him now? She hadn't committed when she'd ended the call, whereas at the café she'd been keen to meet again.

Dreading the next conversation, he dragged his feet all the way back to the lounge where Will pretended to be absorbed in a football match.

"This ref needs glasses."

"Will, please don't be angry with me."

A shrug. Eyes on the TV. "None of my business, is it?"

"It's complicated."

"And I'm just a kid, right? I wouldn't understand."

John slumped onto the sofa, legs as heavy as the shame in his chest. Telling Catherine had been a relief, but the prospect of telling Will killed him inside. He couldn't bear Will's disappointment and that he might topple from his pedestal with an almighty crash. But he'd sworn to be always honest with his brother, even if it meant his ego took a kicking and he had to admit he had flaws.

"One of my pupils has a crush on me, a stoner. Troublemaker. She's been inventing lies, all total fantasy. She's had a go at Catherine, traced her to her brother's bar, and accused me, publicly, of ... all kinds of nasty stuff."

Will bit back the hundreds of questions he wanted to ask. He picked up the remote control and channel hopped. "Report her to social services." John stared at him until Will eventually selected a channel and put the remote down. "She's a kid. Her parents aren't doing their job."

Savvy for a fifteen-year-old, and tough. He'd been so consumed with loving Will as a child he'd missed him turning into a young man.

"If Catherine defended you against a psycho like her, she's worth holding on to. That's if you can talk her into seeing you again."

*

The Bankhouse estate looked grimmer than normal in the fading light. Rows of boxy maisonettes formed a square around a little park containing a one-seated seesaw and a miserable set of swings. A bunch of lads, some of them on bikes, clustered around a broken bench with one remaining slat, while two girls rocked aimlessly on a pair of springy horses, hunched over their phones. Bankhouse was rough but peaceful. The odd car got nicked, the occasional party ended in a scrap. No different to the more affluent estates further from town. The rougher areas were in Toncaster.

At the back of the estate two rows of semis backed onto allotments, and beyond them the river. Easy to pick out the privately owned houses. Private owners tried to make their house not look like a council house. Bobby Trent's house at the end of the row had been upgraded by altering the colour of the rendering from sick cream to white. A compact green van bearing his name, number and a tree graphic was parked underneath the front window.

Robin rang the doorbell and inside, a yappy dog protested at the sound. A man in his late fifties opened the door wearing combats and a flowery t-shirt.

"DI Scott, DS Tanner from Broadstone CID. We'd like to ask you some questions about Ursula Harrison."

Bobby Trent opened the door wider. "Come in."

They followed Trent into a boxy hallway, where a pissed off poodle growled from behind a child gate in the kitchen doorway.

"Rescue dog," Trent said by way of explanation, "She doesn't like people. Me included. Come through."

A huge pine wall unit crammed with books dominated Trent's living room. Books piled up on the coffee table and stacked in every available corner. Robin chose an armchair next to a black hi-fi topped with a record player, topped with more books. For a tree lover Bobby Trent was seriously adding to their demise. Trent took the sofa. Jack loitered in the archway leading to a dining area, preferring as usual to stand and mooch.

"When did you last see Ursula Harrison?"

Trent raked his floppy brown hair and shoved his glasses up his nose. "Last Monday, I think. Why?"

"And how did she seem to you?"

"Same as she always does. Unpleasant." Trent frowned at Jack, who'd ambled towards the open plan dining room, scanning books on another bookcase.

"Do you know she died on Friday?"

"Yes, John told me what little he knew."

"Are you two close?"

"I've known him for years and we're close, yes. He used to come out and talk to me when I was at Ursula's or if I did work at Barbara's. I think he enjoyed the male company and kindness. We've been close ever since."

"What's the nature of your relationship?"

He acknowledged the insinuation with a smile. "Don't we live in a sad world when people mistake genuine affection and compassion for sleaze? Is this relevant to Ursula's death?"

"Wow!" Jack said from the far end of the dining area. "This is incredible."

Robin rose, irritated by the interruption, but he joined him at the patio doors.

Now he understood why Trent had bought this house. The garden was huge. It stretched out towards the river in subtle layers, like a horticultural show exhibit. Pure fantasy, lit discreetly to showcase each feature as the light faded, crafting a visual journey through each enticing tableau.

"Your garden's stunning." Robin knew nothing about gardening, but he recognised the genius of Bobby's art.

"Thank you. I tolerated Ursula because of her garden. Roses grow in her borders like nowhere else I've ever known."

"Tolerated what?"

Bobby took off his glasses and cleaned them on his t-shirt. He had a calm gentleness about him, a touch of casual arrogance. He appeared as at peace with himself as he was with nature. Jack stared out across the garden, listening without listening, like a doodler detaching part of his brain.

"She was vile. I can't think of anything complimentary to say about her. That's how much I tolerated her."

"Mrs Harrison complained about you, but you carried on working there. Are her roses so amazing? Or was there another incentive?"

"What are you implying?"

"You like your plants, but no one puts up with abuse just to grow flowers."

"Or maybe you don't understand passion."

Weird comment. Where had that come from? He glanced at Jack who pulled a 'what's he on?' face from a safe distance behind Bobby's back, just as the poodle began yapping again. Bobby stood.

"Give me a minute, I'll take her outside."

"What do you make of him?" Jack whispered, when Bobby was out of earshot. "Because he's pinging all over my radar."

"I'm not sure, but something's not right."

Jack nodded and they waited for a minute or so. He turned back to the view of the garden while Robin scanned through the books. He tried to pick out a familiar title. Stacks of books about plants and nature; medicinal plants, ancient herbs, rare plant identification. Jeez. Not a chance of a Jack Reacher in this collection. Another minute passed. Silence. Jack spun around, as the penny dropped for him too.

"Shit!"

They both lunged towards the kitchen. Empty. No dog, no Bobby Trent. Robin tugged the back door handle. "It's locked."

He searched the nearest worktop and shelf for a key. Nothing. Trent had locked them in and scarpered.

"This way," shouted Jack from the dining room and the patio door slid open. Outside, they scanned the garden but there was no sign of him or the dog. He couldn't disappear in two minutes.

"Check over next door. I'll do the other side."

The right boundary of the garden bordered a piece of wasteland between the end of Trent's row and the backs of neighbouring houses. Robin ran along the central path towards a seated area covered by a wooden pergola. He managed to get a foothold on the fence and peered over into the dark space. No sign of Trent. No sign of Jack either. They were both pushing sixty and they'd shot off like a pair of greyhounds.

"I found the dog," shouted Jack from the other side of the garden, "it's in next door's garden behind the shed." He emerged from behind a tree, brushing leaves off his jacket. "No sign of Trent."

"He's still here." Robin moved towards the middle of the garden where a circular stone carved with a star marked the central point. He pivoted, trying to spot where Trent might be hiding, but challenged by too many options. "Come out Bobby," he called out, "This is pointless."

A thud, behind him in the direction of the river. Robin spun around and ran towards the noise, along a winding path and up cobbled steps to a decked higher level. A movement in the distance. Branches swayed, accompanied by the crunch of crushed twigs.

"Bobby stop!"

Robin dug in and pushed forward. Where could the guy go? The garden was fenced in on both sides and the back fence hidden by a dense cluster of fruit trees. But Trent continued. Was there a rear exit? He slid over sludgy leaves and branches, following Trent's path until he reached the back fence. Two panels had warped out of line from the rest, leaving a space a dog might squeeze through, but a grown man? Trent was knelt in the dirt, pulling at the panels in sheer desperation. He yanked again then dropped his head and sagged in defeat to the wet ground. He stayed there, unmoving.

"Bobby Trent, I'm arresting you on suspicion of the murder of Ursula Harrison …"

*

Catherine took a taxi back home, the lovely afterglow from her meeting with John obliterated by the run in with his pupil. She believed in his innocence, especially now she'd met the girl, but she resented the intrusion. Simon had tried to persuade her to stay for some Sinatra crooning, but she wanted to be home in her comfies with a glass of wine and a period drama. So, when the taxi pulled up on her driveway and Clive and Cindy were there, her heart sank a little.

"Aren't you supposed to be resting?" Cindy pulled her in for a hug as the taxi disappeared. "We've been knocking for ages. Clive thought you were dead."

Clive hunched in his leather overcoat, holding a bunch of flowers like they were going to bite him. "I hope your heating's on," he grumbled then stuck his arm out, "Cindy reckons these will cheer you up, but I have a hipflask of grappa as back-up."

"I have gin." Cindy yanked a bottle out of her bag, cheesy grin framed by her geometrically perfect bob.

Gratitude for their friendship replaced her initial annoyance. They built a fire in the wood burner to keep Clive happy and camped out in the snug, a tiny but cosy room with the fumes of her Gran's cigarettes infused in the exposed brick walls. For Catherine, this made her love the room more. Her Gran's essence still existed in the fabric of the building around them. When they'd all settled, and Catherine had topped up on paracetamol, Clive gave her his dad face.

"Why weren't you on the sofa binge watching Last Kingdom again? You almost died Cat."

"And it's given me a new appreciation for living in the moment and not wasting another second."

"Cindy swished her G&T around, "Has Robin been looking after you?"

"I've hardly seen him since Friday. Simon's taken time off so he can stay with me. I've left him at Wags belting out Mack The Knife."

"He's such a poor babysitter." Clive fished around in his coat pocket for a little notebook he always carried on him. "I managed to speak to the guy you were going to interview," he licked his fingertip and flicked through the pages of his book, "What do you make of this …"

Cindy stop-signed him. "We agreed no work Clive."

"Really?" Clive huffed like a disappointed kid.

Catherine let them squabble for a minute, her thoughts drifting back to John's issues and the psycho siblings. Such a shame John had all that to deal with. She wouldn't tell Cindy and Clive though. She'd already become protective of John, felt strangely bonded with the person who'd saved her life. Or had she warmed to him because he'd reawakened her need to be around interesting people again.

Discussing the murder of Ursula Harrison became suddenly much more appealing.

"Come on Clive, hit me," she interjected, ending their dispute, "But I'll 'no comment' you if you get giddy."

"As if. OK, so this guy Alan Renshaw was a bookkeeper at Harrison Engineering back in the nineties. He worked in the finance team under Barbara Rickman. Ursula was nearing retirement, but still around. Get this; she used corporal punishment."

Catherine almost choked on her gin. "Fuck. Off. You can't be serious?"

"She had a walking stick in her office, a fancy gift apparently, with an elaborate handle."

"And what? She bent them over her desk for a spanking?"

Clive shook his head. "No, but you're not far off. Across the knuckles mostly. Or just threats. Humiliating ones."

"I don't believe it. How did it never leak?"

"It did," said Cindy, "In 1997 the Chronicle ran a news story from an ex-employee claiming to have been 'punished' by Ursula, but the following day the paper printed an apology."

"Why?" Catherine asked.

Clive shrugged. "I knew the editor back then. Anthony Lamb. He was with the paper until it closed in 2003 and he would never apologise for printing a story he believed true. Someone leaned on him."

"Or leaned on the publisher."

"Also possible. But this was only one instance of it. Now she's dead, people might be more willing to come forward. I had a run-in with her once." Clive stretched out in the heat from the fire like a cat basking in the sun. "A bloke on a Harrison site was injured in an accident involving a digger. We ran the story and she kicked off, threatened the paper and me personally."

"Did she punish you?" Catherine purred, and Cindy snorted her drink as she laughed.

"Fuck off, she was about three feet tall."

If Catherine had gleaned anything from Robin, it was his way of reading someone's expression and understanding repressed emotions behind the mask. Clive was holding back.

He topped up his drink from his flask. "I reckon she had issues, floated around on some spectrum or other. Narcissist maybe?"

"So, what did Ursula or the Harrisons have on Alan Renshaw? How did she guarantee his silence?" Intrigue was an astonishing healer. Her journalist's intuition shook off its mothballs and climbed out of hibernation. "She bought it," she said, "Money had to be her weapon."

"I asked Renshaw," said Clive, "but he wouldn't budge. I'll work on him though."

"Bit embarrassing," said Cindy, "Admitting you let your boss give you a whack for cash."

"How does that conversation work?" said Catherine, "You're having a discussion about a misdemeanour, she gives you a crack but you don't tell anyone? And what's in it for her? The power kick?"

"The sexual kick," suggested Cindy, "It's bloody pervy you have to admit."

"No, I don't buy it. I think it's more what Clive said earlier. Narcissism fits, or sadism even. Most people play out their kinky shit in private."

"I wonder how much her family knows?"

"Got some news for you there; I met John Rickman earlier, that's where I've been."

"No way! What's he like?" Cindy asked. Clive raised his bushy eyebrows, curious too.

"I liked him. He's lovely," she conceded, "Interesting. Funny. Unusual."

Cindy leant forward.

"You like him."

"I just said that."

"No. You *like* him."

"Pack it in Cindy."

"This would make an amazing front page," Cindy ignored her, on a roll now, "Post reporter falls for her hero. Saved from death by murdered woman's grandson."

"Ex-reporter, and that's wrong on so many levels."

"Romance doesn't sell papers," Clive ventured, "But 'my wealthy Grandma's kinky exploits' does. I need to lean on Renshaw harder, especially now Ursula's corpse is all over social media …"

"Wait. What?"

Cindy and Clive stared at her like she'd announced she was really a guy.

"Keep up Cat. Look at this." Cindy did some swiping then handed her phone over. "Posted by her homecare worker."

Every second that image had been live was a second too long. She doubted she'd be the only person wishing she could unsee it. She gave the phone back to Cindy.

"I know you're creaming for a story here and I'm not stupid, I understand the nationals will be on this too. But he's a nice person, and I won't be pushing him for any insider info. Or fetish insights."

They both gave her their 'who are you kidding' stare.

"Well, OK, I might ask questions when I know him a bit better, but Ursula Harrison's death wasn't mentioned today. No reason to bring it up."

"Shoddy." Clive shook his head as if she was the greatest disappointment he'd ever met. "There's always a way to ask about a relative's murder. What the heck did you two talk about?"

"Life. The accident. I wasn't probing for a piece."

Cindy unfolded herself from her armchair and left to top up their drinks. Clive shoved up his sleeves and opened the wood burner door. "Want my advice?" he asked, rearranging logs.

"No."

"Funnily enough neither did Robin." He sank back on the sofa as the fire roared into action again. "Life's short, and I like Robin far more than he likes me…" He held up his hands when Catherine inhaled to protest. "Let me finish. You need someone who understands why you write fiction no one else will ever read because it's how you handle stress. Someone who understands how you can be lost for hours reading a five-hundred-page book about heraldry. He'll never truly understand you."

"No one's perfect Clive. If we all hung around waiting for the one person who ticks all our boxes, we'd all be lonely."

"Maybe. But I saw your eyes shine when you described John Rickman."

"Like when I first met Robin?"

"Yeah, but this time they shone brighter."

Chapter Eight

No escape

"What the hell are you playing at?"

John stared back at Barbara as she fumed on his doorstep, with a quiet calmness he knew would wind her up. He didn't invite her in this time. He'd barely slept since his late-night call with Bobby from the police station.

"William stayed here and don't try to deny it. He told me himself."

No chance. Unless Will had slipped up and told Barbara by accident. Barbara inched forward, right onto the threshold of his home. He fought the urge to move back and regain his own space. No way would he give her the satisfaction of intimidating him.

"Let's discuss this inside." She shoved past him. He didn't move, angry she'd forced her way into his private space.

"He stayed here, yes. I collected him from training and took him to school this morning. He's my brother and I won't stop seeing him just because you don't like it."

"He has prospects, a bright future," she spat, "I don't want him to end up in kind of the wishy-washy, fantasy land you live in."

"Why don't you let Will decide what kind of life he wants, what kind of person he wants to become. He's a good kid."

"Yes, and that's down to me."

"No, it's despite you."

Barbara opened her mouth to retort but stopped as John pushed away from the door and moved towards her. Heat flushed through his chest. This woman had passed judgement on him since the moment she'd first met him, never accepting the good in him and always focusing on the bad.

"You've resented me since my dad first told you he had a son. You've resented me more since he died."

"I raised you, you ungrateful bastard ..."

"You didn't raise me. You tolerated me until I escaped. It's to Will's credit he's the amazing young man he is today, not yours. You don't have a maternal bone in your body. What woman stands back and lets her mother bully her child?"

Barbara's face scrunched into a snarl, and she slapped John hard, punctuating the blow with a guttural screech. He'd expected this too, and he didn't flinch. He wanted her to hit him. He became energised by the sudden surge of adrenalin and the pain shooting up his face. Infuriated by his lack of reaction, Barbara raised her arm a second time, but he caught her wrist. She pulled it away from him and stumbled backwards into the hall table. A lamp at the end teetered from the impact and crashed to the floor where it shattered into pieces across the floorboards. He enjoyed her fight to remain upright, how she floundered to retain her haughty composure. Her heels crunched on the shards.

"Don't you dare speak ill of my mother."

"I have photos of the bruises."

"A little discipline never hurt anyone."

"It hurt me!" John yelled, "And it hurt Will."

"Bullshit! You've poisoned my son. He's lied to me because of you!" Barbara kicked the lampshade up the hallway.

"No, he lied to you because he's trying to protect you. Can't you see that? He wants a relationship with his brother, but you can't bear him needing people in his life other than you."

"He doesn't need you; he worships you like a pathetic little sap. And I won't have it!"

The screeching height her voice had now reached took him back in time, to when she'd screamed at him for throwing up Ribena on her white bathroom rug. She turned away from him for a second, grabbed a large wooden candlestick from the table and launched it at him with another scream of fury. It missed its target and smashed into a picture on the wall beside him. The frame crashed to the floor. Glass shattered.

"Get out of my house."

She stared at him for a few seconds, her shoulders heaving, then she headed for the kitchen. She'd deflected any responsibility for Will's suffering and heard only John's criticism of Ursula. Typical Barbara. Couldn't see her own faults. He wanted to tell her what he thought of her, to let years of simmering resentment boil over but it would all be wasted energy. She didn't care about the past, or what he thought of her in the present. Too preoccupied with protecting Ursula, even after her death, ignoring the truth.

"I don't need this, John." She stared out of the kitchen window. "Not on top of what's happened to my mother."

"Don't apologise for wrecking my house."

"Fuck your house!" She spun around. "You haven't paid for it all anyway. You've always been a leech, feeding away at what my family has worked for."

"And do you know what? I'll carry on leeching as you call it. I know my dad would have wanted me to have what he isn't around to give me. But mostly because I know it pisses you off. You think I'm such a poor role model for Will? Look at yourself."

A loud knock on the door snapped him out of the moment. He left her and crunched his way over bits of broken vase back down the hall. What now?

Two uniformed police officers filled his doorstep, one of them talking into a radio on his lapel.

"We've had reports on a disturbance coming from your house Mr Rickman. Are you OK?"

The policeman peered past John and stared at the broken lamp scattered over the floorboards.

"I think we should come in."

*

Robin had spent the night at his flat. When he'd checked in with Catherine, she had Clive and Cindy round, and he sensed the evening could get messy. He was usually up for a blowout, but he wanted to train at the dojo for a while to release some tension, plus he'd been longing all weekend for the peaceful calmness of his flat. More than ever, he appreciated the large space and the silence. Two hours of training gave him the refresh he needed. By the time he arrived home, his body wallowed in post-exercise glow, his mind invigorated.

The lead Darwin had given him, the ex-employee from Harrison's, was a dead end. Alan Renshaw back peddled so much on his story that, by the end of the interview, Robin wasn't convinced he'd ever worked at Harrison's at all. He was reading through Ursula Harrison's post-mortem report again, hoping for some inspiration before interviewing Trent, when Jack came in.

"Have you seen the latest system update?"

Robin closed the file and logged into his PC. The alert blinked on his dashboard.

"Domestic disturbance?" Robin read the first line and looked at Jack, puzzled.

"Read on. It flagged on the system because of the people involved. I nipped downstairs and had a word with PC Johnson who attended. He said the neighbours at Rickman's place heard one holy row going on next door and called it in."

Robin scanned the report again.

"Well, bugger me. And Rickman admitted Barbara had hit him?"

"Yeah. Johnson says he didn't want to report it, but he logged it on the incident report anyway. He thought the reaction was strange."

"What's going on with that family?"

"Barbara Rickman has a nasty streak." Jack headed for the door to answer his phone, "I'm still more in favour of Trent." He pinched one of Ella's biscuits on the way to his desk, ignored her loud 'oi' and picked up the call.

Robin stared at his screen for a while, specifically at the words 'Attending Officer'. An uncomfortable suspicion had been lurking in his brain since Karen Taylor's interview. He clicked out of the report and opened the archives.

Ursula Harrison's record on the database listed a mind-numbing catalogue of complaints as lengthy and nit-picky as her care file. How much police time had she wasted over the years with her reports? Numerous complaints of intruders in her garden, security lights coming on, alarms going off, 'strange' phone calls, excessive dog barking, people arguing in a parked car, scaffolders across the street setting up at 8am on a Sunday. She'd lived in a quiet area with low crime rates and few disturbances. Her record made Billingham sound like a ghetto where people got kneecapped and did crack in bus shelters.

He clicked into the first couple of incidents and didn't find any anomalies. They were the most recent contacts, the latest one being four months previous when she thought her shed had been broken into. He scrolled further until he found a series of five calls to the station, all within a three-month period and all relating to the same issue; Ursula had been convinced an intruder was sneaking into her house. Ornaments moved, biscuits disappeared from the tin, a rug mysteriously shifted. And after each call, she'd had a visit from her local constabulary.

PC Vic Mason, had attended every time.

Should he stir up this nest or leave it be? He was still churning it over when CSI Collins strutted into CID in another tweed two-piece, working the room and smiling like she'd won best in show for her gooseberry jam. He closed the report. Time to speak to Trent and escape from Collins before she started on the inspirational speeches.

"Ahh, well done Robin," she cooed, as he headed for the door, "I heard about the arrest on the Harrison case. Excellent news."

"Just off to interview him now Ma'am." Robin continued towards the interview suite and left her to Vic, who sprung to life and dazzled as she praised the team. Probably wondering if she offered outside extras. He shoved the bitchy thought away, still not sure about challenging him on it.

Bobby Trent sat at the table in the interview room, legs crossed and relaxed like he was waiting for his meal to arrive in a restaurant. As Jack took Trent through the preliminaries Robin studied him, scrutinising the minute signals he wasn't aware he transmitted. He had calm stillness and answered Jack's questions in his soft timbre. He was intelligent and articulate, and he reminded him of John Rickman. John had grown to emulate the man who'd become his father figure.

"Mr. Trent, can you describe your movements on the night of Ursula Harrison's death?" Robin asked.

"I went through all this with PC Smith when she came to my house."

Robin opened the file in front of him.

"You were in York. Working on a regular contract you have over there."

"Yes."

"Staying at The Spinnings B&B, owned by your friend."

"I usually stay there, yes."

Robin closed the file. Trent crossed his legs and swept his wavy fringe out of his eyes. "Your friend, Mr Marshall, did confirm you've regularly stayed there, but he hasn't seen you for several weeks."

"Correct, I didn't see him last week."

"There's no record of you staying there. A business client took all the rooms for staff attending a meeting at their head office in town."

Trent opened his mouth to speak but stopped himself. He stared for a long time at a scratch across his left wrist then covered his nose and mouth with his hand, pushing back words he didn't want to say.

"You've been arrested on a murder charge Bobby, this is serious. Aside from your attempt to avoid arrest - let's not forget those fun and games - there were footprints outside the house matching your Hunter Wellingtons. Fresh footprints. This is interesting too."

Robin opened the file again and took out a photograph. "This saw from the shed, which you use exclusively I understand, was used to cut Ursula's walking stick in half. She was beaten with the pieces."

Trent was already shaking his head. "That happened years ago. I glued the stick back together. It was a gift from an old friend of Ursula's. She was outraged when she found it'd been broken."

Which did explain how it had snapped so easily. More surprising to hear she had a friend. First one they'd heard of.

"Do you know who did it?" he asked, "Or why?"

"No. We never found out."

"Who did Ursula suspect?" asked Jack.

"Everyone. In fact, I'm surprised she didn't call the police."

Or Vic. Robin glanced down again, ignored the uncomfortable possibility. "Mrs Harrison complained about you, several times."

"She complained about most people."

"I'm not concerned about most people. My priority now is you. How do you explain the footprints outside the front door?"

"Someone set me up, to throw you off the scent. And it worked."

"To implicate you in a murder? They made a smart choice. You've provided a false alibi, done a runner and been, at best, loose with the truth."

Trent folded his arms and sat back, "I've never been in trouble with the police. My worst crime is a parking ticket."

"Where did you stay in York?"

Big sigh. "I stayed with a friend. She's married. Her husband was away on business."

"We'll need her name to confirm this,"

Trent didn't respond. Robin waited until Bobby made eye contact again. "Were you in a relationship with Ursula Harrison? Or did you ever take money from her in return for sexual favours?"

"No to both. Absolutely not."

"It's not an offence, by the way."

"I find it deeply offensive..."

"So, you had no intimate relationship with her of any kind?"

One side of Trent's mouth hitched up in contempt. "She was eighty years old."

"Do you know of any other people who took money from Ursula? Tips, backhanders. Bribes?"

"I tended the gardens, that's it. I chatted to the care staff if they were around, but I mostly kept to myself. Working with nature opens my mind, so I stick on Audible or a podcast and drift away. The carers just want to bitch about people or dissect every second of Love Island, so I wasn't in the clique. I occasionally talked to Ursula about her plants or the gardens in general, and she was almost pleasant. But the idea of being intimate in any way with her is abhorrent, and I'm not desperate for cash. Or anything else."

Maybe Trent wasn't involved with Ursula, but he must've seen or heard about the other stuff going on, no matter how far away he'd drifted. An intelligent introvert like him quietly observed from the background.

"What about the family then? Describe your relationship with them."

"I worked for them."

"What about John Rickman?" Was it relevant to the investigation? Probably not, but curiosity triumphed, and Bobby Trent gave more when pushed.

"He was different. I took him under my wing when he needed a friend."

"Do you make a habit of befriending young boys?"

"Not this again…"

"Handsome lad, beautiful even …"

"Are you sick? We're talking about the man who saved your partner's life!"

Robin's stomach lurched, and for a moment he couldn't speak. How did he know who Catherine was to him? He hadn't mentioned Catherine to Rickman, so she must've told him, and he'd then told Bobby. Or Bobby had read it somewhere. He'd asked James to keep an eye out for any references to her, or their relationship online, but he'd not said anything.

"I'm grateful for what John did. But this is a completely different matter." It sounded weak, and Bobby didn't hide his disdain. "So, you were in York, with your 'friend' on the night of Ursula's murder. And she'll corroborate your story?"

"It's not a story."

"Could you explain then how a hair matching your blood type was found in her bedroom?"

Trent took off his glasses and rubbed his eyes. "She held court in her bedroom when her legs were bad. There's probably more hair on her carpet than a barber's floor."

Jack leant in. "The cleaners had been in two days before, on Wednesday, so no. It was spotless, and according to you the last time you were there was the Monday before."

"Yes. Court summons - bit of a private joke between John and me - she wanted to know why her willow was wilting."

"Can you remember where you were in the room?"

He looked upwards momentarily as he thought. "By the left window, the one framed with ivy. She could see the tree from her bed."

Everything they had now seemed flimsy. Neither the footprint nor the hair provided conclusive evidence which would convict him.

"Why did you try to run from us?" asked Robin.

Trent shook his head. "Old habit. I'm not good with confrontation. And I knew where the conversation was headed."

"Did you kill Ursula Harrison?" Trent didn't even look up from studying his hands.

"Of course not. Do you mind if we take a break?"

Robin headed straight for the cave and coffee. If Trent's alibi stacked up it was impossible for him to have been at Ursula's house at the time they'd identified. They'd basked in glory too soon. Well, Collins had. Christ, she was not going to be happy.

"I don't want to get on the wrong side of you today." Jack scowled into the empty tea bag container. "Sodding hell, who's had all these?"

"I don't think he did it."

"Me neither."

Robin kicked away from the worktop but in the tiny space, he had nowhere to go. He stared instead at the noticeboard, looking without seeing. *We're talking about the man who saved your partner's life.* Those words wouldn't go away. Could Catherine get dragged into this investigation? He needed to see her and find out if John Rickman had spoken about Bobby. They were missing something, mainly a big fat reason why she'd been brutally murdered.

"Guv?" Vic loitered at the door and both he and Jack stared at him, like they'd asked a question he hadn't heard.

We're talking about the man who saved your partner's life.

"Round up the team."

*

"Flowers and dinner in the same day. I'm a lucky girl."

Did sarcasm rumble in her tone or was he looking for it? He'd barely seen her since the accident, and he should've been around more when she needed him. Her eyes were shadowed, cheeks pale. Not great calling her so late in the day either, to arrange dinner for selfish reasons when she should be resting. Impressive relationship skills.

"I'm glad you hadn't eaten. I thought I'd be tied up until late, but I spotted the chance to get out of there for a while."

"How's the investigation going?"

Robin sipped his wine. They were in a quiet corner of the restaurant with only one other couple by the window, both on their phones.

"Slowly. But I'm hoping for a result in the next day or two."

Catherine nodded at the corporate response. She looked gorgeous tonight in simple black jeans and a shirt, effortlessly attractive as always. He missed her. They'd snatched time for a few days but already it seemed longer. It felt more of a mental distance than a physical one. He found it hard to switch off his brain and be in 'home' mode. He wanted to be there in the moment, but he was still processing the day's challenges. In a lovely restaurant with the woman he loved, but his brain wanted him to be with the woman nailed to her bed.

"You didn't have to come over. I understand how busy you are with all this."

"I wanted to see you. How did it go with Clive and Cindy?"

"Great. I didn't think I wanted a gin-fest, but it did me good. What did you do?"

"Kicked the shit out of a punch bag, sparred with Kai, then went home and ironed a shirt. I know how to have a fun time."

Was she there, but not there, or was he projecting his own mental distance onto her? He couldn't work out what had changed. They were silent for a second as the waiter brought over their starters. Robin's stomach skipped with joy at the smell of the food. He hadn't eaten since breakfast.

"Are you staying over?" Catherine asked.

"No, I'm going to head back to mine. I have an early start."

"I don't mind early starts. Stay. I'll make sure you at least get a slice of toast in the morning."

"But little sleep," Robin said with a grin, "No, I'll go home. I'm out of clothes as yours."

She hid her disappointment well, but not well enough. After all this, he would make it up to her. Take her away for a long weekend, surprise her with a break in Europe. She'd always wanted to go to Florence.

"Have you thought about replacing your car?" he asked, trying not to wolf his scallops like a savage.

"I'll wait to see what the insurance company say first. I'm not sure how I'll feel getting behind the wheel again." She pushed back her hair, and the cut on her forehead reminded him of what she'd been through. He put down his fork and studied her more closely.

"No more bad thoughts?" he asked.

"Some, but meeting John helped."

"Oh yes, I forgot to ask. How did it go?"

Robin hadn't forgotten. He'd been dying to ask but couldn't find a way without sounding like a jealous prick.

"Good. I liked him. You were right, he's a nice guy. Talking to him made me feel better about the crash."

"I'm glad. How's he dealing with it?"

Their waiter appeared, checking on their food and drinks. Robin refused a second glass of wine. Catherine finished hers and ordered another.

"Did John mention his family?" He asked when the waiter had gone. He tried to say it casually, as if he'd never planned to ask her the question all along.

"His family?" She stared at him. "Why do you ask?"

Robin fished around for an answer, but it didn't come quickly enough.

"Is that what this impromptu appearance is about?"

"No. Well, not entirely. I wanted to see you, but an issue came up today and you might be able to help me."

"Help how?" Her mood had switched. He'd pissed her off already.

"I wondered if he'd spoken about his gran or step mum, Barbara. Or his friend Bobby."

"In what way?"

She was making him work for it and he already regretted asking the question. "Like, if Barbara had a temper maybe or what his home life was like."

"I met this man for the first time yesterday to thank him for saving my life, Robin. We didn't chit chat about our childhoods." She stared at the stem of her glass, avoiding his eyes.

"I'm just trying to understand the Rickmans better. His grandmother was murdered. I thought he might have mentioned it, that's all."

"What's this issue that came up?"

"I can't really talk about it."

"But you expect me to?"

She had him there.

"This is between us, OK?" Catherine stared back at him, waiting. "Uniform called at his house today because his neighbours reported a disturbance. It turned out to be an argument between him and Barbara."

"And you think this is connected to Ursula?"

"I don't know. They claimed it was a domestic issue regarding his younger brother. She hit him, but he didn't want to press charges."

"She hit him? Jesus. Is she the suspect you've arrested?"

Robin waited while their main courses were served and for the waiter to disappear again, chewing back his annoyance. They'd told the press about the suspect that morning and he wished they hadn't.

"No. We arrested someone on suspicion, but we'll have to release him tomorrow. Collins is dishing out the congratulations and I feel like a fraud."

"Who is it?"

"The friend. Bobby Trent."

"Really?" she prodded her food, ate none of it and put down her fork. "I don't get it. He mentioned him, spoke fondly of him. And what would be his motivation?"

Precisely what Robin was struggling with. "How did he describe their relationship?"

"Surrogate dad was the term he used. Jesus Robin, are you suggesting …"

"No. Well, I don't think so. But the family dynamic is off."

She ate, but with a detached lack of commitment. He let her churn for a moment and picked at his pasta. "How did Ursula Harrison die? Not the press release. The truth."

The blunt question surprised him into a rare, unguarded response.

"She was beaten in her bed and ... crucified. Nailed to the headboard."

"Oh my god." Catherine gaped at him in shock.

Regret chased the relief to have said those words. He shouldn't have told her about the MO or Bobby Trent. Not just because she had enough on her plate, but because her two closest friends were journalists. She, despite her new foray into a different field, was a journalist. But he didn't want taboo subjects or boundaries with her. Conflict clanged in his head.

"Cat, you can't tell Clive or Cindy any of this. We haven't made it public."

Her glare intensified. "Do you need to say that?"

"Sorry, but I've had Collins on my case wanting a quick conviction, and I'm twitchy."

"What's up with her?"

"Oh, I've had the empathy talk, telling me she has every confidence in me, then offering me time out."

"Because of me? Tell her to fuck off, Robin. It's a passive aggressive tactic from some feminist empowerment book she read in the eighties."

He smiled, loving how her sass had returned even if she was pissed off with him.

"And what you described; a woman wouldn't do that. But Barbara could've persuaded or paid someone else to do it."

"Crucify her own mother?"

"Oh come on, you hear of people who kill their own kids. Nothing would surprise me. And you said she was cold."

Had Barbara been in on it with Bobby Trent? Robin hadn't picked up on any connection between them, but they were both smart enough to hide it. His phone vibrated. "Sorry," he said, and fished around in his jacket. She carried on jabbing at her food. It was Jack.

"The hair is likely to be Trent's based on pigmentation, length, stiffness and the appearance of the medulla."

"OK. And the ex-wife?"

"They cited the old 'irreconcilable differences' on the divorce papers. It didn't say much except they had money problems."

Catherine pretended she wasn't listening. Robin told Jack to call it a day, ended the call and put his phone away again. He wanted to be there with Catherine, but his mind inhabited a dozen other places, and she knew it too.

"Do you need to go?" she asked.

He shook his head. "There's nothing else I can do tonight."

"But it sounds like there's progress."

"I hope so."

She wanted more information, but he held back. He didn't want her involved more than necessary, because now she had a direct link with the family. Hypocritical though. He'd tried to exploit the same link over dinner tonight.

"John didn't say anything helpful to you," she offered, unprompted, "We discussed the accident, and he talked about being a history teacher. He mentioned his family briefly and said apart from his brother they weren't close."

"So, you did do some chit-chat."

Catherine pushed her meal aside, half eaten. "He's offered to help with my research."

"I'd maybe hang back until all this is over. His relatives are under scrutiny …"

"And you don't want me involved with them."

"No, I don't, especially after … you know."

He didn't have any right to tell her who she could and couldn't be friends with, and John was definitely the arty type Catherine gravitated towards. A fleeting shadow of insecurity brushed over him. He wasn't arty. He'd taken a razzing at school for using a ruler in art class to draw a tree.

"I'll be careful."

Translation: I'll do what I want.

"What's wrong?" she asked.

"Nothing. Do you fancy going away after this case? Do a city break, or find some sun maybe."

A lengthy pause. She was too perceptive to believe hopping on a plane was all he'd been wondering about.

"Sounds good. If you ever get the time off."

Ouch.

"I'll make sure I do."

Chapter Nine

Bad words

John woke feeling more positive and optimistic than he had for the last month. Marcia was being dealt with, he had the rest of the week off work, and only Ursula's funeral darkened his otherwise sunny horizon. He wanted to be there for Will, who would be forced to go, regardless of his own wishes, but the idea of watching Barbara wallowing in sympathy made him feel sick. It would be well attended. Plenty of sycophants around, eager to show their support of the Harrison empire; the charities who still received donations, the clients who depended on their business and the employees who relied on their salaries and pensions. The local florists would have a good week. Ursula's love of her garden was common knowledge.

He put on his training gear and tried to shove his toxic relatives out of his mind. He'd planned to go for a run then out with Rich later. He'd tried to cancel after Bobby's arrest, but Rich persuaded him that he needed the distraction. And Bobby would be out soon enough, leaving them to apologise for their ridiculous mistake.

The fresh, crisp morning had chased away the endless rain. The rush hour traffic had subsided. Children in the primary school two streets away shouted and squealed in the playground as he stretched on the front steps.

At the gate, he stopped dead in his tracks and stared at his brand-new car. Scrawled across the entire left side, in bright red paint, was the word 'peedo'.

The day closed in on him. Rushing blood throbbed in his head. He panned around, but whoever had done this was long gone. The paint had dried. He scanned the surrounding houses. Had his neighbours peered out of their windows and seen the graffiti? Of course they had. This was a working neighbourhood.

Everyone had left for work or done the school run and seen this. John edged into the road and inspected the other side of his car. Both sides. He took a few clumsy steps backwards and plonked down on his front wall, staring at the violent red word.

He didn't know what to do. Cover the car up? Hide it? He couldn't ring the police. He'd avoided speaking to the police about Marcia and now he had a flashing beacon parked right outside his house.

He dug out his phone in the pocket of his hoody.

"Rich?"

"Hey, you'd better not be bailing out on me. I'm ironing creases into my jeans ready for our date night."

"I have a problem."

"What's wrong?"

The word stuck in his throat. "One second. I'll show you."

John took a photo and sent it straight to Rich.

"Drive it round the back of your house. I'm coming straight over."

*

"Why do this Rich? I've never touched her." John squeezed his wet sponge into a bucket, watched red soapy water froth through his fingers. Rich stopped and leant on the bonnet. "Stuff like this sticks. You hear of guys getting arrested on suspicion of looking at child pornography and even if they get cleared the stigma never goes away. People know I'm a teacher. There're families in this street …"

"Tell the police," Rich held up his hands as John shook his head, "Hey, I know you don't want to, but this is getting way too serious."

John continued rubbing at the paint, wiping away every speck. Red rivers streaked his t-shirt, smeared across his joggers. "The rumour's out there now, spreading. If this gets posted on social media I'm ruined."

John threw his sponge into the bucket and sank down on the steps leading back to his garden, depleted. Rich usually had a calming influence on John, but today he couldn't eradicate the panic squeezing him like a tightfitting coat. His world had contracted and created a narrow path forcing him towards a dark and grim certainty; it wasn't going to get better. His neighbours would grip their children tighter when they saw him, slag him off behind closed doors or shout abuse at him as he passed. He liked where he lived, he'd loved his job until Marcia had fixated on him. Now the foundations of both his home life and work life had shifted.

"Let's get some perspective. You're not ruined." Rich perched on the front of the car. "Say you were pranked. You've talked to most of your neighbours, they know you're a good bloke."

"I wish I had your faith in people. How often have you heard 'I never realised he was a paedo, he seemed like such a nice guy'?"

"Nah, they're usually as weird as fuck. Nothing's happened yet so deal with it in the moment. You have more bollocks than this John. Where's your Henry, where's your fight? When he was accused of cheating with witchcraft what did he do? Bet he didn't cave in and give up."

"He was either executed or he impaled himself on his sword."

"OK, shit analogy. Don't be him then. But don't let the bastards win. I know you've had a shitstorm but you're tough. You've been through worse."

Not strictly true, but he knew what Rich was trying to say.

Rich adjusted his ponytail, lecture over. "What's happened with Catherine?"

"She texted me yesterday to ask how it had gone with Maloney, but I've not seen her again."

"Ring her. Get her over. She wouldn't text you if there wasn't a spark there."

"You sound like Will."

"Then Will's even smarter than I thought."

*

"I didn't think you'd come."

"I almost didn't."

John opened his door and Catherine stepped inside. Her sensible side poked her in the ribs hissing 'what the hell are you doing?' Her impulsive side gave her multiple high fives.

If she didn't have the cottage this would be the kind of house she'd like. Lofty ceilings, ornate mouldings and dusky, period colours offset against stripped back floorboards. She wanted to stare for a while, but she wasn't there to admire the décor. John had made a brave move asking her over and he'd sounded shaken on the phone. He looked it too. Even casually cool in black jeans and t-shirt, his hair damp, cheeks pale. The t-shirt hung from his slim frame.

He led her down the hallway towards the kitchen, past two doorways on the right. She followed him, conscious of her heeled boots clunking on wood while his bare feet were silent. The kitchen's freestanding units painted in a muted olive green gave a modern twist on an old-fashioned style, and for a large room it oozed a warm welcome.

"Did you drive?"

"No, taxi. I'm still carless."

John turned, one hand on the fridge door. "I'm having a glass of wine. Do you fancy one? No offence if you don't, and I'm not trying to get you drunk. I just"

"Maybe a small one. I have a meeting tomorrow and a ton of prep to do."

Odd, being in the house of a stranger, drinking wine on a Tuesday afternoon. But he didn't feel like a stranger. Their lives had slotted together with smooth ease, and she enjoyed his quirks. She'd always been drawn to people who didn't fit in.

"Sorry for hijacking your day. I appreciate you coming over."

"I wasn't sure if coming over added to your complications or not. You said the other day you had a lot going on."

"It doesn't, but I'd understand if you don't want to get involved."

"I'm already involved." She took off her coat and hung her bag on the chair as he poured the wine. "You sounded upset on the phone."

John pushed his hair back and drank his wine. "I feel like an idiot for ringing you. I don't regret it, I'm happy to see you. But I … ah, I don't know. This isn't coming out right." He took another sip, and his fingers quivered. "Someone spray painted 'pedo' across both sides of my new car today."

Her glass clunked against the tabletop as she put it down abruptly.

"Marcia was taken into temporary social care yesterday. She had drugs in her locker and at home and was known to social services. I thought that would be the end of it, but obviously not. My friend Rich came over and helped me to clean the paint off but … yeah, I was upset. He persuaded me to ring you." He blushed. "I don't know … I felt like I should tell you. Rich is brilliant, don't get me wrong but … I wanted to talk to you."

"I don't know if I can help, but I'm happy to listen."

"Do you still believe me?" he asked. It was challenging, and yet the vulnerability in his expression was stark.

"Yes, completely." She didn't think, she just knew. His distress clung to every breath. But words couldn't soothe him, and it surprised her how much she cared.

"I know it's an unfair ask, you don't even know me," he sighed, "But I feel like I need to keep justifying myself."

"Understandable, but I think this will blow over now. Why don't you get away for a few days? Don't you have the week off?"

"I suppose I could go and see my Gran, my dad's mum, but I promised Will I'd take him to a gig on Friday with me and Rich. I don't want to disappoint him."

He seemed younger today, the pain of Marcia's accusation draining his energy. She had to support him after what he'd done for her. Not out of duty either. The injustice of his situation and his plight moved her.

Time to come clean.

"John, I know about your connection to Ursula Harrison."

He didn't seem surprised.

"DI Scott. I wondered how close you were."

His response stunned her for a moment. Good old Google. Impossible to have an invisible digital footprint, and if he'd researched her, or Robin, he would also know what had happened to Simon. It was all there. Simon's assault, how he'd been targeted because of her actions. Clive had tried to rescue her with balanced, thoughtful coverage but social media had been brutal.

"When he interviewed me, he didn't say he knew you," John continued, "Don't you find that strange?"

A door opened and an elephant moseyed into the room. The glug of pouring wine, the fridge door swooshing back into place, punctuated the shift in mood.

"He's wary about mixing work with his private life." Catherine didn't want to betray Robin, but the excuse was sketchy. When John offered her a top up, she covered her glass.

He stiffened. "Well, I guess you know all my demons. I was surprised you came; now I'm astonished."

"I guess you know all my demons too."

"What happened to you and your family was horrifying and unforgivable. None of you deserved it, and I'm terribly sorry for you all."

She'd received countless offerings of condolence, shock, and support over the events of the previous year. Most were well-intentioned and genuine enough but lacked empathy. John's words and compassion made her skin tingle. The intensity of feeling he conveyed was breath-taking.

"Thank you." On impulse she took her own leap of faith. "If you were me, would you have quit the job?"

John didn't break eye contact, just silently shook his head. No explanation offered, no need for one. He confirmed what she already knew.

"Mind if I have a top-up?"

He smiled and refilled her glass. The dishwasher beeped. He stared into his wine, she necked half of hers.

"Does Robin know you're here?"

"No."

"Will you tell him?"

"I don't know. Probably not."

John spun the stem of his glass around on the table, concentrating on twirling it between his fingers. "I was arsey before, sorry. I think the stress is getting to me."

"It's OK, I understand. It's an unusual, horrible situation." Total understatement. Her head clanged with it all. "Look, do you fancy a distraction? I'm going to a meeting at the castle tomorrow morning then for a walk over the back meadows toward the woods. I want to get a better feel for the area. Why don't you come with me?"

A spark of interest illuminated John's eyes and he leant forward. A spontaneous invitation, but it felt right to offer it.

"There were jousting lists on the meadow. There's a local poet, he wrote a poem claiming if you lie with your ears to the ground, you can still hear the pounding hooves."

"Anthony Collins. Journey's End. I came across it in my research."

The worry and strain etched on John's face ebbed away, and his physicality changed, as if he'd shrugged out of a heavy coat.

"I'd love the distraction. Thanks Catherine."

Chapter Ten

Breaking out

Jamie Clarke was at his mate Gringo's flat checking out his new electric guitar when his phone rang. Unknown number. He never answered those. Then two more calls, one straight after the other. For fuck's sake. He sneaked off to the bathroom and left Gringo fawning over his new toy. Jeez. Cool guitar, but he was going overboard on it. He'd give it one if it had a hole.

Jamie locked the door. The unknown number called again, and he swiped the screen to answer. He didn't speak.

Pissed off sigh. "Is that Mr Clarke?"

Was she trying to get hold of his dad? Why not call him on the loser line and enjoy his fascinating conversation directly? Most likely shitfaced and not answering.

"No. Jamie Clarke."

"Yes Jamie, it's you I need. I'm Anna Martin, Marcia's key worker from Brock House. We've tried your dad, but we can't get hold of him. Your sister's gone missing."

Not a huge surprise. "How long's she been gone?"

"About an hour, we think. She climbed out of her bedroom window If you can't help us, we'll have to call the police. Do you know where she is?"

"Just a sec, I'll check my crystal ball."

"She's missing from legal care Mr Clarke. This is serious."

Jamie stared at a row of Gringo's skiddies drying on the radiator. He didn't want Marcia getting into even more trouble, but he also didn't want them to reach her before he did.

"Can you give me half an hour?"

Another, more pissed off sigh. Anna Martin wasn't enjoying the Clarke family experience

"30 minutes or I'm calling the police."

Jamie left Gringo creaming over his Les Paul rip-off and headed towards the outskirts of Toncaster. He parked outside a boarded-up school a mile or so from Brock House. The building was about to be converted into trendy flats, but for the last few months, it had become a regular hideout for bored teenagers. The locals had complained, fences had been put up and security lights fitted, one of it effective.

The kids used a boarded-up cellar window to get in and out. Jamie hooked his fingers behind the piece of wood and slid it out of the frame. He jumped down from the desk that had been shoved up to the wall and shone his phone around the basement, a furniture graveyard full of old wooden desks and chairs doomed to never get repaired. The place reeked of cigarettes and weed. He headed straight for the door, into a second larger room, empty except for a couple of old gym mats chucked in the corner. Marcia sat on one, leaning against the wall, smoking. A small string of cheap fairy lights hung from a nail behind her, casting a weird purple glow over her face. Two emo kids, a bit older than her, were necking in the other corner, lit by a couple of candles on a broken plate. Tinny crap music played from Marcia's phone.

She glanced up, took a drag, said nothing.

"What are you playing at?" A shrug, another drag. He glared at the emos. "Can you two do one? I need to talk to my sister."

"You got any fags?" asked one of them.

Jamie tutted, but he took out his packet and threw it towards him. Only two left anyway. The kid caught it in one hand, pulled his girlfriend up with the other. They disappeared with a swish of long coats, Doc Martens clumping on the stone floor.

"I'm not going back," said Marcia, when they'd left. "It's all his fault."

Jamie crouched next to the mat. "Whose?"

"Mr Rickman's. He got me banged up."

"You're not 'banged up'. And it's because of Dad being a total loser and the weed, not because you fancy your teacher."

"Is it because I'm fat?"

Jamie stared into the purple haze, his brain trying to follow Marcia's mind shift.

"Is that why he likes Catherine Nicholls and not me? But I bet she's a size 12 at least …"

"Marcia …"

"Or is it because she's clever?"

"No, it's because you're fifteen and he's your teacher. That's it. If you were five years older, he'd be all over you."

"It's so not fair."

Her voice cracked. This wasn't about the teacher. Marcia had to have what she wanted, even if none of it made her happy in the end, at least she'd won the prize.

"Get him out of your head and focus on sorting your life out."

"He planted the weed, I'm sure of it."

"He didn't plant the weed at home though, did he? I rang your mate, Steve. He told me you had some."

"I didn't have a massive baggie at school! Why does no one believe me? It's him, I swear to God."

"Why though?"

"Because he's scared shitless people will find out he likes me."

She'd spun such a story she'd become webbed in her lies, and the only way out was to come clean. But pride and stubbornness were stopping her.

"He doesn't like you, Marsh. It's all in your head and you need to let this drop now. Look at the trouble it's landed you in."

"He was OK until I grassed him up to his girlfriend, but she should know what he's like."

Jamie dropped to his knees on the mat and grabbed her arms, yanking her towards him.

"Get off!" She tried to pull away, but he was stronger.

"No. Listen to me."

He gripped her and searched for the right words. Their dad would've given her a smack by now, and as much as Jamie hated it when he hit her, sometimes it was the only way to get through. He'd nurtured that in her, and Jamie despised him for it.

"When we went to his house, you told me he hadn't touched you. You made up what you said to Catherine Nicholls because you're jealous. Fucking reality check Marcia. You can't make shit up about people."

She pulled her arms away and slumped back against the wall. "I'm telling the truth about the weed."

"You lie so much it's hard to know what's true."

"Right. I get it." She wiped her nose on the sleeve of her sweatshirt. "But I'm telling you now, he did it."

"If he did – if – it's because you're trying to ruin him." A broken little girl stared back at him; the ferocity gone. Tears streaked across her cheeks. "Take responsibility for yourself. You've got the chance now to fix all this, to sort your life out." He checked his phone. "I'm calling Anna. She's worried about you."

No argument. A positive sign. He scrolled to his call list. Anna answered on the second ring.

"I'm bringing her back."

*

Hidden down a Broadstone back street, Blue Room hid well off the tourist map. Steep, cracked steps led down into a dingy bar, with indie pop art on the walls and murky booths lit by blue lightbulbs. Robin liked its simplicity, plus they played a curious mix of obscure indie label bands. He liked it more because no one in there knew his name. He could be in his own head and drink a few pints without having to make conversation or listen to tourists stressing at their kids.

On a Tuesday evening the place was dead apart from a group of lads at the pool table and a young couple in a booth who were almost having sex. A beefy guy in a polo shirt stretched across his muscles and a tiny girl with fierce titian hair, absurdly fake breasts spilling out of her denim dress. Robin took his whiskey and chaser to the furthest booth away from the show and slid into the womblike darkness. Music banged through the sludge-coloured floor. He closed his eyes and enjoyed the whiskey burn as the bass pounded into his feet.

Vultures were circling. Anna Collins badgering for a conviction. John Rickman, the tragic and mysterious charmer. Clive Darwin chomping for information like a dog at a never-ending bone. And then his ghosts drifted around in vignette shadows, barely perceptible but ready to swoop in should he have a moment of weakness. He needed time alone, and not at home in his peaceful place. He wanted loud music, whiskey and beer, to stare at nothing and speak to no one. He'd considered going to the dojo but hadn't done for the same reason he didn't want to go home. He never trained on anger or brought negativity into the artform he loved. Sacrilege.

When he decided to find a taxi at ten, he'd had enough. The slight tilt to the floor hadn't existed earlier. The couple he'd seen earlier were still in their booth as he headed past, and he was almost gone when a shriek from behind made him spin around. The woman was trying to get away from her bloke, but he yanked her back. Robin didn't hesitate. In two seconds, he was back at the booth. Beefcake held back the teary girl with the ease of a parent restraining a toddler.

"Are you OK?" Robin asked her.

"Who're you?" snarled the man.

Robin ignored him and kept his focus on her. Beer from the guy's glass and white wine from hers pooled all over the table, the front of her dress wet. She shook in her skimpy dress. Christ, up close, she didn't look old enough to drink.

"I'm going home Jay." She made another attempt to escape.

"No chance!"

'Jay' jumped to his feet and Robin put one hand out towards his chest. He was chunky, but in width, overcompensating for his lack of height by pumping his muscles to freakish proportions. Robin towered over him, but Jay wasn't intimidated by height. He did a squaring-up shuffle and deep-set piggy eyes squinted up at him.

Robin gave him his best bored sigh. "I think it's best if she leaves, don't you?"

The girl tried to edge out of the booth just as Jay shoved Robin back, putting all his considerable weight into it. Impressive. The guy could shove. He stepped backwards and Jay fluffed his feathers, pleased with his little manoeuvre.

"I'm warning you. If you touch me again, I'll retaliate."

Beefy bastard laughed. "Who are you? Liam fucking Neeson?"

Robin turned to the girl. "Come on, I'm leaving too. I'll walk you out."

The air shifted before Jay snapped. "Like fuck you will!"

Glasses clattered to the floor as Jay lunged at Robin, knocking everything in his path out of the way, and the two of them crashed to the floor. Robin dragged himself back to his feet.

119

He'd cracked his head on a table as he fell, and when he touched his temple, his fingers came back bloody. Robin couldn't remember the last time he'd bled in a fight, and it pumped his pulse more than Jay's first proper punch, which landed on his shoulder before pulled himself upright.

Right, this guy was having it. Instinct took over. He launched a barrage of blows at the man-mountain, fist after fist connecting with rock-solid muscle, and he didn't stop. Not even when Jay hit the deck, to a noisy cheer from the pool guys who'd gathered around to watch the fight. The girl screamed at him to stop in a pitch only dogs could hear, and he was sucked back into reality. Jay's chunky fists had stopped flying around and now shielded his face.

Robin rose to his feet and scanned the little audience. The group of lads who stared at him with a mixture of fascination and awe. An older couple watching with bored disinterest like they'd seen it a dozen times. The barmaid on her phone. Fuck. Robin shoved through them and a short skinhead with a face full of make-up gave him a congratulatory slap on the back. The girl knelt dabbing at Jay's bleeding nose with a folded up sanitary pad.

He pushed open the fire exit at the back of the bar, out into a little yard full of empty crates. Up the steps back to street level and down the narrow alleyway leading away from the town centre. He continued until Blue Room faded away and stopped outside a scruffy sandwich shop. He wasn't sure who he saw in the reflection. A familiar face scowled back, but who had he become? Since when did he start fights in shitholes, like the tossers he'd arrested time and time again? How many dickheads had he shoved into a van to cool off? He'd read somewhere about becoming an amalgamation of the people you spent the most time with. Had he spent so much time in the company of dickheads he'd become one too?

He called a taxi and straightened himself up while he waited. Other than the crack on the head from the table, he was a bit crumpled but otherwise unscathed. On impulse, he gave Catherine's address in Camber to the driver and popped her a quick text to say he was on his way. Simon had gone to a gig so they would have the place to themselves again. Presumably. He checked his phone, but she hadn't replied. Maybe Clive had appeared, mining and probing for information, or John? Had Rickman nudged in with his killer chatline? Oh yeah, 'helping with research'. What a joke.

The lights were off at Catherine's, and he'd left his keys at work. Once he'd made the decision to go to Blue Room, he'd take off his flat key and left the others in his desk drawer. He knocked. Maybe she was in the snug around the back. Hopefully alone. He needed her to be alone. And the longer he knocked the more he needed it until he was banging on the door, his palm slapping relentlessly against the wood.

At last, a light came on and the bolt scraped back on the inside of the door. Catherine, hair everywhere and dressed in a bathrobe, squinted into the dark. "What happened to you?"

"Are you on your own?"

"Of course I am. Robin, what's wrong?"

He took Catherine's cheeks in both hands and crushed her lips against his as he pushed her against the wall in the hallway. Her flowery scent infused deep into his lungs, and he kissed her, releasing her cheeks to remove the bathrobe.

"Robin …"

"Sshhh."

Warm, jasmine scented skin smooth beneath his fingers. So soft. He ran his hands around her back, underneath her bare arse and lifted her upwards. He carried her into the sitting room, sensed no resistance. Fully awake now, her breath quickened as he lay her on the shaggy rug and pinned her beneath him. His night, the fight, melted away. It all melted away. Collins, Darwin, Rickman. Gone.

"Cuff me, Catherine."

Her hand skimmed his hips then plunged into his pocket. Oh yes, she knew where they were, of course she did. Metal chinked.

"What did you do?" she whispered, and she eased herself from beneath him, leaving him face down on the floor. She straddled his legs and grabbed his right wrist. Metal bit into his skin. Ah, lovely, mellow Catherine. Not so gentle and placid when as horny as fuck.

"I got into a fight."

"That's fucking bad."

Snap. Ratcheting metal teeth.

"Turn over."

She lifted up and he flipped himself over, then she settled back onto his hips. His cuffed wrists dug into his back. The sweetest pain, a pain he craved and deserved. She looked magnificent as she unfastened his trousers and pulled them down his thighs, naked breasts swinging in rhythmic harmony, nipples hard. Of course he was ready for her. How fucking remiss of him would it be to get her steaming hot and not give her what she wanted? He might be the one in restraints, but he was the one in control. No submissive, no game.

Catherine threaded her fingers through his hair and pinned his head to the floor as she ground on him, and he loved her nakedness while he remained clothed. He wanted to close his eyes and be fucked by her, but he needed to drink in the sight of her too. Glorious sensory overload. She made the decision for him by easing down and rubbing her breasts over his face, balancing on the tip of his cock. How could he miss that? He stuck out his tongue and lapped at the deliciousness brushing his lips.

When she took him inside her again, she was hot. She wanted him and she didn't hold back. Each thrust of her magnificent hips took him harder and deeper than the one before and she dropped her head back as she shattered over him. Those exquisitely explosive pulses around his cock sent him over the edge seconds later. She collapsed on his chest, and her heart pounded against him as her rapid breaths slowed.

Robin would've fallen asleep right there, with Catherine as his gloriously naked blanket, if his hands hadn't still been cuffed behind his back.

"Cat, you need to uncuff me."

"Huh?"

"There's a pin in my wallet. In my coat pocket."

She grumbled and rolled off him. When she came back from the hall, she wore her bathrobe again. She rummaged around in his wallet for the pin, found it, and he rolled to his side obligingly so she could release him.

"Why were you carrying handcuffs? You hardly ever do."

"Psychological. If I'm carrying cuffs, I feel like I'll make an arrest."

As soon as she freed him, he pulled her into his arms, and she curled in around him on the rug.

"You've been drinking."

"I know."

"And you've cut your head."

"I know that too."

"I think we should get you in bed."

"Again? You're insatiable. OK, give me a minute"

"For fuck's sake."

Catherine's exasperated muttering made him chuckle, but he stopped chuckling when she hauled him to his feet and the room did a weird tilting motion like it had in Blue Room.

His last memory was of obediently shrugging out of his shirt sleeves as Catherine undressed him. Seconds later he passed out.

Chapter Eleven

Nature's poison

"We've picked up the suspect at the corner of Willow Crescent and Moss Lane. The suspect is not in the house."

DS Robin Scott glared at Ali Mussadi, the cocky little fucker who'd been running dealers, from his council house, using kids to do drop-offs or teenage girls with packets of crack wrapped in clingfilm inserted in their vaginas. He'd used his own baby and put packages in her nappies. Hopefully he would never get to hold that precious child again now they'd caught him. With his history, he would be going down for a while along with a bunch of his scumbag mates and his girlfriend and her brother who were already back at the station snitching like schoolkids.

His radio crackled.

"PC Scott and PC Morrison, approaching on foot. We're almost there."

PC Erin Scott, his wife. It still sounded weird years after they'd married, despite plenty of opposition and speculation from everyone around them. Robin couldn't give a shit. He'd never experienced love like he did with Erin. She was his home, his world, so who cared how old they were? Not them. Every day blessed because he'd found a woman who made his heart burst, and if that was wanky then so what? They'd fiercely committed to spend their lives together.

"Suspect in custody," said Robin, "Seal it off for SOC."

"Received. Standby."

Someone handed Robin a coffee and he sat on in one of the open cars, listening to the exchanges over the radio. Five separate teams in various locations across the city, sweeping up a gang they'd been tracking for months. The check-ins were reassuring.

"... house empty," Robin listened to Erin relaying back to dispatch, "Clearing last room now. Looks like a nursery. Shit, there's something in the cot, is that ..."

Robin physically recoiled from the thunderous blast erupting from the radio as particles of bone and flesh, house bricks and clothing blew into his face through the heating vents. Hot blood poured through the radio, splattering on his cheeks, filling his nostrils. Coco Chanel. Erin's favourite perfume.

"PC Scott, 387 come in. Come in PC Scott. Acknowledge. Erin, Erin ..."

Robin woke abruptly like he'd stepped off a cliff, gasping, disorientated, and it took a few seconds for reality to return. Next to him, Catherine stroked his hair.

"Have a drink, Robin." She passed him her water from the nightstand, her voice soft. "You were dreaming again."

He sat up and tried to shake off the nightmare, but it lingered, along with the Coco Chanel, as real as if it had sprayed onto his face seconds ago. He forced a smile, but the tiny gesture made his head clang.

"What time is it? I need to go."

"It's just after seven. I'll make you a coffee."

He reached for her arm as she pulled back the duvet and drew her back in towards him.

"About last night." As Robin spoke the shattered pieces of the previous night reassembled in his head. "I'm sorry I woke you, and for being pissed."

"I'm glad you came here and didn't go home on your own. What happened?"

Robin rubbed his face and winced as his fingers skimmed over the gash on his forehead. What had he been thinking? His entire career could be screwed if they realised he was a copper, and a black belt. He couldn't go in there again. He groaned into his hands.

"Some dick in Blue Room was being shitty with his girlfriend, or date, whoever she was. I tried to help her, and it kicked off."

"Shit. When you said you'd been in a fight last night I thought you were just playing the bad boy."

Mischief flashed momentarily but evaporated just as quickly. She rummaged around in her bedside cupboard and found a packet of wipes. She took one and dabbed at the cut on his head. Her mood shifted. "Robin, why do you still dream about Erin?"

He didn't want this conversation. He didn't want to acknowledge what a total dick he'd been last night or why he'd turned up at her house pissed and angry. In his skull, Nirvana drummed on his brain.

"Can we talk about it another time."

"Sure."

He sighed. "Don't be pissed off with me."

She dabbed, less gently this time, then threw the packet of wipes on the cupboard. She climbed out of bed and pulled on leggings and a vest top, slammed some drawers.

"Cat, please …"

"No Robin, be straight with me. Because last night you showed me your vulnerable side. I took it as a good sign. Then in your sleep you call your dead wife's name, and there's pain in your voice. Yearning. And as always when I ask you about her, you shut me down."

Robin stared at her. He swung his legs out of bed.

"I can't do this now."

"Fine." She snatched his phone up from the pile of his clothes pooled on the floor and threw it on the bed. "You'd better ring a taxi."

"I'll come back later, and we can talk."

She left and slammed the door behind her. He jumped up, lunged across the room, and wrenched it open again, smacking his head on the low beam which he'd forgotten to dodge. He wanted to go after her but instead he crumpled and sat back on the bed waiting for his brain to stop clanging. He needed to get his shit together, but now he would have to leave on rocky terms with Catherine, which he hated. The conversation she wanted wasn't happening until he had a clear head and wasn't on the clock.

Downstairs, she was on the phone in the snug, writing in her notebook. She glanced up as his taxi beeped outside.

"I'll call you," he mouthed, finger phone to his ear. She didn't respond.

He turned away and left.

*

"What the hell have you done?"

"You don't want to know."

Robin had been home, shaved and showered, and eaten breakfast on his way in. The paracetamols had kicked in and he'd edged closer to feeling human. The conversation with Catherine still lurked in the back of his mind, but he'd learned a long time ago to compartmentalise. No point stewing over it until he could act on it. Right now, he couldn't.

Jack accepted Robin's lack of explanation. "We can't hold Trent any longer," he said as they headed up the stairs to CID, "As soon as his brief arrives, he'll pick apart what little we have. His alibi is solid, the rest is circumstantial. The hair could've been transferred, anyone could've worn the boots."

Robin pushed open the doors into the investigation room. They were heavier today.

"Call from Joseph Carling Guv." Ella had a post-it note in one hand, a packet of Doritos in the other, "He wants you to call him straight back. He said it's about the 'unknown substance' you discussed."

Robin took the note and stared at the words. He'd been so absorbed in trying to incriminate Trent he'd forgotten about the substance. In Robin's office, they pulled two chairs up to the desk and called the morgue.

Joseph came on the line immediately. "I've never seen this before, and I've made a few calls. No one else has seen it either. It's fascinating."

"What is it?"

"Conium maculatum."

"English please Joseph." There was a smile in Joseph's voice. He enjoyed bouts of occasional smugness.

"Otherwise known as hemlock."

Jack looked as puzzled as him. "Hemlock? Sounds like something from the dark ages."

"Dark ages? Try 399BC and the death of Socrates. It's one of the earliest references to its use. Hemlock's primary function is to cause paralysis followed by respiratory failure. I did some quick research. Socrates drank a hemlock-based liquid – which technically makes his death a suicide by the way – and gradually became paralysed from the legs upwards."

127

"Which explains why Ursula Harrison laid there and took the beating."

"It must've been injected from the site I found behind her left ear."

"Cause of death?"

"Heart failure. There would've been an initial period of a trance-like state, followed by excessive salivation and vomiting. Traces of both were on her bed linen and clothes. She had extreme mydriasis – dilation of the pupils – and there's evidence of the onset of respiratory failure. She died before it happened though."

So, whoever did this kept her alive long enough for her to be aware of what was happening to her. She might not have felt the full effects of the beating, but she would've been conscious.

"The hemlock anaesthetised her limbs. Both patella smashed to shit. All pre-mortem injuries."

"Does this help us to narrow down who our suspect might be?"

Joseph deep breath crackled from the phone's speaker.

"I don't know. Anyone could do a quick Google search, but you'd have to have good understanding medically of the effects of the hemlock. Someone with a knowledge of botany? That would help. Someone smart. Too much and she could have died too quickly. Too little and she might not have died. There are far easier ways to kill."

Robin leant over and disconnected the call. Someone with a knowledge of botany?

"Looks like we get to hold onto Mr Trent for longer," said Jack.

*

"Well, can you hear anything?"

Knelt on a carrier bag with one ear to the ground, Catherine grinned. "Just worms laughing."

John rippled with joy as he laughed at her and took a moment to be thankful he'd met this remarkable woman. Because no matter how complicated the situation, she was good for him. Every fibre of him sensed it.

She had one hand holding back her hair, the other bracing her weight as she leant close to the damp grass, still attempting to listen for the sound of hooves.

"You mustn't be doing it right. Let me try."

He offered her a hand and pulled her to her feet. Autumn-coloured hair blew around her shoulders in the gentle breeze, her cheeks flushed. He held onto her fingers briefly before letting her go.

"We need a proper historian. You have to take it seriously," he teased, and he knelt on the bag which had protected her pants from getting soaked.

"Watch you don't mess hair your hair up."

John pulled a face at her. He didn't care about his hair, or his jeans. He couldn't remember when he had last been so relaxed and happy. Maybe with Will or Bobby, a different contentment.

He put his ear to the ground and closed his eyes. Swishing trees, the sweet smell of damp earth. He lifted and sat back on his heels. Catherine waited, hands on hips, glowing in the sun.

"Well?"

"I feel a bit cheated by Anthony Collins."

Catherine laughed again. "I wonder if he was kneeling on a carrier bag when he heard those 'pounding hooves'."

"I think Mr Collins was wrecked on gin, halfway down his second spliff and picturing a pair of gullible idiots testing his theory out. It's a con."

"I like the idea though." She panned around, scanning the landscape. "That the past is imprinted on the land."

"Me too."

In the shadow of the castle on the hill, the countryside painted a stunning landscape. Untouched meadowlands reached out towards the river on one side and banked steeply towards the woods on the other. Camber nestled against the castle, out of their view, with just the church spire visible. Each step took them further away from civilisation and all its problems, and he'd been right; the distraction, her company, and the fresh air healed him. His brain fog had begun to disperse.

"He was right; the jousting would have taken place here."

"I assumed it would've been within the castle grounds." She looked over at the castle, its south tower gleaming in the sun.

"No, the land slopes." He rose to his feet. "This is the nearest flat area. Imagine the people gathered for the entertainment, sitting on the hillside to watch. We're in a basin so it's like a natural arena."

"Maybe Collins was imagining the echo of the horse's hooves. You're right, the sounds would have been amplified as they bounced around. If the Heritage Trust goes ahead with the re-enactment, it should be here."

"I'd love to help, if I can. Sorry if I sound like a tosser, but tournaments are one of my passions."

"Never apologise for passion. It's what makes us feel alive." She picked up her bag and they headed further away from the castle. "So, what appeals to you about tournaments? Weren't they the Middle Ages version of extreme sports?"

"Later on, yes. At first the tournaments were organised so the fighters could practice their skills when they weren't at battle. Later, they became more for entertainment and the knights who fought them became celebrities, touring the country and travelling overseas to compete and win larger prizes, gain further kudos. Most of the knights were bound to their liege, but others were 'freelancers' – it's where the modern-day term comes from."

Catherine glanced over at him, her expression unreadable.

"Sorry. Am I teaching?"

"No, carry on; I like listening to you. I can feel you're in flow."

"You're humouring me. You must know this stuff."

"It's different hearing about it from someone who has an affinity with the history rather than just reading the facts. You're like my private audio guide."

"I'll want royalties."

"Oh not you too. The voice artist doing the castle audio guide ups his fee weekly. He sounds like Prince Charles after half a bottle of gin."

"Here's my fee; let me take you for dinner."

She smiled. "Not really a fee, is it?"

John stopped. She was so fresh and natural he wanted to capture her image in his mind and refer to her at will, like his own internal screensaver.

"I shouldn't have asked."

Catherine didn't seem uncomfortable; she just looked like she didn't know what to say. The lack of an instant refusal reassured him. A hint life wasn't so cosy with DI Scott.

"Tell me more about freelancers," she said, with a smile which suggested she was flattered at least, and perhaps considering his offer.

"Freelancers were effectively hired fighters." He did his best Prince Charles voice, and she laughed. He loved her laugh.

"You're missing the gin slur."

"Way beyond my acting skills." He pushed back his hair and unfastened his jacket. The mild day was a welcome change after all the rain they'd had. "Have you heard of Henry Stanton?"

"Mmm. The name feels familiar."

"He was a freelancer, a brilliant one. The feudal lords offered him all kinds of rewards to fight for them, but he was notoriously aloof. He didn't fight for fancy gifts and promises of titles. There's little known about him, but it appeared he fought for the thrill of competition and the desire to win. A true athlete."

"What happened to him?"

"He was accused of witchcraft and executed. The authenticity of his skills came into question, and he was seen as a threat. He won too much and took too little."

"He intrigues you."

No sign of judgement in her tone. Rare to find someone genuinely interested in others and not themselves.

"Yes. I admire the strength of character and when I first came across Stanton, as a teenager, I identified with the loner in him. An outcast with the strength and determination to fight his way through adversity. Plus, he lived in my favourite period in history. I could go on, but I'll bore you shitless and you'll think I'm strange."

"I like strange." Catherine stopped and pulled two bottles of water from her bag. He took one, enjoying the fresh air and the warmth of the sun on his face.

"I guess there's tragedy in his story too," she said, after taking a drink and returning the bottle to her bag, "Persecuted for being driven, for excelling at his chosen pursuit. Like modern athletes who're accused of taking performance-enhancing drugs. Did he protest his innocence?"

John sat on a cluster of mossy boulders and Catherine shared the view as the fresh breeze swept their cheeks. "Yes. He suffered a trail by pressing. They staked him out in the marsh embankment flanking the river at its shallowest point. His executioners placed a large piece of wood over his chest and piled stones onto it, pushing him into his grave. That's one story. Another claims he impaled himself on his sword rather than pledge allegiance to any Lord."

"Which do you believe?"

"Neither and both! I love that about medieval history. Sometimes you have to read between sketchy lines. It's been a project for years. I've sat in front of microfilm screens and pored over so many old papers and documents it all now blurs into hours and hours of eye ache."

"It would make a great book."

He'd thought the same, and Rich had suggested it too, but irrationally he wanted to keep Henry to himself. He experienced that world through immersion and the depth of his imagination, so it became as real in his mind as his memories and feelings. Like a method actor becoming a character. He could walk like Stanton, speak like him, feel like him. This was his escape, and he'd never wanted to share it. But she was the first person, other than Rich, who he could imagine sharing it with, knowing she wouldn't judge him.

"What's that?" He pointed at a derelict building, visible now from their position, through a cluster of towering trees.

Catherine followed his eye line, back towards the castle.

"It's the old forge. Not much of the original building is left except the back wall. It's been rebuilt several times over the years. Felix has plans for it, but it's not top priority. Be great if he can restore it." She turned back to him, smiling, "I don't think you're strange by the way. When I was a kid, my dad's friend used to dress like Gandalf. That was weird."

"Pointy hat and a long beard?"

"And a staff."

John laughed. He wanted to take her hand or put his arm around her and enjoy their time more intimately, welcome her into a void in his life he'd ignore for too long. He'd missed this.

"Did you tell Robin about coming to mine yesterday?"

She stared into the distance. "No."

"Do you mind if I ask you why?"

"It's complicated." Cavernous pause. "You're complicated."

He took a deep breath and let it out slowly. "I can't decide whether that's good or not."

"Don't overthink it." Her smile gave him a burst of hope.

"Thanks for inviting me today. I enjoy being with you, Catherine."

She dipped her head, and her hair covered her cheeks. What was she thinking? She seemed relaxed with him, and he loved how open-minded she was, how non-disparaging. He'd been surrounded by volatile, critical people throughout his life. Her balance and peacefulness were compelling.

"I figured you needed a break. And I'm enjoying it too."

His soul sang, thankful he'd found her.

Chapter Twelve

Dynamic deviant

Robin had been enjoying some early training when his phone rang, and he ignored it at first, focused on his form as he moved through his katas. The crisp, cool air from the open windows breezed over his skin and chilled the smooth floorboards beneath his bare feet. Centred and focused, he could be truly himself and indulge in his own being. With each breath came clarity and purpose, and the opportunity to reset his mind.

The caller persisted. He stopped abruptly and snatched up his phone.

"Jack."

"I know, sorry. But I thought you'd want to know. Someone attacked John Rickman last night. He's in Broadstone General. 999 call came in just after 1am. No sign of burglary, wallet still in his pocket. He's taken a right pasting."

"Critical?"

"No, minor head injury, extensive bruising, not life-threatening. I'm on my way over there now."

So, not random, but completely different to Ursula Harrison. It didn't make sense. Two suspects operating independently on connected victims? Did this mean the accident hadn't been an accident? Robin still struggled to see how it could've been deliberate, but it did appear Rickman was a target. And how did this affect his situation with Catherine? They'd briefly spoken the previous night, but she'd been tired, so the cross words they'd had still hung between them.

He shoved his paranoia to a space he reserved at the back of his mind for issues he didn't like to deal with. It was getting crowded back there. He'd been pushing his feelings aside for weeks now, and he would have to deal with them. Just not now.

"I'll be at the hospital in twenty minutes."

"Cat, listen to this."

Catherine scowled at her screen, squinting through a pile of hair and pillows towards the phone on the bedside table. Clive barked at her from the speaker in a tinny yap.

"It's ten past seven."

"Are you still in bed?"

"I'm still asleep actually."

"Well, wake the fuck up and listen to this. Ursula Harrison …" H stopped. "Are you on your own?"

"Yep. It's just me and you."

"That gives me a bit of a twinge. Are you naked?"

"Fuck off Clive."

"Right; Ursula Harrison definitely screwed her staff. Well, either screwed them or battered them. Renshaw's agreed to go on the record."

Catherine sat up. "We talked about this the other night."

"We speculated. Now it's confirmed."

"I'm busy."

"I'll be round at eight."

"Oh God Clive, honestly I hate you."

"Put your green top on."

Alan Renshaw had fought the aging process with every inch of his tanned, sixty-odd year-old physique. Skinny jeans, Toms, and a fitted tee with a sprinkle of silver fox chest hair peeking above the V-neck. Well groomed, greying hair styled around a possibly botoxed, friendly face. He welcomed Clive and Catherine inside his home like they were old friends he'd known for years. He made them a cup of tea and invited Catherine to mooch through his cupboards for biscuits.

They settled in his conservatory, dominated by a huge box of toys, piled high with primary coloured tat. Alan was either an older dad or, more likely, a cool grandad. Too bright and perky to have young kids.

"Sorry I couldn't see you sooner, I've been away for a few days. But I told the police what you suggested," he said to Clive. He plucked a block of Lego from under his thigh and lobbed it in the box.

"Great stuff."

Clive looked smug. Christ, what had he become involved with?

"What was your story to the police, just so I'm in the loop." She glared at Clive, and he repaid the daggers she fired at him with a cheeky wink.

"Just that I'd seen Ursula Harrison waggle her stick at people, like in that fairy story. Hansel and Gretel? The kids have it somewhere…" he looked around as if the book might miraculously appear, "Anyway, I told them it had been exaggerated. For a story, like."

Clive nodded his approval while Catherine listened for the sound of the penny dropping. Nope. She still didn't have a clue what was going on.

Free of Lego, Renshaw eased himself back into a rattan armchair and drank his coffee.

"Where shall I start?"

Alan Renshaw despised Tuesdays. More specifically he hated 10am on Tuesdays, when he took the next week's cash flow projections in to Ursula Harrison. They were always positive. Harrison Engineering was successful, profitable and as liquid as a velvety smooth cognac. It wasn't what he was presenting, more to whom. Ursula Harrison intimidated him. Tiny, impeccably presented, and as divinely spoken as a quintessential English duchess but she could scare the shit out of a brick shithouse without raising her voice. Her business acumen and the way her mind worked was astonishing. She led from the front, backed her team and provided the greater vision which made the company such a success. Her strategies were copied throughout their industry, but no one could replicate what she brought to the business.

He'd simmered his trepidation down to one single reason. Unpredictability. No one knew what she would say or do next. Startling to hear such a dainty woman effing and jeffing like a squaddie. And the first time she'd lifted her blouse to adjust her bra had shocked him. She'd looked him in the eye the entire time, challenging him to react, like he was the odd one for finding her antics unusual.

But he dreaded her punctuating a rant with her walking stick. Those outbursts made him feel like a delinquent child and he didn't know how to react to them. He felt like he should retaliate. But he couldn't. And she knew it. Because she had a unique way of bringing people into the fold and nurturing their dependency with team inclusivity, promises of a breath-taking career and inflated salaries. And just when she had the employee snared through the lip on the tip of an unrelenting hook, she would begin to subtly exploit their weakness. But by then they were in. Committed and addicted. How do you go home and tell your family the BMW's gone or the trip to Thailand is cancelled, because you couldn't take a tongue lashing from the tiny woman with the colossal might?

As he approached her glass fronted office, a flicker of hope lightened his step. She had her elder grandson with her, John. A gentle adolescent with dark hair and chiselled cheekbones that made him boyishly handsome and girlishly pretty at the same time. He sat on the floor in the corner of her office, absorbed in the enormous book on his lap. Alan knocked on the glass door. Ursula made him wait before beckoning him inside.

At first, positivity reigned. Classically clad in a navy skirt suit Ursula praised the financial reports, receptive to Alan's ideas on expense reduction tactics. She had a way of listening intently while she turned her gold crucifix in her fingers. She twisted the pendant around, tightening the chain until it bit into her neck and then she released it, only to begin the process again.

"Stop," she said, and her fingers released Christ on his cross, back into his place at the base of her throat, "I didn't authorise any repeat donations to the Broadstone Hospice."

Alan's pulse accelerated.

"Ah. Maybe David Cross…"

Ursula stopped him with the palm of her hand, grabbed the handset of her desk phone and stabbed at a speed dial button. "David. I need you in my office now."

She didn't wait for an answer. She smacked the handset back into place and stared down the corridor which led to her office, waiting for David Cross to appear. Alan didn't know where to look. The boy in the corner glanced up from his book for the first time. Their eyes connected, and he saw pity there, or empathy. The child knew. He pulled his legs in closer to his chest, making himself smaller.

David Cross, currently an unseasoned victim. He'd been on the payroll for three months, still loved up on team solidarity, red wine lunches and motivational speeches. He skipped into the glass lair, not yet schooled on the potential dangers within. Newbies weren't warned about Ursula; an unwritten rule. You hadn't been initiated into the Harrison fold until Ursula had chewed you up at least once.

For twenty minutes Ursula Harrison systematically ripped her new victim apart until she achieved what she wanted. A bite back. David Cross eventually decided not to take her abusive fuckery anymore and gave as good as he got. Massive mistake. Just at the point of each of them declaring the other a total bastard, Ursula snatched her walking stick from the side of her desk and jabbed it in his direction, fingers tight around the intricate, carved handle.

"Don't you raise your voice at me Cross," she snarled, "If you don't like what I have to say put your company car keys on my desk and fuck off."

The tip of the stick banged on the polished wood, indicating exactly where the keys needed to be. Silently, they fumed at each other. Alan reminded himself to breathe. He wished he wasn't there, but perversely enjoyed it too. When she directed the rage at someone else it was mesmerising to watch.

"Put your keys on my desk right now!"

"I think we should discuss this calmly ..."

"Keys!" she roared.

David hesitantly reached into his pocket and pulled out his keys. She tapped the stick on her desk again. His mind must've been spinning. Was she serious? What would she do if he refused to surrender his keys and walked out of her office?

He placed his keys on the desk, his hand hovering over them like a zookeeper placing a piece of meat in front of a lion's nose. Ursula brought the stick down again, pinning his hand to the desk. She hadn't hurt him. She didn't need to. Her ascendancy was implicit. David froze, aghast. Ursula scrutinized him, unmoving, a predatory gleam in her eyes.

"Don't spend my money again without my express permission," she said, but with the same seductive tone as she might have said 'don't stop until I explode on your cock'.

David pulled his hand away taking the keys with him. He glanced at Alan with a 'what the fuck just happened?' expression. Alan gave him nothing. In the corner of the room, the child continued reading, or pretending to read. He'd seen it all before.

As soon as David left the room Ursula swept her arm across her desk sending, papers, pens, a little framed photo of her younger grandson, all to the floor around her feet. The muggy morning heat sucked air from the room, and she sat back in her cream leather chair. Never taking her eyes from Alan, she hitched her skirt up her thighs. Beneath the prim navy skirt she wore delicate, lace topped stockings attached to suspenders. Much more bedroom than boardroom.

"I need air conditioning. Now, pick up this mess Alan."

He hesitated, as his moral compass and common sense went to battle. His boss had given him a task; nothing wrong with that, except really, she wanted him to humiliate himself for her pleasure. He knew it, she knew it, and there was something deeply erotic about a woman like her knowing what she wanted. And it was just picking up bits of paper, right?

Lowering to his hands and knees, he began his task. Piece by piece he returned every item to her desk. Across the room, John watched him, his expression blank and unreadable. Alan cringed as they made eye contact. What the hell must he be thinking?

John turned back to his book.

"Out loud it feels wrong, but at the time it didn't. She carried on working on her computer, skirt up to her thighs, but I knew what I did drove her crazy." He shook his head. "I've never met a woman so in tune with her sexuality."

"Did you finish the job?" Clive asked.

"No, she did. She made me stand in front of her desk and watch. Best hundred quid I ever made." Alan glanced at Catherine. "Incredibly sexy."

"She masturbated in front of her grandson?" Catherine found it an effort to hide her disgust.

"Yeah. I forgot he was there, and she did too. Or she didn't care. She had a huge walnut desk, so I doubt he saw much."

"It added to the thrill," said Clive.

"I think you're right," said Alan, "She loved how wrong it was."

It explained John's reluctance to talk about his family. The image she had in her mind now of the quiet child, absorbed in his book, simultaneously intrigued and disturbed her.

"Did you see her abuse other people in this way?" she asked.

"I didn't see it as abuse." Alan flicked imaginary dirt off the arm of his chair. "Maybe because she stopped short of hurting anyone."

"But you never thought about complaining, or reporting her?"

"To the police you mean?" he laughed, "It would sound ridiculous. A sixty odd-year-old woman, a wealthy and respectable philanthropist, threatened me with her walking stick. It's laughable."

She found it hard to understand why anyone would agree to be humiliated, regardless of the cash. Add in the extra repugnance for doing it in front of a child.

"Were you ever tempted to take it further with Ursula?" Clive asked.

"Good God no, but she offered me money several times for weird stuff."

Catherine leant forward. Like crawling around her office wasn't weird enough? "What kind of stuff?"

"She paid me two hundred quid to drop my pants and let her verbally humiliate me."

Catherine and Clive stared at him. "Didn't she have a partner?" asked Catherine, "She sounds like one hell of a frustrated lady."

"Never." Alan's answer was immediate. "She was devastated when her husband died, but after his death she started … I don't know what the word is … experimenting."

"Maybe she couldn't express her desires with him." Catherine instantly regretted the comment. Clive's eyebrows shot up with interest.

"Sounds to me like she had a fetish or two and fulfilled her fantasies on consensual, at worst reluctant, staff. Staff who were happy to take a bung too, you included," said Clive.

If there was ever any comeback, she had the perfect cover. If they found it offensive, why take money to do what she wanted? Clever really.

"OK," said Clive, and he closed his notebook. "So she bullied people for god knows how long. Intimidated them. Did anyone ever threaten her? Even in passing. At the water cooler, in the canteen. Someone didn't just dislike her, they loathed her enough to murder her."

Alan rubbed his cheeks and stared out of the windows, eventually he shook his head. "I'm struggling to think of anyone."

They finished their coffees, thanked Alan, and left as rush hour eased off.

"Fancy a quick breakfast at Mortimers?" asked Clive as they took the road back towards Camber.

"Yep, it'll have to be a quick one though. I've arranged a meeting at the castle at ten-thirty."

"Suits me. So, what do you think?"

Catherine stared out of the window, spinning her thoughts, not liking any of them.

"It makes my skin crawl. Not about Ursula Harrison being a horny bitch, each to their own. It's the fact it happened around the children that bothers me."

"The family's fucked up." Clive sucked on his e-cig, "But my dad was shagging my cousin so I've no room to talk."

"Ursula had the money to slip people a few quid to keep quiet, or persuade them to perform acts they were reluctant to do. Help charities, give money to worthy causes and no one thinks you're up to no good behind closed doors."

"I think Renshaw secretly liked it."

"Secretly? He got a hard-on just talking about it. I bet he's tossing off over it right now."

"I might do later."

"Ugh."

Clive laughed as he pulled into the car park at Mortimers over the road from the castle. They found a corner table so Clive could vape undetected. The fancy coffee shop served snacks and afternoon tea and exploited the tourist trade, but the food was exceptional.

"What are these repressed desires you can't express then?" Clive rested his back against the radiator next to their table. "Is Robin a bit dull in bed?"

"Like I'm going to discuss my sex life with you." Catherine rolled her eyes. "You seriously need to get laid soon, and no, he's not. Anyway, back on track: we should share Renshaw's story with the police."

"It happened a long time ago Cat. They could waste a shitload of time tracking down David Cross to find out he's forgotten it ever happened."

"But there might be other David Cross's who've never forgotten, who may have felt so strongly about what she did, they killed her."

"So strongly they waited 15 or so years to retaliate? Nah. I don't buy it."

"The human mind is complex. It distorts, and the right trigger can cause any of us to snap at any time."

"Well, it's up to you, but I reckon Robin has enough on his plate without chasing ghosts."

Catherine stared at Clive, at the little smile he did sometimes, which he'd never been able to hide because it wasn't on his lips. "You want the story."

"Of course I do. It's topical, utterly sleazy and a potential career rocket."

"I thought you didn't care about that shit."

"We all have egos." Clive leant towards her across the table. "Tell me you don't like seeing your name in print. And why's that? Because you want validation, approval, admiration. We're no different."

Catherine sighed, conflicted. It did seem far-fetched that David Cross might have decided to retaliate 15 years after his run-in with Ursula. But some people bore grudges for a lifetime.

"You can have David Cross. If it brings you back from that place," Clive jabbed his finger towards the castle, "That's how strongly I feel about this, and about you."

"I still won't sleep with you."

"A terrible fact I accepted a long time ago."

Clive smiled, a real smile this time which accentuated the deep furrows around his mouth.

They threw ideas around over breakfast, like old times, sucked back into the world she'd tried to leave. She didn't know whether to thank Clive or hate him for it. True, her involvement with John contributed to her interest in Ursula Harrison's life and death, but the pull still remained.

A few hours back in Clive's world followed by an afternoon in hers. Today would be the test.

*

John opened his eyes and wished he hadn't. He blinked against the sudden light which flooded his head with a white pain that crashed against his skull. He wanted to sleep again and escape the all over headache for a bit longer. It was too much. With each breath, the womblike blackness welcomed him, and he melted back into the soft embrace of oblivion.

"Mr Rickman? John?"

John jolted out of sleep this time, like he'd stepped off a cliff. Two faces loomed over him from the bedside, swinging in and out of focus. They brought with them a collective smell of woody aftershave, fresh air and leather.

"DI Scott and this is DS Tanner. We spoke to you after your car accident. Can you tell us what happened last night?"

John dug around in his murky memory. He'd had such a good day with Catherine, and a great night with Rich. Hazy memories now shrouded by the grim recollection of being curled up on his hall floor hoping he wasn't going to die.

"I'd been out in town with a friend. I got out of a taxi, just after midnight I think, put my key in the door and he slammed into me. Pushed me into the house. Then he kicked the shit out of me."

"Did you recognise him?"

"His face was covered with a scarf. He didn't speak either."

"And while all this happened it didn't slip down?" Scott's former friendly, approachable tone had gone. Looked like he fancied finishing off the job.

"Who knows? I was in foetal on the floor trying to protect myself."

"Do you have any idea who might want to hurt you?" asked DS Tanner.

"No. I thought he wanted to rob me. And I haven't pissed anyone off, that I know of anyway."

Except Robin Scott. Maybe he hoped the tough figure of authority act would make John reconsider his relationship with

Catherine. Chiselled out of granite, classic alpha male, all in black today like he was MI5 and not tourist town plod. Did he make her feel safe? Was safety the attraction? John's head banged harder.

"Your house was untouched. No sign of any disturbance."

Tiredness dragged him away. He couldn't process the implications or even think anymore. He drifted off, unable to fight it.

"John?"

He jumped and blinked awake again. They were still there. Scott huffed, obviously irritated, and glanced at his colleague, who shrugged in response. "OK, we'll leave you to rest for now. But this may be connected to your grandmother's death."

"I don't see how."

"Your Grandmother is murdered, you're involved in an accident, then you're attacked. And you don't see a connection?"

The implied criticism and acerbic delivery stung. Wasn't he the victim? Scott made him feel like he was culpable.

"If someone murdered Ursula, they wouldn't have a problem killing me too."

"So why didn't he?"

"I don't know. He'd done enough."

"Enough to what? Give you a warning? Teach you a lesson? Maybe we should ask Bobby, seeing as he's still in custody."

A chill swept through John's entire body and ripped him out of the cloying fatigue. "Bobby wouldn't hurt anyone. I don't understand why he's been detained."

Scott stared at him, trying to probe his brain through eye contact alone. John blinked and looked away, and he hated how he'd conceded.

"We'll need to speak again."

They turned to go.

"Would you mind letting Catherine know what's happened, DI Scott? I don't have my phone and I said I'd help her with her research."

Robin Scott looked blindsided, his jaw tightened. He looked about to snap, but his colleague opened the door and manoeuvred him through before he could respond.

*

"Cheeky bastard!" Robin flung open the doors, almost banging into a bloke in a football kit with his arm in a sling. He stomped ahead of Jack towards the carpark, needing to put some space between him and that smug little shit. "Who does he think he is? I'm going back to have a word."

He spun around and collided with Jack, who grabbed his arm to stop him.

"Don't be stupid. Come on, there's a shitload of work to do."

"I don't care."

"Yes, you do. Let it go, Robin. It was probably genuine."

Robin glared at him, seething. "Seriously? Are you insane?"

"No!" Jack snapped back, "You are, so get a grip and stop being a prick. He saved Catherine's life, which is nobbing you off for some reason, and you've turned it into a pissing contest."

"You're wrong." Robin pulled his arm out of Jack's grasp. "He was trying to wind me up."

"And he's succeeded."

Had he really read it the wrong way, or was Jack just trying to get him to simmer down? Robin had always trusted his instincts and they'd failed him this time. He'd liked Rickman, but now the smug bastard had moved in on Catherine under his tenuous 'let's do history together' cover story. Oh, and he saved her life. That took some beating. How could anyone resist the emotional pull of such a weighty deed? It had to double the appeal. In Robin's head it all sounded puerile, like it had when he'd ripped into Clive.

"I shouldn't have snapped. Stupid of me. Sorry."

Jack was a master of the silent expression. He gave Robin his 'so you should be' dad face.

"You were hard on him in there."

Robin groaned and rubbed his cheeks. "A targeted attack, after midnight on a quiet suburban street, in a nice area. No sign of theft. He's protecting someone, but why protect someone who battered you?"

"I don't know. Fear, extortion, loyalty."

"My gut says loyalty. I don't think he'd take a battering and keep quiet without good reason."

"Or he has no idea who did it."

Robin reached his car first and they stopped beside it, both pondering. "What are we missing Jack?"

Jack stared out across the busy hospital grounds. "We don't have long left with Trent so we should tackle him about the hemlock and have one last go with him."

By the time he turned into the station Robin could easily have booked five other drivers, a couple of cyclists and one stupid teenager who ambled across the road reading his phone at the same time. He got out of his car as Jack chugged in alongside him. The Capri shuddered a toxic cough as he killed the engine.

He'd been back in his office for less than a minute when CS Collins appeared, chomping an apple.

"Thought I'd pop in and see how you're getting on Robin," she said between bites.

"We have new leads Ma'am, and I'm about to speak to our primary suspect again."

Collins perched casually on a cupboard by the window and peered out. "His time is nearly up. Can we charge him with the murder?"

Robin sagged into his chair. "No." The word stuck in his throat. He despised defeat.

"Anyone else in the frame?"

"Not yet, but there was an attack last night which could be connected."

"Rickman, the teacher? Yes, I heard about it. I rang a friend of mine from the grammar school to see if she knew him. He's in her SEN group – Special Educational Needs. They meet at Broadstone. He's well respected. Inspiring even. Does a lot for the kids at Toncaster."

Robin kept his expression blank. It took some effort.

"And he pulled Catherine from her car, didn't he, saved her life?"

"What's your point Ma'am?"

"My point Robin, is there could be personal conflict here. And any personal connection can lead to errors of judgement, as you know. You're a hands-on copper still, which I like. It shows your heart's in the job. But this might be one to step back from."

Hackles rose, and Robin had to anchor himself into his chair. "Step back how? I've never 'stepped back' from a case my entire career."

"Let Jack lead from the front, while you lead from the back."

"It's not happening, and in all honesty Ma'am, I'm insulted. I'll pack up and leave if I ever resort to leading from the back."

She gave him a squinty examination, still munching. "You seem tetchy."

"I'm disappointed with our progress, but we'll get there. We have a strong team, and I can lead them to a result. No personal conflict, and definitely no stepping back."

Not a complete lie; he was disappointed.

"Rule Trent out and move on." She threw her apple core into his bin where it clanged against the metal. "He's not your man. Lean on the staff at Harrison would be my advice. One of them will crack."

"We're already on it."

"Excellent. I'm sure you have all angles covered."

She left him alone with the thickening pressure she'd brought with her into the room. James tapped on the door a few seconds later and stuck his head around. "Trent is waiting in room three Guv."

Chapter Thirteen

New suspect

"Are there any mints in here?" Jack asked, rummaging through the glove box in Ella's car. It smelled of pizza and baby sick.

"Why do you root through the glove box of every car you go in?"

"You can tell a lot about a person from what's in there."

"Go on then, what's mine telling you."

They pulled out of the station car park and joined the traffic. Jack sat back, glad of the light relief. He'd known Ella for six years, and she'd come back from maternity leave with a new edginess to her. Maybe she was just knackered.

"Enough snacks to feed a class of ten-year-olds. You like food."

"God, you're good."

"Several pens. You can write."

"Stop it now, you're showing off." She glanced at him, mischief brightening her eyes. "What's in the boss's glove box?"

"Now you know I can't give away insider knowledge."

"I've never seen him look as stressed as he did this morning."

"No surprise. Collins is breathing down his neck."

"I heard his girlfriend's got friendly with John Rickman since the crash."

Jack studied her as she switched lanes, overtook a ditherer and darted back again. "Didn't have you as a gossip."

"It's not gossip. It affects the case."

"Rickman saved Catherine's life, Ella."

"I'm just saying."

"It's bollocks. If he thought there was conflict with the case, he would sort it."

Ella gave him an unconvinced sniff. "What's Catherine like? I've never met her."

"She's lovely. Interesting, warm, funny. You've been watching too many soaps and reality shows."

"Not much else to do when you're breastfeeding." She turned onto the road heading out to Billingsborough, slammed her palm on the horn and swore at a Corsa with green 'L' plates. "Take your test again, prick!"

"Are you OK?"

"Green plates piss me off. You've either passed or not."

"You're very … prickly."

She shot him a steely glare. "I'm fine."

Barbara Rickman's car was on the drive as they pulled into her street, outside her impressive, detached house. She shared her mother's taste. The period villa-style property occupied a large corner position, partially shielded from view by a high wall topped with stone lions. She answered the door on the second knock wearing smart trousers and a peach blouse. Definitely not loungewear, but she didn't come across as a person who lounged. Was she attractive? He couldn't decide. Impossible to disconnect her appearance from her personality.

"We weren't sure whether you would be at the hospital," he said as she allowed them into the hall.

Barbara stopped. "What?"

"John was assaulted last night. Didn't you know?" He didn't wait for the answer. Her eyebrows shot up with surprise. "We're looking into potential links to your mum's death."

"That's not possible." Her voice sounded strained, the clipped haughtiness gone.

"I've seen him myself this morning."

"No, that there's a link. John has no real connections with my family."

"You raised him, he has your name – your late husband's name - and he has an interest in the family business." Jack waited as she stared at him coldly. "Would you like to know how he is?"

"He's still alive, isn't he?"

"You sound disappointed."

"What a disgusting thing to say." Mrs Haughty was back. "It's no secret, there's no love lost between John and me. But I wouldn't wish him dead."

"Not even to get at his shares? With your mum out of the way he's the only threat, isn't he?"

"Are you implying I was involved in my own mother's murder?"

Jack countered her annoyance with a shrug. "You would gain by having both of them out of the way."

"Look around you. Do you think I'm short of money?"

"No one ever has enough money. I don't," Jack glanced at Ella.

"I definitely don't," she said.

"I'm fifty-six and still waiting for my inheritance." Jack enjoyed winding Barbara up. He'd met few women he disliked as much as the one who fumed in front of him, trying to keep a grip on her temper.

"No chance for me. My Mum and my Nan like the bingo too much." Ella was enjoying herself too. More like her old self again.

"You can cut the double act with me, I'm not impressed by your games," Barbara sneered, "If you've finished with your questions I'd like to get on."

"Here's the problem we have." Jack ignored her dismissal. "Motivation. Why would someone want to kill a wealthy, elderly woman and her fairly wealthy grandson? Step grandson. No sign of robbery in either case and no connection between the incidents and Harrison Engineering. So, whoever perpetrated these crimes has a personal motivation."

That hit home. Her frozen glare melted into concern. "Do you think I'm at risk, and my son? Is he at risk too?"

"That's what we're trying to figure out."

"I think you'd better come in."

*

When Jack and Ella returned, Robin and James were in the major incident suite. They all got drinks and gathered around the case information boards. Trent had been released. He'd heard of hemlock but couldn't identify it. CCTV picked up his van in York around 10pm on the night Ursula was murdered and on the motorway cameras travelling back on Saturday morning. Not enough to charge him.

"William sawed the stick in half," said Jack, "Did it in anger one day after Ursula whacked him with it. No one else knows about it and she hasn't used it since."

Robin sat back and absorbed the information.

"The prodigy." Ella fished in her bag, came up with Maltesers. "Barbara was droning on about how smart he is, Got all twitchy when she heard about John."

"She didn't know?"

"Nope. Didn't give a shit either." She glanced down at her top and pulled her cardigan over her chest where a wet patch bloomed over her breast.

"What do we know about William?"

"Err … he's into kickboxing," she continued, an embarrassed flush creeping up her neck. "Brilliant in maths, science and art. Impeccable student. I rang his school on the way back, but they wouldn't go further without a warrant. Student confidentiality."

"And Ursula hit him?"

"A 'warning tap on the knuckles' according to Barbara," said Jack.

Like she gave Karen Taylor. The door opened and Vic blustered in, windswept and excited. "Just picked this up on the way in Guv." He handed Robin a sheet of paper. "There was a print on the cigarette butt found at Rickman's house and it's a full match."

Robin scanned the report. The name didn't ring a bell.

"Bring him in."

*

Jamie Clarke was a lanky lad in his early twenties with jet-black hair, tight ripped jeans and a complexion that didn't see much sun. Quirky, with deep-set eyes and cherub cheeks. Shaky fingers toyed with an unlit cigarette and his left leg jigged under the table. He'd picked the side of his thumbnail so much it had bled.

Robin introduced himself and Jack for the recording, then opened the file on Jamie they'd scrambled together since identifying him as a suspect.

"Jamie, do you understand why you're here?"

151

"Something about an assault." He sucked his cigarette and pretended to take a drag. An intricate tattoo snaked out from under his black leather jacket, ending in a coiled around his wrist.

"You're from Toncaster, yes?"

"Yeah."

"Where do you hang out?"

"The Grey Mare mostly, near the market."

Made sense. The Grey Mare was a known hangout for the alternative crowd and Jamie slotted straight into that bracket.

"So, you come into Broadstone rather than going into Toncaster?"

"Tonky's shit. Full of chavvy kids listening to R&B. Makes my ears bleed."

Jamie sounded tough enough, but his body gave away his anxiety. He continually rubbed the back of his neck and didn't sit still.

"Where were you last night?"

"Out and about."

"Out and about where exactly?"

He searched upwards for an answer scrawled on the ceiling. Didn't find it.

"Were you in Broadstone at any point? In the Grey Mare maybe?"

Jamie tapped the cigarette on the table while he thought. "Nah, I don't go in on Wednesdays. They have a quiz night for the silver crowd," Jamie glanced at Jack.

"What about Castleton?"

Jamie fake laughed. "Way too posh for me. It's all wine bars and gastro pubs."

"You own a Mini Cooper, registration number VEK 615G?, which has no tax or MOT so it's also uninsured."

Jamie put the cigarette to his lips again. "Been a bit skint."

"You were in Castleton last night. You were caught on camera parked in a residents-only zone, and you were booked."

"The wind must've blown the ticket off. Proper windy last night."

Robin fought a smile. The little shit was cute; he had to admit. "Were you there?"

"If you're telling me that was Castleton, then yeah, I must've been in Castleton."

"Why? 'Too posh for me', you said."

"Lost probably."

"This was last night. Surely you know why you were there; in an area you've admitted you never go to."

"I don't read the signs. I'm dyslexic."

Robin stared at him. "Are you taking the piss?

"No, it's true."

"Listen Jamie; you can do the clever stuff for a bit longer if you like. It's fun. I'm having fun, I really am. But your delaying tactics aren't going to last much longer. Do you know John Rickman?"

One hard swallow. "Who?"

"John Rickman. Shall I spell it for you? You know, with your dyslexia?" Robin paused, but Jamie just glared back at him. "He was attacked last night at his house. In Castleton. Two streets away from where your car was booked at 11.42 pm."

"I didn't see anything."

"I'm not after witnesses. I'm looking for whoever kicked the hell out of him. Do you know him?"

"John Rickman or the person who battered him?"

Robin gritted his teeth. "Either."

"Like I have mates in Castleton."

"I didn't ask if Mr Rickman was your mate. I asked if you know him. Answer the question."

"The name doesn't ring a bell."

Robin put an evidence bag containing the cigarette end on the desk. "A fag end from John Rickman's garden. Your fingerprint's on it."

Jamie stared at the cigarette. "This tiny dimp has my fingerprint on it?"

"We matched the print to the ones we already have on file. From when you were arrested for ..." Robin flicked through his file. "Assault. You were in a scuffle in the Grey Mare – what a coincidence we were just talking about it, eh? A fight over the jukebox, it says here. You punched a guy in the face."

Jamie's jerky knee drummed on the underside of the table, and he probed a spot on his neck with a dirty nail.

"Mr Rickman was seriously assaulted; in fact, we could treat this as attempted murder." Jack nodded his agreement, playing along. "Your car was booked shortly before the attack. This cigarette places you at the scene."

"I didn't try to murder anyone, not that I can remember."

"Why wouldn't you remember? Were you wrecked? Smoking a joint maybe?"

On top of the infuriating jigging, Jamie's jaw had clenched close to snapping and his thumb was bleeding again. "Can I light this?" He waggled the cigarette in his fingers.

"Did you assault Mr Rickman?"

"No."

Robin's pushed the file sideways to Jack and leant on the table. "Jamie, I've listened to your sarky, smart-arse responses and to be honest, I'm not convinced. You were at the scene on the same night, driving a dodgy motor, you have no independent witness, and you've plenty of previous. I think we'll keep you here overnight while we continue with our enquiries."

"Aww, come on. I didn't twat the teacher."

Ah, at last. "Teacher?" Robin looked at Jack like he'd missed a bit and was being thick, "Teacher, Jamie? Who said he's a teacher?"

Jack acted vacant and shrugged, mirroring Robin's fake stupidity. Jamie swallowed something the size of a fist in his throat and jigged so hard he knocked Jack's coffee right off the table. Everyone ignored it.

Robin waited while Jamie waded through the swamp in his head. When he was right, he could wait all day long for his prey to hang themselves. Jamie Clarke was measuring the gibbet and knotting the rope right before his eyes.

"If you didn't know Mr Rickman, and you didn't dump your cigarette ends at his house, and you didn't almost murder him last night," Robin leant closer to the pallid, gulping young man. He slid a photo out of the file without breaking eye contact and pushed it in front of Jamie. It showed a bloody handprint on the door frame of John's house. "Can you explain why your hand was covered in his blood?"

Jamie's face paled further.

"I want a solicitor."

*

Catherine basked in history heaven. The sectioned off parts of the castle, currently closed to the public, always intrigued her. What hid beyond the red rope? What secret or dangerous space couldn't be explored?

There was a guy she loved to follow on Facebook who broke into abandoned buildings and photographed them. Fascinating to see places frozen in a bygone time, and even more appealing when you're not supposed to be there. Today she found the real castle, down the narrow passageways and uneven staircases. Health and safety nightmare but an explorer's dream. Away from the great hall with its simulated décor a different building existed, where she could feel what it would've been like to live there centuries ago. No lighting, no information signs, just the atmospheric spaces and their unforgiving nature. She soaked up its legacy and fell in love with the place again.

Immersed in her imagination, she almost missed her phone ringing. She answered just in time, expecting it to be Cindy, who she'd called several times. It was Clive.

"Missing me already?"

"Have you heard?" No preamble. Very unlike Clive. "John Rickman was assaulted last night."

"Shit. Is he OK?"

"Yeah, he's at the General. Do you want a lift over there?"

Clive's speedy offer took her aback. "Won't that be weird? I've only known him for a week." And yet her stomach knotted. Their day together had been lovely, and he'd texted the night before, while he'd been out with Rich, to tell her again how much he'd enjoyed it.

"Quote Cindy; you like him."

"Cindy's full of shit. And aren't you busy?"

"Admit it; you're intrigued."

"No, you're intrigued. I'm concerned." She stared out of the arrow slit across the undulating land where they'd walked together the day before. What should she do? She *was* concerned, but she shared Clive's intrigue too. The crash had catapulted her into John's world, and not for the first time, she questioned the coincidence.

"I found David Cross by the way "

"Jesus, you don't mess about."

"LinkedIn, easy win." She rolled her eyes at Clive's old cheesy catchphrase. "Semi-retired, breeds fancy cats. And he's up for dishing some dirt. Now she's dead obviously."

"He's an unlikely murderer."

"I think all he could murder is I Will Survive at a naff wedding. Bitter as fuck though."

"Is this our style Clive?" He seemed oddly enthusiastic about what he would usually pass off as unsubstantiated gossip. "It feels like cheap news, and more haters will crawl out of the woodwork."

"I have papers and subscriptions to sell, readers to engage. Now, if I can find a local MP riding this bandwagon, I'll be a happy man. This is what's happening in our town Cat. We can't get snobby about it. So: Rickman. Are we going?"

"I do the talking."

"See you in ten."

*

"We know you attacked John Rickman. What we don't know yet, Jamie, is why?"

Jamie glanced at the duty solicitor Lee Dunn, who sat forward in his chair, ready to pounce. Sludge brown suit, squinty eyes, prematurely balding.

"My client hasn't admitted to the charge." Dunn's smug satisfaction suggested he'd won a much longer argument.

"Oh, come on," Robin wasn't in the mood for a semantic battle, "Fingerprints, DNA, evidence of being in the area."

"Circumstantial."

"Under what circumstances do you leave your fingerprints in someone else's blood? I'll answer for you," Robin cut Dunn off as he began to speak, "When they're guilty." He turned his attention back to Jamie who ignored the indignant huff from Dunn, pinned by Robin's stare. He bowed his head and stared at the table.

"Do you know Ursula Harrison?" Robin asked, clinging to the last morsel of hope that these cases were connected.

Jamie shook his head. "No. Who is she?"

"John Rickman's grandmother. Murdered last week. It's all over the news."

Jamie froze. "I don't watch the news. Why are you asking me about her?"

"Inspector, is there a charge against my client relating to that case?" asked Dunn, "Otherwise, I can't see how this is relevant."

"It's relevant because Mrs Harrison was murdered, and within a week her grandson's been assaulted by your client. These cases are, literally, related."

Jamie sank further, his face hidden by the mass of black hair in need of a wash. "He's my kid sister's teacher. She has a crush on him, like, a really bad crush."

"OK …"

"She's stupid over him, turning up at his house, following him around and stuff."

"Was she having a relationship with him?"

Jamie laughed, didn't look up. "In her dreams."

"So why attack him?"

"She's been taken into care. They found skunk in her locker at school and in her bedroom. She was stitched up."

"And you think John Rickman did it?"

"He wanted her out of the way."

"Does your sister do drugs?"

"A bit of weed, yeah."

How was this all linked to Ursula Harrison? Jack leaned towards Jamie.

"Let's get this clear," he said, "You attacked your sister's teacher, who she's obsessed with, because you reckon he's responsible for her being taken into care?"

"I went to have a word with him, but I got angry. He's not the only one to blame, but I saw red. Fucking fancy car, nice house, nice clothes. We live on a shitty council estate with a pisshead dad and fuck all. Our mum left us with him, you know? Just left her kids. Is it any surprise Marcia's gone wild?" Jamie rubbed at his face, eyes shiny. "I was thinking all this when I was kicking him, and I got more and more wound up, so I kicked more." He swallowed hard. "But he must be a decent guy if he didn't grass on me."

"I'd like a word in private with my client." Dunn rose but Robin ignored him, leaving him standing awkwardly at the table. "Can we break for five minutes?"

Robin shoved his chair back and gave Jack a nod towards the door. Jack suspended the interview and followed him outside.

"I can't see a connection with Ursula Harrison."

"Me neither, and I don't think he's lying." Jack scratched at his head. "When he talked about kicking Rickman, he dropped the cocky act, and it seemed genuine to me."

Robin had sensed it too. When Jamie's guard had dropped, he spoke from the heart. "Why did Rickman protect him?"

"I don't know. I'm not sure Jamie knows either. Do you want to talk to Rickman again?"

Robin shook his head. "Later, but I don't want to lose focus on the main case. We still have a murderer to find. I'm sure Rickman has reasons for dicking us around, but I'm not interested unless it helps us find Ursula Harrison's killer."

"Would Catherine know?" Jack shuffled as he asked the question.

"What are you implying?"

Jack held up his hands. "You said she met him, and they may've talked, that's all."

"She met him for a coffee to thank him for saving her life."

Jack put his hands up. "Fair enough."

"I haven't seen her properly for a few days," Robin conceded, "She didn't mention anything significant over dinner the other night. I'll talk to her again."

"What do we do with our friend in there?" Jack nudged his head towards the interview room.

"I don't see how he can escape an assault charge, even if Dunn gets off his arse…"

The door to the major incident suite down the corridor opened and Vic came out backwards, carrying a tray of mugs. He spotted Robin and Jack and dithered for a moment over what to do with the tray. He put it on the floor then headed towards them at speed.

"Guv, I've just taken a call from a woman at Broadstone Grammar. Her sister-in-law works for the department of agriculture, who we contacted about the hemlock?"

"Go on," said Robin, wishing Vic had multi-speed fast forward.

"The school has a large playing field backing onto the canal. A few years ago, a woman walking her dog on the canal path rang the school and told them poisonous weeds were growing on the verge. It's not uncommon apparently – there's a bush with berries on, can't remember the name, but it's poisonous too, and there's one outside the science block …"

"Vic! Get to the point."

Quick fringe twiddle. "Yeah, so nothing happened, and it was all forgotten. Anyway, after I'd spoken to her, Judy went over with a couple of uniforms, and she reckons she's found it. Hemlock."

Vic swiped at his phone and flashed a photo at Robin and Jack.

"How far is it from Trent's?" Robin asked, feeling his stomach lurch. Trent. Who they'd just released.

"Ten minutes on foot," said Jack, "it's a popular route with dog walkers."

Vic pocketed the phone. "William Rickman goes to Broadstone Grammar."

"And there's the walking stick," said Jack, "We've said from the start this was personal."

"And he's smart," added Vic.

Robin wasn't convinced, but the Vic and Jack tag team seemed to be. "Before we make impulsive decisions, let's work this through. Would a fifteen-year-old boy drug his grandmother and beat her to death because she clobbered him once with her walking stick? Suit up and use Trent's Hunters to confuse us? Trent's close to his brother; he wouldn't do that."

Unless he'd become jealous of their relationship, denied a father twice.

Vic still buzzed like an excited spaniel. "I reckon it's the grandson."

"OK, we need more on William Rickman before we take this further. He's a minor, which means a potential whole world of shit. I don't want any more cock ups." Robin levelled this at Vic.

"We should do a press update," said Jack, "Tell them our suspect has been released without charge, but another arrest is imminent blah blah."

"Agreed." They needed to get back to Jamie Clarke. Robin turned to Vic. "I want to know more about William Rickman. Discreetly, Vic."

"Guv." Vic rubbed his hands together and headed back towards the office.

"And find out where Bobby Trent walks his fucking dog."

*

"Jamie, while we were questioning Mr Rickman's neighbours, we found out about this." Robin slid a photo across the table. "Someone defaced Mr Rickman's car last week. It wasn't reported, but the lad over the road took this photograph to send to his friends so they could have a laugh about it. Did you do this?"

"It was only cheapo paint."

"That's not the point, is it? If you knew Marcia had lied, why did you do it?"

"I was pissed off."

"You've spelled it wrong," said Dunn. Jamie glared at him.

"I don't give a shit about spelling, OK?" he rolled his eyes in Dunn's direction. "Look, I realise now I went off on one without thinking."

"Twice. First the car, then you attacked him. We haven't asked Mr Rickman about this yet, but I reckon he'll claim not to know who did it. Like he claimed not to know who attacked him. And accusing someone of being a paedophile is serious."

"I've told you; I made a mistake."

"But now we have to look into it. Mistake or not, we can't ignore it. Your actions, because you were pissed off, will now take up more police time to investigate."

Jamie's chocolate brown eyes were full of bad-puppy remorse.

"Are you charging my client with criminal damage?" asked Dunn, "Otherwise, perhaps we should get back to the main charge."

"I'll get back to that when I'm ready," said Robin, "My interview, my questions. Sorry if I'm ruining your evening."

"My client wasn't asked a question."

"Here's one; what's going on here? All of this, the car, the attack, seems a bit much considering you claim nothing happened between your sister and her teacher. What's the real reason?"

"I've told you. I was pissed off and I took it out on him. I know I was stupid."

Robin sat back from the table, inclined to believe him. "I'm sure Mr Dunn will explain what happens to you next. In the meantime, keep out of trouble."

Jamie stared at his hands, nodding in silence as Robin spoke. "Will I be allowed to see my sister?"

"Possibly. I mean it though, no more stupidity. Stay away from John Rickman."

Chapter Fourteen

Hurtful truths

Catherine had been so engrossed she'd lost track of how long she'd been holed up in the snug. Researching John wasn't easy. Classic online arctic fox, no social media presence anywhere. She had a couple of friends who taught, and they kept a low profile too, not wanting their private lives visible to their students or parents who might question their suitability to teach their darlings if they got wrecked at the weekend or had a scruffy house.

He did feature on Toncaster High School's website though, and the history department was rich with art and quirky projects bringing the subject to life. Easter dioramas with eggs decorated as characters enacting iconic historical events, fake tweets between warring leaders, Roman forts built in Roblox. Her favourite video showed his class rapping songs they'd written about slave abolition. She enjoyed his evident love of the subject and how engaged the kids were.

However pleasant though, researching John just distracted her from the even more fascinating life of Ursula Harrison. Not her public, professional career, which was impressive but dull. She skimmed over the corporate stuff. Much more compelling was Ursula's secret existence as a reviewer.

It had taken some burrowing and patient, diligent code-cracking, but she'd worked out that Ursula masqueraded as prolific reviewer Carabelle4210. It made sense. The woman had time to kill, and she had the arrogance to believe the world should be subjected to her opinion.

Ursula unleashed savage attacks on places she'd visited, restaurants she'd patronised. Brutal product reviews on a wide range of purchases from pens to pillowcases, hand warmers to handcuffs. She must've spent thousands on Amazon and reviewed every item, most rewarded with less than three stars except a silk nightdress costing almost £300. As a writer, Catherine found her exposition fascinating. Articulate and descriptive, she expressed herself with beautiful fluency. Christ, she was ruthless though. Her wrath oozed from between the lines like poison from petals.

Had she pissed off a business owner, destroyed their company or their reputation? Bad reviews could cripple a company.

She was reading about a hair salon (and huge Post advertiser) who left Ursula with hair 'the style and shade of a Nazi helmet' when Simon put his head around the door.

"Fancy a chippy lunch?" he asked, "I can't take any more of your tofu and kale felafel or whatever they are. He perched on the sofa and scanned the chaos. "This isn't marketing stuff. You're writing for Clive, aren't you?"

"No." Even though his tone wasn't accusatory, she was cautious. "I'm just intrigued."

"By the tempting teacher or the dead dominatrix? What've you found while you've been 'just intrigued'?" He crossed his legs as he sifted through some of the photos and articles she'd printed off. His knee poked through the hole in his ripped jeans, puckered scars from surgery, bone-white against the black denim. She panged with guilt at the reminder of what he'd been through. Both knees reconstructed, the two sides of his face stitched back together, the dental implants replacing his smashed-out teeth. Emotional scars no one could see.

"I've found stuff Robin hasn't mentioned. Not in the papers either. Interesting stuff."

"Well, thank fuck for that."

She pushed away from her laptop and leant against the sofa, surprised by his positive response.

"What?" He ruffled his messy spikes, puzzled. "I haven't seen that look on your face for months. Welcome back."

"We've been through this … "

"No, don't give me any of your martyr bollocks. I'm cool with it, always have been. I never wanted you to jack your job in, and I should've been more vocal. Unlike me, but I had a lot going on and I figured you're a big girl, you can make your own decisions. Looking back, I let you down. So, if you've changed your mind, great, everyone will just have to get over it. Anyway,

I'm the important one." He winked, picked up mug of tea from the table, and drank.

"Oi!"

"So, which one is it?" He ignored her protest and had another swig, studying a photo of John's class constructing a fortress. "John's serious eye candy. That's not why you like him, though. He's got under your skin. I can see how a guy with depth and a bit of a dark side might intrigue you …"

"Christ, you make me sound like a Twilight-watching teenage goth."

"You'd be a shit goth with that hair." Simon grinned. "Look, I know you're not reckless, but you're drawn to complex characters."

"Perhaps. But this isn't about him. Ursula Harrison's even more complex. and I've got a dilemma. I think I've found an angle no one else has picked up on. Do I give it to Clive, write the story, or tell Robin first?"

"Two secs. We need wine not tea." Simon disappeared in a flash, came back with a bottle and two glasses. "Hit me."

"I'm driving to Robin's later."

"Just have one then, or get a taxi. I've taken time off to babysit you. Entertain me."

She laughed at his unusually camp flourish as he flopped onto the sofa. "You're such a dick. And I thought you were going to the chip shop?"

"We'll have felafel."

*

"Sorry I can't get the weekend off."

"I didn't think you would."

Catherine had been there for five minutes, and already the tension between them had intensified. They'd barely spoken since he'd left her house on Wednesday morning and, while they needed to clear the air, he didn't feel like he had the energy for it. He hated long conversations where each word and action were analysed. Get to the point, resolve, move on.

"Someone's parked in my guest space," Robin said, peering out of the windows.

"Yeah, me. It's my new car. I bought it this morning."

He took another drink of the rich and blackcurrant red he'd opened just before she arrived. She looked like she wasn't supposed to be there. She sat on the sofa, her overnight bag still packed at her feet, sipping her wine like a designated driver.

"What's on your mind, Robin?"

Weighty inward sigh. Time to get this over with, "This case, the case," he sat on the sofa opposite her, "It's become messy." He shook his head and avoided eye contact. "Dead ends, red herrings, lack of forensics … and I'm uncomfortable with you being involved."

"I'm not involved in your cases."

"You know John Rickman, so inadvertently you are." He met her eyes. Get to the point, right? No protracted conversations. "Have you seen him?"

"What if I have?"

"And Cindy?"

"Are you asking if I've seen my friends?"

"So he's a friend now? Well, your friend's grandmother was murdered, and he was assaulted a few days ago …"

"Which you knew about and didn't tell me …"

"And your other friend's a reporter who's asking a lot of questions. Details only family or friends would know."

"Like you did at the Italian the other night?"

"I'm investigating a serious crime."

"She's doing her job; you're doing yours."

Robin sighed in exasperation and looked away from her.

"Why didn't you tell me he'd been attacked?"

"I wanted to get the facts straight first." He replied too quickly, and it sounded like he'd practised the response, which he had.

"I think I'd better go." She put her glass down and reached for her bag. "Give me a call when all this is over, and we'll see where we are."

What did that mean? He stared at her, stunned by her reaction.

"I understand how major these investigations are for you, so I'm backing off to give you space. I don't want you to feel obliged to pop round. I don't want to grab a quick meal, watching you constantly check your phone. Focus on your case, and I'll see you on the other side."

Catherine rose to her feet, eyes glassing, just as Robin's phone rang. "It's Judy. She's on my team …"

"Take the call. I'm going."

"Wait," Robin threw his phone onto the sofa, then reached out for her and took her arms, "I need your support, not for you to bail out at the first tricky obstacle."

"I can't support you if you don't let me in, and you can't let me in if you don't trust me."

"Oh, not that shit again. I'm sick of hearing it. I do trust you."

"I don't believe you."

He lowered his head, but he didn't let her go. "This is hard for me, OK? I'm under pressure. Bear with me."

"It's not about your job; that's the bit I get. It's about us."

"I don't need this right now …"

"Neither do I. We need time to think if this is right."

Slapped by the sudden realisation of where this all came from, he let go of her and stepped back.

"This is because of him. Rickman." He snatched up his wine again, "We were fine until you met him."

"Were we?"

"I was."

"Really? Because I feel like I don't get all of you. You go right to the kerb's edge, but you won't cross the road. This isn't about John."

"In your own words; I don't believe you."

"If you want someone to blame, fine." Catherine shrugged. "But you're wrong."

"What is it? You want more commitment?"

Catherine shook her head, "I don't feel I truly know you. I only know the bits you let me see. It's OK to be vulnerable, like the other night. Like what happened in the morning."

Her eyes bore into him, mercilessly drilling for more. He drained his glass.

"You mean all the questions about Erin?"

"Is it unreasonable for me to want to know about your wife?"

"Yes. Because she's gone. It's the past."

"She isn't gone. She's as present in your life now as before."

"No she isn't Cat; she's still fucking dead!"

Robin couldn't watch the hurt on her face as his words smashed into her. He refilled his glass, needing something to do. "What do you want to know?" He plonked down on the sofa. "Ask your questions, satisfy your curiosity." It sounded defensive and hardly the soul sharing she wanted.

"It's much more than curiosity."

"Either get to the point or let it go. I'm sick of you probing my brain for stuff that will be painful for both of us."

"What's the big deal?" her voice had risen a pitch, green eyes ablaze now, cheeks reddening. She tossed her coat back on the sofa. "You want me to let it go, but why can't you?"

"I don't want to let go!" he snarled back, matching her anger.

"Why not? What's so good about hurting?"

"You don't understand."

"Make me understand!"

"It was my fault! OK? My fault she died. I killed the one person who made me feel complete."

"How? You didn't plant the explosives …"

"I gave the order to enter the premises. I sent them to their deaths." He slammed down his glass. "And I sat in a car and listened to her die over the radio. Are you happy now, Catherine? Does it make you feel better now you know why it still hurts as much as it did sixteen years ago? I killed her, and every new day is as painful as back then. People say, don't they, we all have a soul mate? Erin was mine."

His words hung in the air between them like a smokescreen. She stared at him, completely still.

"Now I understand." Her voice wavered, pale and broken. "And I can't compete, can I?"

He didn't reply. He wasn't sure she could. That anyone could.

She scooped up her bag.

"I'm going home."

Chapter Fifteen

Sealed confession

"Vic. Have you seen the Post? How did we miss Alan Renshaw?"

Robin sat in his car outside the newsagent's, holding the chunky Saturday edition of the Post. Ursula Harrison's murder still dominated the front page. This time the angle they'd gone for stirred the cauldron even more at Harrison Engineering, mixing a noxious stew of hearsay and bitching.

On the other end of the phone Vic stammered and spluttered. "We didn't Guv. Err.. I'm checking the system, and you spoke to him. A lead from Clive Darwin? Your note says …"

"Shit!" Robin threw the paper onto the passenger seat and rubbed at the red wine throb building in his temples. Stupid idea to neck a full bottle on a work night, more stupid to chase it with Peroni.

"Do you want me to follow it up?"

"I want the names of everyone who's worked there in the last twenty years. Everyone. Directors to cleaners, and I want them all interviewed. Thoroughly."

Overly long pause.

"On it."

"What's up?" Robin snapped.

"Just … we're talking hundreds, maybe thousands of people. Current payroll is eighty-seven, but they've scaled back in recent years …"

"You'd better get cracking then. Prioritise those who were around when Ursula still ran the company. That should whittle your list down. Most of them are probably dead."

Apart from Alan Renshaw, who must've been one of the younger ones back in the eighties. Robin disconnected the call and snatched up the paper again. He turned to page three, where the cover story continued, all under Darwin's by-line. He would need

168

a rottweiler of a lawyer to fight in the pit if the Harrisons sued him for defamation. Barbara Rickman had kicked off over the photograph on social media, and he couldn't see her keeping silent over this either. Harmful to Harrison's reputation, even if it did happen thirty years ago.

Robin scrolled through the calls on his phone and found Renshaw's number. He didn't answer at first, and Robin had to try five times until he did, sounding pissed off by the intrusion.

"What?" Not enjoying his sudden fame, obviously.

"DI Scott, Broadstone CID. We spoke a few days ago regarding Harrison Engineering."

"Ah, yes … well…"

"I'll be at your house at 1pm today, Mr Renshaw. Be there."

Robin ended the call, cutting Renshaw off mid-protest. Next; Darwin. Unlike Renshaw, Clive sounded like he'd been waiting for the call.

"Robin, how's things?" he answered, far too cheerily for a Saturday morning call from the police.

"You withheld information." Robin wasn't in the mood for preamble.

"I told you to speak to him."

"I did, and he concocted some half-arsed, back-peddling story like he'd been prepped. Are you so desperate to get fluff for your regional rag you'd potentially hinder a murder investigation?"

"Is he a suspect now?"

"No, but my guess is he saw a lot more than he let on in your article. Critical information. Is there a follow-up? That's your usual style, isn't it? Get those circulation figures up."

"We all have a job to do. Yours is catching the bad guys, mine is giving people the truth."

Robin clenched his fists until his nails carved half-moons in his palms.

"Look, I'm not stupid. I've been in this game for a while," Darwin continued, "If I had concrete facts to help the investigation, I would've told you."

"So you're a detective now?"

"At worst, it was a bit sleazy. Don't take my word for it though; ask Catherine. She interviewed him with me, didn't she tell you? I thought she was up for writing the second part, but she

169

flounced off to the castle and dumped me for the late Robert St Stephen and his family of medieval reprobates."

Robin felt his patience snap like a fine elastic stretched beyond its limit. He embraced the relief. The struggle to suppress his feelings was becoming more of a challenge than voicing them.

"This is your only warning, Darwin; don't think you can piss about with me."

"A senior police officer threatening a member of the press. Are we on or off the record here?"

"I'll give you something for your record: be careful where you buy your Charlie. In your position, you've a long way to fall if your dealer decides to snitch, especially when it's not a first offence."

Silence.

"Enjoy your weekend Clive."

Robin stabbed the disconnect button. A low punch, but the smug bastard deserved it. Robin had found out about Clive's little class A habits a while ago but had kept quiet, knowing Catherine valued her friendship with her ex-boss. He didn't want to get him into any serious trouble. He'd always known Darwin wasn't squeaky clean; no great surprise given the circles he moved in. It had been a handy card to have tucked up his sleeve, although he did feel dirty he'd played it. It was out there now though. Served him right for being a cock.

Robin drove around the outskirts of town, crossing the river over into the Northern Quarter, where the All Saints church broke majestically through misty rain. He crunched his way across the uneven car park towards the side entrance. Robin stepped through the open door, out of frenetic normality into tranquillity. Aside from the chilly temperature and utilitarian seats, All Saints had serene beauty. It was highly ornate, but the light was its most striking feature. Pools of light flooded the dramatic arches leading to the altar, chandeliers lit the decorative ceiling and multicoloured beams of sunshine radiated through the stained-glass windows. He'd never been particularly fond of churches, but the effect moved him. He'd transported to a calmer world.

He hadn't anticipated such a youthful priest to greet him. Or perhaps it was more the youthful air Father Heath had about him. He stood tall and slim, with wavy hair swept around in a tousled and trendy style, and had the strangest eyes Robin had ever seen.

One appeared darker than the other, a stigmatism that added to his appeal. He greeted Robin with a confident, quirky charm, momentarily disarming him. He'd expected a cuddly old priest who might be persuaded to spill all to the local constabulary over a cup of tea. Heath looked like he'd be more at home with artisan gin and some folk-rock music.

"Come through to the back Inspector, I've put the heater and the kettle on."

Robin followed him down the aisle, stopping to admire the chancel and the stained-glass clerestory.

"Exquisite, isn't it?" said Heath, "Parts of this church date back to the seventeenth century, although most of what you see now was from the late 1800s."

"It must take a huge amount of upkeep."

"It does. A few years ago, we had to have the top half of the bell tower restored. Nature and time had taken their toll. Harrison Engineering funded much of what you see, which I'm sure you know. I expect you're here about their donations."

Robin admired his directness. He followed Heath into a tight hallway cluttered with bin bags and a broken pew. Robin ducked under a crooked doorway into a warm and comfortable side room, with a sitting area in one half and a kitchen in the other. He took off his coat and waited while Heath made the coffee. He brought the drinks over on a flowery tray.

"So, you want to ask me about Ursula Harrison?"

Robin took a sip, almost burned his lips, and put the cup back down again. "Yes. I want to know her, the real her, not the persona."

Michael Heath didn't struggle with scalding coffee. He took a long drink before he replied. "Ursula Harrison was hard to know, adept at only letting people see what she wanted them to see. An industrious woman, dedicated to her faith and loyal to her family. Her late husband Maurice adored her."

"I sense a 'but'."

The priest pondered for a while, peculiar eyes shining with perverse enjoyment. "She was complex. Multi-faceted. Just when you thought you had a handle on her she would slip from your grasp. Fascinating really. Scary but fascinating."

"Scary how?"

"By being such a bundle of paradoxes, I suppose."

Robin massaged his temples, not in the mood for clever games. "Let me give you my theory, and you tell me if I'm anywhere close. Ursula was a control freak, with a much shadier hidden side. That's the Ursula I want to know."

Michael Heath shifted. "And you hope getting under her skin will help you find her killer?"

"Do you think it will?"

"I'm here to support my parishioners and spread Our Lord's word. It's not my place to have opinions."

"But you do have them."

"Of course. As do the people who worship here. They want all associations severed. Despite the fact her money paid for much of the very building they're so protective of. Even so, a church is its people, not its fabric."

"And what about you? I'm asking you as another man, two blokes batting ideas around over a coffee. I'm interested in your honest opinion."

Robin leant forward. Heath transmitted his inner conflict by self-comforting, with subtle strokes to his neck and face.

"Are you a catholic, Inspector?"

"No."

"Then perhaps you don't know about the confessional seal."

"As a man, Michael," Robin pushed, ignoring the reference.

"I can't divorce myself from my position, and what you ask breaches the seal."

"Does it apply when the penitent is deceased? What a priest reveals is discretionary when it relates to serious criminal activity."

"It's not so simple. A priest would be excommunicated for revealing the contents of confession and can't be forced to testify in court with any information he might have."

"OK, I understand about reliable evidence and hearsay. Let's put the confessional aside for a minute. Did Ursula ever say anything to make you question her or anyone else *outside* of the confessional?"

Heath's eyes narrowed, and Robin waited. Heath might not be what he'd expected, but Robin had anticipated the confidentiality argument.

"I found myself watching her," he said, after giving it some thought, "She was intriguing." He paused, stopping himself from going further.

"And what did you see?" Robin pushed.

"I saw a devout woman who struggled with worship in its literal sense. She couldn't do it, despite her beliefs and need for Our Lord's approval. She expressed her devotion through outward displays of benevolence, usually involving money, but she wouldn't kneel in church, ever. Wouldn't genuflect. The conflict in her must've been exhausting. To feel a connection you can't express, to be incapable of humility."

Classic narcissism. More pieces of Ursula's puzzle clicked into place. Inability to empathise, superiority, vanity. Her bedroom. Christ, she'd created a shrine to herself.

"So her faith was fake because she couldn't accept a superior being existed."

The priest was shaking his head in protest. "No, no, she believed in God, attended every service …"

"But she denied the existence of a higher entity? It sounds like she only gave what she was willing to give - the superficial stuff - to elevate herself."

"A troubled soul, undoubtedly."

"If 'troubled' means to know your behaviour is wrong and use your phoney faith to try to excuse it." Michael Heath stared downwards, shoulders slumped. "I'd like to believe I reached her heart in all the time I spent with her."

Robin didn't want to tell him he was deluded, that he'd failed at the impossible. Heath was the first person he'd spoken to who'd liked Ursula. Maybe he'd also been on her private payroll. Robin cringed, not proud for thinking Heath might be one of Ursula's gimps. But repressed desires had a way of finding expression, Ursula being a prime example. Would Heath have been willing or unwilling? Probably willing. The priest had an experimental vibe.

Power had given Ursula autonomy to the point where she hadn't needed to listen to or be influenced by other people. She'd been aware of her mental state, enough to try to cover up her actions. To avoid judgement,

"I'd like your views on a different, confidential issue." Heath sat upright, steeling himself for more burdening. "Ursula was injected with hemlock, her legs beaten and a bible placed in her hand. Her murder has clear religious subtext."

Heath's expression darkened, and he dropped his head. "May the good Lord protect her soul," he whispered. His eyes had lost their playful sparkle. "In the Old Testament, 'rosh' is the Hebrew word for a poisonous plant of the time, although possibly the poppy. I can't recall the passage exactly, but it's about speaking falsehoods or false judgement."

Robin made a note. James had done several searches, but Heath's suggestion didn't sound familiar. Heath rose to his feet. "Let me think a moment. More coffee?"

Robin waited while Heath messed around with the cups and kettle again, his cool demeanour gone. He opened the coffee jar and closed it again without taking any out. When the kettle boiled and flicked off, Heath stared at it, transfixed.

"Father Heath?"

"What?" He flinched and flashed Robin a forced smile. "Sorry, I was miles away."

When he returned to his chair with their cups, Robin leant forward. "I understand you're conflicted, and I won't pressure you into betraying a confidence. But I have a murderer to find."

"I stand by what I said earlier. I can't break the seal of the confessional. I can offer you an opinion based on what I've seen or share my view on the religious references."

"Do you know of anyone who might have wanted her dead?"

Heath crossed his legs and straightened the crease in his trousers. "I'm not aware of anyone specifically, no."

Robin bit back his frustration. The priest squirmed with discomfort, and his left foot pointed towards the door.

"Father Heath, did you ever see Ursula Harrison abuse anyone?"

A moment of hesitation. "I never saw her, no."

"But you heard rumours. Or she confessed to the abuse?"

Heath shifted and checked the time. He smacked his hands on his thighs. "I'm so sorry, I need to get off. I have an appointment across town I can't miss."

Robin refused to let him go, "Michael, do you know who killed her?"

"I'm sorry …."

"You know!" Robin jumped to his feet, fuelled by a burst of energy he couldn't contain.

"I don't."

"But you have an idea." Robin suspected his discomfort came from a deep seated approval he couldn't admit.

Heath stared up at him, his face darkening with annoyance. "Why do you want to know?"

"What? Are you serious? A crime was committed …"

"No," Heath's unsettling gaze stopped Robin dead, "Why do you need to know? Not Robin the policeman. Robin the man. For your own gain? For validation and respect, the pat on the back? Because it won't change the outcome, believe me. Ursula will still be dead."

The attack on his values stunned Robin into silence. His moral stance was absolute. Of course, he had ambition, but the desire for justice drove him harder.

"Her killer must be punished. Law exists for equality and parity."

"Correct a wrong with another wrong? Job done. Order restored?"

What the hell? Robin refused to debate the higher purpose of the penal system. "I do the job I vowed to do, to the best of my ability, to serve my community, not my own needs."

"And I'm doing my job too." Heath stared at his hands, and Robin could feel the weight of whatever load the priest carried. The dismissal in his tone provided a note of finality, suggesting Robin had pushed him to the outer extreme of his comfort zone.

"Please give my highest regards and the Lord's blessing, to John and Will."

*

Has the Alfa blown up yet?:-)x

Catherine smiled as the text from John pinged on her new phone. The first smile she'd managed all day. She'd parked her bright red machine of gorgeousness next to Felix's filthy Land Rover in the castle carpark. It hadn't been a sensible choice, but she loved it.

Currently underneath it in my overalls. X

Are they dirty? X

Someone was feeling better. And flirty. An interesting development. She took a bite of her sandwich, giving him a minute or so of anticipation while he waited for her response. Could she be reading too much into those three words? Tiredness and a post-argument hangover dulled her enthusiasm, but she didn't want to deflate him. Her mood wasn't his fault.

Very dirty X

Three dots rippled for ages as he composed his reply. A lot of deleting going on.

I'd love to see it. Fancy meeting up? X

She had loads to do. She'd made herself busy; otherwise, she would disappear up her arse analysing every word of last night's argument. A bit of flirty texting seemed harmless, but she didn't feel like she'd be good company after her argument with Robin and a rubbish night's sleep. She hadn't heard from him, and hadn't contacted him either. Their argument hurt, and she still couldn't process the implications. She would never be to him what Erin had been - a deal-breaker. They needed space so not a great idea to fill her space with someone else.

But he'd only suggested a car ride. It would distract her, plus she did have work stuff to talk about with John.

Oh God, who was she kidding?

Ping.

It's ok if you're busy ... X

I'm at the castle, working. Why don't you come over? The owner's stocktaking in the shop, but he won't mind. x

Sounds perfect X

*

"You lied to me."

Alan Renshaw gulped and managed to pale beneath his spray tan. He was just about eye level with Robin, although he stood on his doorstep, and he seemed to shrink even smaller.

"Withholding information. Three years in prison."

"I didn't, I just ..."

"I want a list of anyone you saw Ursula Harrison screw over – in every sense of the word – and I'm not leaving without it. I don't care what deal you have with Clive Darwin either."

"It was all gossip."

"Fine. Give me the gossip."

Renshaw led him inside to a stark white kitchen accessorised with copper utensils and appliances, all shiny and matching. The morning newspaper lay out on the breakfast bar next to a large mug of tea and a half-eaten brunch.

"Checking yourself out?"

Renshaw snatched the paper and moved it away with his food. He pulled out a drawer and fished around for a pen while Robin waited, trying not to judge the dainty man with coiffed silver hair. What had Ursula seen in him? Had she found him easy to intimidate because of his slight physique, or had she observed how much Alan Renshaw wanted to please and needed to be liked.

"Where were you last Thursday night between 12pm and 5am Friday morning?"

Renshaw closed the drawer and removed the pen lid with brilliant-white teeth.

"I had the grandkids over while my daughter worked away. She's a sales rep. Beauty products."

Handy.

"So, this stuff with Ursula Harrison. I'm not bothered about the detail, what happens between consenting adults is your business, but I'm interested to know about anyone who didn't consent. This 'anonymous employee' who she threatened to fire and intimidated with her walking stick; let's start with him."

"David Cross." Renshaw wrote the name down, "I don't know where he is now. There was a guy who drove her around too. Ivor. Ivor the driver people used to call him."

"Surname?"

"Mc-something."

"Are you still in touch with anyone from Harrisons?"

"A few on Facebook."

"Any chat? Speculation maybe?"

"The picture posted the other day has done the rounds."

"And what's the general vibe?"

Renshaw pushed the pad across the worktop towards Robin. "People are surprised it took this long."

Robin hadn't expected anyone to be at the mortuary, so he was surprised to see Joseph Carling poring over a sheaf of paperwork, his customary bandanna holding back his hair. He looked up as the door opened.

"Someone else who can't get a day off." He stretched back in his chair and cracked his fingers.

"I wouldn't be able to rest."

Joseph tutted and shook his head. "Not good. How can I help?"

"The walking stick from the Harrison case. What did you find on it?"

"Traces of the victim's blood and skin. Dust and skin in the carvings on the handle. What are you thinking?"

"Are there any close-up images of it?"

Joseph woke up his PC and opened a library of evidence photographs. He scanned through them until he found the ones showing the two sections of the stick. Robin pointed at a close-up, where a tiny crack in the veneer was visible above the main break.

"See this breach in the surface? Could there be trace in there? Old blood or skin? Here too," he pointed to a tiny dent.

"It's a possibility."

"It was possibly used in previous assaults. Blood or skin tissue could've soaked into the slivers of exposed wood."

"Do you want to have it tested?"

"Yesterday please."

Joseph smirked. "I'll get straight on it. I know who I can call on. Lucinda Del Torres, she's a brilliant forensic pathologist. If anyone can extract you a comparative sample, she can. I'll give her a call." Joseph closed the document and spun around in his seat. "Fancy a beer? Unless you've had a better offer?"

He had no other offers, better or otherwise, and he hadn't heard from Catherine all day. She'd unearthed what she'd been searching for, but he regretted how brutal he'd been. He'd tried to ignore the emptiness lurking in his guts every time he mentally watched her leave his apartment again.

"Sounds good to me."

Joseph pushed away from the desk and jumped up. "Great. I'll just change out of my work clothes and call Lucinda. I'll be ten minutes."

Chapter Sixteen

Past lives

From the corner of the office, the security system beeped, indicating someone had used the keypad at the gates to enter the private section of the castle grounds. Catherine had sent John the code, and when she checked the monitor, his car came around the side of the building into the carpark behind. She flicked on the outdoor lights, pulled on her coat and went out to meet him.

He parked next to Catherine's new car and got out of his Audi, looking gorgeous and windswept in head-to-toe black. The wind swirled around them, moaning softly where it became trapped between the two walls at the corner of the courtyard. He took her arms and kissed her cheek, his lips breezing over her skin. He released her slowly and turned to look at her Alfa.

"That's a very sexy car."

"Do you want to come inside for a coffee or check out my instrument panel?"

He grinned back at her, his hair whipping around his face. "Coffee sounds great."

How did he make those three innocent words sound so seductive?

"You must love working here." They stepped over the enormous stone which marked the threshold and led into the first part of the kitchens. She liked his spice-wood scent which filled her nostrils as he drew close.

"I do, but I stop myself from just sitting around in a constant daydream. Every wall, stone and corner of this place has a story to tell. I'm never bored of feeling its spirit; it's captivating."

She finished musing and turned around. He'd stopped and was watching her with the strangest expression.

"You think I'm weird."

He shook his head. "You're lovely. Inside and out."

"You haven't seen me when I wake up."

He raised his eyebrows, and her stomach tripped.

"Coffee then." She tore her eyes away from the dirtiest little smile she'd ever seen. "There should be cups in here."

The kitchen was one of three rooms used by the castle owners and staff. In a newer part of the building, they'd formerly been storerooms built onto the main keep in the late 1700s. John sat in a chair by the fire while she rummaged around in the cupboards for cups and coffee.

"When's this place reopening?" he asked, "There seems to be loads of work going on."

"Next year, hopefully in time for the summer holidays. So far, it's all on track," she found what she needed and flipped on the kettle, "The main challenge is restoring the North tower, but they could reopen with it sectioned off. Kills the experience a bit though."

"Yeah, the views from the top are breath taking. It's an important part of the history here too."

Catherine turned back to him, waiting for the water to boil.

"How do you feel? You look great, but shouldn't you be resting?"

"I'm still sore, but the painkillers are helping."

Catherine made their coffee and nudged her head towards the door, "Come into the office. It's much nicer and warmer."

He followed her into the room next door with two magnificent Chesterfields and a large ironwork coffee table, where she'd spread all her work out. John cleared a space for her to put the cups then looked around in awe. Paintings of the castle covered the walls, some beautiful watercolours, others drawn by children. Above the fireplace hung a collection of black and white photographs of the building and an assortment of replica ornaments lined the mantlepiece.

"Felix, the owner, collects the paintings," said Catherine, "This is only part of his collection. There's more in the tearoom and the shop."

"Some of these are stunning," he wondered across to the wall opposite and studied a line drawing, an artist's impression of the castle as it would've looked to its contemporaries.

"I love this. It's beautifully accurate."

"I'm pleased you think so. I'm planning to use it on the cover of the tourist's guide."

"Another great choice." John took off his coat as she moved her work stuff out of the way. Had he seen the interview in the Post with Alan Renshaw? Clive had stuck to his word and kept John out of the article, but it was still an inflammatory piece. She was about to mention it when Felix Washington appeared at the door in a flap.

"Catherine, I need to shoot." He stopped when he saw John, "Oh, sorry, I didn't realise …"

"Felix, this is a friend of mine, John. He's a history teacher and has brilliant local history knowledge."

"Pleased to meet you, John." Felix shook John's hand. He wore his usual chaotic ensemble of mismatched casual wear, his greying hair flopping around his head, tangled with the glasses he'd shoved up like a headband.

"Do you mind locking up for me?" he asked, turning back to Catherine, "I've just had a call from my daughter. Theo's fallen off his bike, and she's taken him to A&E, but she's had to take the little one with her too. She needs help."

"No problem. I hope he's OK."

"It's not the first time. He thinks he's some sort of stunt rider. Sorry…," he fished around in his pockets for his car keys, "Good to meet you, John. A historian, eh? We should catch up another time."

"I'd love to."

Felix gave a funny little salute, disappeared, then reappeared.

"Oh, I've left a couple of bottles of my latest red batch in the kitchen for you to try. Let me know what you think." He saluted again as he left, and a few seconds later they saw him through the window as he headed for his muddy jeep at a loping jog.

"He seems nice." The old Chesterfield creaked as John sat beside her.

"He's lovely. Scatty and eccentric, but lovely. He makes home-brewed wine, artisan stuff. They're excellent too. Fierce, but lush."

"In the nicest possible way, he doesn't look like he can afford a pair of shoes, let alone fund this project."

"I thought the same, but he's wealthy. He just doesn't show it. His great grandfather bought this place after it had been empty and derelict for nearly twenty years. Well, other than the army using it for storage during the war. Heritage Trust agreed to partial funding, and it's been in the family ever since. They own a stately home and a converted water tower too."

"I'd never have guessed. He must trust you immensely."

"To lock up, you mean? Yeah, maybe, but I've known Felix for years. He's one of my dad's closest friends. Do you want to try his wine?"

"We're both driving," John replied. The dirty smile twitched on his lips again, "But we can do taxis."

She'd no idea where the impulsive invitation came from. Live in the moment, right?

"I'll find some glasses."

*

Clive didn't have to wait long at Barbara Rickman's house for her Mercedes to pull up on the drive. He'd left his days of hovering around waiting for a snippet behind and he hadn't missed it. His stomach grumbled, and his fingers were already numb.

As soon as she opened the door, he approached the car. She froze.

"You've a nerve coming here after the drivel you published today. Get off my property, or I'll call the police."

"If it's all drivel, why don't you put the record straight?"

Barbara grabbed her handbag off the back seat and slammed the car door. She fished around for her keys, dropped them, and snatched them up again before heading for the front door. She tried to ignore him, but she would retaliate. He counted down in his head. Three, two, one …

"I need you to bury this story, Clive." She turned away, jabbing her key into the lock. After a few failed attempts, she dropped her keys again, but this time she left them on the floor at her feet and rested her forehead against the door frame. Ah, she'd been drinking.

"Let me come in and make you some coffee."

"Just go away."

Clive picked up her keys from the doorstep and eased her out of the way. He expected an explosion, but she moved aside compliantly and allowed him to open the door. Inside, an alarm beeped. She pressed her fingers against an electronic touchpad inside the porch and it fell silent. A large grandfather clock ticked its chunky, rhythmic beat in the hallway.

Barbara headed off, snaking her way towards the kitchen, where a pale yellow light pooled in the gloom. How had she driven in such a state? Clive followed her, intrigued by where this might go. Hammered, Barbara Rickman could be gloriously entertaining.

She threw her handbag on the kitchen table and headed straight for the fridge. A bottle of wine banged down next to the bag. Two wine glasses from the cupboard followed.

"Looks like you're staying. So you might as well have a drink. And yes, I've had a few and driven home. Put it in your shit-rag of a paper and completely ruin me."

"No one is trying to ruin you."

"Really?" Her pitch rose. "Do you know how many calls I've had today about your little stories? Dozens. I lost count at twenty. That arse-licking little bastard Renshaw won't know what's hit him next week. If he enjoys a bit of humiliation, he'll be shooting his load all over his Gucci loafers on Monday. And he did Clive. He fucking loved it."

"So you knew about her little sessions?"

"I'm not blind, or stupid. Of course I did."

"And you had to clean the mess up afterwards. Figuratively, of course."

Barbara didn't respond. Clive took off his coat and scarf and pulled out a chair. What did he hope to achieve there? It had been about a story, but seeing Barbara in such a state had changed his perspective. He'd enjoyed their little clashes over the years, their verbal spars over politics or business. He'd first met her at a charity fundraiser, and they'd had a delicious debate over the ethics of using philanthropy as a PR tool. Her vulnerability reminded him of the stakes, the human cost of exposing truths.

"I take it Renshaw wasn't paid to keep his mouth shut. No cheeky little deal to keep the skeletons locked up? At least he waited until she was dead."

The death stare drifted off target, skewed by booze. She plonked down like a dropped sack and her chair teetered. Defeat didn't suit her.

"You can't protect Ursula forever." He poured them both a glass of a lush-smelling, straw-coloured Chablis. "You've done it for so long you don't even know you're doing it anymore."

"I'm protecting my family."

"No, you're not. You're dragging them through the lies with you."

Barbara took off her mint green jacket and loosened the pussy bow tied at her throat. She swirled wine around her glass and drank half of it in one go. A handsome woman. Not feminine or pretty, but handsome, and occasionally he'd glimpsed her softer side. The Barbara beneath the surface had light and shade, a hint of colour. She'd told him a story once about skinny dipping in the river as a teen, drinking cider with a bad boy, Fleetwood Mac on the radio. It stuck in his mind because he'd loved the detail and how she'd relaxed as she enjoyed the memory. Shame the rainbow didn't appear from the clouds more often.

"The prem baby unit want to rename their Harrison ward because of these stories. Like those boring bastards at the church. Happy to take our money but zero loyalty, zero gratitude. You'd think my mother was the murderer, not the victim. This is catastrophic for our reputation. My reputation. She's dead and I'm still cleaning up her mess."

"Was Ursula ever diagnosed?"

Barbara froze, glass halfway to her mouth. "What do you mean?"

It had been a punt, but a few hours of research might've paid off.

"What was it? Narcissistic Personality Disorder, Histrionic, or a bit of both?"

The elegant crystal wine glass slammed back to the table with such force Clive winced in anticipation of the smash. Barbara's glass survived the crash landing.

"How the hell do you know? I'll sue that fucking quack for breach of confidentiality …"

"It wasn't her doctor, calm down. It doesn't matter how I know anyway. I'm in the right ballpark, aren't I?"

"Who benefits from the truth? No one, except your tawdry readers. Bored housewives and burnt-out middle management looking for escapism and gossip. If I can't bury it Clive, what's left for me? A lifetime of lies, for what?"

"The more you sweep under the carpet, the higher it piles until you trip over it every way you turn."

Barbara stared at her glass. "I'm already tripping."

"Do you know who killed her?"

She burst out laughing like he'd cracked the best joke of the evening, the one he'd saved for the encore. "Take your pick!" She threw her arms open, physically implicating everyone, "How many people did she piss off? How many did she destroy, humiliate, or shame?"

"She didn't just piss someone off. She was murdered."

"Do you think I don't know that?!" she shrieked, her voice getting higher and more hysterical, "My own mother. This might be a story to you, scandal to sell your poxy papers, but this is my life, our reputation..."

"I know, you've said …"

"… and I've a son to protect. I won't let this ruin his chances of a successful life, I won't."

"Two sons."

Barbara sneered and refilled her glass.

"That ungrateful bastard is not my son."

"So you let Ursula bully and mentally abuse him?"

Barbara's slate-grey eyes bore into him, and for a few moments she didn't move. Did she even breathe? The possibility of John unleashing the family skeletons had turned her to stone. He didn't want to lean on Catherine to get more information from John. He respected her too much and she'd been through more than her share of shit. When he'd met John previously, he'd been too groggy to say much. He itched to speak to him again and get his perspective but he just couldn't think of a way or an excuse without upsetting her.

Barbara managed to inhale. "Is that what he's said?"

"No. But it's true, isn't it?"

"You need to leave."

In for a penny. No rainbows would be appearing today. If he couldn't get to John, maybe he could squeeze more out of her.

"Were you punishing John for not being your son? Or because his father dared to die?"

"What?! How is any of this relevant to your readers? Go and work for a gossip mag if this is what appeals to you these days. I thought you had integrity."

"Had Ursula started abusing William too?"

Barbara shot to her feet, knocking her chair over with the sudden velocity. She threw her wine glass at Clive, and he ducked out of the way as the wine arced through the air. The glass whizzed past his head, smashing into the fridge behind him.

"Get out of my house!" she thundered, visibly shaking with emotion.

Clive gave it a moment and considered pushing her further. But she'd reached her tipping point. Years of experience had taught him once someone hit their peak, little of use came out afterwards.

He picked up his scarf and coat and headed for the door.

*

"This is good." John swished the cherry red wine around his plastic champagne flute, "In this cut crystal goblet you can see it has great legs."

Catherine laughed. "Don't take the piss out of my fine tableware. It's all I can find."

John shuddered as a flush of happiness rippled through his body. All the stress of the last few days, even the pain from his bruises, were washed away by the heady infusion of wine and bliss. He wanted to drink her in along with the curious concoction they were sipping, and he never wanted to stop.

"Can we look around? Take our drinks into the great hall, maybe?" He wanted to lose as much of the modernity as possible and immerse in the spirit of the ancient building.

"Great idea." she reached for her coat and the wine bottle. "It's chilly in there," she added by way of explanation, "Most of the rooms have heating now but the hall doesn't. I like it though. It makes it easier to imagine living in this place."

"Shame we can't light a fire in the hearth."

"Yeah, I'd love to, but we'd get smoked out. I think the stacks are blocked off."

John followed her out of the office into the dark corridor which connected the outer extension with the main keep. She stopped abruptly.

"One sec." She handed him the bottle of wine and disappeared back towards the staff rooms. She rummaged around, then returned with a box and a lighter.

"Candles," she said, with a breath-taking smile, which flashed as brightly in her green eyes as it did on her lips, "I'm not sure if the electric is working."

They continued along the corridor. It could've been underground, so quiet and womblike. As they transitioned from the newer part of the building to the old one, the only light came from a couple of wall sconces, making the shadows close in further. More pleasure tingled through his core. They'd walked back in time.

"Can you smell the difference?" she asked as they reached an inner hallway, "Like the years ooze from the walls." A stone staircase snaked upwards into pitch-black on one side and an archway on the other side led off into a dim antechamber. John took a deep breath and smelled it too. Although his lungs also filled with a delicate floral scent she'd left in her wake. He tingled with sensory overload.

"I feel such an emotional attachment to this place, always have."

"Maybe you've been here in another life."

"I'm sure of it."

The air became cooler as they entered the great hall. Catherine put down her wine glass and lit two large candles. She took them over to the colossal hearth at the centre of the room and settled them on the stone. She'd two more tucked into her pockets. With all four lit, a soft glow pooled around her and lapped at the shadows beyond. John took the wine and glasses over and sat on a small wooden bench by the hearth.

"Intriguing what you said about being here before."

"Do you think I'm batshit?"

John laughed, "If you are then so am I."

She mulled it over.

"I'm so at home here, and I'm oddly protective of it. Like I am about my Gran's house. My house."

"It could be a past life connection, or you're wonderfully in tune with history. For most people, the past has gone. It doesn't exist anymore. But others have a greater sensitivity to the legacy of what's gone before. Does that make sense?"

"Totally. Maybe that's why you feel an affinity with Henry Stanton."

"I know it's strange, but yes. I sense a connection with him I can't explain."

John refilled their glasses, high on the red wine fuzz and the conversation.

"Did you see the Post today?" Catherine blindsided him with a switch of subject. He'd read the Post, and it had flooded his head with memories he preferred not to revisit. Especially now. He didn't want his past to ruin this moment.

"You mean the article about Harrison Engineering? Yeah, I read it. Rich saw it online."

She waited for more but sensed his reticence.

"Is it all true?"

"It skimmed the surface of truth, yes. I'm not sure what Alan Renshaw hoped to gain by doing the interview. Attention, or catharsis. He was always a needy character."

"I interviewed him with Clive, the editor."

An assault of overwhelming emotions battered him at once, and his next few breaths stuck in his throat. She'd poked into his past, knew what he'd been subjected to. Old shame crawled over his skin.

"You know I was there." Her cheeks flushed as she stared into her wine. "I thought you'd left the paper."

"It's sucking me back."

"And now they can run more embarrassing stories about my dysfunctional stepfamily and me."

"No, that's not why I'm here." She fired up with sudden ferocity, and he liked that she had a fiery side.

"You could've asked me."

"Not really a subject you bring up with someone you've just met. Especially when you like them."

Encouraging, but he still felt deceived. "You've told me about interview for a reason. Otherwise, why mention it? What do you want to ask?"

"Forget it. I didn't mean to upset you. I just wanted you to know, to be honest with you."

"To you they might be intriguing stories, but they're my bad memories, Catherine. I prefer to keep them locked away. But I like you too, so it's fine if you want to ask me about it."

It wasn't fine. Talking about Ursula forcing him to watch her fucking about with people was the diametrical opposite of fine. But he wanted to trust her, which for him meant giving himself to her. He would share his soul if it brought her closer.

"I'd never disclose anything you say to me. I'm not that type of reporter. Once you break trust you're ruined, personally and professionally. You were right before; I'd left it behind. I was lured back because it made me feel like I belonged again."

Her sincerity melted away his anger. The admission had taken balls. John took a mouthful of wine and let the alcohol kick in.

"I told Clive not to include any mention of you."

Touching that she'd defended him when including the detail would've exploded the story. Kinky shit at the office was one thing but adding kids into the mix gave the report a different, darker context. John wanted to talk about other experiences with her, to chat to her all night and find out what gave her joy, what made her angry and what made her laugh.

"Ursula physically and mentally abused me. It began just after my dad died, from me being ten to around thirteen. Well, the physical stopped around then, but the mental continued until I left to go to Uni. Then she started on Will. Who was eight."

"Oh my God, John, I'm so sorry."

"We can talk about it if you want to. It might do me good. But please not tonight. I don't want to ruin this." John took his wine and sat beside her. He needed to be closer. Silence wrapped around them, and he sensed she'd drifted away.

"This smell reminds me of my dad. He used to brew wine too."

"It must've been tough to lose your parents so young."

"People always comment on how much Will and I resemble my dad, but unless I have a photograph, I can't remember what he looked like or sounded like. I loved him so much and he's now a faded memory." He took another drink. "If I allow myself, I can get consumed with anger, just for him even meeting Barbara. And

190

it kills my memories." He shook away the shadows. "Sorry. I didn't want to meet you today to offload. I should shut up."

What was he doing? He'd slipped into an indulgent reverie that sucked him down like quicksand. It took some effort to drag himself out of the mental swamp.

"Enough about me." He'd extinguished her light, and he wanted it back. "Tell me about you. I want to know a secret you've never told another living soul."

"Wow, what a challenge, OK ...." For a few seconds, only the sound of the wind swirling around the old walls trying to find a way, in broke the silence. "I lost my virginity to my piano teacher, a neighbour on our street. He later became the keyboard player in a band. A huge band."

John raised his eyebrows. "I need details."

Catherine grinned and topped up their glasses.

"We're going to need more wine too. OK, he was nineteen, I was fifteen. The band had just formed, and he taught to make extra cash. I fell hopelessly in love with him. He was so cool and interesting, and he had the most gorgeous hands. Anyway, I've never told anyone because it was completely consensual, and I've no desire to destroy his career. It was Nick Ray from Fibre."

"No way! I have three of their albums."

Catherine's laughter had returned to her eyes. "Now you. Spill."

"I don't know if I can compete with that."

John had plenty of options. He wasn't consciously secretive, but he'd had few people in his life who he'd been close to or trusted enough to share himself with.

"This might be full-on, so feel free to vomit or smack me in the face. Pulling you out of your car was the most precious moment of my entire life." He leant towards her to brush a feathery kiss across her lips then pulled away, searching for any sign of protest. She offered none. Satisfied, he leaned in and kissed her again. This time the hesitancy was gone, and the flush of desire increased the hammering in his chest. Her vitality warmed him, igniting something he'd never truly experienced before. It radiated from his core.

Happiness.

He paused again, his hand deep in her thick hair, cupping her head. "You can stop me any time you choose."

Chapter Seventeen

Old shame

"Robin. Wake up!"

Robin dragged himself into consciousness, fighting aside the heavy clutches of sleep. Joseph, bare-chested and tattooed, frowned at him like an irate dad whose teenager had slept in past lunchtime. It was 9.15am. Sunday.

"Lucinda rang me."

"Huh?"

"Lucinda, my friend from the lab. The stick."

Joseph delivered all of this like Robin was a complete dick for not already knowing what he was on about.

"OK …"

"She's at the lab. Gave me a right earful for getting her out on a Sunday, but get this; she's identified two samples which don't match the victim."

Robin sat up; sleep gone.

"They don't match anyone on file either, so don't get too giddy, but there's trace from two people other than Ursula Harrison on her walking stick."

"It's been used in a previous assault."

"Looks that way. I'll make some coffee."

Joseph ambled off to make coffee, like he'd lived in Robin's flat for years. They'd had a few beers the night before, then crashed back at Robin's with a takeaway. They'd talked into the early hours, and Robin had been surprised by how much he enjoyed Joseph's company and outlook on life. He'd talked to him about Catherine, and Joseph had challenged him, brutally at times. Robin felt battered, but the honesty had done him good. He hadn't appreciated how much baggage he'd stashed away until Joseph had sorted through it all.

He pulled on sweatpants and a t-shirt and found Joseph happily mooching around his kitchen making breakfast. Robin pulled out a barstool. No point interrupting him when he was in flow.

"Thanks for letting me offload last night."

"No problem." Joseph cracked eggs into a jug Robin had forgotten he owned. "I had a good night. Hope I didn't offend you."

"Not at all. You should be a coach or a shrink. You were savage, but it did me good."

"Glad to help. What are you going to do about Catherine?"

"I need to be honest and fair with her. She deserves that, and I won't let her slip away from me. She means too much. The tough talk helped."

"I spend my days around dead people, so sometimes I overcompensate when I'm with the living, and you can't shut me up. Although people usually ask the same questions. How can you deal with corpses? I once had a guy ask me if I'd been tempted to touch a dead girl's breasts."

"Really?"

"It's why I'd rather deal with the dead than the living. People are fucked up. You must see it daily."

"You see the good side of humanity too, but yeah, when you see what people do to each other, you question how we've managed to exist as a race."

"What's your hunch on Ursula Harrison?"

Robin mulled it over.

"Let me ask you the same question. I value your opinion. You've spent time with her; what did she tell you?"

"I love how you ask questions like that." Joseph high fived him without taking his eyes off his scrambled eggs, "Best-preserved eighty-year-old I've ever seen, and all natural too. No sign of any work. Someone robbed her of another twenty years, I reckon. Beauty's a powerful weapon. It gives you confidence. An edge. Think about her bedroom. In her head, Ursula Harrison didn't stop being the vibrant, powerful woman she'd been throughout her adult life. Whoever took it from her understood its significance. And she had an impeccable liver."

"Helpful. Thanks."

Joseph grinned. "Occasionally in my profession, I come across someone who makes me uncomfortable. Children. Try performing an autopsy on a baby or child, and I challenge any medical practitioner who says that isn't tough. Crash victims, battered women, a guy with chunks bitten out of his cock – he was difficult. Ursula Harrison made me feel like I shouldn't be touching her. Figure that out."

"She got me too."

Joseph stopped cooking and turned around.

"I almost covered up her breast when me and Jack found her. I had this overwhelming urge to preserve her dignity but ... I don't know. Did she control me?"

"Wow."

"I know."

Joseph put two plates of eggs on the breakfast bar and sat opposite Robin. It smelled delicious, but he'd lost his appetite.

*

Pale daylight filtered through the castle's office window, and Catherine stirred from sleep, aware she lay snuggled on the sofa in another man's arms. At least she was clothed. She shifted, and a vicious red wine headache clanged in her skull, even at such a slight movement. John's arms remained around her, holding her against his chest as he slept beneath a dusty smelling throwover they'd found, and their coats. He looked so peaceful, beautiful even, with long lashes and sculptured cheekbones most women would die for. What had she done? Yes, she found him attractive and yes, she enjoyed his company. But getting pissed with him and spending the night at the castle hadn't been her agenda. John brought spontaneity sprinkled with intrigue, which was both heady and refreshing. But she also sensed fragility beneath the surface. Damaged and fixed but not fully healed.

"I can feel you looking at me," he murmured, eyes still closed. A smile twitched on his lips, and he pulled her in closer, "What are you thinking?"

"I'm thinking I don't want to hurt you."

"Then don't." John rested his cheek on her hair. He inhaled deeply like he could absorb her essence.

"I feel bad about last night. I enjoyed it, don't get me wrong. I love being with you …"

"Then don't feel bad." He shifted and looked at her directly. "Did you enjoy me?"

No one had ever asked her that before, and despite the headache and the shadow of regret, it turned her on. He offered himself to her, submissive but assertive at the same time.

"Yes."

"Good. I'm yours if you want me."

Twang. Another ripple of arousal. And yes, she did want him, but at the same time, she knew she shouldn't. Not with ambiguity surrounding Robin and how they'd parted on Friday night. She'd never played around, and she didn't want to start now. How easy it had been last night after a bottle of wine.

"Are you expecting anyone here today?"

"No. Felix never comes in on Sundays and the contractors don't do weekends."

"Do you need to be anywhere other than here?"

"Starbucks?"

John smiled. "Shall I find coffee?"

"And paracetamol."

"Snowflake," he said, and he kissed her forehead before easing out from beneath her. His bare feet hit the stone floor and he winced through his teeth, jerking his legs back up.

"Wow, that's cold."

"Snowflake."

"Touché."

"Where are your shoes?"

"God knows."

John put his feet down again and inhaled through gritted teeth as he headed for the door. She lay back into the Chesterfield. Don't overthink. Simon always told her to live in the moment, and in this moment, she was enjoying the deviation from normality, the unpredictable fun and the company of this man. Fuck the world for a while.

She fished around for her phone in her bag and checked the home screen. A message from Clive received the night before. So much for fucking the world.

David Cross – dead end. Refused to talk. Admitted he'd signed a non-disclosure agreement as part of his voluntary redundancy package. Scared he'll get sued.

She tossed the phone back into her bag, too hung over and tired to think about the implications. Clive would have to wait until she felt sensible again.

She must have drifted off to sleep again because John knelt by the sofa drinking his coffee when she woke. He gave the other cup to her, and she moved up, making space for him to join her. He didn't. He sat back on his heels and remained on his knees, looking at her with undisguised affection.

"You said the other day I hadn't seen you when you wake, and now I have. You're radiant, Catherine."

"I think you're still drunk."

"You don't see what I see." John drank his coffee and seemed lost in his thoughts. "You know last night, when I didn't want to talk about my childhood?"

"I'm sorry for prying …"

"No, I want to tell you. I trust you, and it's a part of me, although I've tried for years to deny it exists."

She waited for him to assemble his thoughts, and sensed his struggle. He stared into his mug, his face hidden by his hair. He glanced up, then bowed his head again, and she squirmed at his pain.

"Ursula liked to humiliate people. Men and boys mostly, but not exclusively. I'm not talking about an occasional incident either or a flimsy whim. It was pathological. She didn't just enjoy it; she needed it to survive. As important to her as breathing.

"Most people like her are satisfied to keep their kinks in the bedroom. I mean, it's not unheard of, is it? A lot of people like kinky stuff and when it's consensual, erotic, no one cares. But Ursula didn't restrict her activities to consenting adults. She found her kicks in darker places, with people who didn't consent to be degraded by her, including me. And Will."

Catherine stared at him, both horrified and saddened. She took his arm to pull him to his feet, but he shook his head.

"Let me stay here."

"Don't punish yourself, John. Her behaviour wasn't your fault."

"I know. I just …please. I need to get this out."

She couldn't read his expression. Doubt? A desire to trust, but still unsure. Hard to find words to bridge the gap. She couldn't force him to trust her.

"Crying drove her insane because she didn't feel empathy. She would accuse me of being insecure and jealous, or oversensitive. She would deny saying or doing something to make me look like a liar or say something was a joke I was too stupid to get. I was a greedy pig if I wanted a snack, thick if I struggled with homework, filthy when I showered daily. I was the problem, the one who needed help, according to her."

"Classic gaslighting."

"Yes. I see that now. She was clinically narcissistic, diagnosed by a Harley Street shrink who she consulted over the loss of her first child. She couldn't grieve because she couldn't feel, and he identified deeper issues. Anyway, I found out about that later. The effect of the constant criticism accumulated until I felt so worthless, I tried to make myself die. Through willpower alone. Then I felt selfish because I knew my dad would want me to protect Will. And I did, all the time. I covered for him, took the blame. I was forever on some form of punishment." He smiled, and his features softened. "It's amazing how much yoghurt a twelve-year-old smears on the carpet."

"Did you speak to anyone about her?"

"No, because she repeatedly told me how much I deserved it, that she was trying to help me be a better person because I was too foolish, too clumsy, or just a little bastard who everyone despised. She insisted I was responsible for my dad's death, brainwashed me. I believed her."

"What about Bobby?"

"I told him parts of it. I was too ashamed to tell him everything, although I'm sure he saw enough to reach his own conclusions."

Catherine's fought prickling tears as she listened to him. He looked so young and vulnerable, so lost. "Do you still believe her?"

"Mostly no. When life's good, I can function normally, but when I'm stressed, the conditioning kicks back in again, I weaken and my sense of self drifts away. It's hard to explain."

"You should be proud of how you've come through it all John, and of the person you are now. You're stronger than you think."

"That means a lot, thank you."

"Who do you think killed her?"

John stared into his cup for so long Catherine wasn't sure if he'd heard her, and with each passing second, she became more convinced he knew, regardless of his answer. Eventually he shook his head.

"She damaged people, so who knows?"

"She was nailed her to her bed. Crucified."

He stared at her, his expression frozen. "How do you know? Oh, of course. Robin." He rubbed at his eyes. "Well, she tried to do it to me once. It's the least she deserved."

"Seriously?"

"Really fucking seriously!" John rose on his knees, and his sudden vehemence surprised her, "Don't feel sorry for her."

"But it's a horrific way to die..."

"Let me ask you this: if Ursula forced your child to rub deep heat into his penis because she found a lads mag in his bedroom, would it be justified?"

"I'm not saying what she did wasn't horrendous ..."

"If someone hurt your child, what would your tipping point be? Would it be justified then?"

"I'm not a mum, so I don't know. In my heart yes, I could justify it, but my head still says it's wrong."

John curled into the corner of the huge Chesterfield. She'd had a glimpse of what John the child had been like, and she put her hand on his knee, unsure of how to console him, wanting to hug him but sensing he wanted space. She had no experience of the abuse he'd described and struggled to find words that weren't meaningless platitudes.

"You're a good person. You have morals and integrity." He covered her hand with his and squeezed her fingers. "I grew up with two women with a veneer. An exterior layer of respectability. But all the charitable donations and philanthropy don't cancel out the wrongs."

"Is Barbara the same?"

"She has elements of it. I don't like Barbara, but I can respect how she took me on when my dad died. If you want to write about Harrisons, I'll give you what I know. As long as you keep Will and me out of it."

Tempting. But it was half a story without the personal side. "It could damage Harrisons and be disastrous for Barbara. Which affects Will, and you."

"Dad made sure we're covered. And I don't care about Harrisons. I'm grateful Barbara provided a home for me, but she was culpable for allowing it to continue."

"Wasn't she a victim too?"

He looked at her like she'd suddenly started speaking a different language.

"I've honestly never thought of her in that way." John released her hand and rubbed his face. He pushed back his hair and the memories lingering in the shadows. "I'm sorry for offloading all of this onto you. I didn't want you to think I was avoiding your question from last night, and you deserve to know what you're dealing with. If you want to kick me out can you help me find my shoes first, please?"

Catherine leant in closer and whispered a kiss across his lips. "I'm not kicking you anywhere."

*

Jamie and Marcia Clarke hid from view at the bottom of Brock House's overgrown dump of a garden. They'd had to fight through bushes to find a private spot and an effective smokescreen. Jamie watched Marcia drag on her cigarette like it provided critical life support. The grey joggers and pink jumper were strange, but they gave her a cute vulnerability and made a change from her usual grunge. The shadows had gone from under her eyes, and her skin looked fresher and clear.

He steeled himself with a lungful of nicotine. "I got arrested a few days back."

Marcia froze. "What? Why?"

"I gave your Mr Rickman a kicking."

"You did what?!" she shrieked, then glanced towards the house, "Why? He's done nothing wrong."

"I know. But after I saw you, I was angry. I suppose I took it out on him."

"I can't believe it. What did you do?"

"Jumped him on his doorstep and laid into him. I was high on anger, like in a trance. I must have knocked him out because he wasn't moving. I got out of there and rang 999, pretended I was a neighbour."

"Fucking hell." Marcia's tone had gravity because for once she held the moral high ground. She rolled her cigarette. "I can't believe you did that because of me."

Getting taken into care had changed her already. Chilled her out, scared the attitude out of her. She looked worried now, fighting back tears.

"Hey, I'll be OK. I might speak to him, say sorry. He could have a word with the police."

"Don't go near him again Jamie, I mean it."

"But he might help. He told the police he didn't see who attacked him, but he must have known." Another fortifying drag. "And I vandalised his flashy new car."

"Oh for fucks sake ..."

"I was angry. I know it was stupid."

"I thought I was the stupid one ..."

They smoked in silence. Jamie shifted his tree trunk seat, cold in his t-shirt and thin leather jacket. What a mess. Marcia was stuck in this place for God knows how long, and he faced a potential prison sentence. How could he look out for her if he was inside? Then again, maybe she'd be better off away from him and their dad. These people could guide her back onto the right tracks and get her through her GCSEs.

"The police asked me about Mr Rickman's grandma too. She died last week, and they thought there was a link. They asked me all sorts of stuff about some weed called helmlick, did I know anyone called Ursula, even what size shoes did I wear. They sounded desperate."

"Ursula. That's a totally posh name."

"Yeah, like I'd know anyone called Ursula."

"And its hemlock, you dick."

"Huh?"

"It's poisonous."

He stared at her. "How the hell do you know?"

"Did it in school. This guy in olden times was forced to take it. He died a horrible death where he kind of knew what was happening and could feel it, but he couldn't move or speak."

"You learn some weird shit at school."

"Torture; that's sick! There were boots with spikes in and these tables that stretched you until your arms and legs popped out. Made me feel bad about pulling the legs off daddy long legs …"

He hunched into his coat as he listened to Marcia babbling on. He tuned out most of her stories about school. He wasn't arsed that suchabody had dumped suchabody by text and someone had thrown up cider into their school bag. Actually, he didn't mind the cider story …

Jamie sat up suddenly as Marcia waffled on about dunking witches. "What lesson was it, where you learned about this hemlock stuff?"

Marcia scowled at the interruption. "History. Why?"

"Mr Rickman taught you about hemlock?"

"Err yeah." Marcia rolled her eyes at him. "Why?"

"It's weird. The police mentioned it when they talked about his grandma's murder."

Marcia froze. A car roared past, heavy revving a souped-up engine. Jamie had the strangest feeling, like a roadie had plugged his heart into an amplifier and cranked up the bass.

"Oh my god, you think he did it. Why would he kill his own grandma Jamie?"

"I don't know, do I?"

"And he's a nice guy. Nice guys don't go around battering old ladies. Oh shit, maybe she made him sick. I read it in 'Real People' magazine. This woman did horrible stuff to her kid, so she could take him to hospital all the time and get loads of attention. There's a word for it, munch something …"

"I need to speak to DI Scott."

"Behave," Marcia laughed, "Do you think you're a hotshot detective now? You're obsessed with him."

"That's rich."

Marcia rolled her eyes again, "Well, I'm not anymore. Loads of people learn history and know about poisons and stuff. And you can Google." She shuffled around to get comfortable on her tree stump. "They'll piss themselves at you."

She had a point; they would laugh at him. But what if he was right? Motive. They always talked about motive. He dug out his phone and Googled it.

"You're not ringing the police, are you?"

"No, I'm Googling." He scrolled through the answers. "What makes someone do something?"

"What?"

"Motive."

"Jamie, this is stupid."

He put his phone away. What had been his 'motive' for attacking John? He'd been angry. Defending his sister, getting justice for what had happened to her. Revenge. Great motive. Or money. Psychos kill people because they enjoy the power, or it turns them on.

"Well?" Marcia's tone suggested he was a dumb slug.

"None of it feels right."

"Because it's stupid. If you want to play being a detective, you should stick to working out how to keep yourself out of prison."

*

"You look like shit."

"Just remind me why I like you Clive."

Clive grinned and stepped aside so his enormous Irish wolf hound, Storm, could give Catherine a much kinder greeting. He licked her face then stuck his head in her bag, hunting for the treat she always brought him. He came out with a squeaky penguin and bounded back inside the house, thwacking everything in his path with his tail. A tall vase holding a collection of umbrellas teetered in his wake. Clive steadied it with his leg. A well-practiced manoeuvre.

"I'm sure you choose the noisiest toy you can find."

"Of course I do. I love to piss you off."

Clive's upside-down town house paid homage to wood and leather. He led her into his wood panelled office and shoved Storm off the sofa. She sank into the squishy leather and Storm squeezed back in next to her. He plonked his penguin on her lap and continued chewing its beak.

"So, where the fuck have you been?" Clive asked, feeding a pod into his coffee machine, "The little ticks on my message didn't go blue until this morning. Someone had a late night?"

"No comment."

"Rickman?"

She stroked Storm's scruffy head. How much did she want to tell Clive? John had shared private, painful memories and she wouldn't betray his trust. The weight of his burden rested on her shoulders now too.

"It wasn't what you think."

Clive put her coffee on the table then eased himself into the warm embrace of his office chair, which wouldn't have been out of place on the Starship Enterprise. Padding, armrests, heated seat, side supports.

He sipped his drink and gave her some silent scrutiny. "I thought you'd have a spring in your step once you'd spent time with him, but you don't. Was he not what you expected or are you feeling guilty?"

"I don't know." She twirled Storm's floppy fringe around her fingers, trying to make sense of her feelings. "He's intense. Intriguing. Complex." She wafted away the subject with a dismissive wave. "Anyway, I didn't come round to talk about John. I've been digging. Barbara Rickman used to be Head of HR. She introduced the non-disclosure agreements for all new joiners and changed the existing employee contracts. She was trying to prevent anyone whistleblowing."

"NDAs can't prevent whistleblowing."

"Does the average employee know that though? If you've signed an agreement, potentially facing legal action if you breach it, do you take the risk or keep shtum? Plus, Harrisons is a major charity supporter. Their reputation is untarnished, so arguably the strategy worked. What did Barbara Rickman want to hide?"

"Let's get some perspective. We're talking about a £25M turnover business; not a global conglomerate. Barbara's worth a few million, more now Ursula's gone, but she runs an engineering company not a cartel. The nationals have moved on, and why? Because there's nothing there."

For as long as she'd known him, Clive had always considered the Post as equal to national news providers. Yes, they covered local issues, but he'd striven for a quality of editorial not usually seen in regional papers. A national story had unfolded on their doorstep and a few days ago he'd been pumped, excited even, by the opportunity to show the Post competing with the big boys.

"I don't get how you can't see it. Off the record: the police attended an incident at John's last week. John and Barbara had an argument and she punched him."

Clive laughed. "She's gutsy. But if she'd meant to hurt him, he wouldn't have been entertaining you last night. She's extremely resourceful."

Catherine stared at him, not sure what to make of his reaction. He took off his jumper and rolled up the sleeves of his gecko and palm tree shirt. She was still conflicted about John's offer to give her more on Harrisons. Uncovering the incidents at Harrisons might give oppressed employees a voice, but were they happier maintaining their silence, and was it her right to make the decision for them? There was no pleasure in exposing the truth if it brought people a world of pain or embarrassment. Ethically it didn't sit comfortably either. Tell the truth impartially, minimise harm – that was the code. Well, she wasn't impartial. But Clive was. She'd thought he might pick up the scent and go hunting, but maybe he'd lost his hunger.

"Look, I've dug around Harrisons too," he said, "All I've found is an affair in the marketing department, some expenses fraud and a possible dispute with over-invoicing a client. Jack shit in other words. No one's arsed about that stuff."

"What's their advertising spend these days?"

He froze, cup midway to his lips. The muscles in his jaw tightened. "It's an editorial decision not a commercial one."

"What decision?"

"How about you lean on your new fuckbuddy and find something more exciting than Amazon reviews."

"Right, I'm off." Catherine eased Storm from her lap. She rammed her arms into her coat sleeves then picked up her bag. "Do what you want. I only popped round to borrow a book."

He swept his hand towards his bookcase, eyebrows raised. She found the one she wanted and dropped it into her bag.

"Curious choice, What's the connection?"

"Why does there have to be a connection? I had a weird dream, OK? Black crosses, purple skies." A total lie but she wouldn't tell him why she really wanted it.

Clive raised his hands in silent self-defence.

"And he's not my fuckbuddy. Grow the fuck up."

Chapter Eighteen

Skeletons

"What the hell did you do?"

The day had begun so well. Relaxed breakfast, cooked by someone else, which was always a winner, followed by an excellent ninety-minute session at the dojo. He'd missed training over the last few days, and it had been invigorating to release all the pent-up energy. It had an instant effect on his mood and clarity.

However, it all disintegrated in the space of one furious phone call from Barbara Rickman, which had ended the fantasy of having time off. Robin glared at Vic, demanding an answer, which he already sensed would come bubble-wrapped in bullshit.

"I thought I could get useful info out of Will, and you did ask me to go digging."

"You questioned a minor without a parent present, without the proper authority. Barbara Rickman is threatening action. I've had to repeatedly apologise and pretty much beg her not to issue a complaint. I don't do begging!"

"Sorry Guv."

"Not good enough. William Rickman needs careful handling, and you've gone steaming in like the FBI on crack."

"I wanted to come back with a breakthrough."

"No Vic, you wanted to come back fist-pumping, with the case solved. In a way I don't blame you, I know you're eager to impress, but we still have to proceed in the right way. And while you're in the spotlight; tell me what happened between you and Ursula Harrison three years ago."

Vic's face faded from colour to mono in seconds. Jack leant forward from his perch on the windowsill

"What are you talking about?"

Robin kept his eyes on Vic, "Vic knows."

Vic couldn't maintain eye contact. Denial might have been an option, but whatever story he concocted would be belied by the guilt his entire body was projecting.

"It only happened a couple of times."

"Once is too many."

"I was skint, OK?" He glanced up. "My flatmate met a girl and moved out. I was trying to pay the rent on my own with a maxed-out credit card and a student loan."

"How much did you take from her?" asked Jack.

"I don't know. A grand, maybe a bit more."

"If this gets out …"

"No one knows. I was careful." He gave Jack a plaintive glance, desperate for an ally.

"What did she ask you to do?"

Vic shook his head, staring at his immaculate nails. "Does it matter?"

It probably didn't matter. A police officer had taken cash from an elderly woman who might be seen as vulnerable. The detail was irrelevant.

But Robin had a perverse curiosity. It took balls from Ursula to proposition a young copper. How did you get from talking about ornaments mysteriously moving to offering money for kinky shit? Robin gave Vic some silence, and Jack remained quiet, perhaps curious too.

"She liked the uniform. She wore my jacket and cuffed me to the door. Then she wanked me off."

"Jesus Vic …" Jack sagged back against the window frame.

"One time, she got me to strip and kneel in front of her – cuffed again - and she used her vibrator, telling me I was a dirty copper while she got off …"

"OK, I've heard enough." Jack smacked his palms against his thighs to underline the finality. "What do we do about this?" he asked Robin.

Ursula and Vic had both been consenting adults who'd got what they wanted from the deal. There had been no complaint from Ursula, and although Vic was mortified by recounting the detail, Robin suspected he'd found it hot too.

"I think we keep this between us. But you should've told me Vic. I can't stand lies, and by omission, you lied to me."

"Sorry, Gov. I did find useful info on the Rickman brothers."

"Which was what I wanted." Robin sighed. "Sit down. Tell me what you have."

Vic sat, his face still dusty grey. He flipped through his notes, his hands shaky. Robin bit back his irritation. It was already 10pm and they'd been working long hours without a proper day off for over a week. Fatigue was beginning to show.

"I talked to William's form teacher, Ray Bevan. Very complimentary about William. He described him as above average academically, a little shy but an exemplary student with enormous potential. However, he's been concerned on occasion about the injuries William picked up in his kickboxing classes.

"Now it gets interesting. Harry Quinn runs William's kickboxing class. After he saw unusual marks on his arms in the changing rooms, he pulled William to one side. Oh, he was quick to emphasise he doesn't make a habit of looking at teenage boys, and he checks out. He's ex-military. Served in Afghanistan. Anyway, William didn't want to talk about it, so Quinn phoned Barbara Rickman and she brushed it off, saying she'd seen William and his friend 'pretend fencing' in the garden with bamboo canes. She promised to speak to her son and thanked him for his concern. Quinn figured he'd done what he could. Afterwards, William left in his kit rather than showering and changing at the club."

Robin leant forward. A tingle of excitement prickled over his skin. This sounded like more than a knuckle rap with her stick. Barbara had covered for her, allowed her to beat her son.

"She was afraid of falling out with her mother and losing her inheritance, and I bet Ursula hit Barbara when she was growing up." Robin imagined her taking it with calm defiance. "She thinks it didn't do her any harm, so she turned a blind eye when it happened to her son. We need to match the samples Joseph's lab found on the stick to William, and I want to speak to this young man."

"He'll deny any beatings," said Vic, "I didn't get long with him before Barbara came steaming over, but he's smart."

"I'd expect whoever murdered Ursula Harrison to be smart."

"Barbara will be expecting a visit now." Jack glared at Vic. "We've given her time to think. And William "

"True, but we can check medical records. We might get lucky. People around William have spotted these injuries. Maybe he confided in a friend about his home life. Or his brother."

Robin relished the prospect of questioning John again. Nice or not, he was a slippery fucker who'd been lying, or withholding information, from the start.

"It's late. I'll go and apologise to Barbra Rickman tomorrow, do the whole PR piece and speak to William. You dropped a bollock Vic, but there's some good work here. Let's get back on this in the morning."

"Sorry Guv." Vic left Robin's office at speed, clearly glad to escape the bollocking.

Jack pushed away from the windowsill. "Are you getting off?" he asked Robin.

"Not yet. I want to check a couple of things first."

"Need help?"

"No thanks, I want to go back over what we have and see if it plays with William Rickman as a suspect. I want to make sure our case is rock-solid. After what's happened with Trent and now with Vic cocking up, I don't want any more slips."

"I'll get a few hours and be back for 6am. I have your back, you know."

Robin sank back into his chair. Jack's words were laden with emotion, and although Jack was always supportive, he it touched him to hear him express it. He was defensive of his team, so why did he find it so difficult to ask for, and accept, support from other people?

"I know, thanks Jack."

Jack pulled out the chair Vic had vacated and plonked down. "I know how much you take on board, and I don't want you to think you're on your own getting shafted by Collins and taking one for the team."

"Are you saying you want a shafting?"

"Always open to new experiences."

"For Christ's sake don't tell me Ursula had a go on you too."

"No, I missed out there." Jack grimaced and stared through the window across the office. "I didn't know about Vic."

"Good. Looks like no one else does either."

"Professional Standards would go to town on him."

"Well, unless he confesses, there's no proof it ever happened."

Jack nodded. "What's your gut on the kid?

"I'm trying not to get giddy. I can't picture a teenager having the strength to hold her in place and nail her hands to the bed. Then chop her hair off, stuff it into her mouth and glue up her lips? I'll be happier if we match the blood sample on the stick."

"I've just about had enough of you lot."

Barbara Rickman scowled at Robin and Jack as if they were two thick shits who'd arrived at her house asking if they could rob her. Her ability to wordlessly communicate 'you are pond life' was impressive.

"Understandable, so I've come to apologise in person." Robin dialled up the charm. "I'm sure you can understand, we're keen to find who did this to your mother, and DC Mason was a bit over-enthusiastic, shall we say? But his intentions were good."

"He upset my son, who's grieving for his grandmother …"

"Mum, I'm fine." William appeared behind his mother, a younger version of his brother with a complex hairdo and a peppering of spots.

Barbara turned her scowl towards her son, allowing Robin to step in.

"William, I'm DI Scott. I came to apologise for my officer upsetting you yesterday."

"It's ok thanks, he didn't upset me. He was sound."

Barbara's scowl morphed into a livid glare at her son's casual betrayal. "He had no right …"

"He was doing his job, trying to find who killed Gran."

"You're a minor."

"Right." Will rolled his eyes, full-on disdainful teenager. "I'm happy to help," he said, and Robin admired his balls. Barbara's mouth tightened. She was a human Vesuvius, seconds away from an apocalyptic eruption.

"Thanks. If it's OK with your Mum, we'd like to talk to you."

"No, it's not OK!" Barbara barked.

Will flinched, but he held his ground. Why was she so against it? He understood her defending her son, but Will was managing the situation well.

"William was right, Mrs Rickman. I know it can be distressing, but we do need to ask questions as new lines of enquiry emerge."

"Mum, chill out. It's fine."

"Mrs Rickman, I'd like your opinion on a few things while DI Scott has a quick chat with William." Jack continued the charm offensive with a dazzling smile.

Barbara hesitated, then spun around, inviting them inside with an unimpressed huff. Jack followed her, leaving Robin with William. William didn't look like he was grieving. He was texting on his phone with the remarkable speed teenagers had and Robin resisted the urge to snatch the phone. William shoved it back in his pocket and opened the door to a sitting room off the main hallway. The room was pristine. Surfaces gleamed, everything had its place. William sat in the chair furthest away from the door and pulled out his phone. He sent what could only have been a one-word text and put it away again.

"Is there someone you need to call?"

"No, sorry. I'm done now."

William had the gangly self-consciousness of adolescence, but his air of maturity belied his years. He was so like his brother, but their similarity ran deeper than physical resemblance. Old souls? It was a phrase his granddad always used, and he remembered asking him about it as a child. Both John and William projected a calm authority, as if they possessed knowledge beyond their years.

"Thanks for what you did there, William. Brave move standing up to your mum."

"She'll give me shit for it later."

"When I spoke to your brother, he called you Will. Do you prefer Will to William?"

"Yeah. Only Mum and Gran call me William."

"Will it is. Let's start with your Gran. What was your relationship with her like?"

Next to Will's chair was a side table with a landline handset, notepad and pen. Will began doodling on the pad. "It was OK. We played cards sometimes. She liked quiz shows, so we watched quiz shows."

"When did you last see her?"

"The day before she died. I saw her almost every day, and I had to stay with her in the school holidays. Mum didn't like her being alone all the time."

"What did you do together in the holidays?"

"When I was younger, we visited museums or walked in the woods. Went to church a bunch too." Will stopped doodling and looked up. "Why do you want to know this stuff?"

"Will, I'll be straight with you. People have suggested your Gran had a nasty side. What's your opinion?"

Will's expression didn't change. "It's common knowledge. It wasn't a side. It was just her. She had a horrible temper. Bitched about people. Had to be top dog."

"Did she ever hit you?"

Will glanced towards the door as if afraid Barbara might hear. "Yeah, a few times." His voice lowered.

"You're a strapping lad. Did you never stand up to her, defend yourself?"

"Are you kidding?" Will shook his head and tore a page off the pad. Continued scribbling. "When she was on one you took the shit and waited for it to be over. She'd scream, and spit like an angry cat. I'm surprised she didn't have a heart attack."

"So, she would get into a rage and lash out with her stick?"

"Yes."

Robin waited and let Will process his thoughts. He was looking increasingly uncomfortable. "I understand this is difficult, but you're doing great. What else can you tell me about your childhood?"

Was he going to answer? He was so absorbed in whatever he was drawing he seemed to forget Robin was there. Robin tried to see the notepad, but his view was obscured by the large antique-style phone.

"It was good sometimes," Will said finally, "Apart from Gran dragging me to church all the time. I've always had … stuff. I wish I could remember my dad, but I'm glad I have John. I just wish my Mum liked him more but she wants me to herself. She does it with my friends too."

"Do you think she's scared of losing you like she lost your dad?"

"She wants to control me and my life. Probably because Gran controlled her. And she's like Gran. Control freak."

Father Heath had been right about William; he was insightful and mature for his age.

"Did your Gran help out when you were kids?"

"In her own special way." William's tone was laden with sarcasm. "It wasn't tough for my Mum because either John looked after me or Gran took over. Mum could just get on with her life. Anyway, the odd smack was nothing compared with the other stuff."

A ripple of goosebumps crept up Robin's arms. "What other stuff?" he asked, matching William's hushed tone.

"Punishments."

"Physical punishments?"

William shook his head and stared at his hands.

"I wish. No, all mental, embarrassing stuff. Head fucks." He glanced up as if checking the swearing was ok. Robin didn't react.

"She did things the hard way. If you wet the bed you slept in it. If you screwed up your homework you stayed up all night until you did it right. I got the kitchen floor muddy once. She went nuts. Told me she always kept the floor so clean you could eat your dinner off it. She made me clean it, then she cooked dinner and put my plate on the floor. If I wanted it, I had to eat it right there. That's what my Gran was like."

"It sounds like you've had a rough time. No one would blame you if you hated your Gran for what she did to you. Did you hate her?"

Will nodded and fiddled with the bottom button of his blazer.

"Enough to want her dead?"

"I've wished she would die a million times."

"Where were you the night she died?"

"Here. With Mum," William's head snapped up and the colour drained from his cheeks like a plug had been pulled. "Oh my God, you think I killed her? That's what all these questions are about."

He jumped to his feet but remained rooted to the spot, compelled to flee but with no options.

"I have to ask Will, it's my job. I've asked everyone who knew your Gran the same question."

He hoped he'd done enough to earn William's trust. It took a moment for the fear to fade but eventually he slumped back in his seat.

"I did hate her, and do you know what? I'm glad she's dead. But I didn't kill her."

There were no deviations in his behaviour to suggest he was being untruthful. The phone next to Will began to ring and they jumped at the unexpected shrill noise. They both stared at it until it stopped.

"Like I said, no one liked her. I think it was business related, or one of the carers."

"What makes you think that?"

A shrug. "Could just be a randomer."

"Can you tell me about what happened to your Gran's walking stick?"

Will hesitated and looked away. "I lost my temper and sawed it in half. Most of the time I could handle her being vile but that day I snapped."

"Do you snap often?"

"No. But I hated that stick almost as much as I hated her."

Pain pierced through his words even though he was adept at containing his emotions. Must've been grim if he'd been pushed to a point where he'd taken his anger out on the object so central to his abuse. Snapping was different to planning a murder though.

"One last thing. I spoke to Father Heath the other day. He suggested you might have information to help us with our investigations."

Will gulped. "Confession is confidential."

"He didn't betray your trust, the opposite in fact. He respects and admires you. But if you do have information, it would be advisable to share."

"I don't know who killed her."

Robin waited, hoping to draw more out of the silence, but William had morphed into a sulky teenager and was chewing his nails.

"You've been amazing, thank you. I appreciate how honest you've been," Robin rose to his feet. "I may speak to you again though."

Will folded up his sketches.

"Are you good at drawing?" Robin pointed to the pieces of paper.

"No, they're just doodles. I do it without thinking."

"Can I see?"

Will unfolded three sheets of paper and hesitated for a second before he handed them over. The first was a doodle, a series of spiky lines firing outwards like fireworks, the second a sword with a twisted handle and a snake curled around the blade. It looked like a tattoo design. The last drawing was of a long-haired man holding the same sword, without the serpent this time. The man looked remarkably like John.

"Will, these are brilliant. Is this your brother?" In minimalistic pen strokes Will had captured the essence of his brother perfectly.

"Kind of. He's a knight though."

"Is this how you see him?"

Will took the drawings back from Robin and shoved them in his blazer pocket.

"You think I'm a stupid kid …"

"Whoa, no way do I think that." Robin held up his hands. "You're smarter than half the adults I know."

Barbara who opened the door, face still clenched and stormy.

"I need to get my son to school," she said to Robin, leaving no margin for disagreement.

Robin smiled at Will. Fuck Barbara the control freak. He didn't want to leave with Will feeling like he'd been patronised.

"If I offended you, I apologise."

"You spend a lot of time apologising," said Barbara.

Robin ignored her; his attention focused on Will.

"What did he say to you?"

Will ignored her too. "We're good," he said to Robin, and he left the room.

"Anything useful from Barbara?"

Robin pulled off Barbara's drive and headed back up the street.

"Not much. I asked her about the stuff Karen Taylor mentioned, the special favours. She just laughed."

"Did she seem surprised?"

"Not in the slightest. She shrugged it off and said 'she was always a bit frisky'."

"I expected her to say it was a lie."

"Me too, but she implied it was common for Ursula to add a couple of benefits to her care package."

"Money knocks down barriers. You can buy pretty much anything if you're minted."

"I asked her about the article in The Post too. The one about Ursula and her savage reviews." Robin glanced over, not sure what he was talking about. "It'll be on the website." Jack scrolled through his phone. "Barbara said she didn't know about it, but I reckon she did."

Jack handed Robin his phone when they pulled up outside John's house.

Murder Victim's Secret Reviews Cause Chaos For Local Businesses

Harrison Engineering CEO Ursula Harrison, who was murdered in her home last week, secretly slated hundreds of products and services using an online alias. She wrote vicious reviews on a variety of platforms, including Trust Pilot and Amazon, over several years. The last one was posted just four days before her death.

One review of award-winning 'Moorcroft Manor' in Hanstead described its menu as 'over-priced, mostly inedible plate art' and its gin cocktails as 'reminiscent of nuclear waste'. Michelin starred 'Eatery' fared no better with its signature gourmet steak roulade declared to have 'the consistency and appearance of a urine-soaked beer mat'.

Owner of Bra Boutique, Jemma Farley, an Amazon trader for over fifteen years, saw sales slump following a series of reviews of their 'Intimate' high-end lingerie range …

Robin looked up at Jack.

"I'm surprised James hasn't picked up on this. Whoever wrote it is a good investigator."

"The article says Ursula used an alias. I rang the paper to speak to the reporter, but the receptionist hadn't heard of her."

Robin scrolled to the by-line.

By Florence Hunter.

"I'm not surprised. She's been dead for five years."

Jack's brows knitted. "What do you mean?"

"Florence Hunter was Catherine's Grandma."

*

"Why did you question my little brother?"

John Rickman had recovered well since they'd seen him in hospital after the assault, and he'd brought home with him a new edginess. He glared at Robin and Jack with undisguised contempt.

"Mr Rickman, we've some questions regarding the death of Ursula Harrison. Do you mind if we come in?" Jack's amiable question didn't have any soothing effect on John, but he opened to door to let them in. He led them to the kitchen. Catherine would love this house, and Robin had a pang of missing her. Had John seen her? Had he touched her, kissed her, slept with her? Did he know she rinsed a glass three times before using it, or she hated crispy bits on her fried eggs? Had he kissed her appendix scar and told her how her skin smelled like summer?

John offered them both a seat at the kitchen table, effortlessly suave in jeans and a floral shirt. Robin glanced down at his trousers and jumper. Excellent quality but unexciting. Was he boring? Next to John, he was the prick at school in uniform on non-uniform day. And why the smart casual appearance, when he'd been in the middle of doing some DIY? There was an open toolkit on the worktop by the sink alongside a drill and a selection of screwdrivers.

I've spoken to your brother. He's an impressive young man, mature and articulate. He explained what Ursula was like to be around." Robin scanned the stylish, retro kitchen. John had good taste.

"Was he OK?"

"He was fine. And I can see you're upset we spoke to him, but his insight was useful."

John swallowed, and the tension in his shoulders eased a little.

"You didn't mention Ursula's behaviour when we spoke."

"I don't talk to anyone about it, and I don't see the relevance. It was years ago."

"Well, that's our job. We can decide if it's relevant."

John jumped to his feet and began to tidy away the clutter on the worktop. "Sorry about the mess," he said, suddenly distracted, and he slotted the tools back into the box. He checked each piece first, wiping them with a cloth. Jack shrugged, equally bemused.

"John, did you know how Ursula treated Will?"

"Of course I knew."

A large drill bit dropped to the floor and rattled on the tiles. It rolled under the table and John yanked a chair out to reach it.

"We need your help here. I can understand why this is difficult for you. But we're trying to find who killed her, and although no one liked her, and several people were abused or exploited by her, we're still no closer."

John rinsed a spanner under the tap. Who washed their spanners?

"Did Will want Ursula dead?" asked Jack, "Did you?"

The spanner dropped into the deep Belfast sink, and John rested his hands on it for a moment, eyes closed. "You don't understand. When that shit happens to you, the goal is to reach a stage where you can live like it didn't happen. You don't blame the other person, no matter how much you hate them. They're not the target. You blame yourself, hate yourself. Are we happy she's gone? Absolutely. But it doesn't make any difference. You can't change the past. It still happened."

Robin had experienced similar feelings when Erin died. When the perpetrators were found and convicted, it didn't take the pain away. Justice was done, but the outcome remained the same.

"I saw the stuff in the paper about Alan Renshaw. There were others."

"Can you give us some names?"

John stared out across the garden, watching a squirrel hop along the garden fence until it disappeared over the other side.

"There was a guy in the computer department, Tom Moss I think was his name. Little and skinny back then, like he hadn't developed fully. Ursula would say stuff about the size of his cock, call him a girl, ask him if he still wore nappies. She had a driver too. A Scottish guy with a tattoo on his thigh. She used to make him drive her to places naked from the waist down."

"Why did no one report her?" Robin asked.

"My boss wanked me off while I drove her to meetings. My boss called me a sissy boy and said my cock was tiny," John laughed without humour, "That's why."

"They're serious allegations and not the first we've heard about either."

"You'd have to ask them, but I reckon shame or embarrassment stopped them. Self-blame. No proof, no clear definition of whether it was consensual or not. If a guy complained about a woman abusing him, he'd be ridiculed. Or called a lucky bastard."

"Women can still be abusers. It's still a crime."

"No offence, but that's incredibly naive."

"It's not naive, it's the law," Robin snapped, pissed off by the derisory tone in John's voice, "What about you? Why didn't you speak up?"

It sounded accusatory and critical as he said it. Tension tightened around the three of them. John stared at him.

"I was a child."

His words hung in silence.

"There were people around you," Robin continued, "Teachers, relatives, friends' parents even. Bobby."

"You don't get it. Unless you've experienced it, you have no idea. It's the loneliest place, and you make it sound like I was at fault for not speaking up."

"No, you were a victim ..."

"I'm not a victim!"

"We appreciate you don't want to discuss the details," Jack cut in, "We just want to understand Ursula's life."

John dragged out a chair and sank like he'd been drained of energy. "She rubbed some sub-contractors up the wrong way. Robert Argyle from Timpson Argyle Ltd sticks in my mind. She pulled out of a huge contract with his company, and they went into liquidation. Francesca Lewisham was another. Ursula's private GP. And the guy from the paper who wrote the story about Alan Renshaw. Ursula went nuts because she found out Barbara was shagging him. They had a stinking row one day in the office over a story about a site worker getting injured."

Robin's jaw dropped in astonishment. He'd never experienced the sensation of his face slackening like a semi-deflated balloon. "Clive Darwin?"

"Yeah, Catherine's friend, dresses like an Antiques Roadshow presenter." Robin stiffened and forced himself not to react. "It's funny how people assume kids don't hear or see the things adults try to hide. Whispered conversations, coded words they think you can't understand. That argument was epic though. No code-cracking required. She threatened to get all the main advertisers to pull out of the paper unless he printed an apology, said she would crucify him for damaging her business."

Robin's slack jaw slackened further. "What happened?"

"I'm not sure, but I know she also threatened his predecessor. He caved in, not sure about Clive Darwin. From what I remember, I doubt it."

Robin glanced at Jack. They hadn't released the crucifixion reference, and his mind set off on a wild spin. Clive? Really? Catherine couldn't be aware of whatever happened between Clive and Ursula. Pissed with him or not, and even knowing how loyal she was to her friends, she would've told him if she'd known. Clive had mentioned nothing about knowing Ursula or being intimate with Barbara either. And crucify? Interesting choice of word. Although people use the phrase 'I'll kill you' all the time and rarely mean it.

"What year was that?" asked Jack.

"2010. I remember because I went shopping with Barbara after she finished work, for a suit for the leaver's prom. She never let me choose my own stuff."

They talked with John for a while longer, but Robin drifted away. Christ, he would never have put Clive and Barbara together. Clive could be a dick, but he was a decent person underneath. Catherine chose her friends carefully. Usually.

As they moved to leave, Robin glanced across the other side of the kitchen. John and Jack had headed out already, but he stopped dead. There was a bottle of wine on the worktop, the label a distinctive bright green with a row of turrets in silhouette across the top. Washington Wines. Home-brewed and not available in any shops. Did John know Felix Washington well enough to be drinking his home brew? Catherine had known him for years though. She loved a weird white he made which tasted of nutmeg.

Robin hadn't known jealousy until that moment. It nailed him to the spot while he stared at the green label with the perky, home-printed font he'd once found charming. Now it mocked him. John and Jack were waiting for him at the door now and John knew what he'd seen and what it meant.

"What's up?" asked Jack as soon as they were away from the house.

Robin's jaw clenched so much his words were trapped. "I need to make a call. Give me a sec."

Jack looked perplexed, but he got into the car. Robin took out his phone. Catherine's number rang out then her answerphone kicked in. He tried again, same thing. Probably out dredging up more dirt on Ursula under her new alias, more stuff his team had missed. That would go down well with Collins. He sent Catherine a quick text, pocketed the phone and got into the car.

"He's lying."

"Who?" Jack frowned. "About what?"

Robin stared at the quiet houses. "Rickman. And I don't know."

Jack took a packet of gum from his pocket. Took one, offered Robin one and put them away again.

"Are you conflating issues here? Personal and professional."

"Possibly."

"Do you want a lecture?"

"I'll pass, thanks."

Robin started the car and pulled away.

Chapter Nineteen

Thin edge

"Are you going to eat?

Will stared at his plate of congealing fish pie. His Mum tucked into hers, but she looked elsewhere, eating for fuel rather than enjoyment.

"I'm not hungry."

His Mum scowled at him from the other end of the table. Why did they have to set the dining table and eat formally? Ridiculous just for the two of them. He'd be happier at the kitchen table or even better on his lap in front of the TV. But TV dinners were banned unless he was at John's.

"You must eat, William."

"Are you going to force me like Gran used to? It tastes like hers used to."

"It's the same recipe actually …"

"Or scrape it off my plate and make me eat it out of the bin." Barbara's fork clattered onto her plate, and she stared at Will in dismay. "Why do you think I hate it so much?"

William shoved his plate away, sending it gliding down the table. The plate skimmed off the polished surface and hit the wall. It clunked to the floor, leaving a trail of fish pie slop behind it.

"You didn't tell me." Barbara for once ignored the mess.

"I tried to tell you what a bitch she could be. After a while, I gave up."

"Do not use words like that William!"

"It's why John despised her!" William jumped to his feet, "He protected me, and you hate him for it."

Barbara pushed her plate away. "Stop shouting and sit down."

William plonked back into his chair, surprised by her uncharacteristic, subdued tone. He'd expected an argument, needed one. He wanted to yell and let go of the anger writhing inside him, searching for an outlet.

"You have such potential, and I can help you achieve your dreams."

"Your dreams. What if I want a different life?"

"What do you mean?"

"I want to be normal, do normal things, have normal relationships. Like with John. We watch sport, eat take-aways, go to gigs, laugh. Normal stuff Mum."

"So, you want to waste your life being average."

"No. I want to enjoy my life my way rather than the way you want."

"All I've ever done is try to encourage you …"

"Rubbish. You don't encourage. You force and push."

"Well, aren't you full of home truths today?"

"Why didn't you stop her Mum? Why did you let her bully everyone?" His mum was fighting back tears now, and he'd never seen her cry before. "How could you watch her abuse the sons of the man you loved – and you've said it so many times. You loved dad, but you didn't protect his sons from your evil mother!"

"Stop it!"

Will's emotions erupted in one spectacular purging. "You allowed it, which makes you as bad as she was, and she deserved to die a horrible death after what she did to people. So, you'd better watch out."

"What do you mean?"

"Karma. The sum of a person's actions, or in your case lack of action."

Barbara stared at him in horror, make-up smudged. "What's happened to you? You can't speak to me like this."

"You can't tell me what to think or say!"

"Calm down …"

"I don't want to calm down. I want to know why you didn't stop her."

"Because I couldn't."

"Why not?" Will demanded, but Barbara was shaking her head. "You were afraid of her too, weren't you? What did she have over you?"

"Everything!" Barbara snapped, "She could've written me out of her will, cut your inheritance. I had to keep the peace with her, whether I liked it or not. I covered up her mistakes, but I was protecting you too. Protecting your future."

"But don't you see? I don't care about all this stuff. I don't care if we never have a holiday in the Caribbean again or have a boring old car."

"I mean it much more literally. You think you know it all, but believe me, you don't."

There was a new tightness to his mother's voice, and it shocked him into silence. She took a deep breath and seemed to gather herself together. She wiped her cheeks and reached for her wine.

"What did you mean, literally?"

Barbara emptied her wine glass, refilled it and stared into the dark red liquid. Half a minute passed. She drank a huge mouthful, gulped it as if she was parched.

"Your Gran had another child who died. I don't know how or why; I never got a straight answer when I asked, but when I had you, I felt like … she looked at you and saw her own child. They tried again, repeatedly, to have another child, but she miscarried seven times – then she had me. A girl. Not a replacement for the precious son she'd lost. When I was pregnant and I found out I was having a boy, I didn't tell her because she would've persuaded me to abort. She wouldn't want me to have what she lost."

Will waited for more. He'd never heard this stuff.

"My brother was never mentioned. Taboo subject. I'd already seen how she treated John, and I was thankful. When her hate was directed at him, she wasn't directing it at you. As you grew up, I relaxed. She loved you, wanted the best for you, and you were always so eager to please her. I turned a blind eye because I knew it would make you strong, and I also knew you'd reap the rewards. Yes, she was tough on you, but much tougher on John, and look at what she's left you, William. You'll never have to worry about money. How many people can say that? And was it so bad?"

Will shook his head, stunned. "You honestly believed money was more important than your child's happiness?"

"Oh, don't exaggerate. You're happy. You have everything you want!"

"I want to be sick," William pushed back his chair. He couldn't breathe, and disgust congealed in his stomach. His mum was as cold as his gran. He'd wanted some insight into his gran's behaviour to help him understand, even forgive. Perhaps she'd loved her baby son so much his death had caused devastating damage to her basic functions, cauterised her senses so she no longer had feelings, numbed by grief. Controlling people put her back in command.

Out in the garden, Will hoped the fresh air would flush away the nausea. He took the path to his favourite part of the garden, a bench tucked away out of view of the house. There was an archway over it, overgrown so it looked like part of the wall. He liked being alone there when the last pale moments of sun reached into the shadows. He'd slept on the bench once in his sleeping bag, sneaking back inside in the morning so his mum didn't know. He closed his eyes and let the quietness surround him.

When he'd been younger, he'd missed John dreadfully when they were apart, so John had taught him a trick. Well, more like meditation than a trick. John taught him to relax his body bit by bit, and then imagine they were together, wherever he wanted to be. Will wasn't relaxed enough to focus, but he tried to imagine John next to him, talking like they used to. He wanted to feel him there so much, but the harder he tried, the more frustrated he became. It wasn't working. Will squeezed his eyes shut tighter, holding back the tears behind his eyelids. Eventually they broke free, and Will let his emotions gush out with them, sobbing like the child he'd once been and still was; lonely and lost.

What would John say? If he was there right now, what would he say?

Will, the time has come.

*

Walking didn't have the same therapeutic effect for John as running. He enjoyed the bite of the wind as it blew away the day, but still missed the simple freedom of running through the woods behind his house. Not much fun with bruised ribs though.

Today he wanted to enjoy the seclusion of the other-worldly environment where nature existed freely. Untouched and wild, as it had been for decades, maybe centuries.

Except, he couldn't. And it was all down to Robin Scott.

After spending time with Catherine, he'd been on a high, pumped with positivity. He could imagine her in his future. She hadn't been put off by all his baggage. She'd listened, wanted to understand, and had the rare gift of empathy. No judgement and no fear. She was a precious find. Then Robin Scott arrived at his house and killed it all. Protecting Will was his top priority, and he hated how he'd been exposed to some nasty questions. But he'd dug around in John's mind too, hellbent on unearthing truths John had buried long ago, like he'd a right to know. Staggering arrogance. A police badge shouldn't give him the power to probe around in his core.

When he'd been in hospital, after Jamie jumped him, he'd questioned the attraction. He kept coming back to her need for protection, which was all he saw as appealing in Robin. OK, he wasn't bad looking and he was ripped under the dull clothes; a dig around had provided plenty of insight on Robin's success in karate circles. Multiple black belts, dozens of trophies. A police commendation. Alpha male stuff.

Self-doubt crept in. He had to stop comparing himself to Robin, but he couldn't help it.

There was an old bench by the river. Moss consumed it and one of the boards was missing, but he was thankful when he reached it, ready for a break. The light had faded, but he'd brought a torch purely to light his path. He enjoyed darkness.

No messages. Full signal. Nothing from Catherine since the previous night.

They'd left the castle and had breakfast in a café over the road. Then they'd parted, and he missed her. He sent her a text before going to bed, and she'd replied instantly. All had seemed good.

So why had she been silent all day? Because of Robin? John stared at his phone screen. He hated this. The best and the worst part of meeting someone new: the flush of excitement coupled with agonising guesswork. Factor in an adversary pecking from the periphery. Torture.

Catherine showed online on WhatsApp.

Hey, how are you? He typed.

Too needy? Or just crap? John deleted.

I'm missing you x

Even needier, but honest. He hit send.

She was 'typing' forever. The wind whipped his hair around his cheeks as he waited, the chilly night nipping at his fingers.

Hectic day, sorry. Are you ok? x

Six words, a hundred connotations. He'd hoped for a 'missing you too', and the excuse felt lazy, which wasn't Catherine. Robin Scott had got to her, warned her off, staked his claim on her again like a marauding Viking warrior claiming his woman. And what should he reply with? Was he OK? No, not really, and he was becoming less OK by the second.

Feeling a bit stupid for spilling my guts yesterday. Have I put you off?

He wanted her honesty in return for his, and he had to trust she would give it.

Not at all. I admire your openness.

Better.

I need to ask you something. She hadn't wanted to talk about Robin when they'd been together, but he had to know. *Have you discussed me with Robin? Today, I mean.*

Instant regret. Should he delete it? He hovered over 'delete for everyone' but she would've seen it already.

I haven't spoken to him today.

Cagey. They hadn't spoken, but maybe they'd messaged. She didn't want to lie to him, but perhaps she didn't want to give him the whole truth either.

John, stop worrying. We're good.

That felt more like her.

Can we meet up?

Long pause.

Busy few days, but yes. Thursday/Friday?

The paranoia returned. He'd hoped they might meet later or the following day. Then he would know if Robin Scott blocked his path, and despite her denial, he suspected he did. He didn't seem the type to back away without a fight.

His turn for the long pause. His turn to mask the truth.

No problem x

Chapter Twenty

History repeats

Clive Darwin's office smelled of old cigarettes and Pot Noodles. Filing cabinets predating Robin's birth lined the walls, and he half expected to see a typewriter on the desk. While the office beyond Darwin's yellowed window was spacious and modern, he remained sequestered away in the 1980s. He found Clive in the middle of moving one of the cabinets into a space offering a millimetre each way for manoeuvre.

"Help me with this will you?" he puffed, struggling to shift what looked like half a tonne of metal. He swiped sweat from his forehead.

"What?"

"Get the other end!"

Robin shouldered the cabinet from his side, and it inched into place, dragging wrinkles of carpet with it. "What the hell is in here?"

Clive shouldered it in further. "A body."

"You only weight them down with bricks in water, you know."

"I'll bear it in mind for next time."

The cabinet reached its final resting place. Robin pulled the top drawer, and it scraped reluctantly open, probably for the first time in centuries. It was rammed full of thick magazines.

"Love that you checked," said Clive.

Robin slammed the drawer shut again, "We need to talk."

Clive sat in his battered chair, sweaty and reeking of animosity. "More observations about my private life?"

"I don't care what you do in private. I'd like a word with Florence Hunter actually." Clive stared at him, said nothing. "Yeah, thought that might be tricky. Talk to me about your confrontation with Ursula Harrison instead." Robin remained standing, pumped with an energy he couldn't release. Clive's expression didn't change. "I'll help you remember. Summer 2010, you printed a story slagging off Harrison Engineering. You had a massive argument with Ursula Harrison, and she threatened to destroy you if you didn't issue an apology. No, not destroy. 'Crucify' our witness said."

"Seventy-year-old woman behaving like Don Corleone. Laughable really."

"Did you apologise?"

"No chance. And I didn't find a horse's head in my bed either." Clive began impaling bits of paper and post-it notes from around his desk onto a spike. "I didn't mention it because I barely remember it. That's how significant it was."

"Why did you go to her office then?"

"Because she made threats, and I wanted to tell her what I thought of her."

"I don't believe you. I bet you goaded her for a reaction so you could dish more dirt."

"Busted," Clive yawned. A notification pinged, and he wiggled his mouse to check his pc. "So, you wanted to ask me something?"

"Where were you on Friday the 19th between 11pm and 6am?"

Clive stopped and stared at him. "Are you kidding me? I'm a suspect now because I had an arsey conversation with Ursula Harrison more than ten years ago …"

"Which you failed to divulge …"

"You never asked me!"

"I'm asking you now."

Silence as quiet as a snowy morning. Robin waited and ignored his phone buzzing in his pocket. They would have to wait.

"I went to an open mic night at the civic hall. A group of us from the paper went with a supplier. I arrived home about 1am. Alone. Pissed," he shook his head and hunted around in the pocket of the jacket hanging on his chair. He found his vaper and dragged. "Can't believe you asked."

"Just doing my job. I hunt for killers, you write stories."

"Can you smell testosterone?" Clive sniffed, "Or bullshit. Not sure which. And you know the press plays a significant role in the justice system."

Robin laughed. "Good one, Clive. You do love the view from your high horse, don't you? Talk to me about the 'significant role of the press' when you're the editor of The Telegraph. Until then, I'd like to know what happened after you refused to apologise to Ursula Harrison."

"How naïve and insulting."

"I don't care!" Robin slammed his palms on the metal cabinet, and the heavy clang caused people in the office beyond to turn around and stare. "Answer the question!"

Clive leant back in his chair and studied Robin. "Who told you about this?"

"Doesn't matter. What happened?"

Clive sighed. "Nothing. No motive for murder anyway. Well, I shagged her daughter, which riled her. God knows how she found out. I received a letter from her lawyer telling me to stay away from her family. They accused me of having a vendetta against them and her business, claimed I'd slept with Barbara to get information from her. She invited me to go back and apologise, can you believe that? Invited."

Robin couldn't see Clive being intimate with Barbara. He couldn't see her being intimate with anyone. She was like a fridge, gift wrapped in broken glass and finished with a barbed wire bow.

"And did you?"

"I was tempted for the sport. But no, I never saw her again."

"No way would you miss such an opportunity."

"What? To go crawling to the old bitch with my tail between my legs? Too fucking weird for me."

"Do you remember who the lawyer was?"

"Austin something or other. I might still have the letter. Anyway, if we're done, I have a deadline …"

"No, we're not done. Why did Ursula say she would 'crucify' you?"

"I don't remember her using that word. Who said she did?"

Robin stepped into rocky waters of potentially compromising a witness. "It was John Rickman."

Clive blinked, gulped and vaped in succession. "He heard us arguing?"

"Yes."

"And that's what she said?"

"Allegedly, yes."

Clive opened the bottom drawer of his desk, took out half a packet of Marlboro's and a lighter and sparked up. He opened the window behind his desk and exhaled into the chilly fresh air with force. "Why is it significant?"

"It's an ongoing investigation. I can't reveal the details."

Clive loosened off his tie and unfastened the top button of his vintage car print shirt. He took another drag, his mind spinning, and although Robin had reservations about Clive, he was intelligent and intuitive. He would join the dots. He might also be able to add in the bits of the puzzle Robin had missed; information he knew about John Rickman from Catherine. Reliant on Clive Darwin to offer insights into Catherine's life. This case and his shabby private life were screwed up, and he'd some serious repair work to do.

"I can't say for sure." Clive wafted smoke through the window. "I don't remember, but 'crucify' doesn't resonate with me. Ursula was religious, common knowledge. So, if she used that word specifically, I'd expect it to have significance." Clive fished. He knew the game.

"I agree."

"Shit." The implicit weight of that one word slammed into Robin's gut. "When did you last speak to Catherine?"

Robin's turn to swallow hard. "Friday. We had words. Why?"

"I saw her on Sunday evening. She mentioned a weird nightmare she'd had about a black cross …"

"A nightmare? I work with facts. A dream about shoes means you're going on a journey. It's all bollocks. Anyway, her bad dreams are all about water. Rough seas, capsized boats, the Ti-fucking-tanic. It doesn't fit."

Clive rolled his eyes. "Let me finish. We had a tetchy conversation about Harrisons. She found out all the staff had to sign confidentiality agreements as part of their job contracts. Cat thinks they're hiding secrets, but I think Barbara's just trying to keep the shreds of her reputation intact. Anyway, I made a snidey comment – I regret that actually, I was a dick – I should apologise." He looked out of the window for a moment, took another long drag. "She threw a dig back at me and left. Not heard from her since. She'd come round to borrow a book, one she read a while back when Simon was attacked. Remember she went a bit weird on religion? Triggered by something one of those bastards said to him."

"Oh God Clive, please get to the point."

"The book she took was 'The Meaning of The Crucifixion."

Robin froze. "Why did she want it?"

"She wouldn't say. Got a bit pissy with me when I asked her."

"Cat doesn't do pissy."

Unless she was on the defensive. She knew something.

"What's all this about?" asked Clive, but Robin reached for his phone and headed for the door.

*

Catherine had immersed in writing a blog when the car park gates scraped open. She glanced over at the security monitor, surprised to see John's car. She hadn't expected to see him, although they'd texted earlier before she'd gone to the castle. She'd had no contact from anyone since, which was partly why she loved going there. The sketchy mobile signal was handy for hiding away without distraction. No word from Robin either since their argument on Friday, but she'd left his flat and pretty much dumped him, so what did she expect? She'd hoped he would fight more, and his silence suggested he thought their relationship wasn't worth fighting for. Then again, over the weekend, John had nudged his way in through the breach, and she hadn't put up much of a defence.

A gust of wind blew his hair across his face, and he smiled as he did a little jog over to the back door, a bag over his shoulder. He didn't speak at first; just brushed the lightest of kisses on her lips and took her hand.

"Come inside, I've brought a book to show you."

"I didn't expect to see you today."

He stopped, and his smile faded. "Sorry, I know you've been busy, and I won't stay long. I did message you."

"Ah. Dodgy 4G and Wi-Fi. It's OK though. Come through."

The smile returned, but he had an urgency about him today, a vigour she hadn't seen in him before. Whatever had brought him there, he was excited to share it and as he led her past the office into the old part of the building, her nerves prickled. She barely knew this man, wasn't even sure if she wanted to become more involved with him, yet she'd been swept along by his infectious energy. She'd already become part of his world, and he'd imbued into hers in little more than a week.

The last few moments of daylight bruised the hall with shadow. John released her hand and fished around in his bag. He pulled out a camping lantern and flicked it on. A warm yellow light pooled around them.

"You like it here," said Catherine.

"I do. Thanks for letting me in." He turned to her abruptly, stopping again as he led her across the room.

"What's this is about?"

"One second. I need to find the right place."

He stopped next to a section of wall panelled in dark wood. Usually, the area was cordoned off to visitors to preserve the ancient cladding, but the section had been cleared for the renovations. John moved a little stool over for her to sit on, then knelt beside her. He fished around in his bag again and took out an old book, wrapped in tissue and placed in a separate cotton bag. He handled it like his firstborn, and its ancient years were dusty in her nostrils. He put it on her lap and opened the pages to where a piece of soft fabric had been placed as a bookmark.

"This is one of the few books that mentions Henry Stanton, the knight we talked about. It's a catalogue of tournaments. No one knows who wrote it or why they recorded the details of these contests."

"How old is it?"

"Hard to say. There's a famous French book written by King Rene called Le Livre des Tournois which describes in detail the rules for tournaments dating back to the 1400s. This one isn't as grand, and although the language suggests it was written by a noble, the author certainly wasn't a king. This is what I wanted to show you."

John leant on her leg as he scanned the page, and their world shrunk to the size of the soft pool of light from the lantern, as if only they existed. She felt his passion for this subject in the reverent way he handled the book and in the tone of his voice as he shared it with her. He wanted her to join him in his immersion. This was him sharing his soul.

"He was here, in this room, and the passageway hidden behind this wall. The author describes a feast held in this hall where Stanton was hailed the overall tournament winner. But he'd been injured. A lance had pierced his side, and he was in great pain. Once the ale was flowing and he'd accepted the applause and his prize, he left to seek help with his injury."

Catherine peered at the text, but she struggled to read the unfamiliar dialect written in a tight, looping cursive.

"I'd love a glimpse of that evening." She imagined the hall full of revellers celebrating their wins. "The sounds, the smells, the mood of the room. When I write about the castle, that's what I try to imagine and convey. Facts have their place, but I want people to feel what it was like to be here."

"To make history come alive." John's eyes shone in the lamplight. He watched her as she read the page again, picking out recognisable words, piecing together the story.

"I want to ask you a question." His glance away from her seemed like an evocation of courage as prepared himself for the answer. "Do you love Robin?"

Catherine closed the book and shivered.

"You're cold. Here, take my coat."

John shrugged off his leather jacket and draped it around her shoulders. It was infused with the aftershave he'd worn when they'd slept in each other's arms on the sofa in the office. How could she answer his question truthfully without hurting him? He waited, willing her to say no, intense need searing in his eyes.

"I'm not comfortable discussing Robin with you, John."

He nodded, the muscles in his jaw tightening. "He doesn't deserve you."

The warmth had leeched from his words. He uncoiled to his feet and stepped back, leaving her alone in the lamplight. His jacket gave her the warmth from his body, but she shivered again.

"I'm not sure what it means; to 'deserve' someone. Everyone has their qualities and faults, and I'm no different. Maybe I don't deserve him, or I want too much."

"I don't believe it for a second."

She didn't want this conversation. She recognised her cowardice and she'd been living in a bubble over the last few days. She could've called Robin and stayed at home alone. But instead, she'd submitted to the thrill of intrigue with this man.

"He questioned Will." John's tone accusatory tone implied Catherine was responsible for Robin, or she'd colluded in the decision.

Her stomach lurched. "About what?" She didn't want this conversation either, didn't want to find out her suspicions were right. Why the hell had she allowed herself to become embroiled in all this?

He paced in the shadows, arms wrapped around himself. He must've been freezing in his thin shirt. "Ursula's murder."

"It's just routine. They'll question everyone she knew, including relatives."

"And then he questioned me, asked me if Will had wanted her dead."

"They think Will killed his grandmother?"

"It's fucking insane."

Catherine jumped at the venom in John's words and the ferocity with which he spat them.

More pacing.

"And do you know what? Robin did it on purpose to piss me off. Because of you." John stopped, his face in shadow.

"He wouldn't do that."

"I knew you'd defend him," John swept out of the shadows and grabbed her arms, pulling her towards him. The lamp fell over and rolled away, causing the light to whirl around their feet. "See, this is what I mean. He doesn't deserve you."

His sudden burst of passion startled her. It raged in his grasp, blazed in his eyes, and in the dim, womb-like chamber, the force overwhelmed her.

"John, stop it …"

"I want you to understand how much you mean to me and what I can give you. I can take you to places Robin can't ever reach."

"I can't do this." Catherine pulled out of his grasp. She needed to leave.

"Catherine, please … I'm sorry."

She ignored him, pissed off with the Robin bashing. Maybe John did have feelings for her, but where once his declarations had been flattering, sweet even, now he seemed frantic. Too much too soon. Stifling.

And she couldn't ignore her suspicions about his brother any longer.

She'd tried to push them aside and get on with her work, but they were persistent. She'd spent the previous day buried in books, calls and web searches trying to get her head around it. William Rickman had been involved with the church like his grandmother, dragged along judging by the photos she'd seen of him on the church website and Facebook page looking thoroughly miserable. Sunday school, choir, bellringing. And she'd discovered the marketing team at Harrisons managed all the online content. He'd been used as part of Ursula's PR machine.

And if the police were asking questions about Will, her suspicions weren't unfounded.

"What did you mean when I told you Ursula had been crucified, and you said 'she tried that on me'?"

John stared at her. "What?"

"What did she do to you? Because whoever killed Ursula was punishing her for it. 'Without shedding of blood there is no remission'. *Hebrews 9:27. There had to be blood, and lots of it. Sin can't be forgiven unless the penitent pours out their blood to cover the transgression.* Her killer was aware of this. Just dying wasn't enough."

He understood. Like when she'd asked him on Sunday morning if he knew who'd killed Ursula, and he'd frozen up. He knew. He'd been so immersed in opening his heart to her he'd slipped up.

"I've no idea what you're talking about."

"Something's not right here, and whatever's going on with you, I don't want to be part of it."

"I'd never lie to you. You mean too much to me."

"You hardly know me."

Catherine spun around and strode down the hall.

She'd just reached the door when a heavy object cracked into the back of her head, and she stumbled sideways into the wall, grappling in the dark to keep herself upright. But the cold stone walls provided no purchase, and her head swam, black patches of blur like instant inebriation.

She crashed to the floor.

Chapter Twenty-One

More missing

Catherine's car wasn't on the drive at her cottage. Robin knocked on the door and peered into the sitting room window, but the house remained silent, her car gone. Her mobile went straight to voicemail, and when he called her landline, it rang faintly from the back of the house. He'd hoped to find her at the castle, but the place had been in total darkness and the car park empty. He turned his keys over in his hand. The one she'd given him months ago still hung on his keyring, shiny and largely unused. Huge infringement of her privacy to use it, but he could deal with her potential anger more than the prospect of failing her. He hesitated, then opened the door.

He called out her name and checked the sitting room before heading towards the kitchen. Nothing amiss in there. Cold kettle, the worktops tidy, her bag gone from its usual place on the floor by the table. The snug seemed normal. Books covered the coffee table along with bits of stationery and a USB hard drive, no laptop. Clive's book topped the pile, dying Jesus blurred on the cover.

Laden with dread, he climbed the stairs. As the bedroom came into sight, he had a horrible vision of finding her in bed with John, enjoying a lazy day under the duvet. Resentment blazed through his blood. Maybe he'd not been the best partner to Catherine, but the idea of her being with another man burned his bowels. The bedroom was empty. He ducked under the low beam, saddened by the familiarity of the room. His book was still on the bedside table, a hoody on a hook behind the door. He ached to see her again and make amends.

He checked the bathroom, and the second bedroom, then went back down the stairs. In the kitchen, her answerphone blinked with four messages. He scrolled through them on the screen. Two from her parents, two from him. Usual collection of weird veggie food in the fridge, dishwasher at the end of its cycle, light flashing. The house gave nothing else away.

Robin returned to his car. He started the engine and cranked up the heating, but he didn't leave. He took out his phone and searched his contacts for her parents' number. Liz answered.

"I've been trying to get hold of her Catherine, and I know we … well, I'm sure you know about us having words, but … have you spoken to her?"

Liz took a deep breath. "No. And I've called her five times. Is there a problem?"

"I don't know to be honest. I'm at her house, but there's no sign of her."

"She's been at the castle a lot, but she's not there either. Her dad popped up. He's worried. We both are. It's not like her." Her voice thinned to a whisper.

"Look, I know it's … strained between us at the moment, but if she contacts you, will you please ask her to call me? Or pop me a text?"

"I will. Is she in danger? Be honest with me."

Robin stared at the empty house, not sure how to respond. He didn't know for certain she was in danger. So far, any suspicions about the Rickman brothers were speculatory at best.

"Has she mentioned John Rickman?" he asked.

"The man who pulled her from the car. Yes."

"We're investigating his family over the death of his grandmother. Ask her to stay away from him. Please."

Liz's shallow breaths quickened. "I can hear it in your voice," she whispered finally. "Find my daughter, please Robin."

Her words made his chest tighten, and he gulped, fighting a sudden wave of nausea. "I will, I promise."

Find the man who killed my daughter Robin.

As those words had wrenched from her core, Robin heard Erin's Mum's heart breaking, piece by agonising piece.

"I'll find her."

Robin disconnected the call and tried Catherine again. It rang this time rather than going straight through to the answering service. He sat upright, willing her to answer, but after two rings, it went dead. Had she declined the call? He rang the number again, but this time the familiar recorded message answered immediately. What the hell did it mean? Scrolling through his phone, he'd sent her three texts, two WhatsApp messages (both delivered but unread), and called her five times. Plus, her parents had been trying to reach her too. She might be pissed off, but she wasn't so selfish as to ignore them all.

He rang Jack.

"Guv."

Robin hesitated. Were his concerns legitimate, or were they personal? If he introduced her as part of the case, his life would come under scrutiny. Collins might remove him from the case.

"Robin?"

"Sorry Jack. I have a problem."

"Hang on. I'll pick up in your office." Robin listened to silence for a few seconds. "OK. I'm with you."

"Catherine's not at home, not at work, and her parents can't get hold of her either. We've both tried several times now."

"What do you want me to do?"

Robin wanted to kiss him for not making him spell it out. "I don't want this made common knowledge. Not yet anyway. I could just be paranoid."

"I'll be discreet."

"I know. She always uses Star Taxis in Camber. Will you see if they've taken her anywhere in the last 48 hours? Also, could you speak to the owner of the castle, Felix Washington? Ask if he's seen her."

"No problem."

Robin pinched the bridge of his nose. "Am I overreacting?"

"It won't do any harm to put your mind at rest. She might still be angry with you and has gone off to clear her head. Phone off, no contact with anyone, drink wine and read books."

Robin's phone beeped against his ear. "Stay on the line Jack, one second."

Gone away for a few days. Need some space.

Robin stared at the words, then reconnected with Jack. He read him the message.

"Sounds arsey. What do you think?"

"I don't know. It's only a few words, but it's curt. Shit Jack, I don't know."

"We can track the phone's location but ..."

"But not without it becoming common knowledge, I know." Robin groaned in exasperation. "What would you do?"

"Tough call. Chances are it's genuine, but I wouldn't leave it to chance. Especially if this was my partner. Let me dig around."

"I won't be long."

*

Head swimming. Darkness. Blindfolded. Hard, cold floor beneath her. Limbs wouldn't move.

She smelled John. He was stroking her hair.

"Where are we ..."

"Just listen, please. I have to tell you what happened, how it all began."

"My head hurts so much. I need to go home."

Soothing soft hands on her cheeks. Water on her lips. Catherine tried to pull the blindfold off, but she met resistance. Her wrists were bound. A wave of panic flushed some of the grogginess away. She pulled her arms again, but whatever secured her wrists dug in more.

How had they gone from the lovely evening they'd spent together two days ago to this? And what even was this? She took a few moments to just breathe, struggling for clarity, like trying to sober up through will alone. It didn't work. The mind fog clung to her thoughts, smothering her attempts to reassemble her world coherently. Tied up. What had she done or said to end up here? She couldn't remember. Was there an action, some devastating words, back in the fog? They'd become close. Friends. More than friends. Shared opinions and feelings, memories and experiences.

What did he plan to do with her? A fresh injection of fear rushed through her blood, chilling her further.

"Shhh now, just relax."

Relax? Her heart slammed in her chest like a stampeding rhino. "Then let me see you."

She had to get through to him. If she connected with him again, he might not do whatever he'd planned. Even now, she couldn't believe he was bad to his core, and if he was, what did that say about her? Fucking awful judge of character, that's what.

He eased the blindfold away, like a lover readying her for an intimate bedroom game. His hair brushed her cheek, and he smelled painfully familiar. She'd loved his scent, but now it just reminded her of her reckless stupidity. She expected a rush of light, but instead she had to peer into darkness to make out his face. A black void lurked beyond the pale torchlight. No sounds of traffic or life beyond the blackness, just the wind whistling sporadically and an unidentifiable scratchy noise, reminding her of the gerbil she had as a kid that used to dig relentlessly in the corner of his cage.

Focus on him. Focus on finding a way to make him release her. But how? She'd been abandoned by hope, and she longed for its return, but with the futility of trying to wish a loved one back from death. He sat on the floor next to her, hair partially shielding his pale cheeks. His features receded in the dimness, giving him a haunted gauntness. He didn't meet her eyes.

"I just need you to listen."

She shivered, numbed by the cold. What if his was the last voice she ever heard, the cheese salad she had for lunch her last meal? This couldn't be it. There was so much she still wanted to do, to see, to feel. If she could keep him talking, she had a chance of reaching him.

"OK. I'm listening."

He held his fingers to his lips for a moment, stalling the reluctant confession. She already knew she didn't want to hear what he was about to say.

"Ursula started the day my dad died. She'd been given the green light. I think he knew what she was like. He watched her. I've even wondered if the fire at the lab was accidental. I wouldn't put it past her to get rid of anyone in her path.

"She found me crying in the bathroom, smacked me across the face and told me to shut up making a noise. When the slap just made me cry more, she dragged me up from the floor by my hair and rammed my head down the toilet. I was terrified. I cried the entire night, buried under my duvet so she wouldn't hear me. I begged my dad to return from heaven and take me with him. I knew then, she would get worse.

"I've had long hair since I was a kid. She made me shave my head for my dad's funeral, and I was distraught. I believed my dad wouldn't recognise me, that he'd think I hadn't gone to his funeral. I didn't look like or feel like me. She shaved away my identity. Oh, she made me eat it too, as a punishment for my vanity."

"I'm sure he knew you were there …"

He either didn't care what she thought or had immersed too far in his memories to hear her.

"Ursula told me Dad wouldn't have made a mistake in the lab if he hadn't been rushing to get home to me. Said I was demanding and needy, that I'd put unnecessary pressure on him and made him stressed. She convinced me I was to blame, and I despised myself for it. Years later, when I saw a counsellor, I realised what she'd done. He saved me, which sounds dramatic I know, but he did. I could finally see I wasn't responsible for my dad's death."

"I'm so sorry …"

"She had olive trees, you know, like the ones in the garden of Gethsemane, six of them. A craftsman designed the wooden pergola with a cross on the side facing east, made from dogwood. Did you know Jesus died on a cross made from dogwood? Let me tell you how I know…"

It had started as an uneventful evening. Barbara was working late, and Will and John were at Ursula's waiting for her to pick them up on her way home. She was reading a book about flower arranging, Will was on his playmat on the floor, and John was making funny voices with his teddy bear to make him laugh. He was becoming much more fun to be around now he could crawl and toddle about on his chubby legs, more interactive. He'd been cute as a tiny baby, and John loved him so much he thought his heart would burst, but just lying there sleeping or crying was pretty dull.

Will rolled over and crawled towards his toybox. John followed him and showed him a few toys, wondering what he would choose from the massive selection. Will reached in for a chunky blue car and lobbed it across the floor. Launching toys was his new favourite hobby. John scrambled around to collect them, knowing Ursula would be twitchy about the scattered mess on her floor.

"What are you looking for, Will?" John asked his little brother, returning the cars to the box. "You've so much stuff."

Behind him, Ursula's book snapped shut. John jumped, and Will looked up from his rummaging to see where the noise had come from.

"Do you envy your brother John? Are you jealous of him because he has so much more than you ever had?"

"No." John's stomach clenched, "Not at all. I just meant he has a lot of toys to choose from."

"Envy is one of the worst sins of all."

John nodded. She hadn't asked a question. You only answer when she asks a question. She glared at him, eyes fixed and unblinking. Not for the first time, he wondered if she might fire lasers beams at him and turn him into stone or shoot bursts of fire from her nostrils. He was convinced her walking stick was a super-charged weapon, and when she used it, it boosted her energy supply. It was there, by her chair. It was always there.

She jumped to her feet, snatched Will and dumped him in his playpen. Then she turned to him. No hesitation. She dragged him to his feet by his arm, pulling him towards the door. She was strong. He could feel the power in her fingers as they dug into his skin.

"I've told you what happens to people who sin. What happens?" she demanded, not breaking her stride, not losing her grip on his bicep.

"They're punished."

"Worse than that!"

"They don't go to heaven."

She picked up a roll of garden twine from the shelf in the utility, then flung open the back door and pulled him into the garden. Their breath fogged in the evening chill, and now she looked like smoke was billowing from her nose. John stumbled at her side, freezing already in jeans and a t-shirt. She didn't seem to feel the cold.

"You must redeem for your sins. For killing your father, for envying your brother, for your ignorance and ingratitude. I won't have it under my roof."

Ursula shoved him away from her towards her fancy wooden pergola. He backed against the side of it and snatched freezing air into his lungs. What was she going to do? Where could he escape to? A gust of wind blew through the trees, and they roared.

They were as angry as she was. She stared at him, grey-blonde hair whipping around her head and face like tiny snakes.

Had she lost her mind? Her hatred for him was making her crazy. He was going to be sick. Snot and tears clagged his throat and streamed down his face.

"Hold out your arms against the patibulum. This cross is made from dogwood, like the cross Jesus Christ carried and died upon. You should be honoured and grateful because you're about to understand what it feels like to redeem for your sins, like he was the redeemer for humanity."

She'd made him learn that word, the proper word for the part of the cross going from side to side. With one hand, she held his shaky arm up to the wood and lashed him to it, then she cut the twine on the edge cutter and did the same on his other arm. She was crucifying him, like Jesus. She wanted him to die. Well, he wasn't going to beg and plead. He'd wanted to escape. Now he had the chance.

He would miss Will, but he would be with his dad again. John sobbed. Only if he went to heaven though, because Dad was definitely in heaven. He'd been a good man. The best. But John was a sinner. He wouldn't get to meet his dad again because he would go to hell and be the Devil's slave, trapped in misery for eternity. He cried harder.

The trees laughed.

"I changed overnight. Facing death gives you startling clarity, and I honestly believed I would die. She left me there for a while, then came back out with her stick, cracked me across my knees, and told me to be grateful I hadn't been stabbed like Jesus. By then I didn't give a shit. I was numb, inside and out. Afterwards, I knew she couldn't do anything worse to me; except hurt Will."

He eased he blindfold eased back into place. Panic surged through her entire body again, freezing her breath, and she struggled to snatch air into her lungs.

"John please, no …"

"What you said earlier, about covering her transgressions with blood? There was some truth in that. I can't forgive her, but maybe her God can."

Something sharp jabbed her arm. A soft kiss whispered over her lips.

"Thank you for showing me joy Catherine."

*

Gone away for a few days. Need some space.

Robin stared at the text, hoping to find hidden subtext between those nine words, a clue he'd missed the first time. He wanted it to be from her because it meant she was safe, but he didn't want it to be from her because of how cold it sounded.

He knew who could provide the answers.

The roads had clogged up with school run traffic. Robin queued out of Camber and didn't make it out of second gear until he reached Broadstone's outer ring road. He joined the two-lane circular and crawled along until he reached the exit for Castleton. The arty suburb had a narrow High Street buzzing with people. Robin remembered the route and turned down by the newsagents. He swore at someone who'd parked on the corner while he laughed on his mobile. Robin squeezed past. He didn't have time for bollocking idiots.

What the hell?

Robin pulled over abruptly next to the badly parked car. The driver behind him honked on his horn. Robin ignored it and slid the passenger window down.

"Jamie."

Jamie Clarke, cigarette in one hand, can of Red Bull in the other, stopped studying the adverts stuck to the inside of the shop window and spun around.

"Are you following me?" he asked, ambling over.

"Why the hell would I follow you? Get in. And put your fag out."

Jamie took one last drag on his cigarette and flicked it away before getting into Robin's car. Robin quickly found a safer place to park and killed the engine.

"What are you doing here?" he demanded.

"Just … browsing."

"For what? Antiques and deli wraps?"

"Delly whats?"

Robin glared at him. "Don't act thick. I told you to stay away from John Rickman. You know he lives three streets away.

Are you hoping you might bump into him? Planning another little visit?"

Jamie popped the lid of his can and took a drink. "Wouldn't be my fault if he's out and about." He glanced at Robin across the can. "There's something else. You know that stuff you asked me about? Hemlock? Well, I told Marcia you'd been asking me about it. I got the word wrong, and she corrected me because she knew about it. She learned about hemlock at school, in history. Mr Rickman's class."

Jamie waited for Robin to laugh. He didn't. He watched a woman herd three skippy school children in maroon blazers towards the corner shop, as he slotted Jamie's information into place in his head.

"You're going round there, right?"

"Maybe."

"Want me to come with you?"

"What?" Robin stared at him incredulously.

"He's in. I drove past."

"Did you see a woman? Thirties, pretty, big hair."

Jamie finished his drink and crushed the can. "Your girlfriend, you mean?"

"How do you know she's my ... girlfriend?"

"I've met her. Marcia gave her some shit over Mr Rickman. We found her in Wags in town. Catherine was cool. I liked her."

Robin couldn't remember Catherine mentioning a run-in with the Clarkes, but there'd been a lot going on he didn't know about.

"I didn't see her. But we could knock on."

"We? There is no 'we' Jamie. Look, I appreciate your help but go home. Stay out of this."

"Fair enough." He pulled a sulky pout and made to get out of the car, then stopped and turned back to Robin. "If she was my girlfriend, I'd be pissed too," he said with sombre sincerity, "I hope you find her."

He opened the door and loped off towards the High Street, pulling his cigarettes from his jacket pocket. Robin watched him until he disappeared around the corner and out of sight.

*

Barbara sank into hot, steamy bubbles and let the water pull her into its soothing embrace. Candles on the windowsill, expensive bath oils, Phil Collins on low. A tiny part of the world just for her. Even Will never ventured into her private bathroom. She inhaled the steamy, fragranced air. A new oil she'd bought combining the sweet scent of lilies with a spice infusion which reminded her of Thailand. Costly but worth it. If she bathed at night, the scent clung to her skin while she slept, infusing her dreams with memories of happier times.

She'd been to Thailand with Michael, not long after they'd married, for three glorious, child-free weeks. Those few years she'd been with Michael had been the happiest of her life. Michael had been good for her, had handled her like no other man ever could. When she scanned the map of her life laid out in her memory, her time with Michael was a fresh and green oasis surrounded by years of rocky roads.

Michael's death had changed her life. With him around, Barbara had been able to relax. He'd been so protective of his sons. Barbara caught her mother looking at John with bitter contempt. She despised him just for living, when her son was gone. William had been a distraction at first. Ursula had been infatuated with him, or with the management of him more accurately. He had the best of everything.

At the time, Barbara had mistaken excessive spending for love. Ursula lavished him with gifts, surrounded him with luxuries other parents dreamed of. Michael hadn't liked the excesses, but Barbara had been able to talk him round. Life had been good. And then Michael died, and the foundations of her life had been blasted away, leaving everything else precariously rocking in a dangerous breeze.

Could she have done better? She reached through the steamy air towards her wine. Bullshit and bravado aside, yes she could. She envied the mothers who felt the visceral, unconditional love for their children. It just wasn't there for her. She'd pushed William, driving him away with her ambition instead of giving him her love. Another confession: it was why she despised John so much. He acted out of love. John had his father's passion and depth and grew to be so like Michael it hurt to look at him.

Grief punched her, so physically she gasped aloud. Michael had been dead for a long time, and she'd dealt with his passing.

Or had she? She took another drink and braced herself against grief's merciless weight.

The years had raced by, and she appeared successful, but successful at what? What had she achieved? William was her only real success, and John had probably been right; it was down to William, not her. If she hoped to maintain a bond with her son, she had to try to repair their tattered relationship. But he was so damaged by his childhood she didn't know how to fix him. If he saw it from her perspective, he might realise she'd always acted with him in mind. Sometimes it had been like holding back a tiger with an upturned chair, while simultaneously soothing a fretting python.

She had to talk to William again. They'd barely spoken since their argument. He'd been distant. Distracted. Came home from school and hid in his room, refused dinner. She didn't want him blowing the situation out of proportion. She could repair this.

Barbara pulled on her bathrobe and went to look for him. No TV or music from William's room across the landing. She knocked on his door. No response.

"William?"

Silence. Barbara darted from room to room, opening doors she hadn't opened in the last month. All this space gave her claustrophobia, surrounded by air she couldn't breathe. She felt it now because William had gone. Not a teenage strop either. Gone. Barbara ran back up the stairs and flung open the door to William's room. Nothing amiss. It looked as it always did.

Back in her room, she took her phone from its charger and rang William's number. She knew he wouldn't answer, but she rang anyway, several times, then texted. He wasn't technically missing, and the police wouldn't take her seriously if she called about a teenager who'd been gone for an hour or two. DI Scott might listen to her though. He seemed like a man who cared, who would understand William's troubles. Strings were there to be pulled.

Barbara ignored her protesting pride and dialled Robin Scott's number.

*

"Jack. Not heard from you in a while. Surprised you still have my number."

"How are you doing?" Jack leant back in Robin's chair and turned away from the window which overlooked the office.

"Oh, you know, ticking over. How's things your end? You made DI yet?"

"You know me, Jim. I'm not interested in paperwork and politics. I need a favour."

"And there's me thinking the force wanted me back."

"If it had been up to me, you would never have gone in the first place."

"What do you need?"

"If I give you a mobile number, can you do some digging around for me, please?"

A heavy sigh.

Jim would agree, but Jack allowed him a moment to pretend to consider. He owed him one. After all he'd done for him, he would be offended if he refused.

"Running tight on budgets these days?"

"Always. You know what it's like. I'll fill you in over a beer."

Ella giving her PC the evils. She glanced his way, and the frown deepened. Making the call in Robin's office hadn't been a bright idea. She'd be all over him now, fishing for info.

"Give me the dirty headlines. We both know there's no beer."

Silence. This was Jim's price. Like a game of truth or dare, only in this instance, he didn't get to choose.

"My DI's partner has gone missing and it's not looking good. No one can get hold of her, no one's seen her, and she's become close to a possible suspect in a murder case."

"Which is why you don't want it processed in-house. Bet Collins isn't happy."

Jack began to regret the call. Jim wanted to chew the fat and time was ticking.

"Can you help me or not?"

"It beats internal theft and cheating shaggers. Send me the details. I'll see what I can do."

Chapter Twenty-Two

Demons

"Can I come in? I have a few questions."

"I'm on my way out."

John didn't look on his way anywhere. He wore shorts and a t-shirt, his feet bare and his hair wet as if he'd just showered. Robin stared at the black and purple bruises covering his legs, but unlike last time he had no pity. He wouldn't mind adding to them. He met John's eyes again.

"It won't take long."

Without a word, John opened the door and Robin followed him inside.

"Go through," John gestured towards the kitchen, "I'll be one minute."

John disappeared, leaving Robin alone. He edged around the kitchen table, looking for any signs Catherine might have been there. The only person likely to have been in there was a housekeeper. The kitchen was immaculate, toolkit gone. His phone rang. Barbara Rickman, probably to moan about something else they'd done or not done. He cancelled the call.

"So, what did you want to ask me?"

John had changed into tracksuit bottoms and a long-sleeved top and tied his hair back. He must have been self-conscious about the bruising.

"I'm looking for Catherine. Have you seen her?"

"You two broke up, didn't you?"

He asked the question in such a light, casual manner it fired up Robin's insides. Affable John had disappeared.

"Have you seen her? Yes or no?"

"Not in the last few days."

"Let's talk about your grandmother again."

"Will's grandmother. And I'd rather not ..."

"OK then. Hemlock. What do you know about hemlock?"

"I know all about it."

Robin frowned. He hadn't expected such a blunt and candid response, an arrogant one even.

"Where were you on the night Ursula was killed?"

"Here. It's in my statement."

"So, why were you puking in a layby on the A56 at 3am?"

John blinked. It had been a lucky punt. They'd still not found anything conclusive, but Robin saw the first flicker of discomfort. He moved closer to John, who leant on the door frame.

"I've no idea what you're talking about."

"You caught the bumper of a truck parked in the layby as you left."

"Not me I'm afraid. You could check my car, but it's crushed into a cube now."

"Oh, no it's not." Robin matched John's casual tone as the balance shifted. "It's at the scrap yard. Has a nasty scrape, rear passenger side."

"As you know, I was in a crash. The car was a right off."

"Wrong point of impact."

"That car was covered in bumps and scrapes. You don't park a half-decent car in Toncaster High School's car park. It would be keyed before I even made it into the building."

"There's a very nice new car outside."

John shrugged. "Guess I'll have to take my chances, eh?"

"How did you get the spray paint off?"

Another blink. Robin moved closer.

"What paint?"

"'Peedo'. Massive red letters."

John dipped his head and sighed.

"It was a prank."

"Jamie Clarke's admitted he attacked you, but you claimed you'd no idea who your attacker was."

"A misunderstanding, and it's in the past. I didn't see any point in reporting the paint job. I washed it off."

"But you knew he attacked you."

"Not one hundred per cent."

"You're lying." Robin closed in, but John didn't move, pinned to the doorway as if it provided support. "Like your little brother did. You're a family of liars."

"Keep my brother out of this."

"Which one of you did it? Or did you do it together?"

"Get the fuck out of my house!"

John's calm façade shattered as he pushed away from the door and stood toe to toe with him.

"People will understand," said Robin, his fingertips grazing John's chest to keep him just at bay, "Your grandmother was a twisted bitch; she was handy with her stick, she got off on humiliating people, and no one has a single goddammed nice thing to say about her. I can see how you two might want rid of her."

"You've no idea what you're talking about."

"Did she abuse Will, or did he make it all up for attention?"

John shoved Robin away with enough power to make Robin step backwards. John was tall and slim, but he was stronger than he looked.

"Come on John, tell me the truth. Tell me what's been going on."

John lunged. A decent enough punch, but Robin was ready for it. He blocked the fist aiming straight for his nose and pushed John away, sending him banging back against the wall. In one swift, graceful manoeuvre John took hold of the sweeping brush leant against the cupboard at his side, and it arced through the air, cracking hard into Robin's side. He stumbled backwards, crashed into the nearest chair, and went down. He hadn't seen that coming. John had swung the broom like he'd swung it a thousand times before, like he'd been fencing or sword fighting. Robin dragged himself upright again, winded and incensed to have been bested by a sweeping brush, but not hurt. When he turned around, John had gone.

Robin scrambled to his feet. No sign of John in the hall or the downstairs rooms. The cupboard door was now open though. Had he hidden in a cupboard? Robin yanked the door wider and peered inside. A long, narrow space, neatly organised with stacked plastic boxes filled with God knows what, a vacuum cleaner, a set of golf clubs, and a row of coats at the back. He moved the coats aside, searching the floor for him, but John had vanished.

A noise like a tin can hitting a tiled floor, came from below. He froze, listening for more. But the cupboard ended where the coats hung. There had to be cellar access in there somewhere. Robin shouldered the coats aside again and felt around until his fingers found a handle at the edge of the false back. The door quietly opened.

He'd reached a steep staircase, lit dimly by light from below. A low and gentle buzz, like an air extractor or fan, hummed in the shadows. He took the first step, peering into shadows, but the light source was useless, no brighter than a candle. He edged further, nerves tingling. Sensible option: go back upstairs and radio in for help. But he wasn't feeling sensible. The fight had fired him up, and Catherine could be here. Only option: find her.

He reached the bottom and stood motionless, letting his eyes adjust further to the darkness. As he stepped onto a mat on the floor, there was a firm click from above him. Just the door settling back into place.

Suddenly an icy shard of pain stabbed into his neck. He gasped and spun around, one hand clutched at his throat, the other grappling for the handrail as he fell. He fumbled for purchase, leather soled shoes slipper on the tiled floor.

"What the fuck …" Robin tried to speak. His words slurred like they couldn't be bothered leaving his lips. He managed to keep himself upright long enough to catch a glimpse of John standing in the shadows, watching him with blank detachment.

Then he vanished.

*

"No joy with the CCTV." Ella offered Jack a Jammy Dodger as he headed back to his desk, "The footage is shit. It's pitch black, and all you can see are the car's headlights as it moves past the camera," Ella stopped and frowned, "What's up?"

"Sorry. Miles away." Jack swung his chair around to face Ella, "Do you ever stop eating?"

"Not while I'm still pumping milk, no. Where's the boss, by the way?"

"Following up on Rickman's car, I think. What about the truck driver? Can he ID the guy he saw in the layby?"

"No. Too dark, and the guy wore a hood."

Jack stared at his biscuit; his appetite gone. Robin's concern had sent his mind spinning. He trusted Robin's instincts, and struggled now to ignore his own rising concerns.

"What about the car?" asked Ella, between bites.

"It's gone to the compound. Signs of a secondary collision, but it's so battered it's hard to tell. Plus, it's been valeted."

"Forensics might still find something."

"They might."

"What's wrong? You seem … flat." She pushed her sandwich aside and opened a bottle of orange juice.

"I'm just tired."

"Bollocks. In all the time I've known you, I don't think I've ever heard you say you're tired. You're always going on about how you can manage on four hours sleep."

"Where are Vic and James?" Jack looked around, hoping to distract her. He didn't want to betray Robin's trust until he knew they definitely had a problem.

"Vic's taking a statement downstairs, James has gone home." Ella sat back. "Spill, Jack."

"Leave it, will you?" His mobile began to ring, and Jack pushed out of his chair.

"One second Jim." He left the office and headed for the kitchen. "Go on."

"Interesting one this," said Jim, "No outgoing activity until two hours ago. One ping off the EE mast on the ring road and a low powered ping from one on the A56. I'd say it was on for no more than thirty seconds."

"Long enough to send a text and turn off again."

"Just about. The phone would automatically search for other masts, and you'd see varying strengths of signal, dependent on how far away the masts were. There wasn't enough time. One outgoing text was sent. The next time it was detected, it was moving out of Broadstone towards Mallom."

"Is it still moving?"

"Yep. Towards the airfield."

"What?"

"Not much else down the B336 unless you work at the power station."

Mallom was a tiny airfield for private aircraft and flying lessons. Possible she could know someone with a light aircraft.

"Is she having lessons? Shagging a pilot?"

"Do you have the number of the text recipient?" Jim read out the number. Robin's mobile. So, she'd been in touch. All was good.

"Hang on one sec." Jack put Jim on hold and rang Robin. He didn't answer. He tried again and then reconnected with Jim. "Do you have the location of the number you just gave me?"

"The last known location was Northwest of Broadstone. Around Billingsborough and Castleton. Static. It's not responding now."

"So, going back to the original number, Catherine's phone: did you access the call records?"

"No, just location. Do you want me to?"

Jack hesitated. It appeared she'd messaged Robin and headed off for some fun in the sky. Really? Days after a serious accident. Without telling anyone? And he wasn't stupid; active phone didn't always mean active phone owner.

Fuck it. Don't ask for permission; ask for forgiveness. He'd stand by his decision he made the wrong call. Gut feel. Robin always talked about gut feel.

Jack gave the go ahead, ended the call and returned to the office. Ella watched him in puzzled silence as he dug his Airwave out of his pocket and tried Robin via the radio. No response.

"Are you going to tell me what's wrong yet?"

"I can't get hold of Robin."

"Try ringing the compound," Ella stared at him as the lie sunk in, "He's not at the compound, is he?"

"Get your coat."

"Why, have I pulled?"

"Very funny, come on."

"Right, what's happening? Now Jack," Ella insisted, hands on hips. Her eyes fixed on him, firm and demanding.

Jack rubbed his face and plonked into his chair. "He's gone looking for Catherine. He thinks she's missing. She sent him a text saying she'd gone away for a few days, but I don't think he believes it."

"Are we marriage guidance now?"

"Robin and Catherine had a fallout. John Rickman may've been the trigger."

"So, he's gone around there for a pissing contest?"

"I don't know," said Jack wearily.

"Leave him to it Jack. Don't get involved."

"But Rickman's a suspect."

"Since when? We've identified the brother might be, but not him."

"He could be involved, or at least a viable accomplice."

Ella screwed up her face, head shaking.

"He's an attractive young bloke who saved a woman's life. A law-abiding, popular guy who happens to be a relative – a step relative – of a murder victim. Robin even said he liked him when he first met him. Do you want my theory? He's jealous there's a younger guy on his turf."

"What a pile of shit ..."

"No evidence implicates John Rickman."

"What, so you're suggesting he's trying to frame Rickman now? Out of jealousy? Christ, give the man some credit. He's a DI with a spotless record."

"Well, apart from killing his wife."

"Fucking hell, that's harsh Ella."

"True though."

"No it's not. It was a tragic, horrific accident. He didn't know explosives were hidden in the house, no one did. I don't know what's going on with you, but you've surprised me. You're usually more balanced."

"He wouldn't be the first guy to try to set up a love rival. I don't know how you can't see it."

"There's nothing to see."

"I don't think you're willing to see bad in him and it's clouding your judgement."

"OK, stop. This is getting us nowhere." He could rattle off a list of Robin's flaws, but they don't make him bad, just human like the rest of them.

Ella sighed. "What do you want to do? And nothing's 'going on' with me by the way."

There was. He stared at her for a moment and hoped she would cave in to the silence. She didn't.

257

Was there any truth in what she'd suggested? Robin disliked Rickman, and perhaps it did stem from jealousy, but he'd never pushed him as a suspect. He'd been in favour of the brother like the rest of them.

"I'll hand over to night shift and go home. If he doesn't show up here by seven at the latest, we know there's a problem. And I'm pretty sure he'd have my back if I was in the shit."

*

Robin's legs were concrete, his arms glued to his back. Ragged breaths, hasty and desperate. No, slow now, so slow he wasn't sure if he would take another breath. Then he did ten or so gasps, which made his chest rise and fall rapidly, as his body caught up on the air it had missed before. He'd lost the power to regulate his basic functions. His clothes clung to his skin like he'd sunbathed in forty-degree heat wearing a woollen three-piece suit, but he shuddered with cold. Sweat dripped into his eyes, pooled at his throat, slid down his spine. His mouth had the consistency of scorched earth.

He forced his eyes open. Couldn't keep them open. Gave up.

Waves of nausea woke him the next time. Not waves. Crashing breakers tossed him around in an undulating swell. Black voids pocked his memory. How the hell had he got … where? Where was he? Hard floor. Dim lights. Humming. Arms didn't move how they should. He rolled sideways and retched.

When he opened his eyes again, enough time had passed for bits of vomit to dry on his cheek. But the world seemed to make more sense. He lay at the foot of the cellar stairs, his upper body braced against the bottom step. His arms were behind him and still wouldn't move. His legs stretched out towards a huge bookcase built into the wall. Ankles bound.

He twisted his head to the left, with a degree of effort disproportionate to the minuscule outcome he achieved. A bank of floor-to-ceiling museum cases stretched along one wall, their contents cradled in pools of soft light. Swords. Dozens of swords. A leather sofa curved around a circular low table made from a mill wheel. Dark space beyond. Was it another room? His vision swam in and out of focus, thoughts clanged around like coins in a tin.

"Why did you have to come here?" John appeared out of the shadows and sank onto the sofa. Robin blinked, trying to concentrate on being alive.

"Water," Robin said. Tried to say. The word came out as a crushed croak. His body trembled momentarily, then settled back to stillness.

"You think you know me. You think you understand. But you don't have a clue. I didn't want any of this," John dropped his head into his hands.

Robin closed his eyes as the trembling rippled through him again. His lungs grasped at the cool air, dragging it in as his chest heaved. Something grazed his lips. He opened his eyes again and looked helplessly at John who held a bottle of water to his mouth. Robin drank, hating the neediness. That was good though. He could feel again. And think.

"Where's Catherine?" Robin's words were spongy as his brain continued to demist. "She's missing."

"You're so absorbed in yourself I'm surprised you've even noticed she's gone."

"What did you give me?"

"Your concern for Catherine didn't last long, did it?" John shook his head. "All my life I've been surrounded by selfish people who've no concept of what it's like to care for someone else more than themselves. My dad was an exception, Bobby and Will are too, but everyone else? Ruthless, selfish bastards."

"What happened to you?" Robin's heartrate had slowed from a gallop to a brisk trot.

John stared at him for a long time.

"You don't care about anyone but yourself."

New menace had crept into John's tone, and it wouldn't help the situation to antagonise him further. Robin had to focus on getting out of there. Assuming he could get his body back under control. He still had the strange sensation of being detached from it, like he existed in a limbo place between consciousness and a disturbing euphoria. Maybe Ursula Harrison had experienced the same trippy state as she died, flung back to the bygone times she yearned for on the mother of all roofies.

"So, let's talk about you Robin. And Catherine. How could you let a woman like her go?"

"Untie me, John."

"She's amazing in bed. The best I've ever had."

A cold punch of resentment momentarily made his guts clench again. Then snapshots of memories flashed in his mind like an old-style projector flicking frame by frame. Catherine in the shower, obscured behind steamy glass. Beneath him on the bed, head back, eyes closed. The first time he'd seen her naked. Kissing the moles on her neck. The way her thighs quivered just before she came. One after the other, the images loaded then were snatched away. He couldn't deal with the anger because sorrow overwhelmed him. All those moments were lost. Gone.

"Is she still alive?"

"Probably."

Worse than a yes or no. Not knowing added to the torment.

John leant back into the sofa like they were chatting over a beer. This man was a chameleon and Robin wasn't sure which version of John he faced. The coarse reference to sex with Catherine seemed out of character compared to the sensitive and introverted side of him he'd seen before. An act for his benefit, or his true colours showing? Robin couldn't decide. His instinct was still face down in a heap, trying to recover alongside his self-esteem.

"Every woman should experience a younger man. Put it on the bucket list. Jump from a plane, see the Northern Lights, get laid by younger man. They all fantasise about it."

"You're full of shit."

"Catherine said she had."

Don't take the bait. Don't react. If John wanted a reaction, he wouldn't give him the satisfaction of getting one.

"You wouldn't be the first copper to have relationship issues, to let a special woman slip from your grasp. Is that it Robin? Have you become a cliché? Work too much, drink too much, forget how to feel. I'd fight it, channel all my energy into not becoming the kind of partner your loved one can't reach. Being a copper shouldn't mean being emotionally alone."

The perceptive accuracy stung. Robin shifted in his bonds, but it wasn't the hard floor or the ties around his wrists causing the discomfort. Once again, he saw why Catherine had been drawn to this man.

"Am I right?"

"Probably."

John stared ahead at the bookcase, lost in his thoughts. The gentle hum from the display cabinets gave the subterranean retreat a calming atmosphere. It all looked brand new and gleaming, a whole new take on the man cave. It was another world. John's world. An immersive womb of escape filled with books, history and the possessions he treasured. John had trapped Robin in his absolute core.

"I wouldn't expect you to admit it, not even to yourself. Denial is safer. Easier."

"I got lazy, OK? I assumed I was giving her enough. Hoped. I hoped it was enough. But it wasn't, was it?"

"Complacency is a wrecking ball."

"Great name for a rock song."

"Or the theme tune for your life."

Robin stared at him. "What does that mean?"

"Think about it. It's a guess, but I reckon this is history repeating itself. And it will continue repeating itself until you change."

"I don't want to change."

"The stubborn copper, stuck in his ways. Another cliché. Where's the real you? The one not defined by a badge or a belt."

DI Scott, black belt; the weapons he relied on were defunct here. Did they define him? Was he shallow? His head might still be foggy, but he couldn't accept he was as superficial as John made out. He might not be as freely expressive as others, as open with his emotions. But he felt. He thought. Not just made of a badge and a belt. And why did he care what John thought anyway? He'd been drawn into a deep and meaningful when his focus needed to be on getting the hell out of there, finding Catherine and arresting the murderer. But his only tools were his brain and his voice.

"Maybe you're right, and that's why she turned to you. I left her empty. Neglected her. Now you need to look after her. Where is she?"

John leant forward.

"I know about Erin."

*

Jack was almost home when Jim rang him back. He pulled over to answer, wishing he had Bluetooth in his car.

"I don't have much to tell you," said Jim, in his usual straight-to-the-point style, "Except there's been little activity from the device in the last 24 hours, same over the weekend. One text at 2.12pm today. The number's registered to a John Rickman. Five numbers appear regularly. I'll send them over to you now. There's also a landline. I rang it and reached Clive Darwin at the Post. Going back to the first number though, John Rickman's. His and her numbers pinged off the same mast briefly this afternoon at 3.56pm. Location; northwest of the town centre."

Jack's phone beeped as he received the numbers from Jim. "You've been on the job. What jumps out at you?"

"Sod all. Lots of calls with Clive Darwin, no texts though. Possibly a new device and she uses WhatsApp rather than text. Like I said, the activity levels are low, which does suggest she's taking time out. Next step, if you want to go legit, would be a cloud extraction warrant or request to her service provider. I can go deeper but wouldn't advise it if you think this might go legal."

"Thanks for your help. I appreciate it."

"No problem. I hope you find your girl."

So, Robin had gone over there after all, and might still be there but not responding to calls. It had been a few hours since he'd had last made contact. How long did it take to confront someone and say your piece? Not the best part of four hours, and apart from the occasional run Robin wouldn't take personal time out in the middle of an investigation.

Jack turned his car around in a driveway and headed back towards the ring road. A minor diversion, and it would put his mind at rest. Robin was a big boy, but he'd just sit at home churning.

He drove past John's place twice. He couldn't see Robin's car anywhere. The evening was chilly and clear, close to freezing. The biting wind pinched his cheeks as soon as he left the cosy warmth of his car. He passed a couple of houses before he reached John's, nosing in through open curtains to get a feel for the neighbourhood. Most houses had sacrificed their front gardens in favour of a parking space, but John had kept the original walled garden and ornate stepped entrance. A new black Audi was parked on the kerb.

No lights on, no sounds within. A quick look through the letterbox revealed nothing more than a shadowy hallway. He called John's number and listened for it ringing from inside. The hush remained.

To the side of the house a passageway with a gate halfway down led to a rear garden, bathed in complete darkness. He peered through the French doors, cupping his hands around his head. No sign of anyone inside. A sweeping brush lay on the floor, which seemed strange, but no other signs of any disturbance. Did he have compelling cause to enter? He tried the doors. Locked. No sign of anyone, despite the car parked outside.

His instinct bristled. He couldn't just walk away.

Jack found a large stone in a plant pot and broke one of the small, glazed panes at the top of the back door. Looked vintage, but tough shit. He waited for sound, to see if anyone came to investigate. The house remained hushed. He reached inside and got lucky. Key in the lock.

He was in.

*

Robin's past and present collided. John speaking Erin's name wrenched him out of the last tendrils of brain fog. Catherine had talked to him about Erin. She'd asked him to be open and share his pain with her. She'd asked him to bleed himself dry. Then, to discuss it with a stranger, perhaps over a bottle of Felix Washington's wine ... the betrayal stung more than the likelihood she'd fucked this younger man, who was everything he wasn't.

"I understand why you despise yourself, Robin."

"Shut the fuck up."

"If something's meant to happen, you can't stop it."

"That's bollocks."

"What could you have done to prevent her death?"

In his mind, Robin saw himself make the call again, like watching himself in a film, and the image had perfect clarity because he'd replayed it thousands of times. He knew the script word for word. Why hadn't he sent someone else in there that day, someone else's son, daughter, parent, lover? Selfish, and he didn't like himself for thinking it. Honest and human though. No one ever thinks, 'I'm so glad this horrendous event happened to me and not someone else'. He'd shamelessly wished the misery on others many times.

"Every time you fall in love, you'll lose her, because you choose to punish yourself. It's your life lesson, your penance. Do you deserve a lifetime of loss?"

"Yes! I heard her parent's hearts break. I did that. My actions." Robin swallowed a bitter swell of guilt. "I spoke to Cat's mum earlier. She begged me to find her daughter." He looked John smack in the eyes. "Don't do it to her. Please."

"You mean don't do it to you."

"This isn't about me ..."

"You were lucky. You experienced what most people don't get to feel in a lifetime. A love to fill you like the air you breathe. What a gift. And in a way, you've given me a gift by failing with Catherine. Your self-destruction brought her to me."

"A car crash led her to you; let's not over romanticise."

"When I saved her life."

"So don't take away what you've given. If she's still alive … You want to be with her, don't you?"

"Not much chance now, is there?" John rose to his feet, "And if I can't have her, neither can you," John stared at the bottle and syringe he now held, frowning like it had disappointed him.

What would happen with another shot if John hadn't given him enough last time? He'd given Ursula enough to kill her. Robin was much bigger than the elderly woman, which was probably why he'd been able to fight through it. Assuming it had been hemlock.

"John, please don't give me any more," Robin implored, "What do you gain by keeping me here? I understand why you killed Ursula but killing me too … that's not who you are."

He tried to stand. If he could at least get to his feet, he might be able to fight him off if he came at him again. Although the effects had diminished, he quivered still. Muscles tight, nerves stretched to snapping. He hated being restrained too, and the humiliation of it. Nowhere near as much fun as when he asked Catherine to cuff him. The reality poles apart from the fantasy.

"The courts will be lenient." Robin tried again. "There's no excuse for what happened to you. Murder is never right, but they'll understand what drove you to it. If you add in my death and Catherine's … you don't stand a chance. You're a pretty lad. You'll be doing favours for phone cards for the rest of your life."

The bottle sat alone on the table. He didn't want any more of that stuff. If John came towards him again, he had to find a way to fight.

"But Ursula will still be dead, and you won't have Catherine."

"And Will won't have a brother."

John froze. Mentioning Will had resonated. Will was undeniably his soft spot.

"I've just realised; Erin is in Cath-Erin-e." He spun around. "Don't you think that's strange? You really can't let go, can you?"

"It's a coincidence. I've never thought about it."

"Rubbish. Guilt consumes and contaminates you, so even subconsciously, you make decisions based on what you had and lost. I told Catherine you didn't deserve her, and it's true. She never stood a chance of being loved as fiercely as you loved Erin, did she? She could never replace your wife."

"I don't want anyone to replace her. No one could."

"Which is why you didn't deserve her."

"Fine." Robin kept his voice low and calm, trapped frustration squeezing his ribs. He ached for release. "You have her. You win. Be with her and make her happy …"

"She's gone, Robin." His stomach rolled and pitched downwards like he'd skydived from a plane. "Just like Erin."

"No! I don't believe you. You care for her ..."

"Letting people go is painful, but you must be willing to sacrifice your own happiness to be truly selfless. It's best for her. I need to deal with you next …"

He stopped, interrupted by a loud knock from above. He grabbed a roll of tape from a box of tools behind the sofa, then tore off a strip and approached Robin.

"It's probably a delivery, but one knows about this room."

"I won't shout out; you have my word. You can't keep me here forever. This must end."

John bent over and stuck the tape over Robin's mouth.

"It had ended. Then you came along and fucked it all up again," he perched on the arm of the sofa and listened for another knock, but silence had returned. "Meeting Catherine changed my life, altered my self-perception. No coincidence we met how we did. I was blessed by the opportunity to save the life of the woman who, in her way has saved mine. I haven't known her for long, but she completes me. I saw her as Ursula's diametric, her furthest extreme. Where Ursula cursed my life with her malevolence, Catherine cleansed it.

"Which probably sounds like a pile of shit to you." John sat back and stared at Robin. "You don't strike me as a deep thinker."

Robin fought to not react to John's invective. If his hands were in front of him, he would have a chance of overpowering John, presuming he had the strength to stand. He couldn't process what he'd said about Catherine, refused to accept it.

Another sound from upstairs, but closer this time. A bang, followed by a door opening. John lunged for the syringe, and Robin looked around for something to kick over to make a noise. The glass-topped coffee table was too far away. As John came nearer, he lifted his bound legs and kicked out, desperate to avoid the needle, but his body struggled to comply. Like batting feebly at a gnashing lion in an anxiety dream. He carried on trying, fuelled by the burning desire to stay alive.

John edged back and reconsidered. Being backed in a corner worked to Robin's advantage. John couldn't get near him if he kicked and twisted. Out of luck rather than skill, Robin managed to scrape his shoes down John's shin, aiming for where he'd seen the worst of the bruises left by Jamie's attack. John reeled backwards in pain, and his calves connected with the edge of the table. It wasn't enough to send him flying into it, but he knocked a glass ashtray off the table. It shattered on the tiles.

John spun around and edged away from the glass. Bare feet trod cautiously. Robin had an advantage, and he kicked out again at John, trying to send him off balance and towards the shards of glass. But John was swift. He leapt over the table to safety, meaning Robin couldn't reach him, but at least he'd bought himself some time.

The further away from the syringe the better.

*

Jack checked the ground floor and flicked on all the lights. Satisfied the rooms were clear, he did the same upstairs. Nothing.

266

Back in the hall, he opened the door underneath the stairs. A storage cupboard filled with the stuff people usually shove out of the way; coats, shoes, vacuum cleaner. He slammed it shut. Where the hell were they? He left the house through the smashed back door. He couldn't wait to explain that little mishap.

Time to see how nosy the neighbours were.

The lights were on next door, and as soon as Jack knocked, a tiny woman in a flowery dress opened the door with the security chain on.

"DS Tanner from Broadstone CID, could I have a word?"

The woman flicked on the porch light and squinted at Jack's ID. She checked the photo then slid the chain off.

"Just being cautious after what happened to John next door," she said, "Come in. I've given my statement though."

"I'm looking for John actually. Have you seen him or my colleague? Tall bloke wearing a dark blue coat, short hair."

The woman shook her head straight away.

"No. Well, I saw John go out earlier. I used to hear his old car, but his new one's much quieter. I didn't see him come back, but he must've done. His car's outside."

"Is he home?"

Another head shake. "I've been in the conservatory nearly all day. Have you knocked?"

"I have. OK, sorry to bother you." Disappointed, Jack turned to leave.

"He might be in the cellar. I can hear him if I'm in mine. I don't use the cellar much, but I keep all my painting stuff down there."

Jack stopped.

"He definitely has a cellar?"

"Oh yes. He plays music sometimes."

"How do you access yours?"

The woman opened the door under the stairs. Her house mirrored John's, the door in the same place as his. Hers opened straight onto the stairs, while John's had opened into a cupboard. She flicked on the light.

"Watch the handrail at the bottom. It's a bit shaky."

The cellar seemed endless, more extensive than Jack had expected, and neatly fitted out with metal shelves. He squeezed between a tumble drier and a leaf blower and put his ear to the wall which divided the house from John's. A low hum vibrated through the wall.

"The walls are thick." The woman called from the hallway, "Pre-war. Built to last …"

Jack held up a hand, and she covered her mouth, whispering an apology. Jack closed his eyes, concentrating on sound alone. Just the same monotonous drone. He eased out of the gap and was halfway back up the stairs when a clunk stopped him. A heavy object hitting a bare floor.

"What was that?" the woman whispered.

Jack sprinted up the cellar steps, past the shocked woman and out of the front door. He ran back to John's house, through the side gate and into the kitchen again through the back door, crunching over broken glass. Should he call it in? What would he say? He'd no idea what was going on beneath the floor. No time. He couldn't waste a second if Robin was in danger.

He yanked open the cupboard and shouldered his way through coats. He groped around for a door or a handle, a gap, anything. At last, he felt a lever beneath his fingers, and the panel moved away.

"Don't come any further."

His eyes slowly adjusted to the pale light below. The first few steps were walled in on both sides then the staircase opened up with a simple metal rail running along the left side. A bank of glass-fronted cupboards along the far wall lit the room with its subtle spotlights. Robin lay at the bottom of the stairs, thick tape over his mouth. John crouched by his head, one hand clutching Robin's hair, the other holding a syringe to his throat. What the hell? Jack froze, trying to read whatever Robin was saying with his eyes. John was the one in control, but he appeared the weaker of the two, lost and bewildered.

"John, this is over. Put it down."

Jack edged closer.

"Stay back!"

On the floor, Robin grimaced as the needle penetrated his skin. He shook his head slightly, his eyes never leaving Jack's.

Jack held up his hands, "What do you want?"

"I want you all to fuck off! You, him. Just fuck off!"

"Let's all keep calm, shall we? Is that the hemlock solution you used on Ursula? Robin's a senior police officer. You don't want another death on your conscience."

"Her death is nowhere near my conscience."

Jack took another step. "Throw the syringe away and we can talk about it." He couldn't shove John out of Robin's way, and although the plunger hadn't been pushed down, the needle had pierced Robin's skin. It would take less than a second for him to inject Robin with whatever it contained.

"You don't want to kill him, do you? You'd have done it by now and besides, you're not that kind of person."

John shook his head. "She battered the good out of me."

"No." Jack crept closer. "You proved how strong you are by turning your life around, and your love for your brother, and Bobby … you should be proud of that."

Jack checked over his left shoulder, taking in the room. He needed a second, two at the most. If he could distract John, Robin would be able to throw him off. A one-time-only deal, and he had to time it right, or John could push the plunger on the syringe out of panic. His only weapon was his baton. Useless. And his mobile phone.

"Is that stuff legit?" Jack glanced over at the display cabinets, "It will all be taken away; you know that, don't you?"

John swallowed. Robin stayed laser-focused on Jack. For the first time in Jack's life, he wished he could communicate via telepathy.

"They're legitimately mine."

"Really? All of them? Even the one with the fake handle?"

"What?"

"My dad used to trade in antiques. He taught me about fakes. The one on the right there … it's ringing my alarm bells."

John glanced again, and this time Robin reacted. He threw all his weight at John, who stumbled away, thrown off balance. Robin took advantage and kicked him, sending John sprawling over the coffee table. At the same time, Jack pulled his phone from his pocket and threw it at the glass-fronted cabinets. The centre panel shattered, and glass fragments skittered across the floor like an army of crystal ants.

"You bastard!" John hoisted himself upright and stared at his treasures.

Robin pulled himself onto his knees and rolled his arms up behind his back as high as possible. He swung his arms back down into his butt, pushing his hands outwards and snapping the ties binding his wrists. Jack knew of the technique, and it was impressive to see. Apparently, it hurt like hell, but it snapped the cable tie, and Robin freed himself. He tore the tape from his mouth and the needle from his neck.

"Do you have a key?"

Jack pulled his keys from his pocket and threw them to Robin. Robin hacked through the tie around his ankles and snapped it with a growl.

"Call it in Jack."

"I just launched my phone. Shit."

Jack turned around and scrambled back up the stairs.

Chapter Twenty-three

Henry's sword

"Where's Catherine?"

"Fuck you!"

He lunged at John, finding energy he didn't realise he still had. No fancy karate, no clever moves, just a clash fuelled by animalistic rage. They both crashed to the floor, crunching glass beneath them.

Robin punched John, and he lurched beneath him, trying to throw him off. He was strong, but Robin had more height and weight on his side. He shoved John's cheek into the floor, and John bucked as shards of glass ground into his skin. He lashed out with his free arm, but Robin let the blows land, each one enraging him more.

"You won't have such a pretty face when I'm done with you," Robin snarled in his ear.

"Jealousy suits you Robin," John managed, and he made a sudden lunge for the bottle on the table. It smacked into Robin's head, and putrid-smelling liquid dripped down his neck. Christ, the hemlock. Could it be absorbed through the skin? A moment's distraction, but it bought John enough time to worm free. He scrambled on all fours over to the cabinets with astonishing speed. He reached the central unit, lifted out a short sword and spun around towards Robin. His chest heaved, hair now loose around his shoulders like an enraged savage. His hands, face and feet were bleeding, and his sweatpants were splattered with blood around his knees.

For a moment, neither of them moved.

"Put the sword down. This place will be swarming in less than five minutes."

He stared at a different person. Sword aloft, madness in his eyes. Impressive threat display. Robin's pulse pounded as he remained paralysed by indecision. Wait for backup or try to disarm? He sensed John had tipped over the invisible edge between reality and hysteria.

"I understand why you killed Ursula. You love your brother so much you killed to protect him …"

"I don't want your understanding."

"… that you love Catherine and want to be with her. Where did you take her?"

John spun the sword around with exceptional grace, and speed and pointed the blade to his stomach. Robin lunged towards him and grabbed the handle, knocking it away from its trajectory as they stumbled sideways. They grappled over crunching glass, locked in a hold like two spent boxers waiting for the bell to ring.

"Get off me!"

John resolutely maintained his grip on the sword, despite Robin's greater weight shoving against his chest. They slammed backwards into the display cabinets, and for a second Robin had the advantage, cushioned by John's body, which took the full force of the impact. He managed to get his fingers around the hilt, and he pulled with the last shreds of his strength, but a deeper purpose powered John. Now they had the sword between them, the heavy blade pointed upwards, so close the smell of polished metal filled his nostrils.

Robin didn't budge. He stilled and looked directly into John's eyes, inches from his face. Both breathless, chests heaving, neither willing to concede.

"Where is she?" Sweat trickled onto Robin's lips.

"She ran away to escape you because you're dead inside. You're cold Robin. As cold as Erin's corpse."

The sneery insult stung. There'd been no corpse. She's been blasted into pieces, bits of her strewn in the rubble. He swallowed a backdraft of old grief and focused back on John, because slowly he'd managed to angle the sword towards his stomach, and Robin could feel the resistance of bone and flesh against the tip.

"Do it," John whispered, head back. The blade dug inwards. He smiled, welcoming it in, ready to enjoy its company.

"Tell me what's happened to her, or I swear to God I'll ram this through you."

"There is no God."

John slumped forwards, with the instant matter shift of a popped balloon. For a moment Robin didn't understand what had happened. He pulled his hands away like the sword was fresh from the forge and stumbled back. John slid down the cabinets behind him, the sword embedded in his chest. He'd fallen onto the blade.

Robin stared, shocked into paralysis until his sense kicked back in, and he grabbed at John's shoulders to prevent him from falling further. He sagged like a fresh carcass, and he had to settle for lowering him to the floor. In the distance, wailing sirens approached, and he willed them to get there faster, shaking John, trying to keep him conscious. John groaned, already halfway to a distant place, alien words mumbling from his lips.

"What? What are you trying to say?" He shook him. Nothing. "Tell me where she is!"

"Rich …"

Robin smacked his cheek, felt slipping away beneath his hands.

"I'm sorry ..."

People began swarming down the cellar steps. Paramedics, coppers, Jack looking stressed. The space filled up. Voices, equipment, crunching glass. Robin moved aside to let them deal with John, his head banging like the worst hangover ever invented. Jack stared at John, at the sword protruding from his chest, then at Robin. Fleeting doubt, unspoken questions. He had it all to face now.

Jack offered him a hand and pulled him to his feet. He swayed as the room lurched sideways and Jack grabbed his arm.

"Are you OK?"

"I think so. Have you found Catherine?"

"No. I had Joe track her phone, and she was heading for the airfield. Does she know anyone there?"

Robin stared at him, processing. It didn't make sense. "A friend of hers does charters." He rubbed at his temples. "So the text was from her?"

"Looks that way."

"No, it doesn't feel right. She wouldn't just disappear."

Jack did a compassionate head tilt. Sympathy, perhaps with a hint of 'you're losing the plot'. They went back up the steps and emerged through the door as an ambulance arrived. Robin snatched at memory fragments, like catching balls in the dark.

"He had the sword and I tried to get it off him. We fought …" Robin struggled to reconstruct the scene. "One minute we were holding the sword, the next … he was impaled on it."

"It wasn't your fault."

"But it was. Or it could have been. Shit, I don't know. I should've waited for backup."

"You did what you thought right in the moment. This is a different moment; your perspective is different. You've taught me that."

"I don't think it'll wash with CPS when my prints are all over the sword. And the angle it went in..."

Jack's expression didn't change. "Did you stab him?"

"I wanted to, I really wanted to …"

"But you didn't."

Robin shook his head. "Wanting to was bad enough."

"You'll be fine." Jack gave him a paternal arm clamp. "What are you going to do now?"

"We need to call the airfield and Cat's friend. If she's gone away - fine. I hope she has. But I need to know."

"Sit down and I'll get you a drink. What's her friend called?"

"Carter. I can't remember his first name. Carter's Charters. We laughed at how cheesy it sounded." On the floor in the snug, playing Trivial Pursuit, getting all the answers wrong because they were half wrecked on red wine. A fistful of bees stung in his chest.

When Ella and James arrived, they filled them in on the night's events. The airfield had a night service until 6.30am, so Jack left a message using a spare phone James had brought. Robin tuned out the conversation, distracted by the monologue in his head, the one bollocking he couldn't avoid. He squirmed when Jack explained finding him tied up and gagged, then squirmed more that he'd been taken down by a sweeping brush. What a dick. He'd be laughed out of the dojo when his sensei found out.

"There's a desktop PC in the spare room and an iPad," Jack was saying, "Ella, could you go to the hospital please and keep us posted on John Rickman. If he regains consciousness, ask to see him immediately. Put the pressure on."

"No problem. I'll call in on Barbara Rickman first." Ella reached for her bag.

Robin reached for her arm as she headed for the door. "Are you OK?"

"I'm fine," she said with a glance at Jack. Robin knew when fine didn't mean fine, but he let it go. He needed to get out of there before Collins found out what had happened and hauled him back to the station.

They left the house, leaving James to process the scene.

Robin stopped at the pavement. "Where's my car?"

"It's about ten houses down on the left, next to the white van."

Robin stared down the street. His head was foggy, but he remembered parking outside John's house.

"I didn't spot it, but someone rang up to complain about it apparently, said it's blocking wheelchair access. He must have moved it to make it harder to find you."

Which implied John had intended to detain him for a while, perhaps permanently.

"We'll go in mine."

Numb, Robin took his seat without a word, the events of the past couple of hours replaying in his mind in a surreal and disjointed jumble. The streets rolled silently by.

"Thanks, Jack," said Robin finally, as they headed along the high street, "For finding me, for backing me. I don't know if he would have followed through with his threat, but I'm sure he was going to inject me again. The first shot was horrific. I thought I was going to die."

"It couldn't have been hemlock, or you *would* be dead by now, even with a small dose. It might've been Rohypnol."

"Well, thanks anyway." He shivered, and Jack cranked up the heating. Robin stared out of the window, so drained he didn't know how to think. They whizzed past dark houses and empty streets.

"No piss take about my car?"

Robin scanned the dated but immaculate interior. Jack loved his car. "I honestly don't know where to start."

"Wow, you must be feeling grim." Jack smiled. "So where are we going? Vic's at Cat's house having a look around. Cindy Shelby wasn't much help. Said she hadn't spoken to Catherine for a few days. Clive Darwin wants to join the search."

Robin winced. "I owe him an apology. I've been a right bastard with him."

"He can be a dick, but he's a reasonable dick. He'll understand."

"Two people who might know what John had planned: his little brother or Richard Melling. Ella has the Rickmans covered, so I think we start with the friend."

Chapter Twenty-four

Fake friend

"We need a word."

Richard Melling lived in a terraced house not far from John. He answered the door ruffled from sleep. Robin didn't know the time, but morning was close. Richard showed them into a sparse living room dominated by a desk with three computer screens. No other furniture other than the sofa and a flat screen on the wall, but the three men managed to fill the room.

"It's about John Rickman."

"Is he OK?" Richard shoved back his hair and rubbed his face.

"He was involved in an incident this evening. He's been taken to Broadstone General."

"Again? Jesus. I'll get my coat."

"We want to speak to you first."

Richard dropped into the elaborate gamer chair behind the desk, confusion on his freckly face. The seat whooshed beneath him. Robin perched on the end of the sofa close to him.

"How much do you know about John's relationship with Catherine Nicholls?"

"They've met a few times, and she visited him in hospital with a big bloke, a reporter. When I spoke to John yesterday, he said …," Richard hesitated and gave Robin a transient glance, "They might go away for a few days. What's going on?"

Gone away for a few days, need some space.

"We think he might have abducted her."

"That's ludicrous! Abducted?"

"Is she here?" Robin asked.

"No of course not."

Robin looked at Jack.

"I'll check," said Jack, and he left the room.

"She's not here," Richard repeated, "And John wouldn't abduct anyone. He's not a psycho."

Robin leaned forward. "This evening, your friend drugged me and threatened to kill me. I appreciate you're loyal to John, but I need your help to find her

Richard swallowed. "I don't believe you."

He didn't want to believe it. Robin pushed up the sleeves of his shirt and showed him his wrists. "Why would I make it up? Your friend has serious issues." Richard stared at the vivid red grooves around Robin's wrists. "This is real. And if John survives, he's facing serious charges."

"If he survives? Oh, Jesus …"

"Let's say he has abducted her," said Robin, as Richard dropped his head into his hands and raked at his scalp, "Where would he take her?"

"I don't know."

"Think harder," Robin pushed as Jack returned.

"Does this place have a cellar?" Jack asked.

Richard shook his head. Skinny fingers pulled through ginger frizz.

"Who do you think killed Ursula, Richard?"

Richard froze. As Robin's question sank in, he began to shake his head. "No, no …"

"He admitted it to me …"

"No!" Richard pushed back in the chair, and it wheeled further away. "This is fucked up! He wouldn't …"

"Not even to protect his little brother?"

Richard shook his head, his eyes wild with shock. "Yes, he adores Will but … no. He's not a killer."

"And you have no idea where she might be?"

"I don't know. The castle maybe? She gave him the gate code, and Catherine has access to the main keep. He told me about the left-handed stairways."

"What?"

"The stairs. They were built so attacking raiders from below would be disadvantaged. Their swords would be against the interior curve, so they had no room to swing and …"

"First place we checked." Robin cut off the historical rambling, which was of no use or interest. "The entire site's locked up. No sign of anyone."

Richard shrugged. "Her house, his house …."

Robin leaned into Richard's personal space. "Don't take the piss."

"I'm not, you asked …"

"I know what I asked. You're John's closest friend. You're in on it."

"I'm not! All I know is he's into her."

Robin didn't like the slight smugness to his tone, the note of victory. He turned to Jack. "Did anyone search the keep?"

"No, just externally. They're still trying to get hold of the owner."

"Let's go." Robin jumped up, and a stabbing pain shot through his skull.

"What happened to John?" Richard was still in a state of disbelief, cheeks dusty grey.

"He's in a bad way," said Robin, "He … impaled himself on a sword."

"Oh my God … Henry's sword? Was it Henry's?"

"No idea. Why? Is it significant?"

"It is to John."

Uniform arrived to take a statement from Richard. Outside, Jack's replacement phone rang, and he stared at it in bewilderment for a moment before passing it to Robin. Any other day he would've taken the piss. Today all humour had gone.

It was Vic. Robin answered and put him on speaker so Jack could listen.

"Get this: I'm at Catherine's house still, and a taxi just turned up. The driver found a new iPhone under one of the seats, and a receipt, folded into the wallet bit. It had Catherine's address on it, so he's come to drop it off."

"Where did he take her?" asked Robin.

"It's weird. I showed him her photo and he's never seen her before. Said he would've remembered because she looks like his dentist."

"What about a couple?" asked Jack, "Show him a photo of John Rickman then get a list of all his fares in the last twenty-four hours. Ask if he's been to the airfield."

"OK, he's an Uber so his jobs are on his driver app."

"If Catherine sat in the back, he might not have seen her properly. Has he been to the castle today?" asked Robin.

"Already asked him. No."

"OK. Keep us posted." Robin gave Jack the phone. "What do you think?"

Jack thought for a moment. "She, or they, took a taxi towards the airfield, and she lost her phone in the car. I'd borrow a phone and call the cab firm, check if it was handed in."

"She sent the text around 4pm. Let's say she lost it in the next hour or so. She could be anywhere by now."

"If she sent the text."

"If." Robin rubbed his face, trying to clear the exhaustion and confusion, "Ditch the phone for a second, it's a distraction. She hadn't told anyone she planned to go away. John admitted he'd wanted to get her away from me. Just the vernacular of 'get her away'. It sounds like it's against her will." He stopped. "You think I'm crazy."

"I'd tell you if I thought you were deluded. I'm struggling with why. He's only just met her."

"The depth of his affection for her is staggering, but I can understand how he would cling to friendship and love after being so damaged. The stuff he told me about … I don't know how he can function normally, which is my point. His normal is warped; he escapes to other times to mentally escape this one. Trust me Jack, all this is a decoy to throw us off the scent. He took her phone and … planted it in a taxi, or maybe he asked someone else to do it …"

Hang on.

He snatched Jack's phone and knocked on Richard Melling's door again. Richard answered and Robin took a photo of him.

"Hey, you can't do that," Richard protested, but Robin ignored him. He sent the photo and rang Vic back.

"Show the photo to the taxi driver Vic. I'll hang on."

One of the uniformed officers had joined Richard on the doorstep and was listening with bored professionalism to him moaning about his civil liberties and invasion of privacy.

"Positive ID," said Vic, "He picked him up from his house, took him to Starbucks on the ring road, then took him back again."

"I knew it! You lying bastard." The little shit ducked back inside behind the copper. "Book him for hindering an investigation," Robin spat, as Jack pulled his arm from behind, and the officer held out his hands to stop him too. "And conspiracy to abduct. If anything's happened to her ..."

"I don't know where she is!"

"Then why did you have her phone?"

Richard stared at him like he'd lost his mind. "What phone?"

"The one you left in the taxi."

"It was Will's. John asked me to ..." he tailed off and froze. He looked like he was going to throw up. Richard sagged backwards against the door frame. "Barbara bought Will a new phone. Erased all his numbers, put a tracker on it. He asked me to send it on a little trip to confuse her, throw her off the scent so Will could run away. He's had an escape plan for a while now. John's set it all up for him. Bank account, cash, somewhere to go ... I don't know all the details, but he always wanted Will to have a way out if he needed it. I assumed the time had come."

"It was Catherine's phone, not Will's." Robin yanked open the passenger door of Jack's car and threw himself inside, drained by the events of the night and the violent burst of adrenalin.

"Sorry I lost it."

Jack started the engine. "Understandable. Let's get to the castle."

*

The gates to the car park were open, and Felix waited for them beside a police van and two uniformed officers Robin recognised from the station. Felix had either been dragged from bed in the clothes he wore or didn't own an iron.

"Can you open everywhere up, please?" Robin looked upwards at the imposing structure.

"Catherine was here yesterday morning. I'd like to know what time she left and if she was alone."

"Bad news I'm afraid. I've been inside, and the cameras were shut off. They're monitored through the computer in the office, but the programme has been deactivated."

"How many cameras are there?" asked Robin.

"Eight. All external. But they work like live TV. You can rewind and review but only when you're watching. They don't record and store the footage."

"OK, we'll have to do this the hard way. Guys, could you start by searching the grounds?"

"Guv."

As the officers dispersed to begin the search, a Range Rover pulled into the car park and Clive unfolded from the driver's seat. He opened the boot and took out a huge torch that looked a device for killing aliens. He strode over, chunky overcoat flapping around him, scarf pulled up high.

"Jesus, it's cold," he grumbled at Robin, "I want to help, ok?"

Not the time to bear a grudge.

"Thanks, Clive."

"Let's take a floor each," said Jack, nudging his way through the tension, "Clive, can you take the upper floor?"

"No problem."

Robin stared at the magnificent keep, the place Catherine loved so much. And he felt her there, which scared the hell out of him. The feeling only manifested when he missed someone who'd passed.

"She's not here, is she?"

Robin didn't need a reply from Felix, Jack and Clive. Their faces confirmed it.

"This place is too obvious," said Clive.

Robin plonked down on the bottom step of the stone staircase. Clockwise direction. That's what Richard Melling had talked about, and he understood now. It would be so much harder attacking upwards with your sword in your right hand. Something Catherine would've noticed.

Jack's phone rang, and after a couple of frustrating seconds trying to connect, he moved outside in search of a better signal.

"We need a map." Robin heaved himself upright. If he sat around for much longer, he'd never get up again.

"In the office, this way."

Rolled out of the table in the office, the topographic map was a load of mumbo. He hadn't expected an 'x marks the spot' but vaguely recognisable would've been good. He left Clive and Felix pointing at blobs and studied the pictures on the walls instead. Dozens of paintings and photographs of all parts of the castle.

"Search team's here," announced Jack, reappearing in the doorway, "They're starting on the western side, heading towards the river."

"Still think we're barking up the wrong tree," said Clive. He blew into his cupped hands and rammed his chin down into his scarf.

The pictures on the walls all seemed the same. Keep, walls, tower, keep again, more walls ... wait. Robin stopped and studied a black and white photo from around the 1970s. A guy in a flat cap holding onto two enormous shire horses outside of what looked like a stable building.

"Where's this?" he stabbed a finger at the photo, "I don't remember any stables."

Felix shoved his glasses up onto his head. "No. The stables were demolished. Unsafe and unsavable. That's outside the old forge."

"Where is it?"

"Along the outer wall." Felix returned his glasses to his nose and ran a finger over the map. "Here, where the old village would've been. It's not far. The back of the forge is part of the original wall."

Robin looked at the map. It still didn't make much sense.

"Most of the building is intact, but part of the roof is patched up with tarpaulin," Felix said, "It's been rebuilt a few times, and I keep meaning to sort it out, it's just never been a priority. It's full of junk. Half a tractor, some old furniture. An anvil. I was thinking of having a working blacksmith in there at one time ..."

"Is it accessible?" asked Jack.

"You might have to shove your way through the trees, but yes. And it's not locked. Just a bar across the door."

"So, you can get in, but you can't get out with the bar across. It's perfect."

Clive was nodding. "Makes sense to me.

"Take a phone," said Jack, "I'll stay here and carry on with the search teams."

Felix gave his phone to Robin and told him the code.

"This number should be in the call list." Jack held up his new mobile.

Clive stretched and cracked his back. "Do you want me to come with you or keep searching here? Not being funny, but you look fucked."

Looked? He was fucked, and the idea of a hike through the grounds on a hunch appealed as much as eating his own sick.

"Bring your fancy torch."

*

"Do you know where you're going?"

How long had they been trudging in the darkness? A misty drizzle swirled around them, cloaking the landscape, and although Clive's torch provided reasonable visibility, it was heavy going. They tracked the river, which led in the same direction as the outer wall had done, but they hadn't come across the remaining wall or the smithy.

"I got an orienteering badge in scouts." Clive strode on with unfaltering purpose. No way Robin would admit each step was a mammoth effort. Not when Clive was taking an easy stroll.

"Like you were ever a scout."

"I was kicked out for insubordination."

"Now that I can believe." Robin stopped and stared up at the sky, dread rolling in his stomach. "Have you got a weather app on your phone?"

"On a Blackberry, are you kidding? I don't need one anyway. It's raining."

"I think there's a storm brewing."

"Are you Michael Fish now?

"Fuck off. You can feel it." And he could. Like a dark mood at an unpleasant wedding. And he had no music to drown it out, no anchor. What were the options? Go back and hide while Catherine was out there dying or terrified? Have a meltdown in front of Clive? No chance. His mouth became desert dry, but he had to trust his resilience and ignore it.

The meadow sloped to their right, forming a sweeping basin barely visible in the moonlight. "Over there, look." Robin pointed across the shadowy landscape. "In the photo, behind the guy with the horses, there were trees to his left, the building on his right."

Clive peered into the darkness. "But where's the wall?"

"We're only looking for a short section. The trees could be obscuring it. We need to get closer."

They veered off in the direction of the trees, squelching through rougher ground which slowed their progress. Clive ran through his complete repertoire of expletives as chilly water seeped into his shoes.

A dark structure nestled among the trees, unless he'd created his version of a desert oasis.

"Shit!" Clive suddenly lurched over to one side and crashed to the ground like a felled tree. "I've fucked my ankle." He took Robin's hand and tried to stand, but he growled another barrage of expletives and collapsed again. "You go on, take the torch. I've got my phone light. I'll give it a minute, then I'll follow you."

"I can support you."

"You're a big lad, but I bet I'm a couple of stone heavier. Go. I'll be fine. If she's in there, seconds count."

Robin didn't want to leave him, but he was right. And help wasn't far away. He could still see people and lights at the castle. "Put your phone light on so I know where you are. I'll come back for you."

He left Clive, still swearing between groans of pain, and continued in the direction of the trees.

Chapter Twenty-five

Don't die

Something moved in her hair.

Rummaging.

Semi-conscious, she stirred, dragged from a fitful sleep where she'd dreamt of being trapped in ice, refrigerated into a frosted floor.

Pain on the left side of her head. No, not pain. An agonising grinding, gnawing on her skull.

A tail whipped across her mouth. Claws skittered against her cheek, tangled in thick curls.

Catherine's scream struggled out of her parched throat as she jumped to her feet. She batted at her head, shaking away the last clutches of unconsciousness along with a writhing rat. It dropped to the ground with a thunk and disappeared into the shadows. Another one still writhed in the ends of her hair. With a shriek of horror and revulsion, she batted at the squirming black mass, and it bit back as she tried to smack it loose. Hair tore from her scalp. The rat clung on.

Tears, more screams, hysteria like the climax of a terrible nightmare. She lurched sideways and tossed her head with all the strength she could summon, hair swinging around her shoulders. The animal crunched against the stone wall beside her with a screech. It dropped to the ground and crawled under a pile of broken wood.

Relief, fear and panic collided with the agony caused by the sudden and violent movement, and she stumbled backwards. She banged into the stone wall of … what? Where the hell was she?

Get a grip. Get a fucking grip. You're still alive. They've gone. No sound other than her snatching breath and the wind whining outside. She stilled and tried to control her breaths. Chunks of her memory were missing. She touched her head where the pain drilled most acutely, and her fingers came back slick, knotted in chewed up strands. Clumps of it. Christ, the rats had been eating at her scalp.

She doubled over and retched. Her stomach muscles clenched around an empty space.

A yellow torch in the dirt a few feet away dribbled out a pitiful puddle of light, the battery almost spent. John. Had he left it there so she wouldn't be left in pitch blackness? How very fucking gentlemanly of him.

Disorientated. Groggy. So unbelievably cold. She snatched the torch and pointed it into the shadows. They remained hunched around her and refused to retreat.

Her blood chilled to the same icy temperature as her flesh. Deep groves around her wrists throbbed, but at least he'd untied her. She turned around and scanned the darkness. All manner of junk piled up against the walls: farm equipment, mounds of bricks and slates, more piles of logs. Something skittered close by. Then the same sound, from behind her this time, near to her. Rats. Christ, how many were there? They could smell the blood in her hair, on her fingers.

Was anyone searching for her? It might be days before…

A body moved against her ankles. She jumped and shone the pathetic torch around her feet. She kicked with random inaccuracy, hoping to boot one of them, kill it preferably. Beyond the dim light, the floor undulated. Black bodies withdrew.

He would come back. But then what? And if he cared about her, why had he left her in this rat-infested shithole? The old forge, it had to be. In the middle of nowhere.

Half a tractor knackered tractor corroded in shadows. The cabin part seemed intact, but the front end looked like it had smashed into a wall, part of the engine missing. If she could get into the cabin at least she would be able to escape the rats. Or should she check around for a break in the wall, a gap to squeeze through? Trying to find a way of escape would be better than slowly freezing to death.

How had she been so disastrously stupid?

Maybe Robin would be searching. Unlikely. He was caught up in his case and she'd walked out on him, jealous of a dead woman, jealous of his passion for his job. She'd demolished her relationship with a grenade of envy and bitterness, then launched straight into a dangerous game with a screwed-up time bomb. Nice one, Catherine. Great choices. She didn't deserve Robin's forgiveness if she ever had the chance to ask him for it.

What if John came back? Why would he hurt her though? He'd saved her life less than two weeks ago. He'd taken her there for a reason. Or he hoped she would die of hyperthermia before anyone found her.

She had to get out. The possibility of never seeing Robin again, of never being able to apologise and make up, made her guts wrench more.

But he'd been so lovely, so warm. Fragile though. Exterior intact, broken inside.

Or a brilliant actor.

Arghh, she needed to shut off her clattering thoughts and focus.

One hand in front of her, the other clutching the dying torch, she stumbled over to the tractor. The rusty door resisted, but she yanked it open a crack. She nudged her shoulder against it and tried to hold onto the sides to pull herself up, but she couldn't get enough purchase. Fresh panic crawled through her blood. Life seemed distant, her existence meshed into fragmented memories. Her house, her parents. Friends. Cooking with a glass of wine and dancing around the kitchen. Singing in the car. Writing by candlelight She hadn't cherished it enough.

Don't give up. When had she become a quitter?

With shaky hands clutched around the metal frame, she tried again and almost managed it, but her fingers slipped away and she fell to the ground. Something sharp ripped into her thigh, and she clutched at her leg, dragging breath through gritted teeth. Warm blood chilled on her fingers. For a moment she lay there, trying to haul herself out of the nightmare, hoping she was stuck in the clutches of a horrendous dream. But it remained. And she'd become weaker.

She wanted it to end.

Scuffling.

She needed to move, but as soon as she put her weight on her injured leg the pain intensified like someone had poured petrol into her muscle and set it alight. She'd get into that tractor even if she had to crawl. If she died in there, at least the goddamned rats wouldn't be able to eat her. Dragging herself backwards, she managed to shuffle to the door of the tractor and drag herself up the steps on her backside.

She collapsed onto the cracked vinyl seat, shaky and weak from the exertion, and it wobbled under her weight. She pulled the door shut. Stupid move or clever move? She'd escaped the rats, but would she hear anyone searching for her? Maybe the tractor had a horn. Catherine shone the torch at the dashboard. As alien as a plane cockpit. The light jumped around as her shivering increased, fingers numb and jittery. She jabbed at the buttons and levers, her movements lacking any coordination. Limbs lazy. Nothing happened. She was no expert on farm vehicles, but it had probably died back in the 1970s.

A loud thud made her jerk upright. A rat, standing high on its back legs, stared at her through the glass. Catherine screamed at it with all the energy left in her body.

Then the light died.

*

The forge had changed since photograph had been taken. It had become embedded in the trees and bushes around it and swallowed by nature. There were no signs anyone had been near it for decades until he shone the light on the ground. Some of the overgrown weeds had been trampled.

Clive's torch lit a large arched doorway and two small windows with wooden shutters nailed over them. Spurred by a burst of optimism, Robin threw off the bar, grabbed the metal door handle, and pulled.

It didn't budge.

He put down the torch and pulled again with both hands. What the hell? There wasn't even a lock. Why wouldn't it move?

"Catherine!"

Robin banged his palms against the door, then put his ear to it to drown out the rustling of the trees around him. Silence. He bashed it again. More silence. Disappointment mingled with the worst fatigue he'd ever experienced. He'd been sure this was the right place. She could be hurt. Unconscious. He had to at least check inside before giving up. Not too much to expect a door to open when you pulled the handle. He kicked it. It still didn't open

Did it slide, maybe? Up and over like a garage door. He pushed and pulled, but it didn't budge. Thanks for the heads-up, Felix.

He shouted Catherine's name again and edged around the building, looking for gaps he could squeeze through in the crumbly walls. Where was Darwin when you needed him? If he took a good run-up, he could shove his way through the walls …

A scream ripped through the night. He froze. It had come from inside the building.

"Catherine!"

He trampled his way back to the door, stumbling over the uneven ground as he ran, torch swinging around wildly.

"Cat? Are you hurt?"

No reply. All he had was that scream, and he never wanted to hear one like it again. It sounded like her eyes were being gouged out. It had to be her. He fished around in the inside pocket of his jacket for Felix's phone. It was slick, but it powered on, and he tapped in the code as the downpour intensified. A chaotic rain concerto drummed on the trees and shrubbery around him.

"Cat, if you're in there, I'll get help. I can't open the door."

"Robin? Don't leave me. Please."

Down by his feet, her voice came from the crack where the door met the frame. The relief of hearing her voice replaced by urgent concern. She sounded hoarse and weak. He knelt on the sodden earth.

"Are you hurt?"

No reply. inches away, but it may as well have been miles He banged his palms on the door and wished to God he could knock it down. He wiped rain from the phone screen and called Jack's number again. One bar of 3G. Not much better than sending a sodding pigeon. He couldn't waste any more time hoping to be saved by technology.

He grabbed the torch, rose to his feet and edged his way around the wall. He squeezed a metre or so down the side, but the bushes were dense. Impossible to go any further without cutting his way through. He traced his steps, back past the doors and round to the right of the building. His clothes clung to him now, plastered to his body with rain and mud, but hope energised him. Shoving through branches, he continued along the side wall until he reached what must've been the original outer wall Felix had mentioned.

He grappled his way up the wall and managed to roll over the top. He landed with an ungraceful thud and lay there for a second as the rain battered his face. A throaty growl of thunder rumbled in the distance. For a moment his world shrunk, and he closed his eyes, wishing the sodden womblike space beneath the trees would envelop him. When would this fucking day be over? He rolled over, head down, and inhaled the fresh scent of damp earth and wet leaves. Another, musty scent crawled up his nostrils. Old sweat on filthy clothes. Christ, he stank.

Back on his knees again, crawling under bushes through mulchy undergrowth someone had trampled before him. No wonder John had been in the shower when he'd turned up at his house. He'd been crawling through the same shit.

At last, he found a section of the wall which had collapsed, leaving a crumbling gap just wide enough for him to squeeze through. Tight, but possible. A rusty wheelbarrow lay on its side by the gap. Must've been how he'd moved her. He'd hidden his tracks well, with help from the rain. He shone the torch inside. A pile of old picnic tables and, beyond them, the top of a knackered tractor. He put one leg inside, ducked his head and shoved his shoulders through. The stack of tables seemed solid enough to take his weight.

"Catherine! I'm in. Where are you?"

Robin slid and bumped his way down the stack to the ground, surrounded by junk and logs, piles of God knows what shit. He climbed over it all until he reached the clearer floor space. The torch pooled over the floor to where Catherine lay in a shallow puddle of rainwater by the doors. As the light reached her, a rat sniffing around her leg scuttled off into the shadows.

Scrambling through engine parts and more crates of junk, he ran to her and dropped to his knees at her side. Her pulse fluttered against his fingertips. He gathered her into his arms and shook her.

"Cat, I've got you." She was colder than dead, but her eyes flickered open. "Stay with me, OK?" He scooped her out of the water and turned his attention to the doors. Obvious now why the door hadn't opened. A piece of timber had been rammed between the end of the door, a single brick and then the outer wall. He pulled them away and tried the handle again. It shifted slightly but it still wouldn't budge. He yanked more, using one leg on the wall to give him more leverage.

A loud bang on the door made him jump.

"Robin!"

Clive. He'd never been so glad to hear another voice.

"She's here, but she's in a bad way. Do you have a signal?"

The longest pause ever.

"No. Shit!"

"OK. The door won't slide back. I'll pull, you see if you can work out what's blocking it."

"Got it."

Behind him, Catherine groaned. He fought the urge to hold her, driven by the urgency to get out of there before she… Could he live with not holding her while she took her last breaths, with not giving her comfort and making her feel safe? No, stop catastrophising. Was she critical? Indecision froze him for a moment. He crouched beside her and touched her cheek.

"Just a few minutes, Cat. Hang on." his voice cracked. "Don't leave me."

The door rattled. "Robin, are you pulling?"

He jumped to his feet and grabbed the door handle, levering his weight backwards again. A scraping noise from Clive's side like he was tunnelling his way in. Robin took a deep breath, pulled again, harder, and the door finally juddered sideways. He stumbled backwards as the rainy night rushed in.

Clive bent over, holding his hand between his thighs, dripping. "I'll come back another time for my fingertips. Is Cat OK?"

"No, but she's alive."

Robin lifted her from the ground and pulled her into his lap. A flash of lightning illuminated the forge for a moment, followed seconds later by a grumble of thunder. He flinched involuntarily and glanced up at Clive, expecting him to take the piss. But Clive's expression softened. He'd joined the dots and knew now why Robin had mentioned the weather app.

"I had a signal when I fell. I'll go on ahead. Give it five."

"Thanks, Clive."

*

Even with muted lights and windows filled with darkness, the hospital relentlessly wheezed and beeped.

"Tell me what's happened, Robin." Catherine sounded dopey and drained. He'd showered and slept for a while, and he still didn't want this conversation. She was exhausted from the mild hypothermia and drugs, but the question was implicit, answers as critical to her healing as the physical recovery. He pulled the old fashioned, winged-back chair close to the bed and the seat sighed under his weight. Her white fingers were weightless in his hand, several nails broken, green polish chipped.

"I will. But first, I want to be straight with you. I've been an idiot. What you said the other day about me holding back, you were right. It wasn't a conscious decision; it was … a defence mechanism, I suppose. When Erin died … I handled it so badly. I became selfish about my grief, and I pushed people away. I was such a dick. Other people needed me, I needed them, and I was too self-absorbed to see it. Luckily, I came out of it before I reached total self-destruction. I've feared exposing myself to the pain ever since. I can't lose again. I can't lose you."

"I'm sorry you went through that." Catherine's voice had faded to a whisper. "Sorry you lost her."

"Can we try again?"

She nodded, and he pressed her fingers to his lips, resting his head on their hands as wave of relief and exhaustion flooded over him. He had so much to tell her still, upsetting truths about the man she'd grown close to. But he had to tell her.

"John is in intensive care. He attacked me in his house, drugged and bound me in his cellar. Jack found me, we fought, and John tried to take his own life." She stared at him aghast. Rhythmic bleeps filled the silence with mechanical percussion. "He murdered Ursula."

"Oh my God …"

"He had genuine feelings for you, but they turned into obsession. Perhaps not with you so much as the idea of you, of the two of you being thrown together by some other-worldly force. I don't know how to explain it, but you soothed his battered soul." Robin shook his head. "Christ, I even sound like him now."

"What he did to Ursula … How can he be two people at the same time?"

"His mental state is questionable."

"To obsess so much when I hardly knew him, and we didn't … do anything. We came close, but … we just didn't."

That pulled him up sharp. He'd tried not to think about it but each time his mind dragged him back again, to a mental image he'd drawn of her naked in his arms. John had been winding him up in the cellar then. It had all been an act.

"Why not?" No chance of playing it cool. The question came out before he could stop it.

"Because of you."

He didn't doubt her sincerity. She stared at him in such a way, as if the depth of her honesty could be measured by the ferocity of her gaze.

"When I walked out on you, it wasn't fair. I let envy get in the way. I enjoyed his company. He was magnetic. Different. But I was stupidly on the rebound."

"Envy of what?" He didn't care so much about the rebound stuff. No one was perfect.

"Erin mostly. How you feel about her now, how she was immersed in your world, but I'm not. And your job. How you do what you love."

Her honesty took him aback for a moment, but he respected her for having the courage to say it. "Did I push you too hard to quit your career?"

"Maybe, but it wasn't just you. Mum guilt-tripped me, Dad too. And I became so busy keeping everyone else happy I forgot to look after me."

"I wanted to protect you, but I was trying to protect myself too. What happened to Simon … it could've been you."

"You can't protect everyone all the time, Robin."

"I know." He released her hand and rubbed at his face. The womblike warmth of the dim room lulled him into an easier unburdening. The back of his mind had opened, and everything he'd shoved back there was seeping out.

"Why do you think he took me when he claimed to care about me?"

Safer ground. She wanted answers, logic. Logic he could do.

"He panicked, so hiding you away for a while bought him some time. He sensed we were closing in on him."

"But he didn't kill you."

"No. Killing Ursula was different. He believed her death was justified. She was an evil and cruel woman who deserved to be punished. I don't think his motivation to kill me was strong enough."

"What Ursula did to him was horrendous. I understand his pain."

"I do too, and there's a lot of good in him. Functioning normally, he's a nice guy. I liked him. I can see how you did too."

Catherine looked away towards the window with its faded blinds providing a glimpse into the corridor beyond. A nurse hurried past the window in squeaky shoes, flipping through sheets of paper on a clipboard.

Robin took Catherine's hand again and shuffled closer on his wheezy chair. "I don't blame you."

"You'll always hold it against me."

"No!" he couldn't restrain his vehemence. "I won't, because it made me realise how much I wanted what we had."

"Me too. After the crash, I felt guilty. Now I feel stupid and gullible."

"It's not stupid to be a lovely person. You were grateful for what he did, you offered him your friendship, and he abused your trust."

"I was attracted to him." She looked him straight in the eye, challenging him, giving him the worst to see if he would break.

"Who can blame you? Jesus Cat, I'm a red-blooded male, but I think I was attracted to him! We're all human. We fuck up. I fucked up too."

"I can't stop going over it, and then I invent different scenarios. What if you hadn't found me? What if he'd killed you too? What would he have done if he'd come back for me?"

"You can't invest in the 'what ifs'. It's so destructive. When you put yourself through a made-up event, your body thinks it's real. You'll become stressed to shit and your body won't know how to cope with what's going on in your mind. Please give yourself a break."

He brushed her hair off her cheeks. He loved her more than he realised but hadn't allowed himself to love her freely. Now he had another chance.

"I want to know you Cat, really know you. I'm not creative, but you are, and that's important to me. I want all of you, not just the bits I understand. Look how much you've invested in my passions."

"All those John-Claude Van Damme films ..."

Robin smiled. "There's that. But you read up on the history, you've supported me at competitions, you've bought me quirky little books and pieces of art. What have I done? I haven't read your favourite book. I've never seen a Shakespeare play. Last night was the first time I've been round the castle, other than to pick you up. But you love it there. I've stopped myself from knowing the real you, and I'm so sorry."

The relief to finally say all this to her overwhelmed him.

"I never told you where the thunder phobia came from. I tried to shrug it off, and you were so lovely with me. I should've explained. When I was a kid my friend Adam lived in the next street. He had a bulldog called Jeff. Chunky, loveable thing with a ridiculous overbite. Lightning struck Adam's TV during a thunderstorm, and it blew up, caused a serious house fire. I remember staring at his house. The smoke on the brickwork, the board over his bedroom window, his mum's burnt sewing machine thrown out into the garden. Jeff's charred dog bed. It fascinated and horrified me, the pieces of Adam's everyday life destroyed in minutes. The horror seeped into my subconscious and made a home. It still lives there."

Her featured softened. He loved how she just listened, riding his emotions with him.

"And one last thing, this is important." He paused, needing the words to come out right. "Please don't be jealous of Erin. It's hard to turn off your feelings because when someone dies suddenly, it's as if your emotions freeze in that moment. We hadn't fallen out or drifted` apart. She was there one moment, gone the next. I had no reason to stop loving her. But now I do."

"You don't need to stop loving her; I don't want you to. There's no capacity limit on love. There's room in there for both of us."

Her words smacked him in the face, and when he recovered from the blow, for the first time since Erin's funeral, he cried.

Chapter Twenty-six

Distant thunder

Bobby took hold of John's hand and turned his back on the police officer who remained ever-present at the door. He'd been pleasant enough, but the constant reminder of John's fate if he ever opened his eyes again, stabbed fear in his core. Which way should he hope? Hope John lives to face life imprisonment or hope he dies to escape the misery? Will's heart was broken either way. Bobby had never expected to love someone else's child like this, but as he stared at John's lifeless face, his heart cracked apart too.

This wasn't how it had been meant to work out. He knew John might go back for Ursula one day, and he'd tried hard to help him leave his past behind. His mental fragility had always been a concern, but there had been times when John had been able to live normally, times when Bobby had believed the demons were gone for good. He'd invested so much in this young man, committed to helping him find peace with the past. He'd been a gift, and so what if he wasn't his real son? Blood and genetics didn't guarantee love. He'd chosen to love John, not felt obliged to.

So, he'd attempted to steer the police away from him. It had given John a little breathing space, wasted some time while they chased red herrings. He'd known they would place him in York eventually, and realise he couldn't be a viable suspect. Stupid, but it had been the only way he could think of to protect him. He hadn't predicted John would fill his breathing space with a new distraction, that his needy heart would fire up all the triggers he'd been trying so hard to suppress.

He was so fragile. Yet, how could this kind, loving, sensitive man attack a police officer and abduct the woman he'd instantly fallen in love with? Tough to envisage him killing Ursula too, although he understood his motivation. He knew John but didn't know him at all. And he'd failed him, stupidly thought he'd been fixed. He'd underestimated the complexity and true extent of John's mental ruin.

The police would be back on his case no doubt. Had he known John had killed Ursula, withheld information, perverted the course of justice with lies? None of it mattered. It wouldn't change what John had done, but he would need support if he did pull through this.

Bobby would be there.

*

Robin plonked a box of cakes in the centre of the table and snatched back his arm as piranha hands grabbed at the contents. He still had sleep to catch up on, but being back with the team invigorated him.

"Does no one feed you lot?" he asked, as the cave filled with the sound of happy coppers trebling their daily calorie intake. He took his usual seat, and James passed him a coffee.

"There's one missing," said Vic, licking his fingers, "You get eight in a box."

"Yeah, I'm not stupid. Right, a quick update, then I'm off to the hospital. Catherine's fine; still no news on John Rickman. He's in an induced coma and functioning by machine. Prognosis, still fifty/fifty. Fag packet psych analysis: able to function normally by mentally 'escaping' or detaching from reality. On one side intelligent and intuitive, able to form genuine relationships and a bit of a charmer. On the other side, desensitised, manipulative, obsessive and capable of violence."

"So, a true split personality," said James.

"I'm not an expert, but yes, it's possible. Those disorders are often caused by psychological trauma. Richard Melling's sent Catherine a lengthy message about this happening to John at uni. Reckons he went through periods of being this Henry Stanton character. Even claims to have video of it."

"I get the theory," said James, "His 'knight side' killed Ursula, but then why didn't he switch to this 'Henry Stanton mode' to kill you?"

"James, you sound disappointed," said Robin, laughing.

"I do have my eye on your office chair."

"No chance," said Jack, "I bagsied it a while back."

"Where are your manners?" said Ella, "Ladies get first dibs."

"Listen to you lot," said Vic, "Right pack of vultures."

"You're just nobbed off because you're right at the back of the queue," said Jack, "You're like an obscure royal who's thirty-fourth in line to the throne."

"Well, you can all sit tight on your uncomfy chairs," said Robin, "I'm going nowhere."

For now, anyway. He still had Collins to face and a few more awkward questions about how John Rickman had been impaled on a sword.

"I find his mental state intriguing," said Ella, "I've never come across anything like it."

"Won't be so intriguing if he gets off on grounds of diminished responsibility," said Jack.

"No way. Ursula Harrison's murder was premeditated. You can't pass it off as manslaughter."

"Maybe not, but he might not be fully criminally liable if his mental functions are seen as impaired."

"It's a possibility," said Robin, "But I'm with Ella. I can't see how he could go to such lengths, be so meticulous, and claim diminished responsibility or abnormality of mental function. And I doubt people with a dissociative disorder can control when they switch to another personality."

"Plus, he had a good job," said Vic, "He functioned normally in most aspects of his life. I'll be well pissed off if he gets off on a psych issue."

"Do we think his brother and Richard Melling are involved?" asked James.

"Inconclusive," said Robin, "Melling was manipulated. He knew about John's abusive childhood and reckoned he had sporadic periods of 'mental absence'. Their friendship was genuine, to a point. It's a guess, but if John had told Melling his plans, he would've talked him out of it. Same with Bobby Trent."

"Which leaves the brother."

"Who's still missing," said Robin, "I had a missed call from Barbara Rickman earlier. Looks like Will activated the escape plan."

"Dodgy," said Vic, "I've thought the kid was involved all along."

"We can't forget Will also suffered abuse," said Jack, "Maybe not on the same scale, but he grew up in the same environment. That must've had an effect."

"Will the confession hold up, Guv?" asked James.

"On its own? Possibly not, if he pulls through and gets a brief who can convince a court he's mentally unstable. But we have the hemlock, and Joseph's confident it can be matched with the samples taken from Ursula."

"There's Trent's involvement too," said Jack, "It's conceivable he's complicit."

"Trent, Melling and Will; all still plausible." A wave of tiredness hit him, but he wanted to carry on while he had the team together. "I need more coffee before we tackle these loose ends. Let's have a quick break."

Robin followed Ella in the direction of the kettle, spotting the chance to have a quiet word when the others drifted off.

"How have you found juggling a major case with a little one?" he asked as she spooned coffee into a line of mugs. She shovelled sugar into Vic's oversized bucket, maybe considering how honest she should be. Robin waited, letting her think.

"It's good to be back." Long sigh. "Except it's not. I love my baby, but I can't enjoy the job anymore. I'm either knackered or leaking milk or thinking about how many nappies I need. I resent it. Him." She glanced at Robin, checking his reaction, but he remained neutral. "Which makes me feel guilty, and a bad mum."

Robin passed her the milk, pleased she'd offloaded. "It's OK to not be OK."

She nodded, but he wasn't sure she believed him. "I've been a bit bitchy too. Even Jack said I wasn't myself. I just wanted to be one of those uber-cool moms, you know? Juggling life effortlessly; nails done, baby weight gone, shopping for quinoa wearing my baby in a sling." There was a beat before Robin snorted a laugh and she joined him seconds later, tears of laughter possibly disguising tears of emotion. "Well, maybe KitKats, not quinoa."

"Don't be hard on yourself. Mummy Perfect isn't nicking scrotes or catching killers, if she even exists. Noah will be proud of you when he's old enough to understand why his mum is different." Robin took his mug from the line-up. "I think you've handled it brilliantly Ella."

Ella laughed, visibly lighter. "Thanks Guv."

Robin's phone was ringing for what felt like the billionth time that day already. Jamie Clark returning his call. He answered, skipping the small talk. "I've lined you up an interview at the music shop on King Street. It's a mate of mine, so I hope your guitar skills are up to scratch. Warren likes his staff to be able to show off his instruments."

The silence was so long Robin checked the call hadn't disconnected.

"Are you serious?"

"Very serious. I'll text you his number, he's expecting a call. Don't let me down."

"I could actually kiss you."

Robin laughed. "I'll pass on that, thanks. Good luck Jamie." He disconnected and checked his missed call list. Barbara Rickman had called again. Twice. Probably demanding to know why they hadn't found her son yet. He hovered over her number, reluctant to return her call and ruin his mood. She took the decision out of his hands by calling a third time. He swiped the screen and prepared for an earbashing.

"I thought you weren't going to speak to me DI Scott."

"I've been a bit tied up."

Long silence.

"Yes. I understand why you might want to stay clear of my family. But I wondered if you could come and search William's bedroom. Personally, I mean. You might spot something the others missed."

"I trust my colleagues to do their job."

"Did John talk to you? Did he say if … did William …" She couldn't say the words. The possibility was too horrific.

"John claimed Will wasn't involved."

"Claimed?"

"He may have been protecting him."

"Please find my son."

Robin stared out of the window at the busy town going about its business Another parent pleading for the return of their child. Only this time he wasn't sure if finding Will and returning him to his toxic home was in his best interest, despite him being a plausible accomplice. Not his place to judge Barbara though. This was her wake-up call, an opportunity to atone.

"He likes you," she continued, her voice laced with pain, "After you spoke to him, he said he might consider joining the police. He even said you were the kind of person he would've wanted as a father." The last word cracked. Was it a manipulative act or genuine emotion tightening her throat? Shame he couldn't see her face.

"I like him too. I'll do my best to find him."

*

Chief Superintendent Collins was sorting out the top drawer of her desk when Robin knocked on her half-open door. She glanced up, beckoned him in with a quick flick of her fingers, and continued lining up her stash of pens. He waited as she assessed three staplers, checked if they were loaded then lobbed one into the bin. It was full of rejected office equipment. Her aim was perfect.

"I love a good clear-out." She simultaneously squeezed two hole punches and squinted at the mechanisms. A squeaky blue one followed the staplers into the bin. She wafted a hand towards the chair opposite her desk, "How's Catherine?"

"Fine, thanks Ma'am."

"And how are you?"

Collins leant back and gave him her full attention. He didn't enjoy her scrutiny. He could never get a straight-up read on what was going on in her head, and he was too worn out for mind games. From her expression, he couldn't tell whether he was about to receive a commendation or a sacking. Either seemed feasible.

"Still processing."

She nodded.

"Good job on John Rickman. It's a good result, regardless of whether he recovers. And he didn't kill you, which is a bonus," she smiled, perhaps at him, perhaps at her joke. As the smile faded, she glanced at her line of biros and selected an orange EasyJet one. She scowled at it like she was remembering a lousy flight. "I think I made myself clear when we spoke last night; going to Rickman's alone was ill-judged."

"Lines became blurred. I had suspicions about him, but I couldn't be sure it wasn't for personal reasons. I didn't want to drag the team into a vendetta."

"Understandable. Any news on the brother?"

"Not yet."

"Well, we've found our killer and abductor all in one night. Great result."

A 'but' was coming, signposted in red, probably using one of the fat whiteboard markers lined up in front of her. Was this the reason for the distraction? He'd never known Collins care much about stationery, yet she was acting like a teenage glitter pen addict let loose in WH Smiths.

"Did you stab him, Robin?"

He'd been expecting the question, but his stomach flipped to hear it spoken aloud.

"No."

She nodded and stared thoughtfully at her collection.

"If we're done here, Ma'am, I need to get back to Catherine."

"Of course."

He headed for the door, and as he turned to close it behind him, she scraped the contents of her desk back into the drawer with one dismissive sweep of her arm.

It sounded like the clatter of distant thunder.

***

About the author

Ever since I was a child, I've been captivated by the power of words to transport readers to new worlds and perspectives.
I grew up reading historical epics and was introduced to mystery, horror and thrillers by my dad, an avid reader who loved Dean Koontz and Stephen King. I was hooked, and King remains a huge favourite for the mastery of his craft.
I've worked in magazine publishing, newspapers and marketing agencies for most of my career, and written about diverse subjects from flower arranging to business acquisitions.
Creatively, my early works were scripts and plays. My two-hander 'We Agreed' was performed at the Lowry, a dark story which began my fascination with likeable antagonists and the grey area between right and wrong.
I now spend my creative energy writing modern-day crime stories featuring DI Robin Scott, set in the vibrant and historical tourist town Broadstone.
When I'm not writing, you'll find me reading some gritty and twisty crime thriller, enjoying time with my family or mooching around a castle. I could also be wrestling a foreign object out of my French bulldog Ernie's mouth …

Wendy Turner-Hargreaves

Afterword

If you enjoyed Justified, please leave a review and let others know your thoughts.

Connect with Wendy at:
www.wendyturnerhargreaves.com

On Facebook: www.facebook.com/wendyturnerhargreavesauthor
On Instagram: www.instagram.com/wturnerhargreaves

Printed in Great Britain
by Amazon

20191144R00180